IN A WORLD OF PRISTINE INNOCENCE, THERE WAS NO SUCH THING AS PASSION. THERE WAS GOD'S WILL—AND MAMA'S. . . .

MARY ROSE—Delicate and sweet as a flower. Would her youth and beauty wilt under the endless burden of marriage and childbearing?

ULRICH—Yearning for adventure. Could he accept his role as manager of the family estate?

TERENCE—Full of mischief and wild dreams of the sea, he submitted to the austere vows of priesthood.

JOHN—He pictured himself the loving husband of his secret sweetheart, but Mama saw him as a soldier in uniform, a saber at his side.

CONSTANCE—Outwardly obedient, a secret schemer. Determined to choose for herself, would she make the worst choice of all?

Defiance came dear. No one dared oppose Mama's will. But Sabrina loved Gerrard. And when it came to love . . . Sabrina had plans of her own!

"A GEM!" —*The Anniston Star*

"A NOVEL DESIGNED TO KEEP THE READER RIVETED TO HIS CHAIR."
—*The Pittsburgh Press*

Madeleine A. Polland

SABRINA

A DELL BOOK

Published by
Dell Publishing Co., Inc.
1 Dag Hammarskjold Plaza
New York, New York 10017

Dell ® TM 681510, Dell Publishing Co., Inc.

ISBN: 0-440-17633-6

Reprinted by arrangement with Delacorte Press
Printed in the United States of America
First Dell printing—June 1980

Thank you, to Charlotte.

ACKNOWLEDGMENTS

The ultimate acknowledgment for this book is, of course, to my mother's Great Aunt Sabrina, who, long before the period in which it is set, did indeed have the courage to leap over the wall and marry her young lover, subsequently rearing a large family.

When I came to writing, I did almost no research from books. For virtually everything I needed to know, there was someone to whom I could go and say, "Do you remember?" In this way I assembled information on everything from elastic-sided boots and nuns' stockings to how to get my wounded home from Arras. I am most grateful to everyone who talked to me, and I immensely enjoyed all the good conversations that arose from my inquiries.

CHAPTER 1

In later life, Sabrina did not often allow herself to look back, for nothing is more fruitless than remembered sorrow.

When she did, she sensed no more than the barest existence before her fifteenth birthday, except in the vague recollection of love and warmth; a childhood so secure and effortless it was hardly noticed in its passing. Even then, she realized, she must have still held a great deal of that childhood in her character. Otherwise she would not have been so unaware, so simple, and taken completely by surprise.

Yet she knew herself possessed of some different maturity, which at fifteen had locked her in one certainty that to many only comes much later.

Her fifteenth birthday was her sister's wedding day. High, perfect summer, when the grasses grew tall enough to hide the children and the calm blue days went on forever. The day before the wedding, she was dispatched with the three smaller children in the ass cart, with the picnic hamper, and Tomasheen, the donkey boy, in general charge. Although, God help him, he was as mute as the stones and more than halfway deaf. The day out was no different, really, from many others, except for the quaking excitement rocking the house they had left behind them. Except of course, for Mama, who had the whole business at her cool fingertips. She had given them strict instructions to go to the shore and not set foot in the house again before half past seven.

That could not be far off now.

The smooth rocks where she sat were cooling, and from her small promontory she could see Tomasheen and the little ones, bent, darkening figures on the yellow strand, still scrabbling in the rock pools for sufficient crabs or maybe even prawns to earn some reluctant praise from Cookie.

Tide was coming slowly in like light spilt, spreading to cover the strand with a thin sheet of shining copper. Far across it, beyond the children and off toward Passage West and the open sea, the long arm of land turned grape blue against the sinking sun and a small sudden breeze of evening niggled at the shallows. Around Sabrina's legs her dress was sodden, sticky with limp starch from where she had been walking in the water. There were green stains on it from seaweed and a dark smear of blood where she had cut her finger on a rock, and already one small, expedient corner of her mind was framing excuses for Biddy Sheehan, who did all the washing—unless the appalling worst should happen and she met Mama on the way in, and then no excuses on this earth would do at all.

It would all no doubt be added to what Mama would be waiting to say gravely to her—after tomorrow when all the uproar was over—about the responsibilities of being fifteen. And duty. And dignity. And all the rest of it. Like being thirteen or fourteen but there'd be more of it.

She stared out over the creeping sea, her long legs in their wet sticky lawn drawn up to her chin. None of these lectures had ever seemed to matter much, washing away with all the other lectures and admonitions that poured from Mama and the nuns at school as if they manufactured them like the sacks and bags for the farmers made in the factory down in the village that Ulick had helped to start, which was going to stop the people being poor forever more. With other places like it, Ireland would never again have to starve simply for potatoes.

Always she listened patiently and politely, as she had been trained to listen to grown-ups. Yet she had an inescapable private sense that all the things that would happen to her when she was grown-up would be different. She would have to learn how to manage them herself. This time, however, she felt more inclined to listen, as if she were coming closer to the need for some important knowledge, hoping that someone would have something new to say. Some inner ear was listening already—to what, she did not know.

Nothing more tangible than the shadows that caught her attention, gathering below the far cliffs, out to quench the color from the deep water. The first small waves found strength to curl along the shore and she looked over at Tomasheen and the small ones. He may not have his ears and tongue but thank the saints he was sharp enough inside his head and already had the three children on their way up out of the pools where the tide would be beginning to hiss and suck, up to their pile of nets and buckets and discarded shoes, and Elizabeth, the donkey, langled to crop at the thin dry grass of the dunes.

When the shadows reached the great rock called the Robin's Egg, it was time to go. Sabrina eased the tacky petticoats from her legs and hoped that in the uproar in the house no one would notice that she had come down to the strand without her stockings. The Mama would flay her if she heard of it. Beyond the mountains the sky turned the clear pale turquoise of a thrush's egg, dragged with furry stripes of rich and satisfactory rose. Thank God tomorrow would be fine. Quickly and gratefully she blessed herself.

It had been Mama's idea, long back, that Mary Rose should be married on her birthday. Darling Mama. She would not have one child eclipsed by another. Thinking always of all of them.

"Sabrina's birthday, my dearest," she had said to Mary Rose. "If you want the wedding in June, then we must have it on Sabrina's birthday. What else?"

Mary Rose had come across the room in a quick swirl of

dark velvet skirts to kiss her. "Of course. I should have thought of that myself!" Her lovely eyes were bright for everyone in her own excitement. "And of course Brin shall be my chief bridesmaid!"

There had been frost that day, Brin remembered, watching the soft shadows of summer on the bay. Hard, bitter frost just after Christmas, and all the horses eating their heads off in the stables, and Tomasheen having to bash a hole for the ducks with an ax down at the pasture pond. Beyond the long windows of the drawing room the grass was stiff with rime, and in the pleasure ground the dark firs were fringed with white.

They were all there except Terry. Even John, on Christmas furlough from the Curragh, limp on the piano stool, idly and mischievously punctuating the conversation. The settling of the date was marked by a light staccato of the "Wedding March" and everybody laughed, but Sabrina noticed that Mama's eyes were very bright.

"A June wedding," she said, a little unsteadily, and Sabrina was touched to see her lose even a fraction of her impeccable composure. "A June wedding, for a Rose."

At the piano John had grinned and launched himself into "The Last Rose of Summer," and then MacGinnis had come in to say the tea was drawn this last ten minutes and would be as black as hell itself if they didn't come to drink it. He lit the lamps and drew the heavy curtains against the dark outside, and then Papa had arrived and the smell of the cold evening was on his clothes, and the little ones had come chattering down the stairs. The room was warm and full and safe, the scarlet winter dusk closed out.

And now the wedding was tomorrow.

She noticed the shadows and stood up. No use to yell at Tomasheen, but she cupped her hands around her mouth and shouted along the shore at the children. Away from the restrictions of school and drawing room, her young voice carried with all the rich authority of the kitchen and stables.

"Con! Maggie! C'mon away home. Tell Tomasheen."

She saw them look at her across the waste of sand, and Constance waved. Margaret took the small, unwilling Denis Mary by the hand. Con would be telling Tomasheen. She was best at the finger talk that brought the world into his silent mind. He was only a month older than Sabrina, but wasn't he the lucky fellow, she thought as she began to pad across the cooling sand. What other coachman's child would have been sent away to the special nuns to teach him finger talk, and then the nun coming to teach the children how to talk to him since he was their donkey boy. Ah God, but Mama was an angel. She knew what everybody needed.

The three smaller children were wet to the waist when she reached them and already looking a little blue in the first cool of the evening.

"For the love of God will you look at you," Sabrina said severely. "What will Mama say?"

"You're wet yourself," Margaret said practically, heaving back the sea-limp swaths of fair hair from which the ribbon dangled loose.

"She'll not see anything," said Con calmly. "There'll be too many people in the house. C'mon Brin. Gran'll be there by now."

"And half the county as well," Brin answered. "And Terry."

Her eyes gleamed with pleasure, dark clear grey, long-lashed, and of uncompromising directness under thick level brows. It was a long time since Terry had been home, and every single one of them together. He had been given special leave from the Bishop to assist at the wedding. Mama, of course. She would go to the Pope himself to get what she wanted, or the King of England.

Brin's face grew thoughtful as she scooped buckets and towels into the back of the ass cart. Now that Terry was almost a priest, the thought of him made her feel a little nervous. Somewhere in the black suit and the severe haircut of the seminary, Terry himself seemed to have got lost. The precious, hilarious Terence of their childhood, five years older than herself, who would beckon her off down the backstairs to go visiting the gypsies in Copper's Hollow or rat hunting with the terriers in the stables. She remembered the time the puppy got bitten almost in half and Terry had cried all night even though he was a big boy then.

Tomasheen took the langle off the donkey, who stretched her brittle legs as if to thank him, and Sabrina bent to help

Denis Mary gather his net off a patch of sea holly and to support him while he squeezed his feet into his wet shoes.

"Me stockings is gone," he said indifferently, and looked out over the bay as if with some memory of them, floating. To six-year-old Denis Mary, with his mother's hair muted to pale gold and eyes like the periwinkles that carpeted the pleasure grounds in summer, things always happened. He was never responsible.

"And where did they go?" his sister asked him coldly. He shrugged. And why, thought Sabrina, indeed, should he concern himself. At some time when the turmoil was over, it was she who would probably be faced with the question of Denis Mary's stockings.

Tomasheen hauled the reluctant little donkey away from the thin grass and the sharp tufts of holly, and took time to wonder why she troubled to resist him. You wouldn't think such stuff would give pleasure even to an ass. He gave her a sharp thump on the nose, encouraging her backward into the shafts of the little cart that, like everything else, had been given a smart new coat of green paint for the wedding. Wasn't Tomasheen himself to take flowers in it to the church in the morning? Inside his head he coaxed her with soft sounds that could never pass his lips, and with wry, sad humor he acknowledged it was no good trying the business of talking on your fingers to an ass.

Nor could he frame words that he would, in any case, have never dared to speak. Half-formed words of deep warm pleasure that he didn't know as love, nor would he think of it, and she in her world and he in his, but it was part of the good evening to see Miss Sabrina there, grown so tall and somehow so different since she was home at Easter, coming along the strand like one of the big framed pictures in the house itself, with the red sun behind her and her long hair loose to the wind, and the little ones all about her like they belonged. The small lad had her hand.

"Look Brin." The water slopped in his red bucket. "I've got some progs."

"Prawns, pet," Sabrina said and felt herself a hypocrite, knowing she would call them progs herself the moment she felt like it.

All her thoughts were on the house now, filling up

through this long day with all the people gathering for the wedding. For Mary Rose. And Dermot. Half the hotels were full too, as far as Cork city, and Mama said the little church would need elastic sides to hold them. For weeks there had been a state of siege and frenzy, with endless councils between Mary Rose and Mama and Nora Grimm, the dressmaker, with her mouth full of pins that only came out to make room for a crawly smile, and every chair in the place covered with bolts of cloth, until Papa threatened to go off to Dublin and live in his club until there was somewhere again in his house that he could sit down. Every time he said this Mama would say Ah, now, Barry, get away with you, and Mary Rose would kiss him, and it would all go on exactly as before.

Somewhere in the middle of it all, Mary Rose had stopped being Mary Rose and had inexplicably turned into someone called The Bride.

Brin smiled her thanks to Tomasheen as he held the donkey's head. Mama had long ago trained them that he must always be smiled at since he couldn't hear, and it was necessary to say thank-you to servants. Sabrina herself would have done so without telling, conscious always of his isolation. Although God knew, and she grinned to herself, he'd been in on many of the wild capers before Terry went off to be a priest, and Mama didn't seem to know that what she always called the servants, at a sort of distance, were some of the best friends her children had.

Brin's mind went back to Terry going off to be a priest. Deciding to be a priest. The children piled in on top of her and settled in a damp tangle of arms and legs. She crushed some chill and inadmissible doubt about Terry that crept too often round the edges of her mind like the first shivers of a sickness. Something she had been too young to understand about. Terry leaving them, her mother said, because he had decided to belong to God. There had been raised voices quickly hushed and Mama wearing that patient face toward Terry, as if he were trying to do her some sort of harm. What harm, for mercy's sake, could Terry do, although his own face in those last days before he went away had been as white as old Sister Eulalia's when they had been allowed at school to go and see her after she was dead, stretched out like a skeleton on the chapel floor with a wreath of white roses round her veil? But Terry. He had not been seventeen. Why should she think of someone dead? And his black suit had been too big for him. Ah, well. Maybe it was hard to go away and be a priest. Hard to go away and leave the bay and the boats and the strand and the horses and Abbeygate itself and the family and the rat hunts and all the rest of it. He must have wanted very much indeed to be a priest.

"Get your feet off my shins, Con. I swear you have the sharpest bones this side of a skellyton."

Con tossed her brown head and shifted her feet, and the little old cart with its coat of bright paint creaked along through the violet evening, out over the sandy fringe that was neither dune nor meadow, where a few scrawny sheep of Barty Nolan's cropped at the poor grass, treading the sea pinks and scenting the soft air. The bay had lost the sun except away over to the east where light still touched it blue; along the shore they had left, the waves creamed the edges of the shallows.

Brin looked at Tomasheen, stumping along at the ass's head in an old pair of her brother Ulick's tennis shoes, his bare toes out through the fronts of them. The quirk of his pale hair never lay down on the top of his head, and his long arms dangled from the outgrown sleeves of his bawneen jacket. She felt a surge of affection for him, part of her loved world, and wanted to tell him it had all been a grand day, to see his eager smile flash. But it was too much trouble. She would have to reach out first to touch him, to let him know she wanted to speak to him, then he must let go the ass to answer.

She left him to his silence and put her arm round Denis Mary, whose warm, sea-smelling little body was beginning to subside against her. They were on the road now, rolling noisily over the fallen blossoms of the fuchsias that grew man-high along the roadsides, scattering their flowers like blood in the dust. Beyond them started the demesne walls of the house.

Con and Margaret were chattering, popping with the excitement of all that would have happened in the hours for which they had been banished.

"Ah, what's the use," Maggie said suddenly, bitterly and practically, and her lower lip came out. " 'Tis all right for you two going downstairs, but all that'll happen to me is bed, and made a baby of to keep Denis Mary happy. It's not fair."

The small hooves clacked along the stony road and the small cartload was tense with emotions and excitement and resentments. All edged with a great languor of the long day beside the sea. Brin could smell them all, salt as the tide itself, and Maggie's stockings flying from the tail of the cart like the black flag after executions she remembered reading about and that she had actually seen one day with Gran, flapping in the sun above Galway jail, and everyone stopping in the streets to look. Con yawned, too drowsy to argue, but Sabrina saw the tears on Maggie's lashes and wriggled to get her other arm round her.

"I'll bring you something up," she promised. "And Gran'll come."

"Please, Brin. Please do."

Denis Mary blinked like a disturbed fledgling, his soft hair tufted by the damp, aware of nothing except that something was being promised to someone else.

"Me too," he cried imperiously. "Me too."

But Brin was thinking again of Terry. Almost Father Terence now. No longer Terry my brother. When she had been on the edge of tears, like Margaret, at being excluded from the carry-on in the evening house, it was always Terry who would come creeping in the secret dark with a bowl of trifle or a pile of frosted grapes that filled the sheets with sugar, and all the gossip of the dinner table spun for her into silly stories, whispering and giggling until she must put her head under the blankets lest Nurse hear them from next door, where she sewed industriously in her circle of lamplight. Terry.

Did she remember his unhappiness when he went away to the priesthood? Or was it all confused with her own at losing him?

"Will you get married, Brin?"

Margaret again, brooding on the crowded house and all the things she might be missing.

They lurched together as the ass cart banged over the center stop of the iron gates at the end of the drive. Abbeygate. Carved in the stone of each pillar.

"Well, not tomorrow, pet." Brin grinned. "That's for Mary Rose."

"I think Dermot's very handsome," said Con, and some associated instinct made her smooth back her shining brown hair behind her ears. Con never seemed to get untidy no matter what she did. For a second Sabrina was acutely aware of her sister's beauty, and some vital quality for living that went with it. People were always aware of Con.

"But ever, Brin?" Margaret insisted. "But ever?"

"Of course, love, of course. I shall want you for my bridesmaid."

The little girl smiled, content, and fell silent, but Brin's eyes grew distant on the dark yew hedges flanking the long drive. Of course. But dimly, yet violently, she felt there would be more for her than the owner of the demesne that marched next door, and nearly twice her age, and all the county congratulating Mama because he was a Sir. And what of Mary Rose? The Bride. Sweet and docile and obedient, Brin longed to ask her if she was really happy and wanting to marry Dermot, who looked a bit like Papa's bull down in the far pasture. Or was she happy only because she was doing her duty as a good daughter. She had always been the one for that. Held up to Sabrina as an example, by the nuns and by Mama. Brin made a sudden noise that was almost a snort, and Denis Mary half opened a startled eye. She knew the nuns did not approve of her as they had approved of Mary Rose, always watching her as she herself might watch one of the new foals, unbroken. Cavorting at the end of a rope with an eye to every chance of escape. What did they think she was going to do? She could have told them that Mary Rose was as wild as any, but they had broken her early and taught her pretty manners and the unquestioning acquiescence that Mama required.

And now she was The Bride, and seemed to find it all very satisfactory.

They came from the shadows of the yews and ilexes, to where the light still lingered on the spread of grass before the house, and the drive—swept and weeded, and reweeded, for the morning—widened to a sweep below the pillars of the front steps. For them and for the ass it went straight on, under a wide grey stone arch into the busy world of the stables.

In the secret hour of the Irish west, when indigo dusk reflected back from the great stretches of the sea and drowned the land in lilac light, the big stone house seemed almost floating, insubstantial as the bats that swooped around the children's heads. Against its pale shape the windows glowed in rectangles of gentle light. To each its color.

The drawing room was brilliant, white and amber.

"Oh, look," cried Con. "There's Gran!"

Candlelight was soft in the long dining room where MacGinnis would be setting out the table for the dinner. Some of the bedrooms had their blinds already down, the lamps lit, and high in the dormers was a small warm glow in Denis Mary's room, where Nurse would be already warming his small nightshirt at the fire, and fretting that he would be late to bed if he had not already met his death in the water at the hands of his careless sisters.

Brin grinned ruefully and felt the small damp body against her and hoped the excitement of the house would be sufficient to protect her from the inevitable holy murder for letting him get wet.

On the second floor was the pink glow of shaded lamps in Mary Rose's room, and as they rumbled past, it drew her eyes in fascinated speculation. What would she be thinking about, up there with her wedding dress hanging in the press, and tomorrow night she'd be up in Dublin in the Shelbourne Hotel. With Dermot. It would be like Papa and Mama and the great forbidden privacy of their bedroom. Could she never again run in to Mary Rose, with whom she had shared a room for so long? And find Dermot there? She felt confused and knew herself blushing.

"Ah, Tomasheen, get on," she cried, as urgently as if she were missing life itself, although she knew well he couldn't hear her, thumping steadily along in those terrible old tennis shoes. They crunched through the big archway at the side of the house and saw their father coming from the side door by the gun room with Mr. Brown McCaffery, the solicitor from Cork, their cigars making small red circles in the deepening dusk beneath the trees. Leaving the rumpus of the house for the quiet ivied walks of the pleasure ground. All of them knew better than to shout at him, and even Sabrina's smile was a little reserved and careful as he indicated them to Mr. McCaffery with a small wave of his cigar. Pride was in his gesture, and yet a certain shamefacedness, as if he might be scorned for acknowledging anything so unimportant as a parcel of his girl children. Yet every child looked across at him with silent respect, the happier and safer for having seen him, apart in his own remote world with another man like himself, settling everything for Mary Rose the way he settled everything for all of them.

The last sun caught a spark of light from the heavy chain of gold across his ample waistcoat, where a big seal hung, permitted plaything for an indulged child, gold-hinged, set with dark crimson marble on one side and the pure threaded green of Connemara on the other. Associated always in Sabrina's mind with the rich smell of whiskey and cigars, and the warm sense of privilege.

There were extra carriages in the yard, and all the lamps were lit, hanging from the lintels above the stable doors and two of them from the gnarled arms of the old mulberry tree above the well in the center of the cobbles. From every box, horses alertly watched the bustle, and confused lads from the village staggered round between them with buckets of feed and water, belabored by the ferocious eye and tongue of the head groom. Immediately opposite as they came in they could see through the open doors of the coach house. Old Patsy, who had sired Tomasheen late enough in life to astonish himself and damage the child, labored under a lantern in the cavernous dark, putting the last loving layers of polish on the carriage that would carry Mary Rose in the morning. Behind the high stone wall of the kitchen yard that bounded on the stables, light and noise blazed out with the same sense of urgency and controlled confusion.

As in the grandstand at the races, they all stood up in the cart to survey the scene, a part at last of the excitement. Resentful at being disturbed, Denis Mary leaned up against Sabrina's damp skirts and went back to his interrupted sleep.

"Mother of God, will ya look at that," said Con in the end, and could have come herself from some stone-walled cabin in the village. She threw out a derisive arm at a small shaven-headed scarecrow racing with a bucket to the well, importance glowing on his pinched face. "Will ya look at that! Finian Dooley from Claremuckett, and he after our horses and not knowing himself a horse from a hen! Get on away home, Finian Dooley, before you poison one of them!"

As the rope churned up, the pale, freckled face rose above the bucket in the lamplight and a pair of sharp blue eyes took one shrewd unintimidated glance at the damp trio in the cart.

"Ye'd do betther," he said tartly, "to be off yerselves and go put yer stockings on and dhry yerselves before talking to a man."

He was off, staggering through the shifting shadows, hard put to carry the bucket of water that was almost the size of himself. The girls grinned amiably and yielded him victory. On the great day tomorrow, and they in all their finery and Mama and Papa there and Finian pulling his cowlick and getting a few pennies for standing at the horses' heads, they'd not acknowledge his existence nor he theirs and there would be no grudge. Tomasheen came round to lift the sleeping Denis Mary from the cart.

"What'll I do with him?" his eyes asked, and in a moment of cowardice Sabrina's fingers told him quickly to take him on upstairs himself to Nurse. To Nurse and the small lamp and the firelight dancing on the walls. And with a bit of luck by the time Nurse met her again, the wedding would have blotted out the sodden state of his clothes and the lost stockings. Nurse thought no one could look after the children but herself anyway. She had only relinquished them today, with obvious reluctance, because Mama had asked her to help with some last-minute sewing for the trousseau of her first baby.

Mary Rose. All for Mary Rose.

The dancing, busy shadows were full of the smell of sweat and leather touched with cool gusts of the incoming salt tide, and restless hooves clattered in the boxes. One of the minions from the village started to unharness the donkey and Sabrina knew that even without words Tomasheen would manage to flay him into shreds when he came back, for touching his one particular authority. She grinned and didn't stop him and looked around her again with the almost frightening sense of perception and awareness that laid its sharp hand on everything for her this evening. She herself was the small brave lad wrestling at the donkey's head; she was Denis Mary wrapped in calm security, and Mama coming later all lace and perfume and loving smiles to kiss him good-night. The pale crescent moon was also herself, rising gently in the purple sky behind the white cupola of the stable clock; and the first stars and the sweet luminous faces of her young sisters. All life was Sabrina, and Sabrina almost unbearably life, and there was nothing beyond her comprehension.

Watching from the coach house door, old Patrick had come over to help them from the ass cart before Tomasheen's inept and self-appointed assistant took the donkey out and tipped them all onto the cobbles by letting down the shafts. Without thought, Con and Margaret held out their arms and he swung them down as he had done since they were babies. Suddenly Sabrina held back and in the end gave him her hand, and the good man politely turned his eyes from the cold bare legs climbing down past his nose. And from the sudden blush, from Miss Sabrina who had never blushed before, did a mare drop a foal at her very feet; but Patrick had seen enough in a lifetime of horses and people to know that these children who had lived all their lives with animals and knew their every secret had no idea when the time came that, God help them, they were only animals themselves.

"God help the child," he repeated affectionately later that night when at last he was unlacing his long boots beside the fire in the small cottage at the back of the stables. Even though it was long past midnight, his wife was still baking, helping out with the immense quantities of bread needed for the morning. "God help her, she's growing up."

"God help her indeed." Bridie took a hand from the heavy mass of dough she was slapping on the table long enough to bless herself, as if the process of growing up were indeed an unpreventable and calamitous judgment of heaven. The sign of the cross stayed white on her forehead from the flour.

Lamplight filled the high-walled kitchen yard as the girls came through like some golden overspill from the house, and Katty Ann, the kitchen girl, clanged frantically by the open door among a vast, disorderly pile of vats and crocks unearthed from the dark depths of the storehouse.

"Was it the deep crock?" she screeched at the kitchen door. "Was it the deep one?" Her hair stood in a distraught tousle round her cap, and the glance she rolled up at the three girls was wild.

"Didn't I say so," a powerful voice yelled back. "What else did I say and God preserve me from eejits and the same crock'll be no use to me the way I might get it in pieces the size of a millimeter."

"And what would that be?" Katty Ann was mutinous.

"There you are, Katty Ann." Sabrina dropped her bundle of buckets and nets and lifted up the top crocks to let the scrawny girl take the one she wanted.

"Don't drop it now."

"Ah, Miss Brin!"

She nearly relinquished it at the very thought.

"I'd need to be on the next steamer for the Australias if I did that!"

"Am I to put the brawn in the kitchen trap for the want of a crock?" the deep voice asked again, and Katty Ann staggered off, aiming a kick that almost unbalanced her at a small grey cat who took it as a threat to her family, leaping at once back into a cardboard box containing an unbelievable number of kittens that almost blocked the door. Everyone would walk round it for the next week before they'd move it from the way.

Constance bent to pet the cat, her hair sliding at last from its ribbon like a shining flag in the lamplight.

The wide back door was heavy and battered, opening by its immense brass latch onto the cold slate floor of the kitchen passage. An ornate bracket lamp that had the look of better places gleamed pale above the doorways of pantries and stores that not even Mama dared go into without Mrs. Cook rumbling and thundering at her side.

On the right, a steep flight of stairs was covered with worn red drugget, climbing past green-painted walls with a white dado chipped by years of banging trays. It led up to all the floors of the house, on every landing a green baize door swinging its barrier between servants and family.

A barrier never accepted by the children of the house. The kitchen was there for the young ones to taste in and beg in for just as long as they could hold the balance of Cookie's fragile temper. To a second they could judge the point at which they became her enemies and must run for it, grabbing whatever they could on the way. Even the older ones could be caught by the rich smell of baking that also failed to acknowledge the barrier of the baize doors and crept along the galleries to entice them down the back stairs; sitting on and around the vast scrubbed table keeping Cookie in chat while they waited for the soda bread to come from the oven and she indulgently laid down a great slab of butter from the dairy, moist and yellow in its crock. Loudly and bitterly she complained of their presence in her kitchen, and would have withered without it.

Not one of them, even Papa, lost his relish for the joke that their cook actually was Mrs. Cook. She had come back home after being in some earl's grand house in England where her husband, who was a gamekeeper, had been fatally shot while beating pheasant by one of the Earl's aristocratic but more careless friends.

"And he big enough." Cookie never tired of thundering out the endlessly repeated details. "Big enough for any eejit to see him, and even he wid' a crown on his head!"

They would head her off from her rankling grievance, and her consequent low opinion of the mentality and eyesight of the English aristocracy, by telling her it was a grand day for the Herons when it happened. She had been with Mama now since Ulick was a child.

Today the girls knew better than to go near her, crowding their tousled heads together to peer from a safe distance into the vast kitchen that swarmed like a beehive with temporary help from the surrounding country. At ordinary times it held Cookie and Katty Ann, who came in every day, and a small wizened fellow who must have had a name but was known as nothing but the Maneen and who could do anything from skimming cream to caring for a baby or mending the punctures on their bicycles. No one seemed to know where he had come from in the beginning or where he lived and slept, and rumor among the children had it that he had had his home destroyed on account of Mary Rose, having set up a fine establishment in the old carriage in the coach house.

As they came in, he staggered out from behind the kitchen door, weaving his way along the passage to the pantry with a huge salmon on a silver tray, fresh with shining glaze, going off to wait on the cool stone shelf for its final decorations.

"Ah, Jasus," he said and didn't even look at them. "Get on out o' me way. D'you want me to drop the thing. An I do that, I'll be spending the wedding in Cork jail. Out of it!"

"Manny," they begged as they retreated, scrambling out of the way onto the bottom step of the stairs.

"We're starved, Manny!"

"Get us a bit of something."

"It's all in there. Go on, Manny."

The Maneen was joshing the pantry door with the salmon, trying to open it, and in the end the fish and tray, and he went suddenly in together, the salmon on a racing slant like a risen woodcock through the whins. When he came back down the passage the sweat of shock was shining on his hollow face.

"Is it all right," Con asked solicitously, "or does it have to be fish cakes?"

"No thanks to you if it is," he retorted bitterly. "Gwon upstairs!"

Brin subsided patiently onto the bottom step and the two young ones dropped beside her. Through the kitchen door came a noise like medieval battle, heavy with crashes and metallic clashing and urgent shouts; over it all the general's thundering voice of Mrs. Cook.

The Maneen staggered through again, his big boots slopping, and this time it was a ham, the glaze shining like the fish, spotted with aromatic cloves and somber with truffles. He cocked one second's eye at the girls.

"Yer nothing," he observed to the passage wall as he

skimmed it with the ham, "but a load of ragamuffins, and ye'll get nothing out of me. Get on upstairs where you belong."

Katty Ann came out next like a bullet from a gun. Her cap had almost left her head and her glance had a look of madness as she hurtled into the yard.

"For the love of God," she shrieked, and no one could be sure if she ever intended to come back.

"Cookie's been at her," Margaret observed calmly. Brin looked at the tiny gold watch pinned to the yoke of her dress. Time was short.

"Manny," she hissed as he ran back from the pantry. The din in the kitchen was wilder and Katty Ann fled back to join it, tacking under the weight of a zinc bath. They collided in the door and Katty Ann won by the size and strength of the bath.

"Manny!" Brin pressed her chance. "Did I ever do you any harm?"

"You did not, Miss Brin," he said. "Nor much good neither."

With which cryptic utterance Brin seemed satisfied, and was a few moments later proved correct when the Maneen came furtively out, balancing three raspberry tartlets piled with cream.

"I'll not say don't get yerselves dirty," he said disparagingly. " 'Tis past me to say that. Put the plates on the stairs when you're done."

"Manny, you're an angel."

"If I'm not now, 'twill only be a matther of minutes to me harp if Cook finds out."

He vanished again, rapidly, into the sound of battle.

Sabrina sighed contentedly. You always had to fight the Maneen for everything, but you invariably got it in the end. She took a spoonful of her tart and felt the summer sun in the raspberries, picked in the far warm corner of the kitchen garden just before the woods, the cream rich and thick and yellow from the amiable Jerseys in the green pasture down below the ha-ha. She heard the bedlam in the kitchen and knew that up above her the house would be teeming too. Her need to savor every moment and sensation was so great, it wearied her, and she knew herself almost unwilling to go on up and through the baize doors into the other world of the house, to be battered by more of the passionate awareness that had held her all the day.

As her sisters finished, she held out her hands for the plates and put them down where she had been told, on the bottom step of the stairs, where ten minutes later her mother's maid, flying down to the kitchen for a can of hot water, would put her foot on them and crash shricking among the pieces on the passage floor.

"Get on now, girls," she said. "Time to go up."

CHAPTER 2

The world changed through the baize doors.

The three girls climbed the narrow back stairs to the second floor, past the first gallery leading to the drawing room and their mother's bedroom and sitting room, not daring to look out lest they be trapped, stockingless, damp, and disheveled.

Even at her own floor Sabrina was cautious, urging the two smaller ones on up the stairs before she opened the door.

"Quick now. Get those clothes off before Nurse sees you."

Giggling, they scuffled up the last flight of narrow stairs, and she pushed her way through the swinging door opening to the long passage running the length of the house, wide enough to be given the name of gallery, rich with the glow of hissing gas jets that had never reached down into the kitchens. Warm, comfortable light from bracketed lamps fell on crimson wallpaper that was itself almost totally obscured by gloom-ridden steel engravings framed in heavy gilt. Between the shipwrecks and the evictions and the harrowing scenes of childish death, doors stood hung against the winter draughts with heavy red velvet curtains clattering on brass rings. At the far end a window reached to the ground, framing the last of the sunset in the same red velvet, roped and tasseled.

Small tables with heavy legs, crammed with bric-a-brac, stood here and there along the walls. And fat, buttoned chairs. And the girl in passing laid a hand absently on the cheek of a Nubian statue in loincloth and brilliant turban. She recalled it for years as taller than herself. A fleeting memory caught her mind of the time Terry had filled the out-held tray in the statue's hand with his rejected porridge. Nurse had been very cross. Touching the smooth black cheek, it was as if for a moment she had laid her hand on the heart of the house itself, physically aware of the strength and comfort round her.

The small girls still had their life upstairs with Nurse and Denis Mary in the long bright rooms behind the dormer windows in the roof, but she had come down when she was twelve to share a room with Mary Rose. When preparations for the wedding had left no room to move in it, her mother had given her what was a small sewing room at the end of the gallery, relegating the sycophantic and unprotesting Nora Grimm up to the attics. Sabrina had been speechless with pleasure, looking out, enchanted, on her own private view over the whin-covered hills to the blue peaks of the mountains and a small, far glimpse of the sea beyond the bay.

She watched the drab little room transformed into a bower of white muslin flounces looped with rose-red ribbons, roses twining thick on the pale green carpet and the crewelwork seats of the mahogany chairs.

Reveling in its emptiness, she had thrown open the doors of the shining wardrobe and then turned and flung her arms ecstatically round her mother's neck.

"Oh, Mama, it's beautiful. And all for me!"

No more sweet persistent dominance from Mary Rose with the sense of being always in the way. "All for me."

Gently her mother disengaged her impulsive arms and tucked back a strand of chestnut hair that she had disarranged. For a second Sabrina was halted by the expression on her face. Sad, and yet sort of exalted, like when she came down from the Communion rail at Mass.

"Well, pet," she said, and sighed, "we must get you used to being alone."

Brin ran her hands along the shelves of the chiffonier, thinking of her few precious books and her shells and the tiny beautiful ivories that Uncle Matt had brought her home from China. She spared no more than a few puzzled seconds to try to understand what her mother had meant.

There was a new dress for this evening, already spread for her on the bed, pale silk the color of turning corn, flounced and ruffled at the hem and sleeves with thick cream lace. The sash lay beside it, deeper gold, the corn of high summer. She pulled her sodden dress over her head and shivered suddenly, with excitement and the sudden realization that she had been cold. Her clammy petticoat followed the dress into the corner, and in bodice and ruffled drawers she poured water from the rose-garlanded ewer into the basin.

Pears soap. Would the Mama ever let her smell of anything but a child? For a long time Mary Rose had had a small secret bottle of attar of roses, dabbing it furtively behind her ears and keeping well to leeward of Mama. After tomorrow, no doubt, she could have what she liked. Or could she? Would Dermot take over from Mama in telling her what to do? Half her eye on her own dress, absently rubbing away at the white, scentless lather on her face, she speculated again on all the mysteries of tomorrow's marriage. The dress for her wasn't too bad, but how old did Mama think she was, making her have a sash like the babies'. Could she not have had a waist!

In her crammed chest, she scrabbled for a fresh pair of black stockings, and as she pulled them up and settled her garters under the frilled legs of her drawers, a tap came to the door and a young girl slid through it with a large enamel can. She looked exhausted, huge dark grey eyes in purple shadows, as if she had been running all day. Her back hurt where she had fallen over plates left at the bottom of the kitchen stairs.

"I saw you come up, Miss Brin," she said, "and I thought you'd like a drop of the hot water."

"Ah, Teresa, that's good of you." Teresa looked after her mother and Mary Rose and herself in that order, and lately there had been little time to spare for Sabrina. "But I'm just finished," she said. Her pale clear complexion with its delicate dusting of freckles shone from rubbing. "But don't go, Teresa," she coaxed. "Tie my sash for me. Wouldn't you think my mother would have let me have a waist at my age."

Patiently Teresa laid down the red enamel can and took a fresh ruffled petticoat from the drawer.

"My best," Sabrina said reverently.

"Indeed. And what else, with half the quality of Ireland down there in the drawing room."

"Well, they're not here to see my petticoat," Brin grinned, but stood quietly while Teresa did up the long row of minute pearl buttons down the bodice and tied the tape at her waist.

"Now the dress. Ah, Miss Brin, isn't it lovely?"

Without envy or regret she slid the shimmering folds over Sabrina's head, and her tired young face was soft with pleasure as she settled the foam of lace round the girl's thin elbows.

Rancor or jealousy against the richness of the house and family had never touched her from the day the parish priest had come to Mama and recommended her as a possible servant. "A bright, neat child," he had said to her, "and you'd be doing God's work to lessen the burden in that house by even one."

Teresa had proved him right, so bright and so swiftly clever with her fingers that Mama had soon removed her from the kitchen and the cleaning and trained her for herself. And then for Mary Rose and for Sabrina as they grew old enough to need her.

"The sash now, acushla."

Obediently Brin watched in the mirror as Teresa deftly wrapped the dark gold folds of shot silk around her waist. She knew a sudden sense of excitement and uncomprehended power, an apprehension of herself, as if she had just met some new Sabrina, richly exciting. She gave a small uncontrollable laugh, a little high, and Teresa clucked as she gave the last twitch to the big stiff bow at the back of her waist. Sabrina knew that the ends would fall exactly to the hem of her skirt. There was no one in County Cork could tie a sash like Teresa.

"Sit down now and I'll brush your hair. You look as if someone's dragged you backward through the whins."

Vigorously and carefully she swept the brush through the thick tawny hair that still smelt of the sea, and then reached for the ribbon to match the sash, gathering the hair at the back of Brin's neck with a few skillful twists. In the mirror she saw the girl's face grow cross, thick brows down to her eyes.

"Wouldn't you think," she said to Teresa, "the Mama would let me put my hair up tonight. I'm old enough."

Above her head Teresa laughed.

"And you fifteen tomorrow."

"Exactly."

"And she wouldn't let you have a waist either. Ah, Miss Brin dear, you're in a terrible hurry. All these things'll come. Sixteen's the birthday for them. Sure you're only a child."

Teresa herself, with her chicken bones and her small face thinned forever by the hunger she had known before being taken to work in the house, was not yet sixteen. She fell silent as Sabrina stood up, looking at her. Straight, she thought, as one of the sally rods beside the river.

"Ah, Miss Brin," she said again, looking at the pale dress and the shining hair, the bright level eyes. She could not express even to herself that this straight one in such a hurry to grow up would have more to offer any man when the time came than the correct and milk-and-water Mary Rose would be taking to the altar tomorrow. There was a long moment of silence as the two girls looked at each other, the younger one almost in inquiry, a little awed by the sudden understanding of her own beauty; the other with the sad wisdom and brutal knowledge of life acquired where twelve lived in one small sod cottage and knowledge came with the light at birth. In the silence the gas jet hissed and popped warmly in the round pink globe.

"You'd turn the head of the archbishop of Dublin himself," Teresa said then. "Now put your shoes on, and try not to get dirty."

She was gone, racing to the next task for Mary Rose,

and Brin turned back to the mirror, excited awareness still flaring in her eyes. She lifted her hands to smooth down her soft bodice under the lace ruffles, frowning at its flatness. Mama forbade them ever to discuss such things but of course they did, and everybody knew that Mary Rose had had a bosom when she was little more than twelve and Nora Grimm had had to remake all her bodices. It wasn't fair. Hastily she said an act of contrition for her immodesty and threw a guilty glance at the grave face of the Blessed Virgin, who watched her from the middle of a cluster of well-fed cherubs in a picture above the bed. It was a bit like having Mama always in the room and she had never dared to say she didn't even like the picture. And the Blessed Virgin's hands were full of lilies for perfect purity and you'd know at once she never gave a second thought to bosoms or anything like that. Brin sighed.

Then her eyes in the mirror fell on the little gold crucifix of her First Communion, lost in the lace ruffles around what she felt to be a childishly high neck. Surely she could wear something else tonight. Mama wouldn't mind for once, she told herself, and was unconvinced. But in the morning they'd all be wearing gold necklaces from Dermot, so what matter tonight? Rapidly she unclasped it, not without a pang at thinking she had never taken it off for seven years. But when she was born, Gran had given her pearls, small and perfect, almost the color of her dress. By some chance they weren't locked up in Mama's room, but here, in her own chiffonier.

As she unlocked it, she thanked God Teresa had gone. She'd have put a stopper on it. The small circle lay on a bed of white satin in a blue velvet box, and the square clasp had a beautiful glimmering blue stone. A sapphire. She had a little trouble with it, terrified of breaking it, and then they were on, a single string, like milk against her throat. She couldn't help smiling, and then knew a little shiver of fear. Mama would kill her—but not until after tomorrow.

The door crashed open and Con came in, all in lace-edged white. Her hair gleamed from Nurse's slamming with the brush.

"C'mon Brin. We should be down. Nurse is fit to be

shackled about my dress and the seaweed on it." As soon as Brin turned she saw the pearls.

"Did Mama say?" she asked unbelievingly, and Brin's face told her no.

"You'll be murdered," said Con with relish. "Murdered."

She led the way to the slaughter, dancing gaily along the gallery to the stairs.

Teresa had said something about Mary Rose being resting, but gales of laughter came from behind her closed door. Brin paused and then passed by, whereas even yesterday she would have rushed in to see what it was all about. Mary Rose would be with the cousins who were to be the other bridesmaids. Brin went on slowly, trying to understand what stopped her joining them, going down the first sweep of the stairs to the large square landing where the two sides met to become one flight down into the hall. A tall vase of Pampas spread its feathery shadows across the ceiling above the rose-red lamps, and she gave a small startled moment of acknowledgment to these familiar patterns of her childhood, touched by some premonition of their passing. Con was already ahead of her, skipping along the wide Turkey carpet to where the double doors of the drawing room stood open on a surge of talk.

Decorous, yet exhilarated, flushed with goodwill and the excellent malt whiskey provided by the bride's father, the two families stood, sat, and circled in the hot, overfurnished room. For the occasion, they gave loving greetings to relations and friends with whom they had little or nothing in common, and with whom the knives would almost certainly be out before the last carriage drove away tomorrow. There was also among them love, and solidity and humor and deep religious strength. Rich people. Upper middle class of Ireland, gathered from their elegant and often shabby old houses scattered through the green country. Like Abbeygate itself. Strong ties to England for education and careers, for the army. Strong old families themselves who had dragged their establishments and their dependent villages through the raw nightmare of the years of famine, finishing as any family that has weathered trouble, with closer bonds. Loved, self-satisfied almost to arrogance, benevolent, and in their perfect self-confident security, selfish.

A warm, mixed smell of perfume and whiskey and fine cigars, of silks and pomade and broadcloth, and the inescapable odor of the hissing gas jets hung tangible in the room over the tide of conversation roaring from the most prolific talkers in Europe. Constance danced in, ready to be uncritically enveloped in kisses and hugs by all the adults and glared at by most of the cousins who had not seen her for some time and in any case resented automatically her looks and self-possession. In the door Brin waited, her eyes roving the crowded room until they met one other pair. When they did, she smiled in calm content and moved into the uproar.

"Ah, Brin! Sabrina *pet*! Will you look at her. Look at her. And she inches taller than last year!"

Brin suppressed the desire to point out that surely to God that was only nature unless she'd been sick, heartily disliking the speaker.

"Give me a kiss, pet. Here's your cousins rearing to see you. They've talked of nothing else all day."

Aunt Bridgie. Mama's brother's wife. Big and hot and already dark with sweat—sorry, Mama, perspiration, horses sweat—under the armpits of her too tight bodice. And all the buttons were strained to desperation. She talked incessantly in such a hurry that there was always a bit of spit at the corner of her mouth that she never stopped to wipe away, as if she were afraid people might walk off. As indeed they did, and had to if they were ever to get free of her. She earned the remorseless antagonism of the children by always telling them what they were thinking and pretending soppily that she knew all of what she called their little secrets. Sabrina put her hands behind her back to stop herself from rubbing the wet kiss from her mouth, and glared at the three cousins who were rearing to see her. They glared back at her with equal hate. Redheaded twins with hair like wire and thick legs, and a ninny of a boy called Peter with pale blue eyes like they'd faded in the wash and could never look straight at you anyway, and even though he was older than Brin couldn't take a bit of a toss from a horse without blubbering. They said his Mama was going to make a priest of him.

"Hallo there," said Brin tersely, and the boy gave a reluctant jerk of his head.

"You're to be bridesmaid," one of the twins hissed, and the wire ringlets bent on her shoulders round her hostile freckled face.

The Peggy one, Brin thought.

"I am," she said calmly. "Why wouldn't I, and the bride my sister?"

"And why wouldn't we?" The other one thrust in a second load of freckles. "And why wouldn't we? The Mama here is very upset. She said we'd be the best of the wedding if we'd been asked. A pigeon pair, she said."

Aunt Bridgie was nodding fiercly beside them, a little thwarted by having the subject brought up so abruptly instead of the long and injured scene she had planned with her sister-in-law. But she would not leave them unsupported.

"A pigeon pair," she echoed. "They'd be—"

"Excuse me please," Brin said politely. "I have to say hallo to everyone."

Skillfully she put a forest of aspidistra between them, pursued by the image of Mary Rose going sedately up the aisle tomorrow with a pair of the fat pigeons from the pleasure grounds waddling along behind her. She was still grinning when she found Aunt Tessa on the other side of the banked plants.

"Ah, Auntie Tessa." With real love and pleasure she let herself be folded sweetly in a soft perfumed hug by her mother's sister. A larger, darker woman, possessing some rich ease of manner very different from Mama's sharp elegance. She always seemed just about to laugh; and tall, fair Uncle Marcus about to laugh at her. Brin looked from one fond face to the other, caught at once by the air of calm happiness that hung about them like the fragrance of Aunt Tessa's Paris perfume. This same feeling filled their rambling white house on the cliffs between Kilfenora and the ocean, where eleven children romped and roared as wild and free as the waves that smashed below the rocks.

"Who's come?" Brin asked them, still holding to both their hands. "Who's come?"

Aunt Tessa and Uncle Marcus never traveled with more than a selection of their children, maintaining that no one, not even the railroads, could be expected to endure the whole gang of their hooligans at once. And smiled with pride as they said it.

"Well." Aunt Tessa smiled, knowing her news was good. "We had to bring the bridesmaids, didn't we? And then of course, Sue for you. She's over there with the birds' eggs."

Brin glanced across, content.

"I've seen Mary Rose's dress," she whispered, leaning to her aunt, whose soft ruffled dress was almost the same color as Sabrina's own, a fine cameo among the lace at her slender throat. "It's supposed to be a secret, but I've seen it."

"I'll tell you what, pet," Aunt Tessa said, and her smile held something close to astonishment. "Bride or no bride, she'll have her work cut out to look as good as you!"

Disbelief touched Sabrina, and then the same excitement that had filled her earlier and made her put on the pearls. But to have a grown-up say it! Instinctively she glanced round for her mother, who was very strict on what she called vanity, and then she grew shy and moved away a little awkwardly.

"I'll be gone to Sue," she said, and they both looked after her with affection.

"The pick of the bunch," her uncle said.

"True for you," Aunt Tessa answered, and her lovely face had grown somber. "The pick of the bunch. My sister should tell her what she wants of her. I've no patience with springing a thing like that on a girl without telling her. It's not—"

She didn't finish. A great rustle of drab brown bombazine rose up in front of her, and a strong smell of plain soap.

"I understand, eh, you are, eh, our hostess's sister, eh. I must, eh, introduce myself. I am the bridegroom's elder sister, eh, the Honorable, eh, Eleanor Fitz, eh, James."

"Well now, that's a great pleasure." Marcus's sigh was

inaudible and he stood up courteously to face the large row of uneven teeth and to take the limp hand in his.

Brin was not making straight for Sue. She could see her, with her head happily buried in the velvet-lined cabinet of birds' eggs, and spared a thought of pity for her if she should break one, for Mama never had any feeling that other people's children should be spared reproaches. But there was someone else she wanted to see first. She had to stop and wait patiently while Grandmama, regal in black silk with fringes of jet, ran her eye over her dress and gave an unnecessary tweak to her sash. Brin told Sue afterwards the sweat was breaking on her like a balking horse, lest the old lady see the pearls. No use saying it was none of her business; Grandmama thought everything her business. But Grandmama was fortunately too busy being Grandmama, with bigger game today, and dismissed her briefly.

The parish priest then claimed her manners, removing his nose from a glass of sherry just long enough to eye her with some thin kind of automatic sociability, condescending with brittle humor, the gaslight green on his ancient suit. She dropped him a respectful curtsey and slid away.

It was necessary to skirt as wide as manners and the crowded room allowed her round her Uncle Malachy, one of Papa's younger brothers. He was known in the drawing rooms in doubtful whispers as a bit of the lad for the ladies, and some of them indeed not even all they should be. Pale-eyed and pale-haired, he was better known to Sabrina and all her girl cousins as a thorough and embarrassing nuisance with a strange bright-eyed smile and as many moist pudgy hands as the squid they sometimes found washed up on shore in summer. To be evaded at all costs.

"I must go and be polite to the Bishop, Uncle Malachy," she said sweetly, neatly sidestepping, and moved sharply to where the old gentleman was standing in a proprietary fashion before the huge frilled fan of paper in the empty grate. Behind him on the marble mantelpiece a gang of Baleek cherubs struggled to hold on their white shoulders an ornate and unreadable gilt clock. Talking to the Bishop was Colonel Sir William Fitzjames; he and Papa had been in the Irish Guards together, the regiment John was in now. He was Dermot's uncle of course, for Dermot's father was dead, and Dermot and Mary Rose were to have the big house now when they were married, and the mother and the old horse they called Miss Eleanor were to go and live in the smaller house across the park.

Where was John, she thought suddenly. And Terry?

Of course, all the young men had gone off to Cork for a dinner party in Stephen's Hotel with Dermot. In the morning Brin had heard Mary Rose hanging over the bannister in the hall, threatening all hell to John and Ulick if they should get the bridegroom drunk, then Mama had come out to see what all the noise was about, and Mary Rose had turned at once back into The Bride again.

Touched again by the dim nagging that Mary Rose and The Bride were not the same person, she frowned. Dermot maybe was rather old, and a bit silly on the drink, but he was very nice and suitable, not like the awful scandal of Geraldine Cuthbertson on the other side of the bay, who fell in love with a draper's assistant and had the whole county by the ears with it until the mother had to take her off to England to get her away from him.

Stiff, dutiful badinage from the two elderly gentlemen was clearly passing over her head, so she smiled to show she had been listening and dropped her polite curtsey, escaping gladly from the smell of age and whiskey and the heat of the two big gas globes sizzling behind their heads.

She passed her cousin Peter again, quickly, before he could manage the pinch she saw in his china-blue eyes. Their dislike was savage and mutual and she couldn't resist an inch of tongue to celebrate her escape, sliding off into safety in the lee of the dark blue velvet of the bridegroom's mother.

"Good evening, Lady Fitzjames."

"Oh, ah, oh." She had the same vocal hesitations as her daughter. "Sabrina, is it? Ah, oh, yes, Sabrina. And how are you this happy evening, Sabrina?"

Her smile was thin and watchful, as if she felt the need to be suspicious of even the youngest members of this family who had at last succeeded in carrying off her only son. Brin only thought how amazingly like Dermot she looked, and she an old lady. It was partly the old-fashioned hair like the king's mother, or to be true, like Dermot and the black bull with the curls down on its forehead. But sure to God the curls shouldn't be still so black. Mama would tell her she was being disrespectful to have such thoughts about a grown-up.

Another pretty curtsey and she was gone, smiling, to the place she had been making for since she came in the door. The second curve of the green buttoned love seat by the window had been held empty, the old lady on the other side of it gently fanning herself with a fragile fan of clipped feathers. In no haste, savoring the moment she had waited for all day, Sabrina sat down.

"Gran," she said contentedly and didn't even kiss her.

Steady old eyes full of love and with an abnormal measure of intelligence and understanding looked back at her, and in the one glance that took everything in, Brin knew she had not overlooked the pearls.

"And who said you could?" she asked her without preamble, flicking shut the peach-pink fan, touched almost to the quick, choking tears of old age brought on by the sudden beauty that had overtaken this most loved grandchild since she had last seen her. Such a look—of quality and strength. That this one above all should open such a promise of what they called earthly beauty! This one. Looking at her with her own level eyes under the same straight thick brows. Although she knew her own eyes dimmed now by the damage of old age, she could still see the uncompromising look in the child's which would accept no falsity, or pretenses, which must have an answer always from the heart. Gran knew a small shiver of uncontrollable sadness and hoped her daughter knew what she was about. Then, as always, she remembered the will of God, which directed all their lives and made everything for the best, and she calmed and waited for the answer about the pearls.

"No one said I could," Brin said uncompromisingly. "I just felt like it. Mama wouldn't let me put my hair up."

Gran looked at the thick tawny mane and the clear beautiful bones of the young face above the creamy lace, and her old mind groped for the child who had been to visit her at Easter. Only at Easter.

"She did right," she said severely, as if even by this support she might slow down the headlong rush. But she couldn't help seeing how well the pearls lay against the child's skin.

"They suit you, pet," she said then indulgently.

Surely it would be wiser to let the child know the plans for her future. Or was her strong-willed daughter in this one thing a coward, recognizing a young strength that might challenge her own? Please God, Sabrina herself might prove to want it, and that would make everything easy.

"You'll fight for me, Gran? If Mama is cross. You'll fight for me?"

She was only talking of the pearls but the old lady was startled out of her own thoughts and stared and fumbled for an answer. Then she realized.

"Indeed I will," she said stoutly. "Didn't I give them to you? And it isn't every day is a wedding."

Now Brin kissed her and leaned against her across the inlaid arm of the love seat. They sat smiling the same smile and drawing from each other the serene detachment with which they surveyed the crowded and excited room, humming and rustling like bees at swarm. And if the old lady knew too much ever to be touched again by flawless happiness, and the child knew too little to protect herself from sorrow, for that quiet moment it was nothing.

"Brin! Brin!"

Sue had left the birds' eggs and come quickly over when she turned and saw her. She was small and neat and eager, a little younger than Brin, with all the rich sense of life and the easy outgoing charm of her mother. She wriggled in beside Brin on the velvet seat.

"I declare to God," she said all in one breath, "I thought they'd never let me come, and Mary and Carmel to be bridesmaids, and me to be left at home out of the whole thing with all the boys and babies. I cried," she stated factually and with a certain pride, and Brin smiled at her, loving her, her favorite cousin, and made more room for her.

"Wait till you see my bridesmaid's dress," she said,

and Gran drifted back into her own world behind the feathered fan. Sue was not to be outdone.

"When I had them bamboozled into letting me come, I made the Mama buy me new shoes. Look." She stuck out a pair of bronze patent pumps with gilded buckles and Brin breathed her admiration. But Sue had something else to say that she could no longer hold back, driven on by the atmosphere of the day. She grew suddenly silent in the thrumming room and Brin saw the change in her face and looked at her questioningly.

"There's something else, Brin." Her light voice was breathless, and wild happiness and doubt chased each other over her mobile little face. "It's news and I suppose I shouldn't tell you yet, but who else would I tell? Don't let on to Mama I told you because she'll be wanting to tell you all herself."

Brin frowned a little and glanced round her, a bit annoyed. This was Mary Rose's day, and nothing else should be important. But she grew quiet when she looked back at Sue's face so close to hers. It must be something special.

"What is it, Sueen?"

"I'm to be a nun." She almost gasped it out. "When I'm sixteen. I've always wanted it, and the Mama has said yes at last."

Almost desperately she searched Brin's face for a reaction, and Brin stared at her with open mouth. The whole bright room receded, out through the green wallpaper and the watercolors and the great oils of the highland stags, supplanted by the picture of the small bright-faced Sue turned into one of the chill, mothlike creatures with their hooded eyes and dry midair kisses that touched nothing. They always walked along the walls and you never saw their feet. She knew all about nuns. She'd been in a convent since she was ten. She was always happy enough there, but wary of the nuns and faintly hostile, even as a child unable to understand their withdrawal, which seemed to her unnecessary. They taught her endlessly that God made the world and everything in it, and shrouded it all in His love. And yet they wanted none of it, turning their backs on all His creation. Sue. She could find nothing to say.

"You know I've always wanted it," Sue said again, a

little defensively, sensing Brin's withdrawal, and Brin nodded, remembering the talk and remembering, too, thinking that she was surprised at Sue, that she wouldn't have expected her to go through the sloppy stage about being a nun that so many girls went through. And grew out of. Sue had not grown out of it. With some instinct to escape, as if Sue were already in some way different, she looked across the room and realized that three couples of their closest neighbors had arrived and that her mother was not in the room, nor her father, nor Mary Rose or any of the boys.

Shyness would normally have made it an effort, but this time she was glad to get away from Sue until she could think of what she had told her and find something to say.

"Tell me again, Sue," she said. "Tell me again. There's Lord and Lady Brackett, and those other people. I must go and say hello to them. There's no one else."

She sidled through the skirts and the frock coats and fans and cigars to where MacGinnis had literally dumped them all inside the door, announcing them hopefully to the empty air and then vanishing along the gallery, his flat feet thumping and his coattails flying in the frenzy of all he had to do.

Gravely she curtsied to them and shook hands, apologizing for her mother's not being there.

"There's a lot to do, you know."

She didn't know them very well and saw in their faces the same astonishment that had been gentler in Gran's. You'd declare to God, she thought, that I'd grown a beard.

Patiently and prettily she smiled through all the same remarks about having grown up and then Aunt Tessa came over to take them off her hands. It reminded her of Sue. Sue a nun. Of course lots of girls were, but not Sue. She flashed her aunt a grateful look behind the guests, and Aunt Tessa winked at her, easing them all into the room with her soft charm.

Brin stood a moment at the door, in the cool air rising from the hall, where the front door was standing open, watching the bright, packed room with all the silks and curls and whirling talk. She felt as if she had climbed out of the colored confusion of her own kaleidoscope, and must wait a while for all the particles to settle before she could find out where she belonged. And what shape she was. And what color. In the bright pattern, Sue had suddenly become unexpectedly dark and strange, sharp-edged with sadness.

"Tch, tch!" Mama's teeth clicked disapproval behind her and she swept in with all the fresh sweet smell of the flower-filled conservatory about her. "Sabrina, child, what are you thinking about? All these people here and myself run off the soles of my shoes and Mary Rose resting, and you can do no more than hang around the door like a beggar at a tea shop."

Brin had a fleeting thought of the gales of laughter coming out of Mary Rose's room, but did not argue with her mother. One never argued with Mama. Sabrina was too frequently struck dumb by the pictures conjured by her flow of speech. This had a bad effect, unless she was careful, of making her twitch with laughter instead of composing her face to the necessary contrition.

"I'm sorry, Mama," she said now, and a small disloyal snake of thought made her speculate on how often Mama was wrong about things simply because she never gave people time to put her right. But then, she was always in a hurry because she was always doing good for someone, so maybe it all equaled out.

"Come on in now, and pick up your manners and make our guests welcome."

She was already gone herself, flashing into the room, little taller than Sabrina, a compact and elegant small dynamo of efficiency and hospitality, trailing the sweet perfume of her daughter's wedding flowers, the frills on her dark green muslin dress crusted with the thick white lace of Connemara. Her soft, piled hair was the same red-gold as Terry's, regal on her long neck. As she wheeled off, already talking to the first people inside the door, Sabrina was aware that in one sharp glance she had seen the pearls and the reckoning would come later.

She sighed, and would have made her way back to Sue and her difficult news when she heard MacGinnis down in the hall, and a woman's voice answering him. Reduced a little even by the brief contest with her mother, she gave way to her reluctance to plough again across the crowd of adults, and waited to see who it was, curious as to who was yet to come.

They rounded the stairs onto the gallery, poor old MacGinnis puffing like a grampus, and at once it was Sabrina's instinct to turn and loose herself.

Cousin Anna. Of course. She should have missed her in there. Not that she was anybody's cousin, but an old school friend of Mama's who lived a little mysteriously in England and came regularly to visit when she was in Cork, where, it seemed, she had lived when she and Mama became friends at the convent.

Brin knew Papa hated her, and there was always strain when she came to stay, introducing into the ordered and contented household some sense of nameless discomfort, and ugliness. As if one should always apologize for being happy or even cheerful, lest it upset Cousin Anna, who for some mystic reason was professional stranger to contentment. Her attitude to Mama was possessive and condescending, constant wordless reminder to all of them that it was she who had known Mama first. All of them had come after.

And curiously, Mama did not resent it, shedding her authority and independence, pleased to close herself for hours with Cousin Anna in her small sitting room, while her dispossessed and resentful family roamed the house, waiting with differing antagonisms for her to go away.

Brin was not trying to analyze it all now. She could never look at Cousin Anna without thinking of the hated Cromwell who had asked to have his portrait painted warts and all. She was just about to turn away, resisting until it was compulsory any contact with the small plump figure—always in black like the old queen, celebrating some endless sorrow—avoiding the dry, critical, and unfriendly kiss. Then she realized that Cousin Anna was not alone. The boy walking beside her was well taller than herself; the gaslight in the gallery fell on dark brown hair and a handsome, alert young face. Well, glory be, thought Brin, it must be the son. She was always talking of him, apparently the best at everything in his school over in England. She was prepared to hate Cousin Anna's son on sight, for you'd expect nothing from him but to be three feet high and warts and all. This tall, good-looking youth with his air of self-possession disorganized her, and she longed to fly to Con, being petted to pieces in the drawing room, to tell her the incredible news.

She had left her retreat too late and had to stand her ground, for they had seen her. A sudden desire to turn and run swept over her, not from shyness or antagonism to Cousin Anna, but from a sudden curious sensation, like the shivers of a goose above one's grave, that the strange tall boy was walking straight toward her, and no one else was there.

From downstairs Papa came booming up onto the gallery with Mr. Brown McCaffery, their voices echoing up the hollows of the stairs, and at the same time Mary Rose and Mary and Carmel came from upstairs in a froth of frills and curls and wild excitement. Cousin Anna realized there was more important game behind her than the still girl standing in the door, and turned back to the three girls, arms out in trilling compliments, black as a crow against their pretty dresses.

Brin could sense the reluctant chill dispersing the laughter, the withdrawal that always surrounded the thick-skinned Cousin Anna. Papa stood with dumb good manners playing with his watch chain and waiting for someone to come and remove her, and Brin suppressed an irresistible giggle. Papa could be so beautifully rude to her, and she never seemed to notice. Or maybe she did, Brin thought with sudden percipience, but thought anything worth putting up with to keep her hold on Mama.

The boy hesitated a long moment and then, after the faintest of smiles as a greeting, turned back after his mother. Mama came out with her unhurried rush, sparing time for the swift, inevitable glance that pointed out that the beggar was still lurking at the tea-shop door.

"Anna! Anna dearest! We have all been waiting for you. And this is Gerrard! So long since I have seen him."

She kissed Cousin Anna with a warmth lacking in all the others and threw her arm about the boy, flattering him about his height and drawing them both toward the other guests.

Poor Anna is aware, Mama had often said to the family, that she is not as attractive as some, and her life has known such terrible sorrow. We must help to make up for it. All of them at times had wondered why they should, and slid out through the nearest door, but now Sabrina stood and watched her mother, beautiful and glowing, and giving all her heart even to the least interesting of guests. She knew a moment of shame and inadequacy, such as frequently touched her, that not only did she not quite reach Mama's standards, she just never would be such a person.

Behind them all, MacGinnis waited hopefully to announce the dinner, order having at last been mustered from the chaos produced by the hired help in the dining room, who all appeared to be possessed of two left hands and as little brains as would sit heavy on a farthing. There would be thirty-four, God help him, for the dinner. The conversation in the drawing room was deafening. At last poor MacGinnis, almost dancing in his efforts, caught Mama's eye and she nodded to him.

The wedding had begun.

Sabrina found herself hoping that Cousin Anna's son with the brown hair had noticed the pearls.

CHAPTER 3

The wedding day itself was a hazy white and silver tide, ebbing and flowing through the long, exciting hours, islanded with sharp peaks of memory.

Mary Rose would take the breath away, she looked so beautiful; but with a mature small pang of compassion Sabrina saw that The Bride had disappeared, and it was Mary Rose herself who stood in the shadowed hall, adrift with lace and flowers, her great eyes dark with nerves, looking desperately young and frightened. Brin found the compassion from some obscure depth of certainty that when she stood where Mary Rose did now, it would not be in anything except secure content. Nor did she understand why Mama, of all people, wept when she kissed Mary Rose and left her with her father at the foot of the stairs, and with them all the servants who could not go to the church, gathered at the doorway, beaming their love and admiration. Cookie wept too, but that was more to be expected, great tears pouring down her fat red cheeks, because Cookie wept as easily as she roared and bellowed, and could cry her heart out at a fallen soufflé.

"Don't forget now to take my flowers when I hand them to you," Mary Rose said and Brin shook her head, herself touched by a sudden sense of loss. Quickly she picked up her own white skirts and followed her mother out into the ribboned carriage, where Mary and Carmel waited, drowned in billows of white tulle and rosebuds. Mama dabbed her eyes with her lace-bordered handkerchief as the wheels scrunched on the gravel, and Brin looked back for a last glimpse of the shadowy white figure standing so still within the hall.

"But, Mama." She spoke softly so the others wouldn't hear. "Mary Rose is going to be happy."

It was a plea for reassurance against the fear of sudden doubts, rather than a statement, and by now Mama was herself again, smiling at the outside servants who were standing in the drive.

"Of course. Of course she is. Everyone is happy who does their duty as God sees fit to call them, and Mary Rose is a good girl. She is my first daughter to leave home, that is all."

Brin fell silent. Her duty as God called her. There must be more than that. It did not seem enough for a promise of a long life. Not enough.

They let themselves fall then into the same happy mood as Mary and Carmel, and under their white-frilled parasols they smiled and waved and laughed and called out that The Bride was coming to all the little knots of people at the edges of the road, all the two winding Irish miles to the little village chapel where Mary Rose would turn into The Honorable Mrs. Dermot Aloysius Fitzjames.

In the porch Denis Mary in his white ruffled Gainsborough suit exercised the privilege of his age by suddenly refusing to do his part in the wedding, bursting into noisy howls and flinging cushion and ring ferociously into a dark and dusty corner, where one of the ushers, composing his face, had to crease and dirty his pearl-grey trousers crawling after it.

Aunt Tessa looked as exquisite as was to be expected, in shell-pink lace, her hat a swirl of bird-of-paradise feathers, but for one second the bright day darkened for

Sabrina at the sight of Sue, beaming at her parents' side in smart blue ruffles and the new bronze shoes. Nuns went up the aisle on their fathers' arms, dressed like brides. Brin turned away.

Not even for Mary Rose could Cousin Anna get out of the rusty black that they all found suspect, and she also wore her customary expression, conveying that everything she watched was in any case doomed to failure no matter how they all tried.

Her son stood beside her just below a window, and the sun struck lights of gold in his thick brown hair.

Dermot was rigid at the altar with his cousin from Mallow who was his best man, and before Brin could see any more, Mary Rose came and the organ nearly burst the little church with hallelujahs, and there was no room for everyone in the small porch with Mary Rose's train, so all the bridesmaids had to scramble past and go outside, and now it was Papa, looking immensely fine and handsome, who was nervous, having already trodden on the hem of her skirt coming in the door. Brin suppressed a giggle, hoping to God when it came to it he wouldn't go up and stand beside Dermot and put Mary Rose away to the side. With a few wild hysterical mistakes, the organ crashed and then fluted into Mr. Handel's trumpets and Papa and Mary Rose were off.

They brought chairs for the bride and groom during the sermon. Mr. and Mrs. Fitzjames, Brin kept thinking, and longed to see Mary Rose's face. The bridesmaids had to stand, and a little way back behind Mary Rose, swamped in the heavy perfume of her flowers, Brin lost touch with the Bishop's homily, half thinking again of what her mother had said about duty, and who, God help us, but darling Mama would think of duty on such a day of sun and flowers and happiness. She abandoned the Bishop's mellow voice and looked speculatively along the two rows of backs that belonged to her family, every single one of them home today for Mary Rose.

Papa had stepped back into the seats from his place beside the bride, his handsome face a little embarrassed by his prominence. He smoothed the waxed ends of his moustaches and eased his shoulders a little in their impeccable suit.

Mama was next to him, the reluctant Denis Mary content now on the corner of her chair, thumbing her silver rosary to some odd litany of his own. It was duty, Brin supposed, as well as love, that made Mama so good and careful with them all, too careful, they all thought at times, rearing eight children and knowing just what to do for all of them. Nine children for a very little while.

Ulick was next. Taller than Papa, and the heaviest of the family, fair and steady and handling the estate for Papa, better, they said, than any landowner in County Cork. Over and over again she had heard him praised, both as man and master, in those panting moments when a fox has gone to ground and there was nothing to do but turn the collar up against the wind and sit and let the horses rest and talk about the master, who was Ulick.

She felt her heart give a little leap of tenderness for John, who came next. Although in the pairing between the top half of the family and the bottom, it was always Con who was his favorite. She and Terry. John and Con. But John was gentle and so handsome and so funny. In his fine red coat laced with gold and his sword at his side, he looked as if he had been born in his uniform. Every inch a soldier, they said of him, with his dark head in the air and his curled moustaches. He didn't come home very much, and her mind shied away from other scraps she had heard about debts and girls and gambling. Sure they said that about all soldiers.

Terence should have come next but he was on the altar, and then Mary Rose, sitting with her white-gloved hands clasped dutifully in her lap beside her husband.

Her husband.

If Mama had had her way, there would have been an empty chair then for Bernadette, but there had been quite a row about it and Papa had in the end forbidden it as morbid. Bernadette had died when she was barely two and the whole household had wept and told each other thank God, for the poor child was far from as she should be. Even Mary Rose barely remembered her, and to the young ones she was only Detta and the small white grave that Mama never forgot, with the white immortelles gleaming through the green glass.

There was herself, Sabrina, and her hands were getting

sweaty in the tight gloves and she couldn't do a thing about it with two bouquets, and she began to be overwhelmed by a longing to get Terry down off the altar and go away with him along the shore and round the Head, where the tide would be coming in and singing among the rocks.

Constance would never worry her beautiful brown head about duty. She listened to all Mama had to say and looked as if butter wouldn't melt in her mouth, and she knew the right way to handle everyone and they all loved her. But Con was for Con and no one else.

The little ones were just babies. Nothing yet. Enveloped in the great warm blanket of love that Mama spread about them all.

As long as they did exactly what she said.

Her eyes at last moved slowly and almost reluctantly to Terence, sitting over at the right of the altar, his head a little bent and the candles of the High Mass shining on the smooth cap of his red-gold hair. Fleetingly she thought again of all the fun, aware of some latent wildness that had been in Terry always. But more, she thought of the hours and days, weeks, they had sat huddled in the attics in the winter and in the summer, warm and secret out in the old ruins that gave Abbeygate its name, the daisies thick on the long grass of the old cloister. Did anyone else except her, his special confidante, know of Terry's passionate curiosity about far lands and strange places and the wheeling of the stars that had guided men from the beginning of the world. All these things he talked about to her, the small Sabrina ablaze with interest because it was Terry who talked; telling her of worlds far beyond her child's imagination. In fearful eagerness he had painted for her the seven seas and all the lands that bounded them. Did anyone except herself know that he had set his heart on being a sailor. Did Mama?

The bishop ended his address and she had not heard one word of it. Dermot and Mary Rose stood up, and he blessed them and meant it, a smile on his kind old face. Terence moved from the candlelight over into the shadow and Brin gave back her flowers to Mary Rose. The congregation behind them rose to its feet in a rustle as heavy as the incoming sea, to sing the last jubilant hymn.

Afterward, as they came down through the crowded church, Brin met the grave stare of Cousin Anna's son, who did not seem to be looking much at the bride.

By the time Mary Rose and Dermot drove away into the limpid evening among a shower of tears and rose petals, Brin had taken off her wreath and the careful curls created by Teresa in the morning fell in a tawny tangle round her shoulders. The whole place had taken on a raffish look of disorder, the grass in the marquee trampled flat and littered with paper napkins and cigar butts, the tables ravaged and already half cleared by the exhausted village help. The tall cake waited for its destiny, the middle layer to be kept for the christening of the first child, the rest to be sent in little silver boxes to the guests who couldn't come.

Mama, pale but still immaculate, was saying good-bye to the guests. Papa was nowhere to be seen, nor Ulick, nor John, and Brin grinned to herself, knowing they would have vanished discreetly with a few chosen friends and the whiskey, to take shelter in the gun room. Across the trampled lawn she could see Terence, surrounded as young priests always are, by boring religious ladies of late middle age, who fastened on the young ones because they had not yet learned how to get away. She thought of going over to try and give him a bit of help.

"Well, I call that a perfectly spiffing day."

Cousin Anna's son spoke at her side. She must stop calling him Cousin Anna's son, because it wasn't fair, and made her immediately feel she should dislike him. Cousin Anna had haunted the day like something loosed from a wake. His name was Gerrard.

"I'm glad you enjoyed it," she said politely, and then looked at him. Like herself, he was a little ruffled, the smooth cap of his hair lifted into sort of feathers and his eyes a bit wild. She giggled suddenly and delightedly.

"You've had some champagne," she said accusingly, and her own eyes were overbright.

"So've you," he said.

"Did they let you?"

"My mother? She'd send me to bed without my supper!"

They both laughed again and Brin nearly said I bet she would, but then spoke another truth.

"So would mine," she said, "but Papa let me. I had to drink it behind his back in case the Mama saw."

There was a moment of silence, and their eyes met speculatively, too young even to know exactly what they looked for, searching a while until Gerrard came down to their common level.

"Mothers are the devil," he said, and once again Brin had to stop herself agreeing with him too forcefully. She followed his glance to where the crow black of his mother was advancing along the terrace above them toward the pale blue silk of Mama. A sudden feeling swept her that she did not want to be under their combined scrutiny. With Gerrard.

"Let's go and see if there's any ice cream left."

He understood her at once and they vanished into the marquee. But the ice-packed bins sat now in warming water, pink and white liquid sloshing in the bottom. The air in the marquee was thick and suffocating and smelled heavily of the little donkey Tomasheen had brought in with the cart to load up all the milk churns that must go back down to the farm. Brin wrinkled her nose, but neither needed to speak of their reluctance to go outside again, where they might be descended upon with humiliating corrections. Two tongues clicking, observing the overbright eyes; corrective hands smoothing the untidy hair. Cool eyes indicating that behavior had not been quite what was expected.

"I know where we'll go," Brin said suddenly. "Let's take some food. I'm hungry."

"Me too." He let her lead, since they were on her territory, and they scooped into napkins a load of curling sandwiches and drying canapés and all the tattered scraps of the Maneen's salmon that lay now like a stranded and decaying whale. Gerrard added a few rich slices of the wedding cake, and all the time Brin kept a sharp eye open. None of the hired help would stop them, or Tomasheen, God love him, but MacGinnis or even the Maneen would have had something to say. Regretfully they eyed an open bottle of champagne.

"It'd be flat anyway," Gerrard said loftily, covering the fact that they daren't.

"Of course," said Brin, and led the way rapidly out the

back door of the marquee, her mind stirring half nervously with her first reaching toward so adult a relationship, the stolen food childishly crushing the rosebuds on her dress.

Tomasheen stood and watched them go, and then turned slowly back to his donkey and his churns.

"We'd better run here," Brin said outside, and they did, never realizing they were more conspicuous for doing so; and up on the terrace, Terry suddenly drew his mother's attention and Cousin Anna's to a beautiful marker some old lady had just given him for his missal. They disappeared where the ha-ha wall ended against the broken stones of the old Abbey.

The daisies were still white in the sheep-cropped cloister, and Brin realized with a shock that she had never come here alone with anyone since Terry had gone away and it had ceased to be their secret place.

Gerrard Antony Grant Moynihan, she found out, as the unwatched shadows lengthened on the grass. Almost three years older than herself. In his last year at a place called Ampleforth, a public school in England, although there was talk of their coming back at Christmas to live in Cork, in which case he would go at once into articles with a Cork solicitor.

Brin felt an unreasonable glow of pleasure.

"You live alone with your mother?"

"Who else," he said and fell silent. The next words would have pleased even Mama for their sense of duty, and Brin's glow faded. "She needs me, you see, since my father is dead."

She could not talk to him about his mother, because her dislike of her was so intense, so she told him instead about herself.

Sabrina Angelica Heron. Fifteen today, she added a little shyly.

"Oh, happy birthday! And did they remember," he asked, "with all this going on?" He waved a hand back at the house. He had a way of talking with his eyebrows that she found immensely interesting.

"Of course," she answered him, and managed to take her eyes off the eyebrows. "Mama made Mary Rose have it on my birthday."

She saw a shadow gather on his face, a sort of bleak composure.

"It must be good to have a family," he said then. "To share everything."

Even mothers, she thought. To take the strain off just one.

They talked on contentedly of themselves as if they had both waited years for just this information, and ate unheeding the curling sandwiches and the smeared canapés, laughing and wiping their hands on the cool grass. She listened to his enthusiasm about being a solicitor and could only think of Mr. Brown McCaffery with his eyeglass, and surely he had never been young like Gerrard.

"I'd like to be something when I leave the convent," she said suddenly. "Do something. Not just hang around and do the flowers and go calling with Mama like Mary Rose. She loved it," she added.

"Why not?" he said. "Lots of girls do things now. Like doctors even."

Brin shook her head, unable to put into words even the idea of confronting Mama with such a suggestion. It would be a bigger storm than the Night of the Big Wind itself. No. She would have to sit and play her part until Mama found someone like Dermot for her. She balked at that, unable even to consider it.

"I wouldn't be allowed" was all she said, and Gerrard looked at her curiously. Such a mixture of determination and submission, hugging her knees, oblivious of her crumpled finery, grey eyes dark on some unknown frustration. He heard the stable clock chime eight across the gardens and looked round him at the advancing shadows. He'd get her into some kind of trouble for just being here.

"Look," he said reluctantly, unwilling to end the small moment of freedom for either of them. "Look, it's been grand, but I don't want to get you into a row. It's getting late."

Absently she looked round her, realizing the cloister was deep in shadow and the roosting birds were already beginning to circle the broken towers.

"Mother of God," she said, and became just fifteen again. "The Mama will take us apart."

Mine won't, he thought. Not mine. Never the satisfaction of a good roaring row. Only the withdrawn and wounded glance that told him that yet once more he had managed to offend; and then the refusal to discuss, the sweet, sad determination to talk about small things to show him that no matter what he did they were not bad friends; nothing that he did could really upset her.

And always about some stupid trifle that really didn't matter anyway, yet he was left with an ineradicable sense of guilt.

He sighed and gave his hand to Brin to pull her up, and both of them grew still, startled for a moment by the contact. Brin felt the blush rising to her face and, furious, made great fuss of trying to straighten her crumpled dress as she led the way over the fallen stones of the arches.

Without speaking of it, both of them knew the futility of running or trying not to be seen on the way back over the empty garden. The whole place was quiet now, and anyone looking out the windows was looking out and that was that. They wandered slowly toward the terrace.

"Its funny," Gerrard said suddenly, looking at her. "All my life I've known about your mother. Honor Joyce. She even calls her that. Her best friend. But she always talks as if she still isn't married. But she must have known the lot of you."

"She has," Brin said shortly, and thought it not surprising that Cousin Anna had never mentioned them. She only wanted to know Mama.

"Your mother talked about you, always," she said, and could not suppress a giggle, thinking of the warts. "I thought you'd be small," she added.

He grinned and his whole rather somber face changed. He should laugh more often, she thought, and could not help smiling with him.

"Because of Mama?" he said then. "I understand my father was tall."

Even the house looked weary as they came toward the terrace steps past the empty marquee where the darkness gathered, and Brin thought fleetingly of Mary Rose, on her way to Dublin, and the lovely dress hanging again in the press upstairs. Perhaps she would wear it, some day.

Inside, the dim house was quiet too, the shadows

weighted with a fresh load of memories. The guests of the day were gone, the others resting before they would all drive into Cork for dinner, to give Cookie and MacGinnis and all the worn-out helpers a chance to get straight and rest their ruined feet.

In silence they climbed the shallow curving stairs; closed in by the house, the quick easy relationship that had held them in the abbey seemed to have slipped away. Sabrina felt constrained and shy, and at the same time angry with herself for allowing her shyness to waste precious minutes.

"We should be here more often if we come back to Cork." Gerrard reached after her in her silence, but even he could not raise the assurance to separate himself from his mother.

"I hope so," Brin said politely, and then realized she meant it, and then thought Con would think her taken leave of her wits, to be hoping for a visit from Cousin Anna.

Gerrard didn't understand the sudden smile, but felt a great impulse to touch her, take her hand again before it was too late. They were at the drawing-room door.

Unheard along the carpeted landing, no one saw them come in. In the big room, still tossed with the day's heavy use, the lights had not been lit, and the failing dusk poured through the long windows, showing palely the faces of Mama and Cousin Anna where they sat talking on the love seat. Brin could see at once that Mama was very tired, by the way she was sitting, she who never allowed anyone to loll or crumple. She was sitting quite silent, listening to Cousin Anna.

Cousin Anna was still bolt upright and talking hard, and Sabrina could see the bright intensity of the dark brown eyes. Like dates, she often thought. The bright dates caught the movement at the door and turned on her and Gerrard. Immediately Cousin Anna slumped against the armrest and began exhaustedly to fan herself, sighing deeply.

"Ah, Gerry." The voice was soft with patient suffering. "I never thought you'd go out of reach of me with my smelling salts in your pocket on such a long and tiring day. No doubt you had some affairs more important to you."

She held up a languid hand as he began to fumble hastily in his pocket.

"No, dearest. Don't put yourself out. I have managed without them."

She sighed heavily and put a hand to her forehead, and Brin could feel Gerrard begin to deflate beside her. Her own temper rose in proportion. Why for God's sake couldn't Mama *see*! But the pale oval of Mama's face was merely gazing in concern at poor suffering Cousin Anna.

Before Brin could burst out with something unfortunate, a long dark figure rose from an armchair in the shadows.

"Brin pet. I've hardly had a word with you since I came. Come and let's go somewhere and have a chat before I have to go away again. I'll see she's ready for dinner, Mama."

Terence put an arm round her and steered her firmly back toward the door just as MacGinnis came along the gallery with a taper, lighting the revealing gas jets.

Once safely out, Terry began to laugh uncontrollably.

"What's the matter?"

Brin began to smile too, her anger subsiding, warming to Terry's very presence.

"For mercy's sake, sweetheart," he said, "get upstairs before Mama sees you in the light. And get Teresa to do a bit of quick work on that dress before she sees it at all. I've no doubt it'll be some sort of an heirloom."

Brin glanced down in some surprise at the crumpled frills.

"Is it that bad?"

"It's like the wreck of the Hesperus."

"Ah, Terry."

How often had he saved her from trouble. She leaned into his arm and laid her head against his shoulder. Could she do that when he was a proper priest? The thought came like a chill of autumn through the summer heat, and she strove with a thousand unframed questions.

He looked down at her and gently released her at the turn of the stairs.

"Has it been a good birthday?" he asked her then. No mention of Mary Rose.

Brin paused and then, rather to her surprise, she didn't think of Mary Rose either. She thought of Gerrard and the way his hair grew and how he talked with his eyebrows and just his face.

"Yes," she said. "Yes. Special."

He watched her up to the turn of the stairs and his thin face was inscrutable and sad. But when she turned and looked back, he smiled, warm with hilarious complicity so that she went on content, dismissing the strange moment of sadness. Terry was just the same as ever.

He himself went slowly back downstairs, past the drawing room where Cousin Anna's voice could still be heard clacking like a reaping machine, and out through the front door. For a long time he walked alone in the pleasure grounds, giving a small warm smile at the hearty laughter coming from the lighted window of the gun room, but staying where he was, only the brilliant white of his collar and the pale gleam of his hands and bent face showing in the gathering dark below the trees.

Cousin Anna and Gerrard—and now she no longer called him Cousin Anna's son—left the next morning in the hired wagonette that took all the guests and their luggage, like a tired picnic party, into Cork city to the railway station, where they would separate to go their various ways.

Gran alone was staying for a few days longer to enjoy the company of her daughter and her grandchildren in the house that lay heavy with anticlimax. Even down in the kitchen there was as near silence as Cookie could ever approach, conversation substituted by heartfelt and hard-worked sighs of exhaustion. All the borrowed crocks and pots were sorted out and given to a groom with the dog-cart who departed distastefully with his load to return them to their rightful owners over the length and breadth of the county.

Pale with exhaustion and terror lest she drop something, Katty Ann sorted the best china back into the closets, and in his mahogany-lined pantry MacGinnis allowed himself the rare luxury of a chair as he reverently arranged the best silver back into its baize compartments.

The Maneen had simply disappeared. No one knew

where, but everyone was aware that in due course he would reappear, pale of the belly of the great fish stuffed on the wall of the back hall, trembling gently and as mystified as anyone else as to where he had been, wincing in anguish from any mention of strong drink.

Cookie lifted her tired head as she heard the wagonette roll from the stableyard around to the front door.

"Shouldn't we all thank the blessed Mother of God," she boomed, "that Miss Mary Rose didn't happen to be born a pair of twins."

Good-byes were general; there were tears and promises, and in the crowd Sabrina tried not to look especially at Gerrard. Sue hung round her like a sad puppy, and Brin felt guilty that she had almost avoided her. In the pale sunlight of a day reverting to the ordinary, she could hardly recapture the revulsion that had seized her, and found tearful little Sue so much herself that she almost thought she had been mistaken. Aunt Tessa had said nothing, nor Mama. So perhaps it was just a sloppy dream on Sue's part. Because of her guilt she was even more affectionate than usual and it did not come hard, since she loved Sue dearly. In the tears and kisses there were happy promises for the summer at Kilfenora and Brin held a sudden choking breath as she heard Aunt Tessa asking Cousin Anna if Gerrard could not join what she called the gang of hooligans.

She allowed herself one glance at his hopeful face, and then looked away again as his mother laid a black-gloved hand on his arm.

"I'm afraid," she said, and the strange brown eyes were lambent with regret, "I shall need my son too much this summer to be able to part with him."

"What for, Mama?" Gerrard did not let it go without a small hopeless struggle, but Cousin Anna didn't even look at him, continuing her sweet apologies to Aunt Tessa.

Brin turned away, unwilling to shame him more by having seen him crushed. There was everyone to say good-bye to, except John, who had raced for a train last night, pleading a short furlough.

Last of all, Terry.

"Good-bye, pet. I'll see you in Maynooth in September. Be a good girl now."

Was there something special in his loving look, some hint of a warning she didn't understand? September. It was then they would all go, every one of them, to see him made a proper priest. To take his vows forever. Removing him surely to some sad unapproachable distance. Impulsively she flung her arms around him, and in spite of Mama's disapproving stare that bored into her back, his answering hug held all the comfort of their childhood, nor did she know why she felt so bewilderingly in need of it.

They were all piling up the ladder of the wagonette, still calling their good-byes and plans, and suddenly in the crush she found Gerrard at her side. His mother was primly occupied in getting her black skirts up the steps while showing as little as possible of thick ankles that would have been no occasion of sin to anyone who saw them anyway.

Quickly Gerrard crammed a small piece of paper into her hand.

"Would you ever write to me?" he said rapidly. "That's the address of a friend of mine. I'd get it." He gave a small nod at his mother.

There was no chance to answer. She had to stand back out of the way, but her nameless sadness had lightened. Quickly she glanced at her mother and shoved the paper out of sight under her sash, making the most terrible grimace of threat at Constance, who had missed nothing and never did.

The high bars of the wagonette crashed into place and the driver shouted to his horses. The big wheels crunched and tore at the gravel and flung it up into the air in showers and the packed vehicle moved slowly off, alive with waving hands and parasols opening like flowers to meet the strengthening sun.

Brin stood and in all the loved and loving load looked only for one waving hand. She felt her mother's eyes on her and, startled at herself, could not hold back a blush.

Mama lifted her hands and smoothed back the red-gold hair from her forehead as if by that gesture she smoothed away all the turmoil of the wedding and calmed herself for taking back her settled world. Even her severe blouse and plain blue skirt made it clear that she had set aside the lace and ruffles of the celebrations, and Sabrina sighed.

Papa was already a vanishing back, making off round the corner of the house for his own domains. Ulick had said his good-byes at breakfast, needing to be off about his work, and from the far side of the house came the shouts and imprecations of the gang of men collapsing the marquee.

The wedding was over.

Sabrina stood with Con and Margaret and Denis Mary, fighting a sense of deflation that she knew would at any moment be increased by her mother, who clearly considered her the next task on her efficient list. Under her brown sash, she touched the piece of paper like a talisman.

After a bit of quick whispering, the three young ones raced off about their own affairs; after one sharp glance, Mama let them go.

"Sabrina," she said, the last vestiges of indulgence and celebration smoothed from her face. "Please come to my sitting room in half an hour. I want to talk to you. You can do your exercises until then. I've watched you these last two days slouching around like a drunkard in a bar."

And how, thought Brin inevitably, does Mama know how drunkards behave in bars? But nevertheless, her mind filled with grim anticipation, she walked the proscribed ten lengths of the gallery with the red-bound copy of Pear's Encyclopaedia on her head to improve her carriage. And then for a quarter of an hour swung her arms and legs ridiculously in the regime of calisthenics favored by her mother and supposed to improve she didn't quite know what, since Mama found it too indelicate to explain.

The small precious piece of paper was hidden away in her Latin grammar, and the interview with Mama was much as she had expected, except for the brave flame of mutiny and resentment that raised its head as it had never done before.

She loved Mama's room. Since most of its furnishing had come from Gran's, it was old, with an air of delicacy and elegance lacking in the heavy stuff around the rest of the house. Inlaid and delicately legged, and Mama's innate good taste had known to surround it with light silks and pale plain colors without bobbles and fringes and buttons. The sun struck in and caressed the fine polished surfaces and the room seemed light and made for happiness, and Sabrina was, incredibly, almost irritable.

"Honestly, Mama, I'm not as bad as that!"

Wincing under the castigations of idleness and personal slovenliness and bad manners.

"I have good reports from school, and I'm to be a monitor when we go back. Mother Antonio said so, so I can't be so very dreadful."

If only Mama did not always look so loving, it would be easier to fight her. Not only did she say that everything she said was for Sabrina's good. She obviously thought so, too.

"My darling Brin," she said, and unfairly stood up and kissed her. Brin noticed that their faces now were almost on a level. And also that she had called her Brin. The ultimate pressures were always made with tenderness. "My darling Brin, I want you of all my girls to be the nearest to perfection."

Why me? Brin wanted to cry out. Why me? You never bother Con like this. Why can't I just be ordinary and happy?

But as always with Mama she said nothing, and received the kiss, which only seemed to set some seal on her determination, no matter what was said to her, to be herself. Mama sat down again at her small beautiful escritoire of mahogany delicately inlaid with the glow of rosewood, now piled with all the bills and papers of the wedding. On top of them lay a wire and Mama picked it up.

"The boy just brought me this," she said and handed it to Brin. She looked down at the flimsy paper.

"All my thanks," it said, "for my loving parents and my happy home and my beautiful wedding. God bless you all. Mary Rose Fitzjames."

Mama's eyes were bright with sentimental tears, and Brin felt a surge of pure anger that she knew to be both unkind and mean. The correct thing. Always the correct thing. She realized that she herself would have forgotten. Mary Rose had always known the trick of how to gain Mama's smiles and sweet approval. As she herself could have them by dropping into the pattern and being exactly what Mama wanted, instead of this wild certainty of being Sabrina.

She thought again of her kaleidoscope. She seemed to be a piece that was coming loose. For a moment, panic touched her and she stared at her mother, caught by her own imagery, remembering that when a piece actually did come loose, you could never get the pattern right again, but had to throw the whole thing away and wait until someone gave you a new one.

Her mother was staring at her, and she quickly handed back the wire, touched by some sudden fearful sense of loss.

"That was lovely to get," she said, and looking at Sabrina's face, her mother felt that perhaps her quick tongue had gone a little far, and she sought to make amends, lest she had been a bit too cruel.

"You can come calling with me this afternoon. I need you, now that Mary Rose is gone. It's time I let you grow up a little," she added indulgently.

Offered as a treat. Mary Rose's shoes again. If only she didn't love her so much, the Mama could well teach her how to hate her. Hats and gloves and parasols and the gold-cornered card case, musty kisses in overfurnished houses and China tea and wasn't Mary Rose the lovely bride until the cows came home, wherever cows came home from.

"Thank you, Mama" she said nicely.

Along the gallery she met Con. Con would never trouble about the pattern except to alter it to suit herself. If she ever acknowledged that there was one. Nor did she care tuppence for what Mama thought.

Con darted her one bright assessing glance, sharp with mischief.

"An' I'll bet," she said, poised for flight, "that on top of all the rest of it, she knows nothing about that fellow Gerrard being sweet on you!"

Before Brin could either answer or pull her hair, she was gone.

CHAPTER 4

One of the golden gifts of vanishing childhood had been the long dreaming summer holidays in the west of Ireland. They had never seemed to be real until they were all assembled on the open windy platforms of Limerick Junction, waiting for the train to Ennistymon, traveling, Papa always said with loving distaste, like the tribes of Israel, their small mountain of luggage guaranteeing the delay of any train they took. It stood heaped on the platform like a symbol of freedom as they waited for the express to thunder through, shaking the fretted canopies to their frail foundations and driving Margaret and Denis Mary howling into the shelter of the waiting room, rattling all the tin advertisements along the palings and leaving behind it the silence and vacuum of its passing.

The children reemerged, beaming after the well-loved terror, in their sailor suits of holiday, dancing along the palings to read aloud and savor the bright tin sheets.

"They come as a boon and a blessing to men, / The

Pickwick the Owl, and the Waverley Pen," and the calm-faced sailor on the Player's Navy Cut and the stupid-looking sheep advising them to wash all its friends in Dooley's Dip. They were never sure if they read them or remembered them, their long hair whipping in the wind, and Denis Mary hammering with his spade on the hollow tin, the polite and patient stationmaster with his gold braid as anxious as they were for the train to come.

"I declare to God," Mama used to say, clutching at her hat in the endless wind, "they must look on our holidays as a penance for the lot of them."

Papa never attended the mass exodus, coming later, kept carefully alone in his first-class carriage by a discreet half sovereign here and there, comfortable and quiet with his cigar and the racing page of the Cork *Examiner*.

Brin smiled at her mother's remark, but was nevertheless nagged by a sense of change and loss. Not only in the way the party had grown smaller; first the boys, one by one, and now Mary Rose. The real feeling of loss was in herself, who had never before embarked on this journey with anything less than a whole and entranced heart, clamoring for every loved simplicity that marked it, like the Pickwick the Owl and the Waverley Pen and the picnic hampers in the dusty train and the porter at Ennis with the brown glass eye.

Apart from Mary Rose, it was all still there. It was she who had moved away. Every mile that had previously led to an enchanted land was now just one more tedious mile from some unformulated desperation to be near Cork city.

She couldn't resist voicing her discontent, standing quiet beside her mother while the rest of them raged up and down the platform, pursued in wrath and anguish by Nurse, who had a reasonable conviction that Denis Mary would inevitably end up under the wheels of the incoming train.

"I wonder that Cousin Anna wouldn't let Gerrard come with us. He'd have had a great time of it."

Mama's holiday face faded at once.

"I imagine," she said chillingly, "Cousin Anna can make plans for her son without any advice from me. Or you."

Brin felt Teresa, neat and subdued in her navy costume

with Mama's little red jewel box in her gloved hand, shoot her a glance of warning above her mother's head. Leave well alone, it said.

The slow train was churning in beyond the curve of the line, and the little ones were going wild. The one thin porter looked glumly at the mountain of portmanteaus and wicker baskets and fishing rods and bicycles and buckets and nets and guns. Brin picked up her picnic hamper and the rugs she had been given to carry, and knew Teresa right. Especially after the business of the letter. But she just could not resist the compulsion to speak his name.

Gerrard hadn't known about convents, for all his caution about his own mother, and had cheerfully written to her school. The first she had known about it was a summons from the sister janitor, known to all the girls as Sister Jailer, to go at once to the headmistress. The old nun's head wagged with all the solemnity and warning that such a message deserved, and Sabrina was properly alarmed, but puzzled.

She was a little frightened that something had gone wrong at home. Or to John. Things happened to soldiers even when there wasn't a war. When they were practicing. Quickly she whipped on the Sunday sash and the white gloves without which she might not appear before Mother Angela. As she took off her pinafore and tied the rich silk round her waist, she ran her mind over her life and behavior at the moment and could find nothing wrong. Since the lambasting Mama had given her after the wedding, she had been trying hard, simply for self-protection. Her class marks were nearly excellent, and at Sunday Reading she had had to do the bow of penance for bad conduct rather less than most. Quickly she brushed her hair back and straightened the black ribbon at her neck and drew her gloves on. Better face it and find out.

Had she known it, the strange combination of her severe black dress and the shining folds of the deep pink sash gave her an aspect of disturbing individuality that did little to help the interview.

Mother Angela sat behind her bare table in a whitewashed room so plain that even the sunlight flooding over the well-scrubbed floor seemed an intrusion and a mistake. A piece of frivolity on the part of God that must be endured but not enjoyed. Before her was an opened letter.

Brin curtsied and made the obligatory greeting in French and stood submissively with her gloved hands folded. Mother Angela's deep eyes roamed over her, looking for faults, and found one disturbing one. The girl did not look as submissive as her attitude. A look of self-certainty and directness that was surely close to sinful pride and must be checked; a gaze as straight and clear-cut as the upright young figure. Self-willed. The nun thought of talks she had had with the girl's mother and sighed a little, foreseeing difficulties the mother dismissed. None of her thoughts showed in her shadowed face, and when she spoke her voice was cool and measured.

"Sabrina." A little distastefully, she touched paper in front of her with her dry nun's fingers, then folded her hands again immediately as if the contact had been unpleasant. "I have a letter here addressed to you."

Brin began to smile. Letters were always exciting. Then fear clutched her again. This must be something special to be called up here for it. Had something indeed happened at home? It did not occur to her that such news would never come by letter.

"It is from a boy."

Mother Angela spoke the word as if she mentioned some long forgotten fear. Real confusion took over from anxiety on Brin's face.

"A boy?" She could think of no one to fill the description. Mother Angela watched her for the signs of guilt, but Brin looked back at her with an open, puzzled face.

"The signature is Gerrard Moynihan."

Sabrina's face cleared to a relieved smile.

"Oh, yes, Mother." She had written him one letter as he had asked. A young, careful letter, given with much secrecy to Teresa to post. "He's not a boy, Mother. He's—"

"I'm well aware who he is. His mother was a pupil here."

"Yes, Mother. His mother was Mama's—"

"I know all that also. So that I know this young man is no relative of yours."

"No." A sick chill swept over Brin as she began to see the chasm opening. "But Cousin Anna—"

"You are aware of the rules about receiving letters only from male relatives."

Some trap was closing, and she had not even seen it; the letter had been given to Teresa simply out of an instinct of privacy from the endless surveillance of her mother. Gerrard. No more yet than a sort of new dimension. Something that made the sun brighter and every day a fresh excitement. Something that had made her painfully vulnerable to Con's teasing.

At that thought a slow uncomfortable blush crept up her cheeks and all her instincts clamored for her to turn and run before Mother went any further. Before she made it ugly.

"You may well blush," said the nun, and the lecture that followed had words like impropriety and immodesty and immorality and a host of veiled hints and implications that Brin did not even understand and did not want to concerning herself and Gerrard. Fiercely she closed her ears; standing straight and careful and concentrating on the mouth that opened and closed in the face so pale with cloistered pallor. Framed in the multiple shelter of wimples and veils, black on white, closed away even from her own hair and her own looks. They said they didn't even have mirrors and had to look at themselves secretly in tins and things and then it was a mortal sin. At the moment the girl thought of her only as a source of ugliness she could not run away from. Hostile to a world she had long thrust away, and in the end, however deeply buried, to youth and beauty.

Sabrina got herself out somehow when she was dismissed. Bewildered and with a sense of being tarnished, trying in outrage to relate the words used to a contented hour in the old cloister among the debris of the wedding. Telling each other about themselves. All Terry had said was for the love of heaven go and change your dress.

"It's not like that! It's not, it's not, it's not," she cried to the calm face of Saint Anthony, tenderly holding the child Jesus in a bower of flowers and candles at the end of the passage. The candles reminded her it was his feast day, and she said him a quick automatic prayer, reminding him of the scissors she had lost last week; never thinking to speak of something she had just then lost by Mother's tongue.

"But it isn't like that," she said to the smiling saint,

directly, as if he had been involved, touched by hot bitter tears at the ravaging of something hardly begun, barely savored or understood. Rapidly she slipped back along the polished corridors, to change before anyone could meet her and demand with the fierce curiosity of their confined lives why she had been to Mother's Parlor.

Of course it all came up again with Mama, but she was ready, something in her having hardened in defense of what was secret to herself, even though in her mind she still hardly knew what she was defending. With Mama wading in after Mother Angela, she had a fierce sense of being under siege.

Mama had come on a Sunday visit, and after the lunch was over in the chill, austere guests' refectory, she sent Con away to play with the little ones. Then she led Sabrina, with small, loving conversation, to a seat in the shade in the convent garden.

"Sabrina," she said when she had settled and spread her lilac dress. Mama always looked lovely.

"May I take my gloves off? My hands are hot."

Mama looked surprised at even so small an interruption when she had begun to speak.

"Yes, pet, do. But put them on again before we walk about. We don't want a bad mark, do we? I want to talk to you."

"I know. Gerrard wrote to me. Have you got it from Mother?"

Again Mama was taken aback by the bluntness. Mother was right. There was much in Sabrina that needed to be watched.

She spoke almost exactly as Mother had done, but always with the undertones of love and solicitude that Mama never forgot. Brin listened and knew that this time she could not believe her, nor could she listen. She closed her mind as she had against Mother Angela, concentrating fiercely on a bed of snapdragons and remembering how they used to bite each other's fingers with the blossoms when they were small. The flowers would have been beautiful had they not been planted with the cold need for order and discipline demanded by the convent. Even they had to have a fence round them and stand in rigid rows. She realized her mother had stopped talking.

"May I read it?" she said.

"I don't see why not," Mama answered her. "When all is said and done, it's Cousin Anna's boy."

Then what, thought Sabrina, is it all about?

Mama answered her thought as she opened her lilac reticule.

"It is the deceit," she said.

Brin took the letter and was taken completely by surprise by the soft thrill of pleasure and excitement she got from seeing the name at the end of it. Strong, tidy writing with big upright capitals. Definite, like himself. Carefully she kept her face without reaction, and when she had finished, stayed in silence staring at the paper. Nothing. Nothing except the fact that it came from him. Nothing that Terry could not have written or John, at the same age. A schoolboy's recital of his doings. He had been playing a lot of lawn tennis. They were performing *Julius Caesar* for the parents at the end of term. He had enjoyed the wedding and they would be coming back to Cork at the end of July to make all arrangements for moving back there permanently, when he hoped to see more of her family.

Carefully she folded it up and handed it back to her mother, who looked at her doubtfully, with a faint unaccustomed feeling that she had lost control of the situation, and at least temporarily of Sabrina.

"You may keep it if you like, pet. There's really nothing harmful in it, we realize that."

"No," Brin said, and astounded herself that she should stand up to her mother. "Nothing except that Gerrard wrote it, and that you cannot take away. But now you and Mother have both read it, it's not really mine anymore. May I please go now and talk to the little ones?"

There was no real reason to say no, and Mama curbed the surge of anger and indignation that Sabrina should defy her, all the quick words that sprang to her easy tongue. Sabrina dragged her gloves onto her hot hands and together they stood up. Between them, Mother Angela and Mama had taught her caution and deceit it would never have entered her mind to practice.

The savor and the splendor had gone from the summer at Kilfenora. The great famous picnics along the flawless strands grown ordinary and without magic. Mystified by her sense of loss, she helped as always with the preparations in the noisy, crowded kitchen, taking the hot rolls from the oven and wrapping them in spotless napkins, packing them in baskets that would go into the donkey cart with the whole ham and the crock of golden butter beaded with moisture under its cover of waxed paper. Bags of fresh biscuits and the half of a salmon that Aunt Tessa grudged, throwing it in at the last moment in her conviction that children were always hungry. Warm scones and fresh strawberry jam, and the thin old cook smiling above a whole new fruitcake, knowing she would never see any of it again except the crumbs in the bottom of the tin.

There were the special crisp iced biscuits with pictures on them that even to this day they squabbled over, remembering their favorites when they were small, ritually nibbling off the icing before they touched the biscuit underneath.

All the food went in the donkey cart, with gallons of homemade lemonade in milk cans, down the green lanes and the long winding slope to the miles of golden strand. The family themselves trailed Indian file down the steep path of the cliffs, laden with ganseys and shrimping nets and fishing rods, sun bonnets and telescopes and towels, their friends already waving from the shore, not to be seen again until they struggled back up in the cool shadows of the evening, the sun sliding scarlet below the vast floor of the Atlantic and dusk gathering around the white house. Sabrina went with all the rest as she had always done, and grieved secretly for lost happiness and magic gone.

It was gone also from the dank majestic rainbows that looped the cliffs on dark wild days of storm. Happiness and loved security had faded from the crowded house. From the evenings of quietness around the great fires of turf and logs lit against the evening chill, and from the times that friends were called from far and wide, still flushed with their long day's sun and sea, and the bedrooms filled with rustling skirts and petticoats and flowers and lovely children in the wild excitement of their first growing up. Fixing each other's ruffles and easing out curls, trooping down to the drawing room, soft with candlelight, where the furniture had been pushed back and Aunt Tessa sat at the upright rosewood piano, Uncle Marcus and one of the lads from the stables taking their turn with the accordion and the fiddle.

The great round moon would come up beyond the cliffs, turning the cold Atlantic to a sheet of silver, and bright excited eyes and sunburnt faces glowed in the gentle light, Con in her element, drifting like a snowflake in her white dress.

To Brin now it was a lot of people whom she surely loved, but only doing a lot of things they had all done a thousand times before.

Brin knew well that there was nothing changed except herself, and drew back even further, lest she be driven to acknowledge this to the approaches of anybody's love. She had seen Aunt Tessa looking speculatively at her more than once. It was not that she tangibly missed Gerrard, for she knew too little of him. Rather was it the sad sense of the withdrawal of something important and delicate that she had barely touched; with it went the resentment against inflicted ugliness, and she needed time to recover not from deprivation, but disgust. Little Sue, calmly happy among her approving family in her desire to be a nun, filled her with moods almost of revulsion.

She felt her mother watching her with barely suppressed irritation and even Papa had offered her several of the wordless pats that were his most active demonstration toward any of his children that he thought to be unhappy, comfort for wounds of the body and the spirit alike.

The holiday passed until the time when Mama was ready to go for a little while to visit Gran in Lisdoonvarna town before the whole family trekked back to Cork. There was a game of hide and seek raging through the attics while the grey summer rain sluiced down outside across the sodden fields. Brin could hear them, boys as old as Gerrard whooping with the rest of them through the deserted rooms. Why was she being such a prig? Mama came into the hall where she sat curled in one of the window seats flanking the front door. Seeing Sabrina alone, she offered her a patient and understanding face that still clearly demanded what fresh nonsense was this, that she couldn't be upstairs raising the roof with all the others. Sabrina was being a nuisance.

"Mama. May I come with you to Gran's?"

Mama looked astonished and gratified. "Now?"

"Please. I'd like to see Gran a bit more."

Aunt Tessa had come in and stood warming her hands before the log fire that had been lit against the streaming day. Brin caught the look of affection and even pity on her face.

"What a good idea, Brin love. There's times I get sick of this mob myself, and it's a good thing to go away, and somehow I get round to loving them all again."

Brin shook her head. She had never stopped loving them.

In the old flat-fronted house on the main street of Lisdoonvarna she was more content, with no more demands than to sit with Gran behind the glittering windows that looked out on the comings and goings of the town between their shrouding loops of lace. But she could not talk, even to Gran, who for all her clever understanding always finished up at the blank wall of the will of God.

Gran asked her in the end what was the matter, and Brin shook her head, close to tears, immersed in an unhappiness and withdrawal she could find no words to describe.

"Is it Terry, my darling?" Gran said then. "You knew it was happening, and your Mama is very gratified to be giving a son to God. It's a great blessing on the household. He'll still be Terry, you know. We just have to treat him a little differently when he's a priest."

Your Mama is very gratified. Gratified, too, to see Mary Rose married to a Sir. Not gratified about Gerrard.

Brin thrust down her thoughts.

"No, Gran," she said."It's nothing. It's just me."

She bent and kissed the loved old face between the high wings of the tapestried chair from which Gran kept strict surveillance of the street. Even as she kissed her she knew she had lost most of Gran's attention to the sedate and dignified passing of a dark-skinned gentleman in a turban and immaculate white clothes, walking from the hotel down to the spa, followed at a respectful distance by two servants.

"There now," said Gran, and for the moment Sabrina's troubles were forgotten. "That's the nabob has bought the mansion at the head of the lake at Ballinacool. Wouldn't you wonder he'd think the waters could do him any good."

"Why not, Gran?"

"Well, look at the color of him, child. He can't be like us inside."

Brin smiled and was distracted, as Gran had largely intended, watching the dignified passing of the nabob, whose wealth and legendary habits had set all Connemara by the ears. Then she excused herself and went away, wanting to be alone, for Gran as always had penetrated through the top layer of trouble and hit close to real doubt and pain.

A fortnight later the entire family converged on the grey blank college of Maynooth, in the flat fields of Kildare, to see Terence ordained a priest.

In the cold, unbeautiful chapel with the hard wooden kneeler biting at her knees, she watched in chill reluctance as he prostrated himself below the altar, assuming the very shape of the cross with his body, in his dedication to adopt it and all it stood for in the fulfillment of his vows.

She felt guilty and ashamed and somehow sinful, that she could not share the obvious pride and happiness of all the others. Mama, elegant and suitable in a dark brown braided costume with a small close-fitting hat, seemed possessed of almost mystic radiance, her overbright eyes fixed on the white-clad figure of her son. Papa looked a little disturbed and embarrassed, never happy with formalities, and had the endearing appearance of being out of his depth among all the priests and longing for a cigar.

Only Sabrina, kneeling with all the rest of them for his first blessing as a priest, could not clear the look of doubt and bereavement from her face.

John and Mary Rose were missing and, of course, Dermot. John had written to say he could not get short furlough, which had roused his mother to flushed annoyance and astonishment, since the Curragh was no more, as she said, than a dog's race from Maynooth. Only shortage of time had prevented her from approaching his colonel with her indignation, John having thoughtlessly written only the day before they left for Maynooth.

Mary Rose was suffering from some complaint only discussed in whispers round the house, baffling and alarming Brin, until Teresa had in the end bluntly enlightened her.

"For the love of God, Miss Brin, isn't she simply sick with a baby."

Brin had blushed infuriatingly, mad that the simple Teresa should know all about these things when she did not. So soon, she thought then. Poor Mary Rose. So soon. She can't even be The Bride anymore.

A bewildering and disturbing summer, and she felt she had lurched through it, fraught with awkwardness. As if the wedding on her birthday had marked the last day of something, like all the periods of the church year in the missal. The last day of Advent, or something like that. But no Christmas had come for her, and she knew it would be nice for everyone if it did, in some shape or form, as she knew herself withdrawn almost to the point of being sullen, and disliked herself as much as anybody else, infuriated by Mama's overt and thinly disguised approaches to what she clearly felt to be a particularly awkward adolescence. Gerrard was almost forgotten in the long weeks of silence, except as part of all that had pushed her so grievously out of joint.

To her complete astonishment, he came to Abbeygate for Christmas.

Mama had arrived at the convent one grey December day when the sky lay thick and dark above the enclosure walls and the icy chill in the visitors' parlor was little less than that in the dead garden outside.

Warmly the girls kissed her, delighted to see her; she brought the warm essence of home, and they were charmed at the unexpected break in the dreary day.

Mama looked in benign approval at the broad blue ribbon that Sabrina wore across her humiliatingly childish holland pinafore.

"And are you being a good monitor, sweetheart?"

The gentleness of the question did not deceive Brin.

Ever since the affair of the letter, she had regarded the nuns with cold caution and distrust. After it, she had not expected to be appointed monitor, with its responsibility balanced by a number of small and valuable privileges. Having got her ribbon after all, she was, detachedly, defensively, as perfect at her task as possible. They might not approve of her, but they would never be able to find any fault she could avoid.

"I hope so, Mama." For a moment, she looked past her mother's loving smile, and their eyes met in an unspoken challenge. Mama's next words astounded her.

"I've just been with Cousin Anna."

"Here? In Cork?"

Sabrina spoke too eagerly and too quickly, and at once regretted it, catching Con's malicious grin. Con lay heedless against her mother, sitting on the arm of her chair with her own arm round her neck. No use or thought for defenses, since she would always do what she wanted anyway—and curiously, was mostly allowed to. Brin found a fault in a fingernail and dropped her eyes to examine it. Mama continued calmly.

"Yes, at the Clonmel Hotel. The house they were supposed to have ready is in some sort of turmoil still. It'll be in no manner comfortable for Christmas. So I've asked her to Abbeygate."

That will please Papa, Brin thought at once, but could not help looking up.

"And the boy, of course," added Mama.

Papa loved his family festivals when all his family gathered round him, and was jealous of any intrusion, however suitable. And no one would consider Cousin Anna suitable. For herself, Brin was aware of a rising tide of pleasure that Mama must not see. She could feel herself flushing under Con's grin. She asked the first question that entered her head, one she had often pondered on.

"Mama, why did Cousin Anna go to England to live?"

Mama answered equably, as though she had not noticed and registered the embarrassed blush. For a moment she wondered if she was doing right, but she couldn't leave poor Anna on the streets of Cork for Christmas, and if the two of them couldn't handle the situation between them they were worth nothing.

"D'you know," she said to Sabrina. "I've never really known. And it's not the kind of thing you'd like to ask, since it was at such a sad time. But she must have had her reasons, poor creature."

Mama paused, her mind obviously turned backward on the close friendship of her girlhood.

"Three years is a long time, you know," she said then, and even Con's idle eyes grew interested. There was always a bit of a mystery about the old black crow. "Your father was still in the army then when we were married, and Anna was one of my bridesmaids. I've shown you where she lived in the city."

She had, often enough. A grey stone house with sash windows in a quiet square.

"She was an only child and goodness knows that's odd enough, but her parents were old. Her father was already dead at this time, and she and her mother were very poor. The convent was very good to them."

Both girls were rapt now in the story that something had suddenly prompted Mama to tell. Sabrina listened with greedy curiosity to anything that might concern Gerrard, but also could not resist a thin thread of distasteful curiosity about the enigma of the strange hostile woman who was his mother. Maybe Mama speculated too, sometimes. She was too intelligent not to.

"But, Mama, I've always understood Cousin Anna was very rich. She's always telling us the price of everything and it's always more than anyone else would pay!"

"Don't be uncharitable, Sabrina." For a moment Brin was afraid she had stopped her. "That was later, later," Mama went on after the rebuking pause. "When I knew her she was as poor as Lazarus up out of the tomb. A charity boarder."

A quick streak of unwilling pity ran through Sabrina for the plump girl with the warts in Mama's wedding pictures, staring into the camera with button eyes. Who had paid for her dress? Probably Gran. Did she really love Mama, or was there jealousy to this day in the darting black glances. Brin stared at her mother, her mind groping round a new dimension in her mother's relationship with Cousin Anna.

"Then?" she asked, fascinated.

"Well now, that's how I left her. I went to India with your Papa, and Ulick was born there. Just before we were there three years, Papa's elder brother died, and Papa had to come home to see to the estate. It broke his heart, resigning his commission. He was a born soldier."

For the moment, she had forgotten Cousin Anna, her mind filled with a closer sadness. For some incomprehensible reason, Brin thought of Terry, flat on his face before the altar, vowing his life away to God.

"But, Mama, why did he have to?" What had moved Mama to this confidence they had never heard before? Her mind roved the family. Papa had brothers. One of them could have done it. And even Grandfather was still alive. He could have had a factor.

"Had it," her mother correctly severely. "And no."

Brin blinked, groping after her mother's conversational darts.

"Had what?"

"The land. Abbeygate. The land must always go to the eldest. It's not just something to give any stray character to look after. It must always go to the eldest."

She spoke as if she had just added an afterthought to the commandments of God.

"Even if he doesn't want it?" Sabrina felt a little breathless.

"Even if he doesn't want it. I enjoyed the army too, you know. The station life. I didn't want to come back."

Sabrina looked with new and immense curiosity at her mother and knew her right. She was made for the glittering competence of something wider than a tall grey house in County Cork.

"But why?" she said helplessly, and didn't want to know the answer, understanding now the trend of all the conversation. "Why not say he didn't want it? Just say no."

Her mother's eyes grew cold.

"Duty," she said again, and the girl shrank to hear the whole wide story of distant happiness that she had begun to believe in, squeezed again into this narrow word that

Mama thought was the whole business of life. She had said it about Mary Rose and now she said it again. "We must all do our duty before God, or what else has he given us life for?" Her handsome face was severe and certain.

Happiness, thought Brin and dared not say it, and Gerrard's way of talking with his eyebrows floated inconsequently before her mind.

"I see no joke," Mama said coolly. "No joke." And only then Brin realized she had smiled.

"The land," Mama said then, suddenly and fiercely, and the look on her face reminded Sabrina of a day she had been out on her bicycle with Sue, and they stopped to talk to a man with a little patch of land outside the village before Lisdoonvarna. Batty Flute his name was, and he stood there in the soft blue evening with a hoe in his hand, teasing at a patch of ground the size of one of the tablecloths at Abbeygate, walled carefully against marauding cattle with loose stones carried from the fields. He had shown Brin, as the stranger, his small proud crop of potatoes and his few cabbages and lettuce and a turnip or two for the cow. In one corner was a tangled plot of flowers.

"For the woman," he said deprecatingly. "She has a bit of taste that way, the creature."

He had leaned on his hoe and his eyes held the same blazing dedication as Mama's. "And all round here," he said, and his gesture was almost as wide as the land between the walls, "all round here is mine. I have it from me father."

Brin had thought of all the hundreds of acres round Abbeygate, and felt a moment of deep shame, child though she had been. Later she knew it unnecessary. Batty Flute had all the kingdom he could handle and could look her father in the eye, and Uncle Marcus, landowner to landowner, and speak together of what they had to leave their sons.

"The eldest son must have the land," Mama said again, as if she had followed her thought. "Everything else follows after.

"The second one can be the soldier," she added then, and Brin sat very still on her hard chair. This bright pattern had not been shaken for generations. "I wouldn't let your father stay in the army," declared Mama firmly. "His duty was to Abbeygate."

There was a silence and Brin had an impulse to rush home through the cold, darkening evening to what she had always thought of as the remote and untouchable rock of strength that was her father.

Con yawned and stirred restlessly, beginning to be bored as she always was when the conversation stayed away too long from Con.

"What about Cousin Anna?" she said, trying to bring Mama back to something more interesting.

"Ah, yes," Mama said, but she had one more shot for Sabrina, and her fixed amber eyes made it personal.

"Duty," she said, but even that didn't have the fierceness of her claim on the land. Did Ulick want it? Brin wondered suddenly. Would Ulick rather be a soldier or a lawyer or a chimney sweep? "Duty," said Mama, "is everything in life, or where would we be with the whole population slithering around like half-set jellies?"

Mama had done it again. Ruined the homily by the ridiculous simile.

"And Cousin Anna?" Brin echoed Con in order to keep the grin off her face.

"Cousin Anna? In those three years she had married and had Gerrard, and then first the mother and then the husband died within the year. I've always told you she had a lot of sorrow. Why she went to England I've never asked."

Enough sorrow, Brin wondered, for these perpetual widow's weeds. More sorrow than her handsome and elegant mother who had watched for two years the sad, flickering life of a child who "wasn't all she should be," her mother who was still able to sit there in her perfumed furs; and wasn't she lucky in the ice-cold chill of the parlor, her face still bright with strength and courage. No wonder Cousin Anna clung to her. Brin felt a surge of love and admiration, no matter how they disagreed.

Mama stood up, drawing her furs around her, oblivious of the cold that paralyzed her children. It had been just as cold for her when she was at school there. She had had chilblains too, and never thought to complain.

"I have to go, pets. It'll be dark before I'm home, and

poor old Patrick'll be frozen to an icicle sitting out there anyway. By the way, Tomasheen's going off to do the heavy gardening in the other convent, the Augustinians. He's wasted on the ass cart. He has green fingers and could grow a coach and four from a horsehair and a splinter. And since they've vowed to almost total silence he should suit them well."

Brin hugged her mother, burying her face in the silken fur of her shoulder. She had to hide her laughter because Mama never knew she was funny and got quite indignant if she was laughed at. Con was kissed and hugged in turn, and it gave Brin time to spare a thought for Tomasheen, going off in his own silence from the place he had been born, into another silent world. No doubt Mama had arranged it all and was sure it was best for him.

"Give our love to Papa and the littles!"

Sister Jailer was unearthed from her minute cubbyhole to let them out. They were not allowed further than the inner hall, after which all the locks began, but as the outer doors stood open to let her mother through, Brin noticed that the grey sky had melted into a slow bitter drizzle.

"Bye, Mama! Bye!"

"Good-bye, my darlings! Thank you, Sister!"

Brin was thinking of Patrick, waiting in the cold beyond the outer gate, which Mama would have to wrestle with herself, since not even courtesy allowed Sister Jailer beyond the last locked door.

"Poor Patrick," she said. "Wouldn't you think they'd bring him in and give him a bowl of soup in the kitchen."

"In a convent?" Con said witheringly. "That'd be kindness. You don't have kindness in convents, only Charity, and all that happens a long way away. Go on in back to the recreation room and sew at those nightshirts for the little black heathens in the Congo and stop slithering around like a half-set jelly thinking about Patrick getting a congestion out there on the box!"

She was gone down the long cold passage with a flip of the dark chestnut hair, and Sabrina followed, staggered. Not only was she making a cod of all that Mama said, but the toss of the head and the bright sharp tone could have been Mama herself speaking. She had already vanished down a gloomy corridor where holy poverty permitted no more than a tiny lantern half-starved of oil at intervals along the walls. When she reached the recreation room, Con was already settled at her place among her class at the long table, and she lifted bright hilarious eyes to Brin above the nightshirt for the little heathen in the Congo.

Whatever hopes Sabrina and Gerrard may have had of seeing each other through the holiday were quickly dashed after his arrival in the bright mild afternoon of Christmas Eve. He looked to her like a stranger, older, handsome and competent at the reins of his mother's well-kept trap, in a heavy brown ulster with a velvet collar and a dashing driving cap to match it. Only when he smiled did he come back to her, and she could see he shared her own desperate longing for some time alone. But the police system of Mama and Cousin Anna worked with remorseless efficiency, and in an atmosphere heavy with surveillance they could not snatch as much as a minute to themselves. Slow, hot rebellion was kindling in Sabrina to be treated like a child who could not be trusted, and through the cheerful clamor of Christmas, she met the same look of mounting anger in Gerrard's eyes.

They could snatch small talk against the family uproar, join hands round the Christmas tree on Christmas Eve with the children, and try to hide their passionate attention to each other's presents. His dark eyes gleaming, he watched her opening a packet containing a small old print he had discovered of the Abbey cloister, and above the children's heads, for one careless moment Brin gave away her ecstatic pleasure. His mother's glance shot from one to the other, and when he unwrapped Brin's gift of a neckerchief of paisley silk, she looked at it with grief.

"Ah," she said sadly. "Isn't it a pity that Gerrard has never been one for those bright colors."

He will be now, thought Brin meanly, and had to turn away before she laughed at the thought of all the times Cousin Anna must see it on his neck.

They sat together in the trap on the bright starlit journey to midnight Mass, Denis Mary wedged beside them. But Cousin Anna sat on the seat opposite, and the magic of the starlight and the silvered sea and the age-old splendor of Christmas night in even the humblest church was brought to them for nothing. When on their return MacGinnis brought in the hot soup with all the servants' wishes for their happy Christmas, they looked at each other in a hopelessness that had grown frank and unashamed. He was longing to talk with her and she with him, hedged on every side by the bright determined affection of their mothers.

MacGinnis had the Crown Derby out for Christmas dinner, the table glowing with ruby and gold, glittering with silver and the precious ancient blue Waterford that was Mama's pride and treasure. It was Brin's neat fingers that made small wreaths from Christmas roses, setting them in frail trails of smilax and the dark strength of red-berried holly from the lane beyond the stables. At each place she laid a small packet of scarlet tissue with a silver star, special presents from her parents.

She was busy there most of Christmas Morning, knowing Gerrard had gone riding with all the others, and she carefully drew out her task until at last she was alone. MacGinnis had gone back downstairs in answer to a hissing summons from one of the hired help. A red, shaven poll around the door, freckled face pale with fright at its surroundings.

"Psst!"

Brin knew him as a ladeen from along the road whose usual occupation seemed to be rolling the illegal and lethal iron ball through the country lanes, with a flotilla of small relations to watch for the police and hold the stakes.

"Psst!"

Brin saw the thunder gathering on MacGinnis's face, and bent over the table to hide her grin. With dreadful determination MacGinnis made for the door.

"Gwon away outa that," he said, but before the messenger retreated, Brin got the gist of his trouble.

" 'Tis the Maneen," he said hoarsely.

"Sir," said MacGinnis.

"Sorr. 'Tis him and the lady at the range and the pots in the kitchen."

Fascinated, Brin recognized Cookie.

" 'Tis likely she'll be doing herself a harm—Sorr—roaring there like a heifer with a stillborn calf. Sorr."

Noticing Brin, he touched his shaven forelock, and before MacGinnis edged him out, she gathered that it was the Maneen who had overindulged in the Christmas spirit or spirits, and was now dead drunk under the kitchen table, "wid the feet of him sticking out fit to thrip anyone, and the lady shouting she'll not lay even one more spoonful of grease on the goose until he's taken out."

Brin grinned broadly. Christmas downstairs was obviously running nicely to schedule. She began to clear up, well pleased with her work, and also aware that for all the turmoil in the kitchen, the dinner would be on time and as wonderful as all of Cookie's Christmas dinners always were.

As she brushed her rubbish into a wicker basket, she saw them all coming back from the morning's ride, strung out Indian file along the narrow path beyond the pasture. Gerrard was in the middle, very much at home on a strong grey of Ulick's.

Longingly she watched him out of sight, near to praying that someone might mention where she was.

Alone.

Unused to dissimulation, her hands shook a little and she caught her underlip ruefully as she rescattered all her cleared rubbish and clippings; and when a few moments later the door opened, she didn't look up, her heart hammering in her throat.

"Ah, so there you still are, Sabrina. You were so long, your mother thought you might need some help."

Cousin Anna. Aware. The currant eyes gleaming, knowing exactly what she had hoped for. And her foolish subterfuges to achieve it.

She couldn't look at her, sick with fury as she regathered all the bits into the basket.

"I've just finished, Cousin Anna," she managed to say, and Cousin Anna surveyed the table blankly.

"I always think," she said, " 'tis a pity to put all that sort of stuff around a table at Christmas. I would think myself the good food should be enough."

Speechless, Brin swept from the room to take her basket back to the conservatory. By the time she came back they were all gathered in the warm, bright drawing room, and through the cheerful talk she met Gerrard's eyes, understanding and echoing her own baffled frustration.

At the Christmas table, Con was put next to Gerrard, and on the other side of him the gently swelling Mary Rose. With her hair up at fourteen and a half, Con shot her sister a grin of wicked malice that would have done credit to Cousin Anna.

The evening games were the most humiliating repression of all, when Mama and Cousin Anna competed in what was to them the most important game—making sure that Gerrard and Sabrina were never allowed outside the door together. Teams for charades were quickly and skillfully arranged so that they were always apart. When Mama and Cousin Anna insisted on playing blindman's buff, arranged to please the little ones, so that they might make sure that Gerrard and Sabrina never caught each other, Brin gave up and sat down in disgust. Quickly Gerrard took her lead, and sat himself, leaving their mothers to their pointless capers. Papa looked at them both shrewdly from under lowered lids, and while Mama and her friend perforce played with the small ones in the middle of the floor, Gerrard moved over and sat deliberately beside Sabrina.

"Merry Christmas," he said, and could not keep the bitterness from his voice; and Brin looked at him helplessly, knowing they would both pay even for so small a triumph.

It was Ulick who saved their Christmas, when the tired children were at last collected by Nurse, her heavy face dark with foreboding for the troubles inevitable upon overeating and overexcitement. He flung himself down into an armchair and declared Christmas Day over by asking who was for the meet tomorrow.

"Where is it?" Mama asked cautiously, feeling her way.

"Castle Brackett. You should know that, Mama. On Stephen's Day."

"That's a six-mile ride," Mama said at once, "I don't think Sabrina—"

For once Ulick wheeled on her.

"What's the matter with her?" he demanded. "Is she

sick? She's been riding Castle Brackett Meet since she was ten, and double the distance often. Do you want to go, Brin?"

Brin merely looked at him. Want to go. On Saint Stephen's Day. And with the hope that Gerrard would be mounted. And without either Cousin Anna, who did not ride, nor Mama, who for some whispered reason had not ridden since Denis Mary had been born. And would never lower herself from one of the finest followers in the county to going after the hounds, as she said herself, in a pony trap like a cripple in a bath chair.

Yes, Brin wanted to go.

Mama for once had no answer. She knew her eldest son to be the kind of Master who demanded every able-bodied member of his household behind him in the field, and there was little even she could do to oppose him.

Brin held her breath and in the silence the last big log of Christmas Night crashed in scarlet sparks into the hearth.

"You'll be out, Dermot?"

"I have my horse," Dermot said, and nodded heavily, flushed and determined, as if he already faced the business of heaving his long day's drinking onto a horse in the early morning.

"And you, young fellow. I've just the mount for you."

"I know," said Gerrard, and dared not look at Sabrina lest their excitement show in both their faces. "I tried him this morning. It'll be grand."

Cousin Anna began to speak, leading to the inevitable repression. Ulick stopped her.

"For God's sake what's supposed to be the matter with *him*? Don't tell me he's too much of a milksop to get on a horse, because he doesn't look it. You'll take Battleaxe, boy."

"Spiffing," said Gerrard and refused to meet his mother's suffering eye.

"What about Mass," Mama said as a last desperate bid.

"Mass?" Ulick was appalled. "They can all go out and string their beads any other day they like. Tomorrow I have my hounds out. What's wrong with you, Mother?"

There was complete silence, and Brin noticed her father

with his eyes down, offering immense concentration to the cutting of a new cigar.

"Tattybogle needs a good run," Brin said. "I've not had her out for long enough." She could hardly keep from laughing out loud in pure excitement. A day out with Tattybogle, and Gerrard there.

Lest she betray herself, or lest anything more be said that could reverse it all, she stood up quickly.

"I told Peter to have Tatty ready for you," Ulick said, betraying his intentions all the time, and Brin felt a tremor of fear as her mother's mouth tightened. Her good-night kiss was chilly. There would be a reckoning sometime.

"Well," she said, "it'll be early for Castle Brackett. Good-night, everybody."

She wanted to grin again at the look of infuriated defeat in Mama and the sheer venom on the face of Cousin Anna. Before God, you'd think them capable of going out to nobble the horses, now they'd failed to nobble her. Her eyes slid away from Gerrard's lest even he should see in them the breathless anticipation of tomorrow.

It began in the warm glow of the kitchen when it was little more than day, dark and grey, with the dead feel of the frost promised by the stars the night before. The sun was just opening the first white slots of unwilling light above the leaden sea.

Since Mama had stopped going out, breakfast on all early hunting mornings was in the kitchen by tyrannical order of Cookie.

"And is it me," she had demanded of them, "and Katty Ann or the poor man MacGinnis to go on destroying our feet tramping the length and breadth of the house in the middle of God's night, carrying food to you for the convenience of a pack of dogs and horses."

No one had argued, nor dared anyone admit that the formality of breakfast in the dining room with Mama on such mornings was something they were all secretly delighted to forgo.

Now it had become part of the day. Hot bread that Cookie had not been too exhausted to make before the sun was even up. Crisp thick rashers sliced down from the sides hanging out in the back store. Strong hot tea in the golden light of the oil lamp swinging gently above the table. The first pale sun of the day, spreading beyond the windows and the vast kettle singing on the range. All the rest of the huge room lost in shadows.

Ulick stamped in, fine and handsome in his red coat, and Brin looked at him and wondered not for the first time why he wasn't married. He looked around them all paternally, and his face warmed as the glance embraced his father, wedged into Cookie's own chair at the end of the table.

"Mr. Dermot'll have a good cup of tea in his room, Cookie. Ah, sure, yes, I know all about your destroyed feet. Give it to me and I'll take it up to him."

"Sit down there and eat your bacon," Cookie said despotically. "I'll manage that far with the help of God."

Brin looked at Ulick as he dragged up a chair, screeching it across the slate floor. She really knew very little about him, but she could see from his tolerant grin that he realized as well as any of them that the complaints about Cookie's feet were so that in Mama's absence, she could have them all down here in her kitchen in the dark mornings, making them special to her own kingdom, and the other interdependent one in the stables beyond the wall.

"You know what to do with it on the way up," Ulick said to Cookie as she poured the thick brown tea in a high stream from the enamel pot.

"Ah, sure I have it here," she said, and when the huge cup was full, she put down the teapot and added a heavy-handed splash of Papa's best Scotch whiskey.

Papa grunted and twinkled at the end of the table, and in the old elder tree out in the yard the birds began to sing in faint hope of a fine day.

"Jaysus," said Ulick, looking at the bottle. "So that's where it goes."

"Don't I have to have it here," answered Cookie equably, "to fill yer flasks. Unless you'd prefer wather."

She slammed a silver hip flask down witheringly in front of the father, and then Ulick, and then with a look of great affection which she tried to hide below a scowl, she padded round on the destroyed feet and put one down for Gerrard.

" 'Tis only half-full," she said crushingly.

"Well then, I'd better only half fall off, or get half-cold," said Gerrard, but he looked gratefully after Cookie, who was slapping out of the kitchen with Dermot's tea. Not for the whiskey, which he honestly didn't much like, but for putting him among the men.

"I'll tell you one thing." Ulick laid down his knife and fork and reached for more soda bread, glaring at Gerrard as if he must not be allowed to get above himself. "Anyone who rides with me keeps out of my way. Understood?"

Gerrard nodded.

Papa's eyes were unsmiling, his attention on his breakfast.

"You'd do well to listen," he said. "He's put meself off the field before now."

Cookie lumbered back through the door.

"I'd need a novena to the Sacred Heart Himself," she said, "to get that gentleman awake enough to lift a leg across a horse this side of sunset."

Ulick grunted and addressed himself to what his father had said, a small smile at his lips.

"It's not that you don't deserve it," he said. "I'll tell you something, Gerrard, and let it be a warning to you."

Gerrard looked quickly from one of them to another, only feeling certain of the joke when he saw Sabrina smiling.

"When you add the size of himself there," Ulick went on, "and the size of his cob, the combined weight would come up there near half a ton, and when he's got it going, he can't stop it. Sure I've lost half my best hounds, trampled underfoot."

Papa rolled his eye at Cookie over his enormous cup with Papa written on it, scrolled in gold. Mary Rose had given it to him once for Christmas long ago.

"Give me a splash of that malt, will you, Cookie, like a good woman, before the children of the house have it all taken. And isn't it a terrible thing, while I think of it, when a man gets no respect from his own children."

"Well, b'God," answered Cookie, heaving out the day's

potatoes from the bin against the coming of Katty Ann. "I'd say the gentleman complaining should ask himself who reared them."

Nothing, thought Sabrina, who felt she could burst with the pressure of unaccustomed happiness and peace. Nothing, other than the smell of bacon and the firelight and lamplight, and a lot of silly talk. But it was as if the last lame months had been looped away and she had found balance and content again. Then she remembered that it was the last lame months that had brought Gerrard there beside her, and for that she would accept all the trouble and discord.

Con was the only quiet one at the table, steadily eating her breakfast without even acknowledging the chaffing of the others: but then Con was often quiet nowadays, preoccupied more and more with her own affairs and less willing to give her confidence to anyone.

"I've told them let Tomasheen have Margaret's pony," Ulick said suddenly as he heaved back his chair. "He might as well have one decent day if they're putting the veil on him after Christmas."

"Oh, Ulick!"

Tears of sheer gratitude were hot under Brin's lids. How good of Ulick. Tomasheen had as good a pair of hands, and a feeling for a horse second to none, but there was no more room in the yard, and it was difficult too for other people to make themselves understood. So he was going to the silent nuns. But Brin knew, as the laconic Ulick knew, that he would give his wordless life for what he was going to get today. Ulick dismissed it with a small gesture and went out the kitchen door.

"I've heard tell," said Cookie to the pot she was heaving down from a high shelf. "I've heard tell that out foreign where the Spanishers are, they kill bulls themselves and then eat them. Now if only yer brother was off after a pig, couldn't we have a great meal of roast pork tonight. Who'd want a fox?"

In tranquil good humor they clattered out of the yard and along the gravel toward the road. The pale sun was already pushing the frost back into the long grass along the edges of the pleasure grounds and the dark damp gravel was safe and easy for the horses. The air was chill and fresh and Sabrina took a deep breath of it and touched Tattybogle on the neck as if to promise her her share of the lovely day. Feeling Gerrard's eyes on her, she smiled, without coquetry or reservation, unable to dissemble. The fact that they had managed to escape was the best of all the bright morning.

Gerrard had been thinking that every outfit he saw her wearing seemed to suit her better than the last, but surely the black habit molded to her straightness and the hard hat down above her lovely face was best of all. For a moment the bright day grew dark, and as if he understood his thoughts the bay horse fidgeted a little, sidling and offering him a small tentative arching of his back. Gerrard held him a little more firmly. God help him if he came to any kind of disaster with one of the Master's horses. Anyway. His face cleared. Today was today. What matter he was only seventeen and a half—or three quarters, really—and would have to be twenty-one before he got a penny. His mother seemed to have plenty of it, although she was always complaining. The smile came finally to his face at the thought of asking Mama to give him enough money to marry Brin.

They turned a moment before the gates, partly to allow Ulick past them, and also to look up and wave as they had all promised to the children hanging out the dormer windows. Maggie had had a cold, and so Tomasheen had the loan of her pony, but when Mama and Cousin Anna came back from early Mass, Nurse and the children were to take the trap and find the hunt as best they could, and many a time Sabrina's day had been enriched by the sight of the dignified Nurse with her bonnet on the back of her head, hounding the pony along the boreens and even across the fields with two screeching children clinging to the sides of the trap and the hunt never far from her determined grip.

They all turned and waved, and the children waved wildly back, and then they turned toward the road and the two Irish miles that they must ride before they could collect the hounds, owing to Mama's refusal, even when Papa was the Master, to have the stench of the kennels any nearer to her home. Brin's eye was caught by a movement in a window further along the house. One of the guest rooms. From behind a curtain Cousin Anna looked down unsmiling, bleak in her black wrapper; nor did she wave. Brin thought irritably that even the woman's drawers must surely be black, but she couldn't expect Gerrard to share that joke. She knew he had seen her, but with mute agreement neither of them mentioned her, as if even to speak her name might damage their day.

Neither of them remembered much of it, except that it was beautiful. And easy. The bicycles and the sidecars and the inevitable tribe of yelling urchins with their sally switches; Nurse, breathing a little hard, with Maggie and Denis Mary urging her on; even the old lady from the house beyond the lake in her donkey bath chair. All these did almost as well as the hunt, pouring itself across whin-covered slopes and rocky fields and open woods, with enough satisfactory banks and ditches not to leave them feeling soft, coming down into gentle land away round in a circle from Castle Brackett, where the water glittered brilliant in the bogholes and curlews rose before them in complaining clouds.

Although they kept close together during the day, Gerrard and Brin spoke little, smiling at each other occasionally; overwhelmed by the consciousness of each other's presence, not yet lightened by the ease of speech that would allow them to break down a little the burden of their astonished attraction for each other. Both of them were acutely aware of every physical aspect of the day that passed them like some mutual dream, never to be forgotten.

A little after three, the third fox was killed at the end of a short run in a small plantation of firs halfway down a sheep-cropped slope from a narrow boreen where they had all been jostling for some time in search of a way out. Ulick took the stone wall sideways with the freedom accorded to the Master, followed with more difficulty by all the others, and that included Tomasheen, whose lyrical grin was partly due, Brin realized, to the fact that among other things, his impediment isolated him from any sense of danger. What Tomasheen could not see did not exist when he was once off. She closed her eyes for a shaken second as an enormous chestnut crashed down a tail's breath from the willing little pony, but Tomasheen had heard nothing, and was away, hell for leather down the green field. Brin smiled, delighted for him. He knew enough to watch and keep his distance.

Half the field decided not to go down for the obsequies over which the hounds were screaming in the copse, but to turn where they were within the narrow walls and make for home.

Brin turned to Gerrard; nor did it occur to her to look to anybody else. A strand of her hair had come loose, and her eyes were brilliant. But she was tired now, and the way they had come round, both she and Tatty had nine Irish miles to jog for home.

"Shall we go too?"

All Gerrard wanted was to get her to himself for the slow ride back.

"D'you know where we are?" he asked her, and she looked down to the long, dark blue lake looping among the trees at the bottom of the hill.

"We're gone round the other side of Castle Brackett. About nine miles home."

The horses were edging and jostling a little in the confines between the grey stone walls, already sensing their stables as their owners eased them round with slackened urgency. Gerrard swore softly to himself. He didn't want the ride home in this crowd, making talk to some stranger, and he searched for a way of delaying to let them get away that would not be too obvious. Brin had something else on her mind.

Gently in the press she edged Tattybogle over to where Con sat confidently on her grey cob beside a pale spotty youth with red hair and badly polished boots who had been following her close all day. Brin noticed that Con's hair hadn't come down, and gave her own an irritable push up under her hat.

"Con," she said, "we think we should go home." She could see from Con's face that the intrusion wasn't welcome, but was still shaken when Con took a swift look all round them and leaned in over Tattybogle's chestnut head.

"Well, do then," she said, "the pair of you, and good luck to you. Can't you see I have my own fish to fry."

With an instinct for an alibi, even though she was

tempted to put the heel in Tattybogle and leave Con without a thought, Brin glanced down the field to see who might be there and considered by Mama within the limits of respectability. She decided it was all right. Papa was still there, and Ulick, of course, and Lady Brackett, the mother of Con's redheaded youth. She turned and rode back to Gerrard, and the small delay had allowed the main body of riders to get away ahead.

Gerrard waited, almost suffocating in his anxiety that something might still go wrong. But at last they were on the narrow road between the sedgy ditches, with the great red disk of the sun beginning to slide behind the skeleton trees, and no sound but the far clopping of the other horses and an occasional voice ringing in the first hint of evening frost. And the wild fading notes of Patsy's horn as he collected the ecstatic hounds. At last there was no one else and all the still perfect quiet needed for talking down the world.

And they found there was nothing they could say.

In total silence they rode for almost half a mile, and then Brin first of all stole a glance and saw Gerrard begin to laugh. She grinned herself and began to laugh too, until they rolled in their saddles like idiots, loosing all the tensions for which their youth and inexperience could not find words.

From then on, no mile was long enough, stirrup to stirrup, and eyes to fascinated eyes, letting the horses take them the road they knew as well as Brin herself.

The edge of the world moved up the disk of the scarlet sun and over the flat fields the shadows crept cold and purple. Brin shivered, as much from tiredness and excitement as from cold, but Gerrard at once drew in his horse. Brin turned in the saddle. He was fumbling in his pocket.

"What is it?"

"Didn't Cookie give us something for the cold?"

"Ah, no, Gerrard. I don't like the stuff."

"No more do I. But the good woman might be hurt if we don't touch it at all."

Brin wanted to point out, practically, that he could lean over and pour it in the ditch, but she realized it was an important and ritual part of the day, a day so precious that no one thing must be left out. She reached out for the flask he held out to her, unscrewed it, and noticed as she took it that it was Terry's, with his name on it from some long-gone birthday. She took a good gulp, to show herself as amiable as anybody else for the conventions of the hunt.

Fire blazed through her as fierce as the blood-red water that ran in the ditches in the reflection of the sinking sun, and she stared at Gerrard with tears brimming from her eyes as he manfully took his own great gulp and pretended no reaction.

"Well, it's warm anyway," she said with truth, feeling it down even in the toes of her boots, and then there was no holding the talk, both of them clamoring in the cold dusk to dredge up all experience and lay it like a gift before the other.

"Why did you call her Tattybogle?" Gerrard asked after many other things, looking at the pale chestnut, beautiful because it was Sabrina's.

"Because I was there when she was born, and she looked like one," she said. "All eight-foot legs and wild eyes and this bit of mane that grows the wrong way." She reached out and touched the waterfall of silk on Tatty's neck. "Only it was much worse then."

Tattybogle. Scarecrow. Only Sabrina would think of it. He stared at her, enchanted. The strange world of purple shadows, shot by the last shafts of light from the ditches and beginning to creep with the frosty mists of night, was no more than the eerie and proper setting for the sudden fairy tale in which they rode.

"Tell me," she said suddenly, "did you get in any row from the letter I wrote you?"

"No." He would not admit, terrified of being thought soppy, that he still had it, every word memorized.

"I did about yours."

"You did? With who?"

"The nuns and my mother. You know they read everything. They gave it to her."

"But why?"

His mind groped for even the most minor indiscretion. "It was as harmless as yours."

"I know," she said. "But you know what nuns are."

"No, I don't. Our beaks are excellent fellows. I don't know anything about nuns. Tell me."

She wouldn't blemish the magic day with it.

"I told Mama to keep it," she said, and there was soft regret in her voice. "I didn't want it after they'd all read it."

He could hardly bear to look at her almost severely beautiful young face. A girl who, in his phraseology, couldn't be messed about with. Fleetingly he was struck with some desire to protect her, some speculation as to whether one day, because of him, she might come up against his mother, and what would happen then.

He was clearly aware, and had been for a long time, of the peculiar and possessive disposition of his mother. But the patience and calm that had made his grandfather so successful a courtier of the old queen lay strong in Gerrard. At no time did he move forward to meet trouble, steadily handling what lay about him, and keeping a clear vision of the future he could not yet deal with. Deep inside him, he knew that at some time he would come into direct collision with his mother. But not yet, when he had no strength to speak from. And since her loneliness was so apparent, Sabrina's mother her only friend, he hoped he would be able to manage the collision when it came without losing her.

He sighed, and they shook off a sudden inexplicable silence and the fairy tale persisted into the lamplight and the welcome of the stable yard, where the grinning Tomasheen was rubbing down the pony, having, like Cinderella, been given a curfew, almost on pain of death.

"Was it good, Tomasheen?" she asked him on her fingers, and he nodded like the clockwork Chinaman on Con's mantel, and twisted his fingers into knots to try and tell her. She smiled and touched him lightly, affectionately, with her crop, delighted in his day's pleasure. They went on with the numb and rolling gait of people who have spent long hours in the saddle, through the shadows of the kitchen yard and up the back stairs. From the kitchen came the rumbles of Cookie snoring by the range, and when they went through at the first door, old MacGinnis was coming across the hall.

He smiled at them gently.

"Was it a good day, Miss Brin?"

"It was. Yes, thank-you, it was."

His benevolence enveloped them both.

"Well, you're the first back. Go on in now to the dining room, and I'll go and wake the old haythen in the kitchen and bring in the tea to you."

The fire was monstrous in the dining room, leaping behind the bars of the black-leaded grate, and on a white cloth the big table bore the spread of scones and soda bread and two kinds of barmbrack; yellow butter and strawberry jam and the hot mat ready for the potato cakes; all the carcasses of yesterday's cold birds, gathered respectfully round a fresh ham; and the grand splendid remnants of the Christmas cake.

"Oh, Gerrard, doesn't it look marvelous? I'm starving."

Brin threw herself into one of the curly high-backed chairs beside the fire, vaguely noticing that in the heat of the room, the warm glow that had held her coming home seemed to be getting just a little swimmy. She must be tired. Without a thought, she held out a foot as she would to Teresa, and after a moment of astonished hesitation, with much laughing, Gerrard pulled her boots off. And then she did the same for him and he no longer thought it strange. They sat down again in their armchairs on either side of the flames and propped their cold feet on the high-railed fender of polished brass, contentedly watching the steam rising from their woolen socks.

"Hot, isn't it," Gerrard said and pulled his sock loose, letting the ends dangle like the long curl of Brin's hair that had come down when she took her hat off. Very hot, she thought. Gerrard seemed to be going up and down a bit. She noticed that she had put her hard hat on the round curly head of a child angel that stood almost life-size beside the fireplace. Now when did she do that?

Gerrard got up and brought them both a leg of chicken.

Then they talked again as eagerly as if they had never found a word to say on the way home, groping their way together into a magic country as old as time with the excited certainty that they alone had laid a print in it.

"Do they ever call you Gerry?" she asked him, and realized that she had scorched the sole of one of her socks. She drew her foot back sharply. Was it smoking or steaming?

"Only at school. I don't care for it."

"Nor do I. I'd never call you Gerry."

"But I like Brin. It's a great nickname."

"Everybody calls me that. Even Mama sometimes when she's in a good mood."

The door opened with immense speed and Mama swept in as if on cue, regal in a dark red dress with cream lace high around her throat. It was obvious at once that this was not going to be one of the "Brin" times. And it was clear that Mama found even more to displease her than she had expected, her furious glance sweeping comprehensively over the hat at a rakish angle on the cherub's curls and the two pairs of boots in the hearth and the ends of Gerrard's dangling sock—no worse than Sabrina's dangling hair. Over everything lay the sharp acrid smell of burning wool.

Oh, dear, Brin thought, and sighed.

Cousin Anna wore her most pained and disappointed expression, fixing her gaze steadily on a high ornate corner of the stuccoed ceiling, in order to make it perfectly clear that in no circumstance would she drop her eyes to look at the grievous and heartfelt disappointment that was her son.

Behind them came Con, coolly beautiful with the cold chill of the evening flushing her cheeks, nonchalant and still impeccable, and followed sheepishly by the awkward youth with the red hair. In the far rear MacGinnis, patiently waiting with the heavy tea tray, his long face expressionless; and last of all the Maneen with the hot potato cakes, craning his skinny neck like a turkey, trying to see round the old man lest he be missing some bit of a ruckus.

Mama had no hesitation about looking at both Gerrard and Sabrina, and withering what she saw. Appalled, Gerrard stood up with a sort of sick politeness, and even in the eye of the storm Brin failed to hold back a helpless surge of laughter at the sight of him. A half-picked chicken bone in his fist and a sort of terrible placating smirk on his face, and the silly look of his breeches without any boots below them. She caught his eye and, sick with horror, he felt the laughter exploding in his own throat. He looked wildly round for somewhere to dump the leg of chicken, each hopeless gust of laughter overtaken by another. He couldn't stop, nor could Brin, and now she was crying with it, her stomach aching, laughing as she had not laughed and cried since the clowns in the circus over in Mallow when she was a child. In the end, the two mothers ignored them in disgust, as they might wait for infants to recover from a tantrum.

MacGinnis stepped gravely in and laid the tea tray on the table, setting out the silver service exactly as Mama liked it for pouring out. Then with equal expressionless gravity he stepped out of the way as he was leaving the room, and removed the chicken bone from Gerrard's nerveless fingers.

"Oh. Ah. Thank-you, MacGinnis."

Both of them shook again, one word enough to start them off, but more quietly now. The Maneen sidled round the table in his big loose boots with his platter of potato cakes, taking so long about laying them down that Mama in the end turned her cold glare on him, and he scuttled from the room like a cockroach.

With the back of her hand Sabrina wiped her eyes.

Mama was shaking almost as much as she was, but with fury. Her red-gold hair seemed to be standing round her head like flames. Some appalled part of Brin realized that nothing angered her as much as what she called lack of respect. But she hadn't been able to help it. She clamped her lips together and kept her eyes from Gerrard.

"I see *nothing*. Nothing *whatever* to laugh about for either of you. I was entirely foolish to let you go, and neither of you with the responsibility of Hottentots."

That sobered Brin. If she allowed herself to be laughing directly at Mama, then God knew where it would all finish. Hottentot? Something to do with Table Mountain?

Beside Mama, Cousin Anna's very warts seemed to proclaim that had she had control of the situation, nothing whatever would have occurred.

Mama flew on, almost falling over her own words, and the smell of hot potato cakes on the table was sheer agony to hungry stomachs.

"And *why* did you abandon your sister? Your younger sister! In the middle of the bog and night falling. Who did you think would bring her home? Who? And yourselves riding unchaperoned the breadth of the county and giving talk to everyone for weeks!"

Brin thought of the cold evening and the sinking sun glittering scarlet in the roadside ditches; the warm occasional touch of Gerrard's leg against hers. The foolish, harmless conversation. Poised on all the fragile emotions of the lovely day, something snapped in her, leaving her in bitter coldness against the fresh destruction. She stood up quickly, and Gerrard watched the change in her face and tried to speak, feeling it was for him to take all blame and defend her. She read his glance and gave him a small quick smile and told him with a gesture to say nothing. It would only make it worse.

She removed the angel's hat and thought it a pity. It suited him. Then she threw her own chicken bone into the fire and bent to pick up her boots; nor did she lift a finger to put back her hair. There was something in her chill deliberation that had brought a silence to the room, and she was halfway round the table before she answered her mother, facing her directly.

"Who would bring her home?" she said then, grey eyes blazing into amber, and her voice was as coldly furious as Mama's own. "Who indeed but Padgeen Brackett over there, and that was what she wanted all the time, and he hanging like a leech to her stirrup the livelong day. Would the county not be talking about them? And if she wasn't in such a hurry to race off with him, there was his Mama there, and Papa too, and half the hunt that'd be riding this way, and be glad to see Miss Heron home!"

Padgeen smirked, and Con's brown eyes shot murder. Mama drew herself up, and even then Brin felt it unfair that she had heels on. It gave her an advantage over herself there in her socks.

"Sabrina." Her voice was careful and her face composed, all temper carefully smoothed out. Oh, God, thought Brin, there'll be all hell later on. "I think you must be overtired," Mama went on. "I think you should go to your room at once. I'll have your tea sent up to you on a tray."

Sent to her room like a baby before all of them. No point in arguing. She'd be defeated in the end and give them the chance to upset her. Nothing to do but obey as best she could without letting go the tears that suddenly choked her throat. She couldn't look at Gerrard or she knew they would break. Clinging to her anger, she picked up her boots and stalked from the room, in passing telling Con with her eyes what she would have to say to her later, and having the satisfaction of seeing that even Con looked a little shamefaced and upset at what she had started. The dark look of smoldering triumph in Cousin Anna's eyes she was unable to avoid, and was grateful that she was the one nearest to the door.

Papa was coming round the turn of the stairs, tiredly and a little heavily, gratefully undoing the buttons of his pink coat. On impulse, remembering like pain the warm happy kitchen of the early morning, she went to him and laid her head against the white folds of his stock, fighting back the humiliating tears.

Papa looked down at the untidy tawny head and sighed. Awkwardly he patted her back, waiting for her to grow quiet.

"Storms, pet?"

She moved away, bright tears spiking her lashes.

"Yes," she said. "I've been thrown out."

Some expression that was almost distaste crossed his heavy face.

"I'll come and have a chat with you later," he said.

She kissed him and went on up slowly. It was unheard of, and she didn't really believe it. Only when they were sick did Papa come visiting. Probably Mama wouldn't let him, she thought, in the end, and was then appalled at the directness of her thought; the truth that had erupted from nowhere. Probably, indeed, she wouldn't let him. She wouldn't let him be a soldier when he wanted to.

Teresa had a hot bath waiting in her room, and her attitude showed the speed with which news got round the house.

"Thank-you, Teresa," she said gratefully, and had a feeling that the hot lovely bath with some of Mary Rose's abandoned perfume in it and the extra special tea in bed, with a best lace tray cloth and a poor brown-edged winter rose that someone had snatched for her from some sheltered corner, was not quite what Mama had intended.

Sabrina lay and thought about Teresa. Although she would admit nothing, and flushed a soft defensive pink even at the mention of his name, the servants' grapevine knew she was being courted with determination by a steady young farmer from out beyond Passage West.

What would she do, she wondered, if Teresa left to be married and she had to cope with Mama without her loving, if almost unspoken, support?

Papa did come. When she was curled comfortably in her mahogany bed with some of the fine embroidery that was both her talent and her pleasure. She laid it down eagerly and with warm content when he knocked and came in, ready to give him all her attention, for she felt it must be something very important for him to have come like this.

But Papa did not talk.

He wedged himself with great difficulty into her rose-covered chair and filled the room with his cigar smoke, his light blue eyes distant and abstracted. In the end he got up defeated, and Brin looked at him with fresh tears rising in her throat, torn for that one moment by the incredible feeling that she herself was in some way older than this loved pillar of her childhood.

He bent and kissed her lovingly on the forehead, and when he reached the door he turned.

"You will remember, pet," he said, as though it were the end of the long conversation he had failed to hold. "Remember that everything she ever does is for the best of every one of you."

And left her, with the thick tears at last creeping unchecked down her cheeks, and she did not really know for what.

CHAPTER 5

Sabrina limped through another year, struggling with the uneven balance in her mind between the dutiful behavior to Mama that her upbringing dictated and a set, secret determination that in the end she would be herself and have her life take its own shape.

She realized that in adult eyes she and Gerrard were very young, painfully young, and it would be almost another three years before he was through his articles with Mr. Brown McCaffery. His name was never mentioned. Cousin Anna might as well have been childless. No discussion was allowed in which she might ask that they be allowed even to meet occasionally, to get to know each other. Did the same hostile silence prevail, she wondered, in Gerrard's home? Probably it did.

Mama, she knew, saw her as she had seen Sue at the time of the wedding when Sue had said she was going to be a nun. Brin had listened incredulous, and waited for her friend to grow out of some sloppy religious phase. Now Mama clearly waited with controlled patience for her to grow out of her adolescent romantic notions about Gerrard.

Brin felt it should be some message to both of them that now, at the end of summer, Sue was actually going, sweetly content, not only to be a nun, but in the bleak, withdrawn Order of the Poor Clares. After her profession, she would never again see her family; and in constant recollection of death, she would sleep every night in the narrow confines of her own coffin, and every day lift a spadeful of earth from her own grave. Sue. Brin's heart grew cold to think of it. Yet before she was fifteen, Sue had known exactly what she wanted. Why should she not know too?

So there was no reason to have lonely doubts of herself and Gerrard simply because they were young; although nothing had been said that Mama herself could not have listened to, she knew Gerrard waited as patiently as she for their future.

She had grown more orderly and quiet, beginning to show much of Mama's own style, and the nuns were pleased with her; but the other girls of her own age who came back from the holidays and excursions in high excitement, rushing whispering into corners, had begun to toss their hair and look at her with pity.

"Nothing romantic ever seems to happen to Sabrina. Not a fellow seems to look at her. Wouldn't you think it a shame, and she so good-looking."

There was only one conclusion to come to, and Con for some lopsided reason never let her down.

"They think you're the driest stick in the grade," she told her once. "They've decided you're going to be a nun and are keeping it secret!"

Con eyed her dryly, and Brin laughed and shivered in one breath.

"Can you imagine it?" she said, appalled.

"No," said Con bluntly. "But you need to watch yourself."

"What do you mean?"

Con was almost her own age. Only eleven months younger. After the death of Bernadette, Mama had seemed to be in some haste to prove that she had been an isolated accident in her otherwise handsome and perfect family.

As she had been.

But Brin felt lately that Con was passing her out, a small twist almost of cynicism touching the corner of her lovely mouth, the dark eyes grown knowledgeable and a little hard.

"What do you mean, Con?"

She felt a small cold snake of fear. For anyone, Mama and Cousin Anna would be formidable opponents. Cousin Anna didn't want to lose her darling boy to any girl. And Mama? What did Mama want or not want? You'd think she'd approve of Gerrard since his mother was her dearest friend.

Con pulled a buffer from her pinafore pocket and began to polish her fine fingernails, a vanity like all other vanities forbidden in the convent. The rich Sunday sashes and the ruffled dresses of high festivals were all obscurely for the glory of God, like the flowers and incense and candles and the embroidered vestments of the priests.

Con polished vigorously, not even bothering to look if she was watched, even though she knew as well as Brin that nuns could see out through the backs of their veils. They were sitting in the pale spring sun on the low wall between the arches of the children's cloister, where the girls on recreation were scattered round the stone passage, forbidden the grass in the center lest they wear it out.

"You need to watch Mama," Con said as she rubbed and breathed and rubbed again. "You're too soft."

Brin was shocked. It was possible for her to be at red war with Mama, and to have all her secret fears about the outcome. But it was not yet possible to speak of it, or of how she harbored her strength for a bigger battle as yet far away.

Possible for Con to speak of anything, buffing away furiously after a faintly pitying glance at her sister.

"Well, you may not object, Brin. You may give in all along the way. But I'll tell you this now. I'm going into none of Mama's jelly molds. I'm going to be the one who does what I like."

By some instinct, Con put the buffer away before the soundless footsteps came along the cloister. The two girls slipped off the wall and stood respectfully as the nun passed them by.

Con grimaced after her, aware of the sweeping, critical glance that had passed over them, but Brin barely looked, full of curiosity about her sister. She never resented restraint as much as Con did, especially now that it was all part of the patient waiting for time to pass.

"What d'you want to do then, Con?"

"Get married," Con said tersely. "And not to some walking whiskey barrel twice my age, because Mama tells me to and he's a Sir. I'll have a marriage for my pleasure. To money. So I can travel and do everything I want."

"But, Con," Brin cried defensively. "Surely Mary Rose is happy. Especially now she's got little James."

There had been no need to ask who Con meant, and Brin felt her heart contract with pain. She was not as blunt and practical as Con, and knew she was still pleading in her deep self for all the legends of security and happiness to be true forever, although sadly she knew they were of childhood. Did she begin to do her own thinking with her conviction that Mary Rose and The Bride had been two different people. Or with Terry? Going away into the confines of a priest's life, when he had craved for all the world.

She stared sadly at Con, who would ruthlessly tear the veils from anything, and knew instinctively that this would in the end bring her sister its own sorrows. Mary Rose was certainly happy now; with the minute James in the crook of her arm, she looked like Mary Rose again, even younger than The Bride. And Mama was in high good humor, beaming over her first grandchild and conveying subtly that she was responsible for this happy consummation.

"Have you decided who, Con?" She was being facetious now. After all, Con was only fifteen. Then she remembered that she had been just fifteen to the day last year when she met Gerrard. She looked at Con with interest.

"Padgeen Brackett," her sister said decisively and matter-of-factly. "He'll do as well as any. And his father is as old as Methuselah and hanging on a thread. Padgeen'll have that castle and more money than a king when he's gone. That'll do for a beginning."

Brin regarded her, not even astonished now. What had made Con like this?

"And the Mama'll love him," Con said then, "since he'll be a lord or on the way to it. If he had seven pairs of legs he'd be all right for her. But you watch out."

"And what do you think," Brin asked then, "that Mama has in store for me?" She was thinking of what Gerrard had said about girls even being doctors, excitement stirring in her.

Con dropped her smart expression and turned her great brown eyes on her sister in real concern. She shoved her hands deep in her pinafore pockets.

"I don't know," she said. "I just don't know. But be careful. Look how you were with Gerrard. Just warned off. You're no fighter, Brin."

Brin put a hand over the pocket of her skirt. She wouldn't even put it inside, lest the rustle of paper attract Con's sharp attention.

Her grey eyes were grave and steady, and she knew a moment of weak affection when she longed to tell Con that she had not been warned off and never would be. Nor Gerrard. Then she remembered Con's treachery after the hunt on Stephen's Day, and held her peace.

"I'll fight," was all she said, "when the time comes to fight for something."

Con shrugged and shivered at the same time. The cold shadows of spring were creeping over the grass, taking the color from the grey stone cloister. As if to underline that day was closing, the hard flat bell rang for Benediction, and the two girls stood up to join the line already forming on the other side of the cloister outside the chapel door.

Sabrina was still thinking of what Con had said about fighting, her hand now in her pocket closed about the three sheets of Gerrard's last letter. They had established communication through Teresa, who came once a fortnight with their washing and a carefully packed selection of Cookie's best efforts in the way of cakes and biscuits; she was driven over by the groom in the trap, now that Tomasheen was gone into a world of silence almost greater than his own.

That was all the fighting that could be done at the moment. To be sure they didn't lose each other. Anything more would earn them only trouble when there was nothing they could do about it.

The phrases of the letter were running through her mind, and she smiled as she went into the chapel, wondering if she dare write to Aunt Tessa and suggest that he be asked to the west this summer. Mama would probably put a spoke in it somewhere and the trouble would be greater than ever. Her smile faded before the blaze of candles. When, when, when would she manage to see him again?

One brilliant morning in June after Sister Jailer had brought the letters, all of them, both for nuns and girls, to be read by Mother Angela, the headmistress sat and looked long at one of them.

It was on thick deckled paper and Mother's disciplined nose lifted away the faint hint of perfume from the lining of the envelope.

Mrs. MacRory Glynn would be delighted if Mother Angela could get permission for Sabrina and Constance Heron to join a daylong picnic on the occasion of the birthday of the writer's daughter Euphemia, who, as Mother Angela knew, was a dear friend of both the Heron girls. The letter lost its burst of formality and trailed off into sentiment. Mother Angela sat before her bare table and considered it.

Mrs. MacRory Glynn. Her daughters were day pupils of the school, therefore already well down the ladder in the social hierarchy. Rumor, to which Mother listened acutely while preserving the unbroken impression of interior silence, said that Mr. MacRory Glynn had made a fortune in cattle dealing, and indeed, God forgive the man, the sense of it was still around his boots. Having amassed this fortune somewhere remote in the north or west or both, he was now spending it on turning his daughters Euphemia and Eugenia into ladies.

He had made it unequivocally clear, pinning Mother Angela with a bold blue eye whose determination she could not but admire, that if the convent succeeded in his plans for his daughters and even managed to keep the girleens happy into the bargain, then the chapel of the community might well find itself the better of a marble altar, and himself he fancied that pink with the dark lines in it that came from Italy.

It would certainly make his girls happy, Mother Angela mused, and their mother too, to capture as guests for a day the two exclusive and protected Heron girls. Indeed Euphemia showed signs of an undisciplined adoration of Sabrina that should be discouraged rather than fostered.

And what would their Mama think of it?

Mother Angela had little doubt, but she sat for a long time looking at the letter and in the end made a note on her list for her secretary, to send the invitation on to Mrs. Heron with the approval of Mother Angela for its acceptance.

Only the smallest corner of her severely disciplined nun's mind saw as she wrote the sun from the high oriel window in the chapel flooding down onto rose-pink marble, dark-veined, from the quarries of Carrara.

Brin's first and only thought when Sister Jailer clanged the huge locks of the outer gates behind them, was that Mother Angela would be peering from behind some curtained window and would recognize the boy who stared down in dumb astonishment from the cheerful crowd spilling over the railed side of the wagonette. Then her common sense told her that no nun would do anything so worldly as to peer out windows, and that probably Mother Angela had never seen Gerrard anyway.

She caught Con's hilarious eyes.

"Now what would Mama say?" she murmured and then was lost, laughing and calling greetings, in the forest of hands that leaned down to pull her into the wagonette. She spoke to Gerrard as cheerfully and easily as to any of the others, making it easier—wittingly or unwittingly, and one never knew with Con—for Brin to follow her, to let her eyes rest easily on him, and to bring his name from her thickened throat.

They did not sit together, lest it be too obvious, as the wagonette with its noisy load lumbered along the little rock-edged roads towards the sea. Sickly, Brin looked forward to a day as carefully chaperoned as such a picnic with her mother always was, just wondering vaguely how they would manage it with so many, and the only grown-ups seeming to be Euphemia's parents and the driver.

But Mrs. MacRory Glynn was not her mother, and Brin realized with dawning glee as the journey wore on, that had her mother met the Glynns, she and Con would certainly not have been allowed to come.

Mrs. MacRory Glynn in tight pink satin for a picnic would have been quite enough for Mama without going any further.

Across the incredible splendid mixture of a meal served by Mrs. Glynn and the driver of the wagonette, Brin kept catching glances of bright determined mischief from Con. She was out to make the best of the day, and although Gerrard edged his way firmly round until he was beside her, Brin was so implanted with guilt and restriction that she dare not look at him, waiting with held breath for some inevitable storm.

"Ah, that's right now, Gerrard. Give Sabrina a cushion. Are you comfortable there, Sabrina? And do you know each other? You do? Well now isn't that grand. Grand," said Mrs. MacRory Glynn, who had not been long in County Cork. "Take some salmon there, Gerrard. 'Twas in the Blackwater no more than hours ago. And there's the fish slice. A fortune in Switzer's in Dublin that cost me. A fortune!"

Sunshine lay soft as milk across the green fields and the rocky beaches of Summer Cove, the soundless sea melting unnoticed into the cloudless sky along a horizon only defined by the dim shape of an Atlantic steamer, creeping out of Queenstown on the long journey to America.

They had only begun to talk, delighted small chat that had grown in courage as they realized that around the spread cloth no one cared.

Gerrard's handsome face grew somber as he watched the long ship draw its slow line between sea and sky, and Brin noticed how even since Christmas his face was changing and losing its roundness, fine beautiful bones beginning to be clear along his jawline.

"We'll have to go away somewhere when the time comes we can get married. You realize that, don't you? Cork won't hold us. Would you like Dublin? Or would you like somewhere far away—on one of those." He nodded at the steamer drawing away into the blue distance.

Brin looked after it and thought of all the terrible tales of the sinking *Titanic* last year, and wondered how many young people at the beginning of their lives like herself and Gerrard had been on her. She couldn't answer, partly because of that chill thought, and partly because she realized he was further on than she was in his practical thinking and planning. She felt a little breathless, making much of the business of breaking messily into a huge meringue, and a moment of panic touched her. She was only just sixteen. But it would be almost three years before they could think of marrying, and Mary Rose had not been quite nineteen.

Her eyes on the still sea and the vanishing steamer, some strength came to her to accept that he was right, and that not only would Cork not hold them, but she would have no glorious wedding wrapped in family approval like Mary Rose. What Mama had once disapproved of was forever.

"We'll have to run away, probably, even then," she said softly and saw in his eyes a strange mixture of humility and pride, understanding what it would mean to her if it should come to that.

Red-faced and perspiring, even his soft collar limp with sweat, Mr. MacRory Glynn was dragging bottles of champagne from a zinc bath of almost melted ice.

"C'mon now," he bellowed jovially, having got himself well advanced on the whiskey, his carefully refined accent slipping fast back to the patois of the cattle fairs beyond the Shannon. "Yez is all too quiet!"

"Ah do, get on now." His wife joined him. "Drink to Phemie's health, the lot of you. Pether, give them all a glass to do it, will you."

Brin and Gerrard could not look at each other as the pale bubbles foamed in their glasses, primed for explosion by the unexpected emotions of the day.

"Don't get drunk, now," Gerrard managed to say then, and burst out laughing. "Will you ever forget your hard hat on the angel!" That was the end of restraint, taking up where they had been severed at Christmas, snatching at every second of the sliding silver day that was vanishing from their grasp almost before they had laid hands on it.

There was bathing, with shrieking and yelling and hilarious modesty as they undressed behind the rocks, and after the bathing, mixed races on the long straight sands. They came to little. The handicappers of such a confused field were left arguing at the start, well aware that the winning post was Mr. MacRory Glynn, prostrate against a carefully chosen rock with his head beneath a newspaper.

"Sure I'm watching the whole thing," he cried against criticism. " 'Tis only against the heat on me skin." Whenever a panting winner arrived, he would thrust a sleepy hand into his trouser pocket and award him or her a half a sovereign. All subsequent claims were settled by giving the same to everyone who ran, down to the three-year-old who arrived panting and protesting in the heel of every hunt.

The dark rocks were beginning to run out fingers of shadow from the west and the color was deepening on the silver sea. Brin, jingling two gold coins in her pocket, was growing nervous and desperate. It couldn't end like this, with no more than snatched whispers in the middle of a yelling pack. When the howl went up for rounders and the inevitable squabbles began over picking sides, Gerrard gave a small jerk of his head against the noise, indicating that they should go off around the rocks. All Mama's training raised its outraged head. Brin's immediate reaction was that it was impossible, improper; impossible. She flushed an embarrassed pink and Gerrard smiled at her.

"D'you really want to play rounders with the babies?" he asked her, and she followed his glance round to see that Con was missing and she hadn't seen her go. That in fact all the older ones were missing. Only the under-twelves clamored round the driver and paced out the placing of large stones for the rounders posts. In the distance, beside the shriveling remains of the picnic, a large hump under a tartan rug marked the slumbers of Mrs. MacRory Glynn. The winning post had ceased to move at all, only the Cork *Examiner* rising and falling in a long swell that matched the rhythm of the sea. All the others had vanished on what was obviously an accepted activity of a MacRory Glynn picnic.

Gerrard read her look and began to laugh, holding out his hand, and with no hurry they wandered off along the shore, round the small headland where the pool's were already cooling in the shadows and evening crept along the bottom of the cliffs. In the distance rose the bedlam of dispute belonging to the rounders, and away beyond them, still in sun, some small children with their nurse were dredging in the rocky shallows with their shrimping nets.

They talked of her last year at school, of his work with Mr. Brown MacCaffery, of his coming summer holiday with his friends in England, and of hers in Lisdoonvarna. Endlessly they spoke of things that were going to occupy and pass their time as though in this way they could speed its passing.

Then in the end they fell silent, their hands together, left with nothing but the bleak knowledge of their separation, making a small beginning on all the sweet foolishnesses of their pleasure in each other that they had never had a chance for before. He touched her fingers one by one as if he were memorizing them.

"Why are we so sure, Brin?"

"I don't know." Her grey eyes rested on his, dark with her own certainty.

"We're very young."

"I know."

Before either of them had time to understand what was happening their lips met, each one almost frightened by the importance of this first feeling of the softness of the other's lips, cool and touched with the salt sea.

They drew back quietly from an experience for which neither was quite ready, and yet were shaken with delight that it had overtaken them. Gerrard touched her face, smoothing back a wandering tendril of hair, and she caught his fingers into hers.

"It's going to be a long time," he said. He was speaking more to himself than to her, and she knew it and didn't answer.

Mixed hunting calls were beginning to split the quiet back beyond the little headland. A clear screech reached them of the Gone Away, and they smiled but still could not bring themselves to move.

The wagonette was almost loaded when they reached it, by unspoken agreement picking their way back along the rocks at the top of the shore to avoid being watched and welcomed up every inch of the empty strand. But there was nothing said in criticism. Only good-hearted approval from the great noisy family for the fact that they had enjoyed themselves, a crude and simple trust—and what was a picnic for if not for a bit of harmless spooning off among the rocks. They rumbled home through limpid purple dusk, between hedges starred with the pale ghosts of wild roses and the rocky sedge-grown edges of the bog itself, stretching away into formless shadow. They sang the old sad sweet songs of Ireland, heavy with sorrows they had never known, and broke off happily to wave and shout at the country people who leaned to watch them over their half doors, behind them in every poor, small room the red glow from the lamp of the Sacred Heart. Gerrard's arm was round Brin, and his other hand held both of hers tightly in his lap. Con had found a young MacRory Glynn who seemed to be doing very well as a substitute for Padgeen Brackett, and she smiled over at Brin, widening her eyes as if to say she was truly glad to see her happy. Brin had never felt closer to her sister.

Mother Angela was about when they came in, saying good-bye to some parents in the hall. From their tousled appearance she revived all her chill certainty that had she met their hostess, Mrs. Heron would not have wanted her daughters to attend the picnic. Then, floating like a prayer in the back of her mind, she recalled the marble altar, and summoned all her worldliness to tell herself that picnics were bound to be a little untidy. She managed her wintry smile that never touched her watchful eyes, and expressed the hope that they had enjoyed themselves.

Astonished, they curtsied, and said yes, they had.

"Very well, then," she said, "go and get tidy for supper."

"Cripes," said Con rudely as they climbed the glacial stairs. "She must be sickening for something."

Sabrina didn't answer, drenched with gratitude that not even the chill disapproving hand of Mother Angela had fallen on the day.

In her cubicle, where beyond the window the full rising

moon managed to bring beauty even to the disciplined regiments of the convent flowerbeds, she took the day hour by hour as she changed into her Sunday dress and brushed her hair, laying it carefully aside in her mind between protective layers of secrecy, as she would lay the soft, bruisable petals of wild flowers between blotting paper, to press them and keep them safe forever.

She paused a moment, her hairbrush in her hand, meeting her own eyes in the mirror small enough to discourage the sin of vanity. She tried obscurely to clarify some fierce feeling that the day had had more innocence in it, and more simple goodness, than a year of Mama's homilies. She thrust the thought away, not wishing to think of the two together, jealously preserving her contentment.

The summer dragged in the white house beyond Kilfenora, tense with the determined cheerfulness of all of them who knew they would never see Sue again, barefoot with them on the beaches, or galloping her pony along the clifftops above the glittering sea with the wind in her brown hair. Brin could not bear to look at her, as ripped with sorrow as if she were already dead.

They will cut off all her lovely hair, she thought.

Sue alone seemed lit with some ineffable content, while even the weather mourned, a windy summer, broken and fitful, quenching the sun for days on end with grey incessant rain.

And Gran was ill. A pale shadow of her strong determined self, easily wearied, but holding to her place beside the window in her pretty lace-frilled cap, lest, unsupervised, the town of Lisdoonvarna might get out of hand.

Brin spent a lot of time with her that summer, talking to her, reading to her, taking her crochet from her when the old eyes grew tired, letting fashionable Ireland drift past outside the windows in its new narrower dresses; she was happier than in the atmosphere of strained hilarity that stalked Aunt Tessa's house like the sad ghost of other summers.

Gran watched her with her own grey eyes that were losing their sharpness and concentration, aware that there was something wrong with the child, and that once she would have had the energy to find out what it was.

She asked her daughter direct.

"Honor, have you told Sabrina what you plan for her future?"

Crisply Mama answered, "No. And I would be grateful, Mother, if nothing is said of it. I want the matter left completely until she is out of school."

"You see no reason to change your mind?"

Mama's amber eyes widened.

"None at all. Is there one?"

Gran fell silent, unequal to battle, her fine old hands, rich with rings, clasped in her lap, keeping all her strength for the acceptance of the will of God both for herself and for the child grown tall this year into a beautiful young woman with some secret stillness in her face that spoke to Gran of strength, and privacy well-defended.

Often she would put a hand out to Sabrina as they sat together, as if she knew the child was now stronger than herself. And they would sit, watching the wet summer clear to a fine blue-gold September, when Brin must go back for a while to Adranmore, to say good-bye to Sue.

Brin was aware, too, that her mother was watching her with a sort of puzzled severity that she trimmed at once to her loving smile whenever Brin caught her eyes. Clearly, at the moment her mother did not understand her. Not fitting the pattern again, Brin thought, and had a fleeting memory of the night before the wedding when she had felt herself a colored piece of her kaleidoscope, not sure what color, or where she belonged.

Blue, she thought she was now. Inconspicuous and protective, hanging round the edges, not sure whether she was going to slip off forever. She had no illusions about the battles when she came to marry Gerrard, but if they were both strong enough, what in the end could anybody do? Mama would without a doubt let the blue piece slip away as unsatisfactory, and reform the pattern more in keeping with her taste.

Con must surely be giving her pleasure, showing at fifteen all the calm self-confident beauty that must inevitably lead to a good marriage, even if nothing better showed than Padgeen Brackett. Con was clever, attracting the boys like bees around a comb, but with an innate discretion that made quite sure the mothers liked her too. She was the belle of the summer on the beaches and at the picnics and in the evening, dancing at the houses round the country. It was even said sadly among the mothers that Sabrina had unaccountably "gone off."

Con told her this with a certain small malice, looping up her chestnut hair in the shadowy bedroom for yet another party. Brin had chosen to stay at home with Sue, and she gave Con her old, contented grin.

"Gone off? What do they think I am? Yesterday's milk?"

Con picked up a small bunch of artificial flowers and turned to look at her sister with one of her rare moments of gravity.

"Still Gerrard?" she asked.

"Still Gerrard."

"And the best of luck," Con said. She held out the flowers, her own affairs back quickly to the top of her mind. "Here, put these in for me. That wretched Teresa's out courting again."

"Jonas Higgins."

"No less. Imagine him following her all the way here. He was probably afraid some buck from Kilfenora would make away with her."

"I'm glad for her. He has a good bit of land there at Passage West. And he's steady."

"You talk like a mother."

Brin laughed, giving the white silk flowers a last small twist in the shining braids.

"I'm very fond of Teresa. But the Mama won't be pleased. Teresa's trying to keep it from her until they're ready to be married."

Con was no longer listening, absorbed in her own reflection, an ear cocked for the sounds of wheels outside.

It was desperate when they all left. Like a funeral, Brin thought wildly, although she had never been to one; never closer than to see one in passing, all the weeping women shrouded in their black shawls outside the churchyard wall; only the men inside, around the coffin and the grave.

Like a funeral, for none of them could hold their tears, yet the one they were losing kissed them all serenely and comforted them, telling them that they had all her life, since none of them would ever be absent from her prayers.

Only Aunt Tessa and Uncle Marcus smiled, determinedly, and as the engine whistled to drown all further talk, Sue stood there between them with the rest of the family grouped round her, waving as the carriages lurched from Ennistymon station. The wind whipped small curls round the edges of her brown hair and ruffled her pink skirt, and Brin knew a moment of unbearable understanding of what it was going to mean to Uncle Marcus when she laid her white gloved hand on his arm and he must lead her, dressed as a bride and crowned with flowers, to the altar of some strange church to give her forever to God and to her grave.

Poised on an outburst that she knew would not be forgiven, Brin met her mother's eye and realized that Mama was the only one both dry-eyed and composed. A mutinous anger born of her pain made her want to demand if Mama would have wept had Sue been really dead. Tiredly she knew that she would only get what she had got before. A lecture on how Sue should not be grieved after, having the courage to take the step far beyond all earthly happiness. To give herself and her life to absolute communion with God.

"For everybody's sins, Sabrina. For mine, and for yours too. For the sins of the world. She is doing her duty as she sees it."

Brin stared out at the green-gold country under a sky as blue as the pictures of heaven in Denis Mary's prayer book. Stone walls, dragged boulder by boulder from the fields, made a patchwork that swept up in grandeur to the yellow hills. Small white cabins scattered the slopes, each one with its frugal turf stack black against the gable end; and men working in the small fields straightened themselves and took off their wide hats to wave a greeting to the passing train. Great majestic shadows floated over the bare shoulders of the hills and turned them blue as grapes, and in a potato patch below the line, barefoot small children with their mother, went wild with joy to see the engine.

Sabrina felt a rush of furious anger, blundering around thoughts so much against all her training that they filled her with guilt even as they careened through her rebellious mind. All her life she had been taught that life itself was God's gift, and to be grateful to Him for everything that went with it, from the golden world the train was clacking through right back through the rich unthinking happiness that was her childhood; and Abbeygate; the love of all her family; Gerrard. Now she was being asked to regard it all as some den of wickedness which she did not understand and which must never be explained. From which people like Sue must fly in expiation.

Lamb of God, Who takest away the sins of the world.

What were the sins of the world? Did little Sue know, and would anybody ever tell her, shut away from them?

Probably Mama would regard the picnic with Gerrard as one of the sins of the world. Kissing him. The nuns, too, would think the same, like over the letter. All the letters, if they only knew. They never left her, packed secretly away among the clothes that only Teresa would touch.

Certainty welled in her that she and Gerrard were in the end part of the sun-striped hills and the light flashing silver in the brown bogholes; the bog cotton like a trembling white foam across the dark land. She squeezed her hands until they hurt with the longing to feel his about them, to feel his warm, certain touch. Completing something. Something.

She stood up with such fierce abruptness that she tore the lace of her sleeve on the window catch. Her mother looked up severely from the *Life of Saint Theresa.* and even Papa, who was traveling with them, opened his eyes in his corner.

"Sabrina!"

"I'm going in with the littles for a while," she said.

Life with them was still uncomplicated content.

"Our cousin is a Poor Clare," they would say of Sue in time, and remember no more.

Con carefully lifted her patent-leather boots out of Brin's way as she charged into the corridor.

• • •

Apart from the children, John seemed to be the only one really cheerful and on form that Christmas, home on furlough for ten days.

"Well," he said when the welcomes were all over and the kissing done and MacGinnis and the Maneen had struggled his long tin trunk upstairs. He straddled the drawing-room fire with a glass of whiskey in his hand, his bright eyes roaming the room with pleasure. Behind him the gilt clock ticked noisily as if it waited for him to go on, and he took his eyes from the room and looked at his family grouped round him. He took a gulp of whiskey.

"You'd better make the most of me," he said then. "It's almost certain there's going to be a war."

"A war!" It was Mama who spoke, appalled, but Papa sat up a little straighter in his chair, and even Con looked interested, as if calculating what it might mean to her. In the background in pantomime, Denis Mary began to fire a gun, knowing better than to make any noise with Mama in the room.

Brin did not know what to think, eyeing John as if he had taken on some new importance, as soldiers did when war was mentioned. As yet to her it was only a word from history. Distant. Heroic stories of bravery against the Boers and the eldest Cunningham boy dead out there from fever. Or old matters of bows and arrows and blunderbusses in some chosen field.

In the silence she looked again at her brother. She did not know him or Ulick very well. The darkest of the family and the tallest and thinnest, wonderfully handsome, but with some pallor in his face that made her think of the heavy Dermot. Of more than that. Of obscure gossip overheard in the kitchen and the stables that brought her back to the sins of the world.

"The Kaiser?" Papa was saying, as one man to another, as if the women weren't there.

"Yes." John rocked on his heels. "They say they'll never hold mad William through this year."

"It's impossible," Mama burst out, looking at John as if he had told her of some dread and unpleasant disease. Sabrina saw his face harden strangely.

"Why, Mama?"

She groped. Her cry had been the instinctive fear of a mother for her soldier son.

"England would never allow it," she said then firmly.

John smiled and wandered over to the chiffonier to pour himself another whiskey, and the fire glittered in the crystal decanter. Papa held out his glass and Mama's lips tightened. She had recovered herself.

John came back to the fire.

"England might not have much to say," he said. "Germany and Austria will find some reason to fly for each other's throats, and I don't think it'll be easy for anyone to be left out.

"Treaties—" Papa was beginning to say, but Mama was before him, having settled everything.

"But you wouldn't have to go, John, dear," she said firmly. "Not from the Curragh. They'd have enough soldiers in England. We could speak to the general. It would be easily settled."

She bent over her crochet again, and so missed the wave of dead anger that swept John's face.

"My dear Mama," he said coldly, and Papa half raised a hand as if to try to stop what was coming. "Since you compelled me to be a soldier because you wanted it, would you deny me the first opportunity to be one, instead of a lapdog in a scarlet coat?"

In the terrible, endless silence, Brin thought of Terry, immolated before the altar in Maynooth. And of Mary Rose, having another baby after Christmas.

Carefully Mama put her crochet away in its ruffled muslin bag; nor did she show the slightest trace of emotion, except for the dull flush that crept slowly up her cheeks.

"I must go now," she said, "and see Mrs. Cook about the dinner."

She swept her brown skirts unhurriedly from the room.

John took another deep gulp of his whiskey and looked suddenly about as old as Denis Mary, who, with Margaret, stared from the far end of the room, aware of some tension he and she didn't understand.

"Sorry, Pop," John said, and Papa made a small helpless gesture and gruffly led the talk to other things.

CHAPTER 6

After a Christmas as tenuous as the tinsel hung on the Christmas tree with Mama's disapproval, John cut short his leave on the pretext of wanting to get back and see what was going on and returned early to the Curragh.

Brin came into the drawing room in the grey dusk of the evening before he left and found him with his back to the firelit room, staring out across the gardens and the ha-ha to where the wild wind streamed across the winter land, even the harsh whins cowering, stripped, before the onslaught.

"John."

Her voice was gentle. It seemed somehow wrong to find him like this, alone in the half dark, when they had him for so few days. He turned and waited where he was until she came to him, then smiled suddenly in the cold light, the same sweet irresistible smile as Con's.

"You cheated me," he said.

"Me? How?"

"You grew up. Behind my back, when I wasn't looking. When did it happen?"

She slipped her arm through his, shaking her head. As if she didn't know.

"John," she said, and her eyes were on the crumbling towers of the abbey, rearing like specters in the gloom. "It seems a long time since Mary Rose's wedding."

He knew exactly what she meant, and was silent for a while.

"Long enough," he said then, lightly, "for two babies."

"One."

"There might be another now if you went and asked."

She laughed, as he had meant her to. The baby was not due for another three weeks. He moved over automatically to the piano, as he always did if he were near it, making a gesture of disgust at the plush cloth and the photographs and china dogs that covered it.

"Doesn't Mama know enough about a decent piano not to do this to it," he said irritably as he put down his glass. It was an old argument.

"It's fashionable," Brin said placatingly.

For a few moments he rambled harmoniously up and down the keyboard, and then, as if holding to their thoughts, he broke into a poignantly nostalgic rendering of "The Last Rose of Summer." The firelight gleamed in his dark curls and carved shadows of unsuitable old age on his young face, and the soft notes faded into the dark corners of the room like memories that crept away to die. Yet Sabrina, her throat closing, knew it to be a moment she would remember when she sat like Gran, her world narrowed to her chair and the calm knowledge of approaching death.

She could not help it. She put her hand across John's on the keyboard and he stopped at once.

"Yes," he said. "Too sad. Let's have a polka."

"John," she asked him urgently and kept his hands imprisoned. "Was it true?"

"Was what true?" He lifted his head. His eyes were expressionless. Why then did they tear her with distress?

"What—what you said about Mama forcing you to be a soldier."

John stood up abruptly and stared out again over the

darkening land, and the girl dared not interrupt him. He turned back again to the piano and with a crashing discord hurled himself into "The Soldiers of the Queen." Brin realized he was more than a little drunk.

Soldiers of the King, he sang it, and finished on a series of agonizing chords, big drums banging in the base.

"What matter, my lovely?" he said and picked up his whiskey, and something in the endearment grated crudely on Sabrina. "In no time at all we shall all be dead. Slaughtered in our brave red coats."

MacGinnis came hustling into the room, and the Maneen with a taper to light the lamps; MacGinnis scolded them for sitting in the dark and went from window to window drawing the green velvet curtains.

"And it's as bleak outside, Mr. John, as would give the shivers to a Siberian."

"And what's a Siberian, MacGinnis?" John asked him.

"Ah, well now, Mr. John." The old man smiled, twinkling. "Sure I don't honestly know, to be exact, but I do know it's one of them very cold characters."

John was immensely gay and cheerful all that evening, making them laugh all through dinner, playing and singing all the latest fashionable songs for them at the piano, twinkling at Mama in all the naughty bits as if nothing had ever lain between them; and he stayed long and late with Papa and Ulick in the men's kingdom of the gun room when Mama and the girls had gone to bed.

When the time came for him to leave next morning, the pattern appeared flawless, with Mama and Papa wrapped against the cold on the steps to see him off; and Sabrina and Con and Margaret and Denis Mary hooking their hoops along the gravel while they waited for the trap. Even Ulick at the last moment came round the house from the direction of the stables.

Mama kissed John as lovingly as always and settled the velvet collar of his ulster, and he kissed them all, giving Brin a long look and then kissing her again.

"No more growing up," he said. "You'll do very well as you are."

He climbed into the dogcart beside the groom and his long tin box, and as they rattled out the gates Brin tried to pretend, under Mama's eyes, that the tears that filled her eyes were from the cold sad wind.

Denis Mary raced up the steps into the hall and seized one of Papa's walking sticks from the hall stand, facing them with it from the top of the steps.

"John says he's going to have a war!" He danced up and down and Brin noticed how long his legs had grown in his black stockings. Even Denis Mary was growing up. "A war, a war, a war!" he shouted, beside himself that he had not been stopped. "I'm a war! I'm a soldier and I'm going to shoot you all dead!"

It was the silence that stopped him in the end, and without a word Mama took the walking stick and replaced it in the stand. Heavily Papa closed the front door.

"Bang, bang, bang!" cried Denis Mary as he stumped on up the stairs, and at the landing, under the pale fronds of the pampas, he shot MacGinnis in the stomach with his fingers. "I'm a war!"

Two days before they were due to go back to school, Dermot's groom came whirling over the gravel in a grey, wet dawn, looking for Mama. Brin was wakened by the urgent wheels below her window and came running along the gallery in her wrapper, to meet MacGinnis scrambling from the back quarters in his bare feet, nightshirt flapping underneath his overcoat, trying to reach the door before the knocking roused the household.

She stood listening to the groom giving his urgent message, knowing before he spoke what it would be, even more sick with terror since she didn't know exactly what to fear.

"She's not dead, MacGinnis?"

She caught him as he pounded up the stairs and he flashed her a look of compassion.

"Ah, no, Miss Brin. 'Tis only the baby is a bit slow in coming, and Miss Mary Rose wants her mother, like any other poor creature in the same state. The groom is gone for the doctor now, so there's no anxiety."

Mama would not even give her the ordinary human comfort that MacGinnis had, bound even on that cold frightened morning by the propriety that forbade her to discuss such matters with an unmarried daughter.

"May I not come, Mama? I might be of some use."

A look of absolute shock crossed Mama's face. She was in the hall by then, as neat and groomed as if she had never gone to bed. Only her hands, gripping each other in their grey gloves as she waited for the dogcart to come back, betrayed her anxiety for Mary Rose.

"You have no shoes on. You'll catch cold," was all she said to Sabrina, thrusting her back among the children, pushing her away from the women's world that the girl strained to enter in more ways than merely her secret and almost strangled love. "I don't imagine," Mama added, "that I shall be very long. Don't forget your calisthenics. Or your Latin."

The wheels of the dogcart crunched on the gravel outside, and Sabrina saw the anxiety deepen in her mother's eyes. MacGinnis came from behind them and opened the front door for her to go out, and the grey, wet mist seeped into the hall.

"Mama," Sabrina said, but her mother either did not sense, or did not accept, the sympathy she was trying to offer.

"Don't make a scene, child," she said briskly. "Mary Rose is in God's hands. I'll be back soon."

Old MacGinnis looked at Brin gently as he closed the door.

"Go on back to your bed now, Miss Brin," he said, "and I'll bring you a good drop of tea."

Mama did not come back soon.

All the long silent day the dank mist closed out the world beyond the gardens, and away in the windless distance, the Atlantic steamers moaned defensively, feeling their way around the Old Head of Kinsale, searching for Queenstown, or for the open sea.

Sabrina was immensely glad to see the lamps lit and the curtains drawn against the blank early dusk, closing them all in a small illusion of security, where their fears became more manageable.

Dinner was eaten in almost total silence, in spite of all their efforts to meet Papa's gallant attempts at conversation. In the end he too fell silent, stroking the long waxed ends of his moustaches, his mild blue eyes staring away into some anxious distance. He sent them to bed at the proper time with a great show of authority, in an endeavor to preserve some order in the house, but long later, they were still loitering wordlessly in the upper gallery, Teresa with them. Her thin face was drawn and anxious, having more knowledge than they as to what could be happening to Mary Rose.

Papa came slowly and heavily round the curve of the stairs, and as he reached the gallery Sabrina saw his face and went to him swiftly, remembering without rancor that out of all of them, his beautiful Mary Rose had been his favorite child.

"Papa," she said, as she had spoken to her mother in the morning, reaching to share fear and possible sorrow. Reaching to share some need of comfort. Papa did not reject her as Mama had done, his big hand closing warm round hers. He nodded to Con and Teresa along the gallery.

"I think," he said, and there was a small shake in his commanding voice that made Sabrina tremble. "I think, we should all say a little prayer for Mary Rose. Come, Constance."

Con came at once, but Teresa hung back, not feeling it suitable.

"Come, child," said Papa, and they all went down and found their rosaries from the drawer in the hall table where they were kept, to be easily picked up on the way out to the chapel. In the lamplit drawing room, because they could not quite think where else would be more suitable, Papa lumbered to his knees against a velvet chair and led them in the Glorious Mysteries for Mary Rose. It was at the third mystery that Sabrina realized there were more voices in the prayers, coming from the hall where MacGinnis and Cookie and the Maneen and Katty Ann had come up from the kitchen to join in, kneeling together beyond the door. Ulick, astonished at finding them, came and joined them in silence.

Still they couldn't go to bed, and MacGinnis made them strong tea and Papa and Ulick laced it with a drop of whiskey, and they sat drinking it in silence, until in the dark late night, with the wind from the southwest whipping the mist to shreds and the stars beginning to light the gaps between the racing clouds, they heard the sound of hooves pounding to the front door.

They all answered it. The groom had ridden over and stood in the flood of lamplight from the hall, a great grin on his tired face.

Mary Rose had a daughter. Both were safe and as well as could be expected. Mrs. Heron would stay the night with Mrs. Fitzjames.

"Go on round," said Papa to the man, "to the kitchen, and tell them, and get them to give you a drink. They're all up, the decent souls."

"And I've no doubt," he said, turning from the door when the man had gone, leading his horse, "that it'll be my best Scotch whiskey he'll be given down there by that pack of rogues."

But Brin watched the slow bright tears coursing down his cheeks before he could find his handkerchief, and was pierced by the knowledge of vulnerability in those to whom previously she had looked only for omnipotent security.

"Well." Papa was recovering. "We'll need now to wish the child well."

He pulled the long fringed bell rope and MacGinnis came, looking ten years younger than he had at dinner, with his master's wants anticipated by a bottle of champagne and four glasses on a silver tray.

Papa stared at it a long moment, as if he couldn't understand what was wrong.

"Four more glasses, MacGinnis," he said then. "And another bottle. For the lot of you. B'God if you can pray with us, you can drink with us too!"

The gilt clock above the cherubs struck a musical three and the fire was low in the grate as they held their small strange party for Mary Rose and her new baby. MacGinnis and Cookie and the Maneen and Katty Ann, flushed with pleasure, stood near the door and could be coaxed no further. Papa's face had swelled again to its customary expression of dignified geniality, and Ulick simply stood there and smiled. And smiled.

"Go on away now, the lot of you," said Papa in the end, and giggling with relief from fear, and with champagne, they all went at last to bed. His daughters kissed Papa, and the servants bowed and bobbed, and he looked over them all with equal benevolence and affection.

"And now, for the love of God," he said to them as they crowded the door, "don't tell Mrs. Heron or she'll have the lot of us on bread and water for the week."

Mary Rose was wan and languid when they went to see her on their way back to school, the little baby white and fragile as a winter flower. The house seemed to be still full of women, although Lady Fitzjames made it clear that Mama's presence had been a matter of unnecessary hysteria all the time. In among all the petticoats, Dermot seemed uncomfortable, lurking in the background with a look of exhaustion and guilt, his black bull's curls hanging low over his flushed face.

From the whispering that was going on, Sabrina gathered that the doctor had said that Mary Rose should not have any more children for some considerable time. Lady Fitzjames clicked her yellow false teeth over this, and made it clear that she thought Mary Rose a disappointment.

"Poor Dermot," she said.

"Poor Mary Rose," Mama answered tartly. "I have no doubt that Dermot—"

She realized that Sabrina was listening and stood up.

"It's time you girls were gone," she said, and Sabrina, looking at her taut and disapproving face, could not but remember that Dermot had been Mama's choice. It was Mama who had turned the lovely lighthearted Mary Rose into The Bride.

On the seven Irish miles to the convent, Sabrina first of all sat quiet, her gloved hands folded in her lap, letting all the experiences and emotions of the event wash over her.

In the end she whispered to Con.

"Did you hear them say that Mary Rose must have no more babies for some time, or she might die? I thought, I thought—" She hesitated to confide in Con, but this was something the easy familiarity with the farm and stables had not taught her, and one could never ask Mama. "I thought, if you were married, you had to have as many babies as God sent you."

Con, ten months younger, with even her school boater

perched on her head in some unsuitable style the nuns could not defeat, turned on her sister a withering glance. Then she offered her a succinct description of the habits and possibilities of the marriage bed that turned Sabrina scarlet, her eyes in agony on the groom's back, lest he had heard.

Con looked her over again. "I don't understand how it is you don't know these things."

Sabrina felt a great calm settle on her, almost as if Gerrard had sat down beside her and taken her hand in his. Her grey eyes cleared, and she smiled at her sister.

"I'll know when the time comes," she said. It was like not fighting before you had to.

Con shook her head, defeated; as if she acknowledged that Sabrina knew nothing about anything, and yet inexplicably knew far more than she did herself, with all her quick information.

At the end of June Brin left the convent, deluged with scapulars and holy pictures scrawled in young hands with loving messages for her future. With patience and even grace born of knowing she was leaving them, she suffered all the dry nuns' kisses and acknowledged without much thought the slightly veiled assurances of Reverend Mother that they would soon be seeing her again.

Arrested for a moment by some tone in the old nun's voice, she looked into the bright, dark eyes, set deep in a withered face that yet held some aspect of unconquerable youth. And innocence. The one nun above them all whom she held in a deep respect that had grown into affection. There was nothing in Reverend Mother's eyes except the penetrating gaze she had encountered, with diminishing trembling, for the last eight years. She dismissed the words as a routine farewell, for of course they would be seeing her again soon if Mama had anything to do with it. She and Cousin Anna were always here arranging this and that.

She couldn't wait to get away, feeling groundless hope that once outside the high grey walls, life would surely present her with more opportunities for seeing Gerrard. As they bowled home through the green sunlit fields with the whins flowing like a yellow tide across the hills and the soft wind touched with the salt sea, she felt an irrepressible surge of excitement and promise.

"What are you going to do now, Brin?" Con asked her across the well of the trap, and if there was deliberate malice in the question in front of Mama, Brin ignored it.

"Burn all my sashes," she grinned, "and throw my school boater from the end of the jetty."

For all her wild vocabulary, Mama was blessed with little sense of humor.

"I declare, Sabrina, you have little thought for anything," she said repressively. "Well you know that Margaret is starting school there in September and will need them all. That would be willful waste." She turned to Con and answered her question carefully. "What else would Sabrina be doing, except to come west with all of us for the holiday?"

"Hoorah for Brin," cried the irrepressible Con, shooting Brin a glance that conveyed clearly that she, Con, was aware how far Lisdoonvarna was from Cork city, and was not unsympathetic.

Nor, through the first week or two of the holidays at home, did Brin lose her sense of euphoria, her feeling that although at the moment nothing had changed, life had begun to open. Even without any contact, she felt the certainty of her love for Gerrard in some way strengthened now that she did not have to think of herself any longer as officially a child.

She spent a lot of time with Mary Rose, as she was allowed now to ride over unescorted on Tattybogle to the big ugly red brick house where Dermot's mother still lived and ruled as if the marriage had never taken place.

"But I thought," Brin said to Mary Rose, "that she was going to the Dower House with Eleanor, and leaving you and Dermot here?"

Mary Rose's lovely face was strained, already a sad and anxious expression gathering in her blue eyes. She spoke with uncharacteristic bitterness.

"Well, she hasn't. And why would she? She's not the woman to trust me with either her house or her son."

"But Mary Rose—"

Brin did not know what to say, touching the edges of matters that even her ten days of emancipation didn't help with. Adults were adults, and in their own world, where no breath of argument or criticism from the young might touch them. But where did Mary Rose fit in? Married and a mother twice, yet still pathetically young against the corseted and dominant personalities of Lady Fitzjames and her horse-faced daughter.

She felt a surge of anger. She had never liked them much, but never needed to think about them. They were just grown-ups. Now loyalty to Mary Rose filled her. No matter what else, no daughter of Mama's could be anything but a perfect housekeeper, each of them taken, one by one, through Mama's iron routines. Mary Rose especially was a most exquisite cook. "Who," Cookie used to roar, "would want me to stay in any house that held that one!"

Now Mary Rose, still pale and thin, sat among the daisies on the half-tended lawn, and her only smiles seemed to be for the little boy scrambling round her skirts, bull curls like Dermot's already dangling on his forehead, and for the tiny flowerlike daughter sleeping in her arms.

On the first day Brin had ridden over, she had looked at Mary Rose, appalled.

"Mary Rose!"

"Brin, darling, what is it? So lovely to see you again! And grown-up, now. Dear Brin, it's wonderful to have you home."

Brin submitted to the soft perfumed kisses, her mind a storm of fear.

"But Mary Rose!" She could only think of the one thing, her face scarlet, not knowing how to express her sick dread, since even to your sister it was not a suitable topic for converstation in the middle of the gloomy hall, where anyone might come. Then Mary Rose realized what was wrong, and her blue eyes darkened. She put her hands defensively across her thickening waist and looked at her young sister, her own face showing, unprotected, the ravages of the battle for resignation and courage.

"But they said—the doctor said—" Clear into the summer day came the memory of the night of freezing mist when they had prayed for Mary Rose.

"I know," her sister said sadly. "And now there is

another in a year, like you and Con. Gran would say it was the will of God."

And Con, thought Sabrina, looking at Mary Rose now with her fear turned to pure scarlet rage, would call it the will of Dermot.

The nurse, chosen by Lady Fitzjames, came down the stairs with the children, and with reluctance and disapproval clear on her narrow face, handed them over to their mother.

With one accord, Sabrina and her sister turned and went from the house, out into the sun.

At the middle of July they all went, according to custom, to Kilfenora, and Brin went more easily this time, conscious of a year gone. Cheerfully she preserved for the children all the treasured rituals of the journey. Letters to Gerrard had become a difficulty since she had left the convent, but Teresa overcame it by sending them to her sister, who lived on the outskirts of the city. Gerrard came every couple of weeks to collect them.

"Ah, Teresa, what would we do without you?"

"You'd tell your mothers and stand up for yourselves," said Teresa tartly, and then at the look on Sabrina's face, regretted it. She stood up from the trunk she was packing, her hands to her slender aching back over the crisp bow of her apron.

"Ah, no, acushla," she said, "I know you couldn't. Not yet. The Mama would slap you into a convent or something."

Brin laughed at that and went on collecting her belongings for the holiday.

One of the things she loved about Aunt Tessa's house was the great wonderful freedom of newspapers, tossed all round the place for all of them to read. As if, Mama once said, they didn't have enough in the print of them to corrupt the world. At home, Sabrina and Con gained their knowledge of the world from *The Girl's Own Paper* and the *Messenger of the Sacred Heart*, and Mama even went through those before they got them.

Uncle Marcus loved to preside over his breakfast table with all the morning papers at his elbow, reading out all the bits he thought of interest to his family assembled round the long table drenched with bright sea light from beyond the cliffs. The chairs had been spaced out to fill Sue's place.

"Um," he said, one brilliant morning, no different from any other, full of the smell of frying bacon and hot bread, with big black lumps of cloud gathering out beyond the ocean for the rain that was bound to come later in the day after so fine a morning. He turned the paper round and folded it over, crackling, at the article that had caught his attention. "Um," he said again.

"What?" asked Aunt Tessa, dexterously fielding a piece of egg off the chin of her youngest child. Except for evening dinner, she would have no cloistered nursery meals for her children, such as Mama favored. "What is it?"

There was a long pause as Uncle Marcus bent his fair head over the paper.

"Someone has assassinated a grand duke," he said. He went on reading, munching his toast. Sabrina knew he liked to be questioned and asked details of what he read, so she asked him where it had happened.

"Um, place called Sarajevo, if that's how you'd pronounce it. In Bosnia—that's one of the small places in the middle of Europe. The Archduke Franz Ferdinand of Austria. And his wife, poor lady. Both of them shot."

"The poor creatures," said Aunt Tessa, staring over a spoon of egg, arrested only by the personal tragedy.

"May God have mercy on them," said Mama.

Uncle Marcus shook his head and turned his paper round to look for something more interesting.

"Can we go now, Papa?" cried Rory, the eldest boy. "Is General Knowledge over? Because the weather's not going to hold, and the Mama wants fish."

"Ah, get on with you, you load of ignoramuses," cried Uncle Marcus, and threw the paper down and reached for his tea. "I wonder if you'd even listen if I was reading to you of the end of the world!"

When the stampede had died down, the grown-ups settled to more tea and their own plans for the golden day, as long as it might last, and no finger of fear touched them yet for the tall boys already marching for the shore.

As day followed blazing day through that perfect summer, and all the young ones grew brown as nuts in the endless sun, Uncle Marcus began to read the news with more attention, gripped by the first cold premonitions that he did not want yet to share with Tessa.

He still reassured them all, although now after that first morning there was no need to shout for their attention when he read the papers, even the youngest aware that day by day there was some crisis growing greater. It would be all right, Uncle Marcus told them firmly. Despite the senile thunderings of the old tyrant in Vienna, none of the great powers of Europe wanted war. Nor did Russia. Wasn't the Tsar still on his holidays, cruising in his great yacht, and the Kaiser off in his sailing boat. Both of them claimed war to be impossible.

There would be a silence and a relaxation. The adults thrusting aside for a little longer the cold horror that now frankly held them. The young ones almost disappointed, ready to be carried on the wave of emotion and excitement that rolled through the newspapers.

Sabrina took the papers and read them for herself, but her interest was always in the people concerned, rather than in the bigger issues. With sad passion she devoured all the details of the murder in Sarajevo, where it seemed the summer was as brilliant and as beautiful as their own. The Archduchess had worn a green silk dress and a parasol to match, beside the Archduke in the carriage in the sun, collapsing into his arms as he fell already dying to the floor.

"Sophie," they heard him say. "Please don't die. Please live for our children." And Sabrina wept.

But Sophie had died, and Brin could not help thinking of the sad children. She knew herself at that time to be wide open and raw to every emotion, writing and receiving almost incoherent letters from Gerrard, triumphant that they had managed two long years and yet feeling the next impossibly eternal. The beauty of the exceptional summer was almost intolerable, the sadness of the Sarajevo murder almost a luxury for the indulgence of her own pent-up feelings that felt the longing for Gerrard in every thought and breath. She searched ridiculously for sorrow, since she could not have happiness, the bereaved children in Vienna tearing at her unstable feelings almost as deeply as if they had been her own, and his.

On the beautiful morning of the twenty-fourth of July, Austria issued an ultimatum to Serbia, and over the daily papers the pretenses slid from the adults around the breakfast table like a shed skin. Beside the picnic hampers by the tranquil sea, or in the heavy sun-splashed woods, the eyes of the sunburnt boys in their white shirts were bright as the weather as they eagerly compared their ages. The younger ones were sullen with disappointment, because even if it did finally come for England—and even Uncle Marcus was beginning to look resigned—then it could only take a month or two to finish it, and they'd never have a chance. The little ones, like Denis Mary, were already drilling through the exciting days, with rifles made of boughs or driftwood, pounding drums ransacked from the attics. Since his brother was a soldier, Denis Mary had an automatic position of command.

The girls were resentful and out of it, sitting useless on the fringes of this new man's world.

"We could always be nurses," Sabrina said one day, growing bored with the endless soldier talk and tired of the unfair competition. "They always have to have lots of nurses in wars. What about Florence Nightingale?"

"I haven't either a lamp or a cardigan," said Con, poker-faced, and Sue's elder brother grinned quickly and then looked over at Brin and spoke like the grown-ups, withdrawing reluctantly from the excitement.

"There wouldn't be time," he said, shaking his curly head, "to train a whole new lot of people. I doubt if they'll want any of us. If England does declare, it'll be all over by Christmas." He grinned again then, and reached for another sandwich. "Anyway, it would take longer than that to persuade your Mama. Besides, think of the poor soldiers looked after by you lot. It would kill more than the enemy would!"

Brin hurled a bread roll at him, his sister followed smartly with a glass of water, and for a time all warfare became entirely local.

Morning after morning the sun climbed perfect from behind the inland hills, bright backdrop to catastrophe, and they listened in growing silence each day to Uncle Marcus reading out the progress of the horror that had been unleashed on Europe and could not now be halted.

Austria against Serbia.

Russia against Austria.

Germany against Russia.

Now the young ones left the breakfast table quietly and gravely, controlling their own fierce excitement before the stricken faces of their parents.

"It's coming."

"Yes."

"You'll be first, Rory."

"Immediately. I've told mother."

They looked at him, as if already it should have laid some mark on him.

On the clear fine night of August the fifth, there were special editions of the *Examiner*, hawked through the dark streets, where lights sprang in the windows at the newsboys' urgent shouts. In the warm night the people flocked from their houses out into the streets, excited and contemptuous, ready to dismiss the one-armed William back into his groveling and defeated Germany by Christmas.

The papers reached Lisdoonvarna on the milk train, and Gran sent her groom over at once to Uncle Marcus at Kilfenora. Disturbed by the sound of urgent hooves, the household came one by one downstairs, and Brin thought again of Mary Rose. They gathered in the hall, even the servants coming up, pale-faced and anxious. The first sun of the perfect new day struck on the back wall of the hall in the delicate fan dictated by the window above the double door, and unconsciously Uncle Marcus stood in its light, his handsome face grown suddenly old.

The headline was simple, six inches high, black like mourning across the front page of the paper.

WAR!

With some solemnity, Uncle Marcus read them the details.

Britain has declared war on Germany.

There was a lot more, about troop movements and the possibility of air attack on London and not hoarding food and other things, but Brin hardly listened, standing in the shadows beyond the golden fan and looking round all their faces; the young ones were wildly excited but trying to hold themselves in because for some reason all the parents seemed upset.

The bootboy, known terror of Kilfenora on a Saturday night, was grinning madly, his red head filled with the promise of unlimited fighting and no one to tell him it was wrong.

The housekeeper wept, and Brin remembered she had six sons, all in their twenties, and no husband to care for her.

Papa looked alert and somehow suddenly thinner and more erect, as if some force long idle had been set in motion. As if even for him the drums might beat.

Aunt Tessa's eyes kept coming back to Rory, who in their secret talks had expressed his determination to go at once. Another chair to be closed up at the table. And Peter John and Antony would not be far behind, twins, less than two years younger. It had never seemed important before that except for Sue, all the older children of this family were boys.

Sabrina's eyes moved over to her mother. Mama's disciplined face showed no expression, but her eyes were wide and dark, looking at nothing, and Sabrina felt the sudden prick of tears, with the urgent wish that she might have another chance to say good-bye to John.

And what of Gerrard? He would be nineteen now. Ignorantly, she wondered if it were the right age to go to war, feeling certain only of the soldiers like John. They might never need the boys like Gerrard and Rory and Peter John and Tony, and Mrs. Daly's six, if it was all going to be finished by Christmas.

Uncle Marcus was still speaking, quiet blue eyes roaming over all of them and carefully never resting especially on his sons. She hadn't heard what he said, but it had brought quiet even to the excited boys, and they all went back up to their rooms.

Brin didn't go back to bed, settling herself in the deep seat of the sash window, to watch the day flow blue across the ocean, Inisheer and Inishmaan touched to gold on the pale sea. She could begin to estimate what it would all mean, but nameless fear was cold in her stomach, and she longed to talk to Gerrard. In the end she went over for her small mahogany writing desk and came back to open it on her lap. They had to call her for breakfast, her long hair hanging round her like a shield as she wrote; the bright perfect summer day crumbled to uncertainty.

Two days later she was driving on calls with Mama, crammed unwillingly into white dress and gloves and buttoned boots. She and Con and now even Margaret had to take turns for martyrdom, and today was hers.

All the drawing rooms had seemed the same, swimming in the airless yellow light of lowered blinds. In one of them a parrot, richly, splendidly blue. In another two small woolly dogs that barked incessantly and gnawed the toes from her new boots. A dull, dreadful daughter to be conversed with in a third. In all of them plum cake and seed cake and two kinds of tea and currant bread. And everywhere, anxious faces, and strained speculative talk about the war.

She herself had only reasoned out one thing through these fearful days of the first thundering advance of Germany through Europe. If Gerrard went to be a soldier, it would make everything different. He would no longer be in Cork, serving out the long days of his articles to Mr. Brown McCaffery. And she was no longer a child at school. There must be a way, in a war, in which she could follow if he went away, although she acknowledged with a wry smile that even the army might have trouble in getting him away from Cousin Anna.

Only later did Sabrina learn subtlety and patience.

Now on the journey home, she took the bull squarely by the horns. Mama was driving herself, with the same controlled skill with which she did everything else, both horse and dogcart neatly under her command. Her white hat of folded tulle, which reminded Brin irresistibly of a meringue of MacRory Glynn proportions, cast a gentle shadow on her face, that could not conceal a look of strain. There had been no word from John since he last went back.

But all today Mama had been affectionate and uncritical, as if for once Brin had measured up to her exacting standard, and the girl felt the moment good.

White-gloved hands tight in her lap, she stiffened herself for the battle, the steady clop of the cob's hooves like the beat of the calling drum.

"Mama," she said, "I have nothing to do since I left

school. Now that the war has come, do you not think I might train as a nurse? Lots of nice girls do it nowadays, and I'm sure they'll need a lot more the way the war is going."

Almost she blurted out what Gerrard had said about girls even being doctors.

She waited for the tirade, on no daughter of Mama's doing anything so degrading at any time, leave such work to the servants bred to it, and above all in a war did she not know about the dirt and the wounds and the totally unsuitable proximity to men who would not even be gentlemen.

She had anticipated it all, with the odd inevitable quirk from Mama thrown in, and when it didn't come, she looked curiously at her mother. Mama was sitting bolt upright, but that was normal. But she was silent, and that was not. She stared out over the horse's dappled flanks, and Brin had the feeling that in her silence she too had arrived at some moment of decision.

"No." said Mama.

"But," Brin said, and took a deep breath to start the fight, but she got no further.

"No," said Mama again, and her voice was calm. "Because I have arranged with Reverend Mother some long time back that you shall become a nun. You shall have the summer, and then after the autumn spent in preparation, you will enter as a postulant after Christmas."

Mama had not even turned around to look at her, giving all her attention to her driving, having stated her arrangements, which allowed no discussion.

For a few minutes Brin sat completely still, and then she lifted her head and looked at the rolling hills, the shadows of high clouds moving in purple masses on their bare flanks. She looked at the green flat fields that ended in nothing at the vast precipice of the Cliffs, where at high tide the thundering spray was spun with endless rainbows. Her eyes came down to the grey familiar ribbon of road, and the steady pounding of the dappled horse. The tangle of flowers along the ragged roadside, pink and blue, and the tall stems of yellow loosestrife.

She opened her fingers and looked down at them, as if

she had never before noticed that they would obey her will, shattered by her total sense of disbelief.

She remembered Con telling her to watch out.

Then, because it was the only reaction she could find to such a suggestion, she began to laugh.

CHAPTER 7

Sabrina knew that whatever passed between them afterward, that laugh was never forgotten.

Having once broached the subject, whether on impulse or not, Mama could not leave it unresolved, and in the following days, although it was supposed to be secret between them, it destroyed the atmosphere of the house more surely than all the dreadful war news pouring in black headlines across the daily papers. Awkwardness and distraint filled the air, heavy and palpable as a sea mist creeping along the Atlantic floor. Worse here than anywhere, Brin thought, furious and embarrassed. Here where their own little nun had gone off of her own free will, longing for it, and the three letters allowed to her in her year as a postulant brimmed with her unshaken content. Brin spent hours staring out her window at the green land rising to the dark blue sky, wondering how she was going to escape, not daring even to think of Gerrard, her need of him was so great.

"No, Mama," was all she could say. "No." And could give no easy reason. Fiercely her mother demanded reasons. Even one. And she could give none. She was convinced that her impetuous mother had been stampeded into speaking by the outrageous suggestion that she might of her own accord wish to do something else. It was all probably meant to be said in September, when they were back in Abbeygate and Mama was prepared and on her own ground. Now the dispute raged awkwardly round bedrooms and empty parlors and contrived walks. Their locked antagonism broke off into strained smiles every time they were interrupted by the unfortunate members of the family who wanted nothing but to extract the last ounce of happiness from this holiday that lay dramatically beneath a monstrous shadow, and might well be the last, for some of them at least.

Mama had forgotten the war. Forgotten John. Her will was being opposed and she could see nothing else. She was still struggling to be what she called cool and reasonable, her light brown eyes trying unsuccessfully to conceal her astonishment and fury that this daughter, raised so carefully to her pattern, should be daring to go against her.

"It is what I have always planned for you, Sabrina. There is no question of refusing."

She was bright-eyed, rigid for battle, almost as if hackles had gone up like those of the brilliant little banty cocks that strutted on the rough lawn.

"You should have said something, Mama. I could have told you always—"

She stopped as she realized that earlier she would not have dared. A.G. Ante Gerrard. A small smile touched her lips, but she knew that even as a child she could never have thought of being a nun. She and her mother were in her bedroom that day, and she stared again out the window at the endless splendor of that tragic summer, when there were so many other things tearing at her mind. She could hardly bear to listen to Mama, wanting to brush it all off like a wasp at a picnic. A picnic. All the others had gone off in the wagonette along the coast. She sighed and spoke again.

"For me, it would not be right, Mama. I would never be happy."

"Happy!" From the rising tone of her voice, Brin knew that Mama had almost asked what had that to do with it.

"If I were not happy, Mama, how could I be a good nun?"

It went on and on and she listened absently, pleating the lilac bedspread beside her fingers. Pale lovely colors in this sea-lighted room. Aunt Tessa did not care for the frills and roses that filled all Mama's bedrooms. She was always a bit ahead of fashion.

Duty was coming up again and what God called you to. Brin couldn't see where God came into it. It was Mama who was calling her to be a nun.

"Mama," she said patiently, and knew she shouldn't, "if you think so much of the nuns, why didn't you become one?"

Then it was all about being called instead to the married state as Mary Rose had been. Brin's eyebrows went up. And doing your duty by your husband and so on and on and on. Brin stopped listening, thinking with only half-comprehended compassion about her father.

She had heard it all before and what did it amount to? John. Drinking himself silly alone in a dark drawing room. Terry. A priest in a bleak parish in the heart of the country. And Mary Rose. Walking in sick fear of the next baby in a house she hated.

She felt curiously gentle, touched almost with astonished pity for the elegant woman in the soft white dress who sat rocking fiercely in her cushioned chair, struggling to keep her temper with this recalcitrant child.

The bounds of Mama's controlled patience were giving way.

"Isn't it the same in any decent family that you look at?" she cried. "The land and the army and the church with both nuns and priests and good marriages for all the other girls. Haven't I done it for all of them, and they good and willing children!"

Good, undoubtedly, Brin thought. But willing?

"What is wrong with you, Sabrina, that you cannot take your place?"

The pattern. Always the pattern. How simple it must

have made it for Mama to rear them all, preparing every one of them for a slot. Like the tall red machines on the station, where you put your penny in and faithfully got out your chocolate bar, always plain for the boys and milk for the girls. Would she have been saved if Bernadette had lived?

"And what have you arranged for Con?" she asked, only curious. It would have to suit Con, or Mama wouldn't have a chance. Did she know about Padgeen? Mama, she wanted to say to her. Give yourself a little peace. You couldn't hope all eight of us would fall into place without a fight. Mama only gave her a withering glare that said the thing had gone too far even for her supernatural patience. In a whirl of her white skirts she left the room.

Brin sighed and moved over to the deep window seat, and sat marveling that she had had the courage to hold out even this far, knowing she was going to need a great deal more. If only she could see Gerrard.

She heard the wagonette come back from Liscannor, lumbering past the house and round to the stables, and then the back door opened and the family burst like a tide through the house. It seemed a thousand years since she had felt like one of them. Con came into the bedroom with her quick light step, flushed by the sun and cool and salty from the sea. Her rich brown hair was tied at the neck by a piece of string, and she was barefoot, carrying her sandshoes. Why is it, Brin wondered without resentment, that she can do anything she likes? Mama would have taken me to pieces for that, even on a holiday. The answer, she knew, was that Con already was stronger than Mama, and Mama was too wise to lose dignity or strength in useless battles.

"Weather's going," Con said. She threw down her sandshoes and a damp towel and loosed the piece of string. She looked at it a moment and ran it through her fingers, smiling, as if it had some special meaning. Then she tossed it on the bed and shook out her hair, a bronze cloud, touched with gold lights from the long summer.

"Well," she said and sat herself on the edge of the bed. She looked critically at Sabrina, as if she surveyed her for damage after some disaster. "What a day you must have had! Liscannor was heaven." She heaved back the tangle of hair with her two hands, and looked at Brin from between them. "But I told you, didn't I? I knew she had something up her sleeve for you. I warned you." She paused. "You're not going to, are you?"

"No," said Brin.

"Good." To Con it was all over, whereas Brin knew that Mama was like the rising wind beyond the window that was dying into silence between gusts. She had only retreated to gather strength.

"And what about you, Con? I asked her what she had for you."

"You never did. Wasn't that very bold?" Con laughed delightedly and stretched her arms above her head, her loose white sleeves falling away from their sunburnt curves. Brin smiled at her. "She needn't plan for me," she said. "I'm out to beat Mama at her own game. I'll do something she wants me to do anyway. She'd have had Padgeen Brackett for Mary Rose if he'd been out of stockings. Dermot was only a bad second."

Brin was no longer shocked.

"Have you told her?"

Con collapsed in laughter.

"Mercy on us, I haven't told him yet. Remember, Brin my love, I'm only a child!"

She didn't look like a child, pulling off her crumpled cotton dress and moving over to the old shadowed mirror to brush her hair, slim legs and bare feet beautifully brown below the ruffled petticoat. Yet there was something about her that made Brin, even as she laughed, feel as old as Gran. And sad.

The next day she was to go with Mama to Lisdoonvarna, to see Gran, but before they left, with a certain sense of desperation, she cornered Aunt Tessa in the garden, where she was nipping off the dead heads of the late roses.

Aunt Tessa looked up and smiled, smoothing back a piece of windblown hair, knowing Sabrina had come to do the talking.

"Aunt Tessa." She took the basketful of brown-edged roses from her and held it, searching for words, and her aunt did not watch her, reaching across the dry flowerbed for another rose. Sabrina stopped pretending that anything need be explained.

"Aunt Tessa. Would you speak to Mama for me? Tell her I don't want to. I know it's hard for you to understand, with Sue, but—"

Aunt Tessa firmly clipped off two more flowers and the secateurs snapped in the silence. She stepped back from the flowerbed onto the grass and put them into the big pocket of her apron. She looked at Sabrina then, grave and loving, yet with some definite chill that told the girl she should not have asked. She felt herself flushing sadly and longed to be away and the whole thing never mentioned.

"Sweetheart," said Aunt Tessa, "I understand everything. But no. I'll not speak to your Mama. How do you think I'd feel if she tried to come between me and one of my children. I'd never forgive her, and she'd never forgive me."

Brin stood there bleakly and knew she was right, and felt as much alone as if she were in the middle of the wide sea beyond the fields. A small wind blew from it and rustled the dry leaves along the grass, frolicking among them as if to apologize for having been away so long.

Mama was calling from the steps of the house.

Mama drove, the same trap and the same cob, along the same road. Like a remembered and unhappy dream. But they had veils tied around their hats against the gusting wind, and big bright umbrellas in the sockets of the trap against the threat of the fat purple clouds piling from the west. As they came down the long straight road into Lisdoonvarna, it was raining for the first time in two months.

Gran nowadays was keeping to her bed, and Lisdoonvarna had to manage its affairs unsupervised; part of the whole breaking pattern to see her, laying down all her trusts; still now in the high brass bed, with her shrinking face the same color as the parchment lace of her priceless bedspread. Only the jewels on her quiet hands winked with undimmed life. Sabrina knew a moment of startled revulsion and retreat as a nun stood up from beside the bed as they came in and melted noiselessly from the room.

"She's a nursing sister from the hospital," Gran said

when they had kissed her. Brin felt the dry chill of the poor old hands and heard the thinness of the voice and could hardly hold her tears. "I was getting too much for Maggie, the creature."

"I'll go and have a word with her," said Mama, and Brin knew that she was being left alone with Gran deliberately, so that Gran might influence her. She looked after her mother, easing through the door almost as noiselessly as the nun, in her neat, correct driving habit, and felt herself shaken by blind fury that she would use even Gran; poor Gran, when they should be thinking of nothing but her, and it clearly not far from the end, and yet Mama would use her, use her. She felt almost incoherent, only turning and trying to calm her face when Gran spoke from the bed.

"Come and sit here, pet."

She moved over to the straight-backed chair the nun had left, and Gran threaded the red beads of her rosary carefully between her fingers as if they could tell her something. Her eyes in the parchment face were fading, but still direct and shrewd, and slowly she turned her head on the lace-edged pillow and looked at Brin.

"She's told you, my darling?" she asked, and Brin nodded, barely able to speak. A gleam of sunshine trailed like hope itself across the room, muted by the parchment blinds.

"Couldn't you tell her, Gran, that I'm not Sue. It's not for me."

It was all she dare say, unable to place the burden of her secret on Gran's frailty, on the stillness and pallor of a room that could speak only of death; no talk of love and hope and life would survive in this pale place, and Brin composed herself to listen quietly. But the wrinkled lids closed suddenly and Gran's face lost all look of life. Sheer terror seized the girl that even what she'd said had been too much and she started from her chair.

"Gran!"

Desperately she looked at the door for Mama. Even for the nun. But the eyes smiled as they opened again, hearing the note of fear.

"I get tired, pet." She lifted one of her folded hands and laid it on Brin's anxious ones. Brin had to speak again.

"Did you know, Gran? Did you know about it?"

"About you? Yes, my darling. Since you were born."

"Since I was born!" A new incomprehensible piece of the pattern. How could she not tell me until now!

"Why, Gran? Why me?"

"That's for your Mama to tell you."

So I should think, Brin thought mutinously.

"There's a reason?" she asked.

"There is indeed."

Brin was silent, and the gold clock on the fringed mantel filled the room with the message that was growing urgent now for Gran. But Brin had forgotten even her, appalled by the sense of helplessness of being merely a part of Mama's pattern: before she could even think herself. Were all of them like that? Did it make it better or worse that there was a reason?

Oh, Gerrard. It all seemed to make him even further away.

"I can't, Gran," she said desperately. "I may have a reason, too."

Gran ignored this.

"Take it all, my darling, as the will of God, then it all becomes easy."

"But Gran." She was anguished now. "It's got nothing to do with God. It's Mama." Like John, she wanted to cry, and Terry and Mary Rose, and even Papa.

Gran's eyelids drooped again. She was growing tired again, but she spoke quite clearly.

"And since when was the will of your mother not the will of God for you, child? And for every one of you she brought into this world?"

No anger. Or argument. Just the calm certainty of the rules that had brought her through all her life and in perfect serenity to this quiet room, her beads between her fingers and her eyes lifted to the statue of the Sacred Heart, on a bracket high on the wall beyond the glittering knobs of her marriage bed.

Brin felt humbled and hopeless, and yet filled beneath it with a smoldering anger that she should not be permitted to be herself, crushed and battered by love and respect toward a life she didn't want.

"I can't, Gran," she whispered. But Gran did not hear.

Mama came back then, and Brin sat quiet while they talked, listening to the rain pounding beyond the drawn blinds. She took the renewed message from Gran's eyes as she kissed her good-bye, already ashamed that she had so troubled her terrifying frailty.

Outside, the nun stood back in her blue habit, with downcast eyes, to let them pass, and Brin knew she was unfair to be so hostile to every one of them, simply because she was threatened with their life.

She tried to smile as her mother said good-day, but the nun merely inclined her head in her white coif and did not look at them.

"No," said Brin to the carpeted landing and to the fragile watercolors painted long ago by Gran along the strand and on the cliffs when she was a young redheaded bride and Lisdoonvarna at her feet. At the turn of the stairs there was a portrait of her husband, handsome and black-haired, the other grandfather they had never known, brought home to Gran on a hurdle one frosty evening from the hunting field, long before any one of them were born. The portrait was life-size, and his merry eyes, so like Aunt Tessa's, stared with some hilarious complicity from the canvas.

No wonder, thought Brin, that Gran had felt God calling her to the married state. What would that determined-looking fellow have said if she'd told him she was going off to be a nun!

"No," she said to the top of the polished stairs. It was cold dreadful misery to go against Gran, confused with this fury that she had ever been involved. She could hardly look at her mother. Please God, Gran might never know.

They had to comfort old Maggie in the hall, her strong, seamed face almost as old as Gran's, and the light through the stained glass of the hall door making soft shifting colors on her spotless apron. She had known Mama all her life, and had no compunction about expressing her poor opinion of being displaced by a nursing sister.

"I don't know, indeed, what Miss Tessa would be thinking of to do it," she said. "What, Miss Honor, can that one be doing for her that I cannot? I'd even manage to give her a bit of a smile now and then."

Brin looked out at the grey sheets of rain and thought of Gran's pale quiet face, and wondered sadly for how long it would matter.

Mama had one other visit arranged for her before they went back to Abbeygate, and Sabrina, with cold anger, realized that Mama was mustering all her possible support.

"This is the big guns," Con said, and Brin grinned.

"I'm glad to see him for any reason," she said.

"Give him my love. And don't let him get round you."

"I don't think he'll try."

Con looked at her sharply, but Brin said no more, unable to put into words her certainty that Mama's big guns were quite possibly trained against herself.

The parish where Father Terence was curate embraced a small dirty town and a collection of outlying and inaccessible farms on the flat windswept plains beyond Loughrea, and they were to go there for a couple of days, ostensibly just to see Terry, and then join the rest of the family on their way home, at Limerick Junction.

The ugly little market town still bore the traces of the cattle fair the previous day, unswept manure drying along the wide main street and the shutters still up on some of the shop windows, giving it a blinded look. When they reached it in the rickety outside car that was the only station transport, the square sandstone hotel, surrounded by a few untended shrubs, looked as bleak as Sabrina's own spirit.

Sabrina was now as tall as her mother, with Mama's innate elegance tempered still by the warmth of the wilder days, and before they had ever climbed the pocked steps, they were the object of embarrassing interest through the windows of the commercial room. Through the thinly carpeted corridors hung an ineradicable smell of boiled bacon and cabbage, slapped down remorselessly every day for the dinner, by country girls with red hands and crumpled aprons. Mama, who was fastidious to the point of hysteria, endured it all with a tight gracious patience that told Brin clearly she was offering it up to God on behalf of her difficult daughter, this visit to Father Terence being the one last influence that should remove all her ridiculous objections.

Watching her, Sabrina longed to tell her not to suffer on her account, and tried to envisage Mama's face if she should do so.

In the afternoon of their arrival they were invited to tea in the presbytery by the parish priest. Terry had written with a certain sad, satirical humor about the exigencies of his new parish, and its church, and when they had negotiated the manure-spattered streets under the curious stares of their inhabitants, Brin realized that only humor could have possibly allowed him to survive it.

The church was grey, surrounded by a waste of grey crushed flint calculated to endure to the necessary eternity the pounding of the heavy country boots of the parishioners. Around the grey waste was a grey wall on the further reaches of which sat a row of ragged little boys, like birds along a branch, putting through their idle days by watching the comings and goings from the station and joshing the passing girls. It was without grace or color, without flower or tree, save for a few wilted lilies yellowing before a grey mournful statute of the Sacred Heart.

The matching Presbytery flanked the church, blank glittering windows shrouded in curtains of heavy lace, doubtless concealing an interior of equal bleakness.

Sabrina had only time to register the astonishing weight and quality of the gleaming front door before it opened swiftly and they were admitted by a plump woman in an apron and elastic cotton sleeves who did not even offer them good-day and gave the appearance of having been waiting behind the door. It was immediately obvious that the austerity of the parochial surroundings did not extend beyond the doorstep.

She was aware at once of suffocating heat from an enormous fire, with a massive collection of glittering brass irons propped in a high fender that also contained two covered dishes on its hobs. She had an impression of overstuffed and crowded chairs and pompommed tables, all overwhelmed by the one in the center of the room, spread with a lace-edged cloth and obliterated by a spread of food that would make a hunting tea at Abbeygate look like a Lenten fast.

She thought quickly that this was something Mama

might have said, but sadly, Mama was no longer funny. As if intensity had blunted her.

Father Peter Jordan was small, but as rotund as his well-kept surroundings and excellent table would lead anyone to expect. The skin on his plump face was red and shining, and curiously ceramic, as if a smile might split it to a thousand fine cracks. This accounted probably for its caution, and its appearance of being little used. When he spoke, small gouts of spit gathered at the corners of his mouth, and he wiped them away constantly with a large, beautifully laundered handkerchief.

Once again Brin could feel the tension of Mama's endurance. The things the child put me through, she could imagine her saying to Cousin Anna. If only the child could be sensible. When Father Jordan announced with his painful and cautious joviality that he would summon Father Terence and the young things could go for a walk while his sister was out wetting the tea, she had a sense of being manipulated that drove her almost to open rudeness. She could visualize word for word the letter that Mama would have written ahead, asking that she be left alone with Terence so he might talk some sense into her.

Only Terence saved her, coming in quietly and kissing his mother with all the respect and deference she regarded as her due. She tossed her elegant head a little, and a small approving smile touched her lips. There now, when all was said and done, this son was all he should be. Terry turned then to Brin and with one small flicker of his face managed to tell her that he knew exactly what was happening and for pity's sake to take it easy, and all about the dreadful church and the porcelain priest and the four different kinds of currant bread. Brin had a sudden certain knowledge that on other days he would get bread and margarine in his own room, and she had to look away before she gave way to the first real helpless grin since Mama had opened up.

In the second-class capacity of curate, Father Terence was strictly prohibited from using the polished hall or the Grand Front Door. As he guided Sabrina down a slate passage and out a side door into the grey world of the unconsecrated, he was aware of her almost hysterical mixture of fury and helpless giggles. He kept her going with parish gossip and inquiries about the family, past the row of boys who touched their forelocks and called good-evening to the priest, looking, Brin realized, as if they liked him. He smiled back and lifted a hand to them. They crossed the railway line below the station and Brin looked along it and thought of Cork, but that was one thing she couldn't tell even Terry. Almost in silence they walked down a little rutted boreen between loose stone walls, leading to the rough stepping-stones over a small tumbling river edged with moss and sedge and yellow iris that grew in the peat-brown foam. Terry gave her his hand across and smiled at her, telling her silently what she knew. That they must wait and settle and then she could talk.

He halted in the end at the top of a gentle slope, where the tumbled remnants of a Norman keep stood square above the little town, hawthorn and juniper growing from the arrow slits, and jackdaws nesting in the stairs.

She saw none of it, lost again in her rebellious anger that those she loved should be used against her. First Gran and now Terry. Maybe Mama would let Cousin Anna have a go. Filled with pain, and longing for their old uncomplicated relationship, she sat down beside him on a fallen rampart and waited furiously for him to talk like a priest, for what else could he do since that's what Mama had sent him here for, and she'd bring in that priest with the china face into the bargain too. Fiercely she dug hole after hole in the soft turf with the ferrule of her ruffled parasol, not looking at him.

"Will you be planting something there?" he asked her mildly in the end, and the voice was the voice of Terry of the rat hunts. But when she turned to him, although the lively eyes were full of love, they were guarded, deeper set, as if they had carefully learned to hold their secrets, and let other people hold theirs.

She began to cry then suddenly, deep heartbroken sobs for loneliness that was just beginning to touch her, reaching out like the cold fingers of winter dusk. Watching her, her brother's eyes were deep with pity, but he sat unmoving, a little way away on the mossy stone, and when at last she would have begun to speak, he raised a hand.

"Tell me nothing, love," he said. "It's better that way,"

and she knew that he was right. He gave her his big handkerchief, and smiled as she blew her nose and apologized incoherently. Then he took her hand and she grew calm, watching for a long time the sun and shadow chase across the windy plain.

"Race you down the hill," he said then, and stood up and grinned at her. Astonished, and with tears still wet on her face, she nevertheless laughed with sudden unstable happiness and fled before him down the long gentle slope, where he caught her to him in the reed-filled grass beside the river and hugged her wordlessly, as he had done for all her hurts when he was Terry and she was little Brin.

"Now for God's sake," he said, and jerked his head towards an ancient woman in a black headshawl who regarded them with toothless malevolence over the half door of her small cabin just across the stream. "Old Peggy Hessian there will have it all over the parish in twenty minutes that the curate is having carnival knowledge of some young female down by the river steps."

Carnival knowledge. She laughed again, and took his hand across the wet stones. Carnal knowledge. All the big words the church used to clothe the reality of love; and her longing young heart told her she had barely touched the fringes of it. The warm, firm touch of Gerrard's hand; and his thigh along hers, horse to horse, in that one frosty evening; one hesitant, almost apologetic kiss and the tremor running through her like a sickness when she looked at the perfect shape of his head, and the way his hair grew above his ears; his foolish eyebrows.

Carnal knowledge. In the catechism. A thing for whispers in the confessional. For the secret life behind her parents' bedroom door, never to be spoken of. For the shadow of fear dark now in Mary Rose's lovely eyes.

But for her and Gerrard surely, the calm certainty of a gateway to some tranquil world of love. How did she know, who knew nothing of it? Why, he had asked her, are we so sure?

"I'll not do it, Terry. I'll not do it."

No answer. Thin, dirty sheep cropped the short grass between the stones, and from among them he stopped and picked up a skull, long bleached bare from some woolly head. His face was carefully composed.

"That's all it comes to in the end, you know. In this world anyway, after they're all finished with us."

"But, Terry!" She was frantic to make him talk. "I'm only seventeen. So long from now till then to be doing Mama's will."

"Or God's."

"That's what Gran says. She takes everything that way."

"She's fortunate." He threw away the skull, and a few sheep raised slow, reproachful munching heads. "Anyway, who knows when 'then' is. Especially now with the war."

She looked at him quickly, horrified that she had barely thought of it, locked and embattled in her own private siege. At least the war couldn't affect him.

"Terry, it's terrible, isn't it? Terrible. They're all over these poor countries like ants. There's Rory and the twins—" She'd said no proper good-bye to them, withdrawn by Mama as if she had some catching sickness. "I thought I could be a nurse," she said abruptly. "Anyway, you'll be safe," she said then. "That'll please Mama. She's very worried about John."

A strange expression crossed his face, but he said nothing, waiting to let her go ahead of him across the sleepers of the railway. They walked in silence again until they rounded the bleak walls of the presbytery, and in the porch outside the door he stopped and turned to her.

"I'm no one to give you help, love," he said then, and the thumb with which he made the sign of the cross on her forehead reminded her that she should never have asked him.

"Anyway," he said, opening the door. "I'll get a good tea out of it," and she could not help smiling back, happy simply to be with him.

But in the suffocating parlor, the ceramic priest made it clear he expected her to kneel for his blessing, and congratulated her in God's name on her decision to become a nun. She dared not look at Terry, but Mama sat on the edge of her red plush chair with a smile of dignified smugness touching her lips, like a gambler who has played what he is sure is the master card and waits tranquilly for the outcome of the game.

She was regally gracious too to everyone they met on

the way back to the hotel, inclining her feathered head as she picked her way delicately between the cowpats, her silver-grey skirt in her hand and the late sun gleaming on her ropes of pearls.

The sweet reek of turf smoke filled the limpid dusk and climbed into the still air, the gusty wind dying with the sun. Over the half doors and through small dusty windows, lamplight shone, hazed in that gentle hour into some soft promise of warmth within and permanence and family life that severed Brin's thoughts from her mother's as completely as if they walked in two different worlds.

Father Terence saw them off at the station in the morning, in the train for Limerick Junction. As it pulled and snorted its way clear of the platform and the streets and the river and the little castle of King John, Mama settled back in her corner, waiting for Sabrina to arrange the small special cushion without which she never traveled. She was pleased with herself and ready to be indulgent, carefully touching into place her neat blue traveling toque.

"There," she said, smiling at Sabrina. "That's all settled." How tiresome the child had been. Such a waste of time.

Brin felt the pit of her stomach grow cold, and folded her hands tightly on the *Messenger of the Sacred Heart* in her lap, Mama's choice now as suitable reading.

"What is, Mama?" she asked politely.

Mama stared at her and the dangerous flush rose up her face. The train thundered through a short tunnel and she waited to speak until it came out.

"Everything," she said. "Everything. You talked to Terry."

"Yes," she said, and thought of carnival knowledge and Peggy Hessian, and, foolishly, smiled. She couldn't help it.

Mama almost spat.

"Well?"

Brin was silent.

"You heard what Father Jordan said."

Sabrina looked her gravely in the face and tried to keep her knees together so that Mama wouldn't see how they were shaking.

"He said it, Mama. Not me."

"Not I," Mama corrected automatically. "You didn't say anything last night!"

"You never mentioned it." She could see Mama was almost beside herself with fury and astonishment.

"And you are not going to enter?"

Brin looked out at the green, rick-strewn fields clacking past.

"No, Mama."

She was never more sure.

CHAPTER 8

To the fury of the family, where the atmosphere lay strained already, a few days after they all got back to Abbeygate, Cousin Anna came to visit.

Con, irrepressible and sure of herself, would challenge Mama now on anything, and where Mama would once have suppressed her instantly, now she offered reasons. As though her failure to exact immediate obedience from Sabrina had managed to dint the surface of even her steel-bright confidence.

"It was arranged, dear, before we went away. I can't put her off now." She hesitated and said no more.

It was the nearest she had ever come to admitting there was anything amiss in the smooth perfection of the pattern, and her attitude to Sabrina conveyed infuriatingly that anything that was wrong was just a temporary nuisance, and Cousin Anna happened to be coming in the middle of it. A little time, and Sabrina would fall into place like all the rest.

So, while the first bright leaves of autumn drifted onto the cobwebbed grass, and her quarrel with her mother was set aside in uneasy abeyance, Brin was compelled to sit and listen endlessly to Cousin Anna singing the praises of her darling Gerrard as he had been when he was at school before she met him, and then automatically hated him and speculated about his warts. Anna's son. No name.

From the bright, watchful malice of her button eye, Brin knew that Mama had told her about the convent, and she realized that if the old crow knew, she wanted none of it; she'd be all the happier to see her driven in. One less between her and Mama.

If you *knew*, she thought gleefully, behind her polite face. If you only knew. She tried to visualize the scene if she were to say sweetly, "Cousin Anna. Mama," and then tell them everything. Like a talisman she fingered the last letter in her pocket. It was full almost of panic lest Brin should give way, assuring her he would find a way to stop such utter nonsense. Foolish words, for what could he do? It was she who must hold out.

"You must be very proud of him, Cousin Anna."

Brin caught the note of mischief in Con's sedate voice, and shot her a warning glare. Con loved to dance too close to danger. Even Mama sat up a little straighter against her cushions, watchful.

But Cousin Anna only smiled the loving smile of the Widow of Windsor at the mention of dead Albert, her black skirts spread to the toes of her button boots. Brin listened to the clacking voice and longed to be able to repeat to Gerrard what a fine fellow he was. To see him grin. She would sometime. Sometime . . .

"I'm not," said Cousin Anna, "one to be going in for sinful pride even over my own son. But he's a great comfort. A great comfort to a woman alone like me."

Con's eyes were enormous, filled with admiration, fixed on Cousin Anna, who clearly thought the Constance one was getting a bit of sense. Brin had to look away.

"And I'm sure, Cousin Anna, he's so handsome, all the girls must be wild for him. Has he any special one?"

The widow's benign mask slipped and the black eyes grew small as currants.

"I'd give him credit for more sense," she said. "Why

would he be making a fool of himself going after girls? Isn't he well enough as he is?"

In the mild September sun they were sitting in basket chairs on the paved and sheltered space outside the dining-room windows at the back of the house, surrounded by the gold and yellow blaze of fresh chrysanthemums and the last tired asters. There was a sound of wheels on the gravel around by the front steps, and Brin stood up abruptly. Con nonchalantly examined the toes of her shoes.

"I'll go and see who it is," Brin said, and even Mama forebore to point out that that was MacGinnis's place. She vanished round the corner of the house and was grinning all over her face as she came round to the front. Con was the very devil. Her smile widened as she saw a hired dogcart drawn up at the foot of the steps, and then fear touched her, chill and sad.

John was paying the driver. John in unfamiliar khaki. The first soldier, Brin realized with a shock, that she had actually seen, bringing all the newspaper articles to life suddenly and desperately, in the person of John. All centered there in him, stooping to pick up his valise, and the smallness of it brought an instant message. He would not be staying long. He put his change in his breeches pocket as the dogcart turned and ground off back toward the station.

"John!"

She ran to him and kissed him, searching his face as if she should find him already different because he was real. His moustache was shorter, and his hair, but otherwise he just kissed her back and hugged her and told her she'd done it again.

"What?" In her mind she was already thanking God to have given Mama another chance.

"Grown up."

This time she could hardly smile, knowing it to be so painfully true, and swamped by all the emotional impact of the moment and what his uniform implied.

"They're round on the pavings," she said. "And John—" Her face gave warning of bad news.

"Mm?"

"Cousin Anna's here."

John used a word that Mama would like to think Sabrina didn't know. She touched his arm just before they came round to where the others sat.

"How long?"

"Three days," he said, and stood a moment, and then moved on, as if there were nothing to be said, into the sun and the rich tang of the autumn flowers and his family's welcome.

Three days. Short and useless, filled with the remorseless strains of Cousin Anna, who had not the sense to go away. And with the brittle brightness of Mama, who never forgot or forgave a child who spoke against her, and would not set aside John's outburst at Christmas. Bleakly Sabrina knew that if in the end she herself insisted on her own way, as she was determined to, she also would be placed outside the bounds of Mama's love. To her, John was still a naughty boy who had spoken out of turn and must in future be kept firmly in his place.

Frantically Sabrina, and Con also, watched Mama giving to Cousin Anna all the time and thought and even affection that she should be giving at this time to John. Apparently completely indifferent to the ravening monster raging across Europe, that might be already hungering for her son.

War talk was discouraged. Table conversation should be light but not frivolous. Interesting but never heavy. This was Mama's ruling and she saw no reason to change it now, over the lamplit table with the big soft moths still whirring in through windows open to the last flowering of the lovely summer.

"We do realize, darling, it's your work," she said firmly to John. "But you must tell it all to Papa and Ulick in the gun room. Cousin Anna is our guest and I'm sure she's not interested. And I've been so glad to see you in your own clothes this two days, that drab olive stuff is so unbecoming, don't you think, Anna?"

"Cousin Anna has a son too," John said coldly. "It should interest her for him." Brin's heart lurched, longing to question John as to whether Gerrard would be likely to go, forgetting to thank MacGinnis when he offered her the meat. She realized that Cousin Anna was smugly and vigorously asserting that she wouldn't allow any newspapers in the house at the present time, full of all that depressing war rubbish. A little skirmish, over by Christmas and grossly exaggerated. Brin could visualize Gerrard clearly, buying papers from the newsboys in the streets of Cork and reading them in McCaffery's office. Every letter he wrote spoke of the progress of the war.

Cousin Anna went on to speak of the insidious manner in which Mrs. Leila Murphy had edged precedence over her in the matter of arranging the flowers for the high altar on Sundays.

The men stared at their plates, and the very moment that decency allowed, Papa's chair went over almost with a crash as he pushed it back.

"I've a good port for you, John," he said. "For your last night. I'm sure the ladies will excuse us."

Gratefully John and Ulick pushed back their own chairs, and Mama looked as gracious as she could, knowing that there was one person only whom she dare not argue with, once he had made his wishes clear.

"We'll have our coffee in here, MacGinnis," she said, "and the gentlemen in the gun room."

"Ma'am," said MacGinnis, and allowed himself a small satisfied smile as he left the room.

"Two trays for the coffee," he said to Cookie in the kitchen, and her thick, cross eyebrows rose to the frill of her cap. MacGinnis anticipated the explosion.

"Ah, c'mon now, Mrs. Cook, ma'am," he said. "Is another tray an' coffee pot too much to give Mr. John a bit of peace in the gun room with his father and his brother? And the black one well away with the madam in the dining room. They'd keep them there till cockcrow."

Cookie slammed down a second silver coffee pot to heat.

"Is it that?" she said. "I'd make enough coffee for all the sorrowing souls in hell only to give anyone a bit of peace against that one. Wouldn't you think she'd have enough sense to go home and Mr. John here?"

But MacGinnis had gone as close as he would go to gossip about the family, and his long face closed.

"I'm obliged to you, Mrs. Cook," he said.

Up in the dining room, Cousin Anna settled in her chair, ready to resume after the interruption.

"I always say," she said comfortably, "it's better once we're away from the men, although the creatures have their uses, God knows."

There's Mama, thought Brin, trying to ram me into a convent, and that old harridan ready to strangle any girl who comes in reach of Gerrard. How in God's name am I going to fight them both? Happiness seemed receded to an impossible distance, lost in the shadows, all the light held by Cousin Anna's opening and closing mouth and Mama's attentive face. As so often, she wondered what it was that Mama saw in her, and watched their relationship with amazement. Con kicked her sharply under the table to tell her her face was showing, an old expression of their childhood, so she smiled and straightened it out into polite interest until they were free to go.

Later the boys came and found them where they were sitting together in Brin's room, speculating openly now on Mama and Cousin Anna.

"We'll get out," said John at once, "and hear no more of her."

Almost without speaking they crept down the stairs and out of the house, going across the garden and the little road, and took the wandering steep path down through the wind-bent pine trees to the shore. Their silence was heavy, weighted with words that none of them wanted to say, the dark shadow of Germany reaching its fingers to the moon-drenched Irish shore, where the strand stretched milk-white under the full harvest moon, the calm sea bleached to silver and the hills no more than sleeping shadows far across the bay.

Even the cynical Con was somber, burdened by the truths and sorrows that were being glossed over by a layer of despotic pretty manners in the house behind them. For a few minutes they walked side by side in silence, down to the damp, firm sand along the water's edge. Brin looked slowly all around the familiar silver world and wondered with chill sadness where John would be when the hunter's moon was full.

They began to talk then, idly, standing in the creaming edges of the waves, jumping back from them as they had done when they were small to madden Nurse. They talked a little, sadly, of the war and then, after a while, of their childhood. Foolish things and shocking escapades and wild disgraces with Mama, and great days in the field when Papa was the Master and Terence forever being bellowed off the field for one offense or another, laughing and capping each other's stories. Con told John then with much detail and relish about Brin and Gerrard getting drunk on Stephen's Day, including the smell of Brin's burning socks and the chicken bones and the silly grin on Gerrard's face. John wouldn't believe it, shouting with laughter and Ulick smiled contentedly. Whatever his family did was right.

"That old bundle of weeds," John cried. "She couldn't have a son fit for anything but a eunuch," and Con and Brin didn't have to be shocked since Mama wasn't there. Then Con went too far and said if they only knew it, they were laughing at less than half the joke, and Brin got frightened and joshed her to shut up, and Con sat down, giggling, in the sea.

John was a little drunk and thought it immoderately funny, laughing too much even to help her up. With Ulick's hand she finally staggered to her feet and took off her dripping shoes, and John took his off too, rolling up his trousers. In some sudden reaction, they walked off together along the shore, Con holding up her dripping dress and the water splashing light around her lovely legs. Back to Brin and Ulick came broken snatches of "The Walrus and the Carpenter" and "The Owl and the Pussycat Went to Sea," until they stopped some distance away and stood looking out at the sea, their arms around each other. Inevitably in a few moments, John began to sing, and Con joined him, clear and sweet above his tenor, the pair of them fluting away in the gentle night with the strange sad pleasure that was their heritage, all the grieving songs of Mr. Thomas Moore, who had taken the drawing rooms of distant London by the heart. When he started on "The Minstrel Boy," word for word in the silence, the ancient tale of the long-dead child who had strapped on his father's sword and stumbled over it forth to war with his old harp slung across his shoulder, then Con fell silent, and Brin sat down abruptly on the sand and laid her head on her knees.

"Oh, Ulick, I wish they'd stop. They're making me cry. Not tonight. It's too much tonight."

Ulick thumped down heavily beside her and she felt his big hand on her shoulders.

"Ah, God, yes, we're a melancholy lot, and revel in it too. But you must let a man say good-bye to his country in his own way, and John was always one for lifting up his voice and baying at the moon like some wandering dog. C'mon, let's skim stones."

Brin didn't move, and with the bluntness of the emotional moment, she lifted her head and asked Ulick at her side the question she had often asked herself in the last few months since she had got older and known him better.

"Ulick, why haven't you married yet?"

There was silence, with the murmur of the voices of Con and John coming clear along the shore, and Ulick picked up a handful of stones from beside him and flung them one by one to make small circles on the calm sea. Obviously he was deciding whether to answer.

"I wanted to, once," he said briefly then. "But the Mama didn't approve and it was her house."

Papa's, Brin's mind cried. Papa's.

"But, Ulick," she said hopelessly. Obviously since she knew nothing of it, it had been a long time ago. "You could have gone away, lived somewhere else."

Again there was silence, save for the small splashes and bursts of laughter where Con and John were losing their melancholy.

"Ah, well," said Ulick in the flat voice that thrust away pain. "The father needed me on the estate. He never had the heart for it."

"He wanted to be a soldier."

"He did."

They looked over together to where the silvered shadows of Con and John were themselves skimming stones; hoops of spray on the dark water.

"And you now?" Brin pressed him. "Now that there's a war?"

"Me? Come now, the red coat's for John. I've to stay here and double up the pigs and the cabbages so that no one starves once they start blockading us with these submarines."

He stood up with surprising agility for his bulk, just as he swung himself effortlessly onto a horse, and began searching for flat stones among the shingle. The other two came racing along the breaking foam, the water around them dark now in the declining moon, arriving beside Brin laughing and breathless and, to her eyes, unbearably handsome and beautiful. Unbearably.

"I know where we'll all go now," John said. "The good man'll not be gone to bed yet."

They made their way back to the house, this time in one ungainly line with their arms around each other's shoulders, and up through the wood John sang again, old whispering Gaelic love songs in the tongue. He steered them to the side door, the light from the gun room window bright beside it.

"Be careful now," John said. "Or the eunuch's mother'll hear us!"

Brin had to hold Con up, she laughed so much, and in a bunch they stumbled in the gun-room door, where Papa sat alone before the fire in his worn leather chair, surrounded by a litter of books and papers in the only room in the house that was permitted to be untidy—all except for the guns, impeccably clean and in order, racked in their glass-fronted case along the wall.

"Well, there you are, sir," said John. "And look what we brought you. A pair of mermaids we found down along the shore."

Brin's throat tightened at the look of warm pleasure that flushed Papa's face. He stood up slowly and looked the two mermaids up and down, and his eyes gleamed under the heavy brows.

"I've always been told," he said, "that if you have the singular good fortune to catch a mermaid, you have at once to give her something sweet to hold her."

Gravely he put out two more of his crystal glasses and poured them each a small quantity of his finest port, glowing like a jewel in the lamplight.

He eyed them again as he handed them the glasses.

"I'd think it'd do no harm," he added, "to keep them a bit warm as well,wet as they are from the sea."

He eased his own chair and another close to the fire and turned to his grinning sons.

"And the fishermen," he said, "I have no doubt, are chilled and exhausted after hauling them in."

He filled the glasses they had left earlier on the green baize tablecloth, and John sank into a chair, Con on the arm of it beside the fire.

They sipped their drinks a few moments in silence.

"Jesus God," said Con then, and no one rebuked her. "I'm steaming! At least I don't smell as bad as Brin's socks at Christmas."

"You do," said Brin. "You do. You smell like a salt-water laundry!"

John stretched out his long legs past Con's cloud of steam, along the brass fender, holding his golden drink to the light.

"You know what this is," he said. "It's mutiny." He spoke with great content. "It's no more than rank bloody mutiny, and the lot of us'll be lined up and shot at dawn."

The war came rushing into the small, warm room at his light remark as if the German hordes that now clamored only thirty miles from Paris had broken down the door and flooded through it, reminding them all that tomorrow had to come.

It was two o'clock when they at last crept furtively up the stairs, even their father with a faint pleased smile on his face and his brown boots in his hand, padding along the crimson carpet in his stockinged feet.

In Sabrina's room, Teresa dozed in the rose-covered chair, and the girl came in so quietly that she didn't wake. Brin stood a moment, looking at the thin, tired young face. When she and Gerrard were as old as Time and their children all grown up, they would remember that it was Teresa who kept everything alive for them through these bleak years of separation. She reached out a hand and touched her gently on the arm.

"Teresa."

Teresa started up, full of apologies, but Brin stopped them, offering her own.

"You shouldn't have waited up, Tesa," she said, using the old name of childhood. "You won't be pleased. I declare to God we're filthy. My dress is all seawater and Con's lost one of her shoes and the Maneen'll never get John's suit fit to be worn again."

She pushed back a falling strand of hair and beamed at Teresa with bright eyes that were anything but apologetic. The last hint of fatigue left Teresa's face and it was soft with affection as she began to unhook the crumpled dress.

"Ah, Miss Brin," she said contentedly, "to be sure, for me it has all the aroma of good days gone by."

They all slept late, and when they woke, John was already gone, taking the dogcart alone in the misty dawn and stabling the horse at the station.

He had left a note under Con's door.

"Con-con, I'm not much good at farewells to soldier son going off to war. Bless the lot of you, last night was grand. Be good mermaids. John."

Con brought it into Brin's room and woke her, and even her vital face was still.

"Shall we show it to Mama?" she asked Brin, and Brin didn't know what to say.

"It would be too cruel if we didn't," she said in the end. "She'll think John just slipped away so as not to have to say good-bye to her."

"Which he did," Con said flatly.

"Yes, but she loves him. She loves us all really, you know."

"By her own rules only. Only if you do everything to please her."

Now it had been said, out in the open, and for a while there was silence between them.

"I'll show it to her," Con said then, and at breakfast she used it to counter the cool reproaches for being unpunctual.

She was blank-faced and unhelpful about the pieces Mama did not understand.

"What happened last night?" Mama asked sharply.

Con shrugged.

"He must have been out somewhere."

"Mermaids? What mermaids?" Apart from being incomprehensible, it was nonsensical, and that to Mama was far worse. She passed the note to Papa.

"Barry, what do you make of that nonsense? Do you understand it?"

Papa gave the perfect performance as the severe and

baffled father, snorting at the piece of paper through his eyeglasses and even turning it over to see if there was anything else on the back.

"I suppose," he said heavily in the end, his voice weighted with sarcasm, "we have to be grateful the young man consented even to leave a note."

Con and Sabrina addressed themselves carefully to the food on their willow-patterned plates, and across the table Cousin Anna champed methodically at her man-sized breakfast and made it clear without even lifting her eyes that of course she wouldn't be asked, but should the thing be shown to her, she would know exactly what it meant at once.

Brin lifted her head when she felt safe, and was startled to see Mama's hair caught in a shaft of the clear morning sun. With a shock she realized that in the merciless light, half the strands that still looked as if they shone red-gold were in fact touched with grey, and the lines on Mama's face had deepened.

Am I doing that to her? she wondered sadly. Or John? Or just herself?

She was interrupted by Mama's precise folding of her napkin, embroidered to match the willow pattern of the china, thereby declaring the meal over and no pity to those who had come too late to finish.

"Constance, you will help Mrs. Cook this morning with the blackberry preserves. The children are going down with Nurse to the back lane to pick more blackberries. You are finished, Barry?"

Con looked with distaste at her hands, seeing them already purple, and Papa, who was daring to lag, nodded over the last of his toast. Mama stood up.

"Sabrina," she said. "I want you to come out with me. I shall be ready in half an hour."

Now where or what? thought Brin drearily, and the moon-drenched magic of the previous night receded to the dimension of a dream. Probably to the convent to be talked at by Reverend Mother. That hadn't happened yet, and must surely come.

No, her mind said as she folded her own napkin and slid it into the silver ring. No and no and no. But somehow she must see Gerrard. His letters were still wild with protest and warm with love and all the strength he could offer her to resist, and even alarming plans for trying to get married now on whatever work he might be able to do. Hopeless plans and he must know it as he wrote them. And they were only letters. She needed to see him, to touch him, and to know him real, and to understand afresh what she was struggling for. Longing washed over her like last night's tide along the shore.

"Don't keep me waiting, Sabrina," said Mama from the door, and behind her the black shadow of Cousin Anna nodded her head as if to ask what else you could expect.

The day was cloudless, touched by the wind with the first faint promise of the cold to come, and beyond the gardens in the demesne the beeches had their first light sheets of gold. Brin sniffed the sharp sweet air and the salt wind coming from the sea, and thought of John, and then of Gerrard, and wished desperately to be somewhere else than where she was, facing the same arguments with whatever reinforcements Mama had decided to summon up today. Mama was driving, and from the set of her mouth Sabrina knew she was displeased with John. And with her, of course. Mama would always be ready for a real flaming row about trifles, like Con's missing boot, which had blazed just before they left, but something important always produced this atmosphere of taut yet patient hurt, making it clear that the child concerned was not only darkening her days, but destroying her organization, which was infinitely worse.

Brin observed that the occasion must be formal, since Mama had put on dark clothes; navy blue, with only a soft drift of white lace around her throat, a close navy hat covering most of her bright hair. Surely it must be the convent. Those were convent clothes. Suitable to the mother of a postulant being interviewed by Reverend Mother. Mama never put a foot wrong about such things.

Then she realized that Mama's gloved hands had turned the pony down a small road toward the sea, little more than a lane, leading to the little church where Mary Rose had been married on that brilliant day that already seemed so long ago. It stood alone some distance across the fields from its small draggle of houses, surrounded only by a space of weedy gravel on a small promontory above the sea, with a small overcrowded graveyard at its side. For the wedding it had all been cleared and tidied, and as they reached it Brin tried not to see anything symbolical about the grass grown rank again around the leaning stones, and the last wild roses on a briar sprouting green with life from the darkness of a cracked tomb. Blackberries ripened richly over the rough stone wall from which the coat of wedding whitewash had long been washed by winter rains.

"We're not going to Cork," she said, unnecessarily, to her mother.

"Did anyone say we were?"

"Well, no, but—"

The parish priest, Brin thought then. Oh, Lord, surely not. Mama couldn't be as desperate as that. Not that it would be like Terry's china priest, but although he was a dear old soul and they all loved him, he was long past anything but the comfortable holy platitudes that had kept him safe and happy for forty years.

But Mama passed the presbytery door, and the church as well, and carefully took her black elastic-sided boots along the trodden grass between the graves, incongruous in her neat coat and skirt in the sad untidy place.

Detta's grave then, Brin thought. Well, I'd have come here with her any time she wanted, but why all the mystery?

Mama stopped at the tiny grave, conspicuous for its neatness, small among the marble tombs of the bigger families of the district. At its head was a weeping child angel, on whose gentle head an old hawthorn tree dropped flowers and fruit in season, and now shed its first dying leaves. Mama blessed herself and said her customary prayers for her ninth child, and Brin followed her, greatly mystified as to what it was all about.

Her mother lifted her head and looked at her across the marble angel, and the wind whispered in the ancient tree and drew a hand across the tranquil sea. Brin had a sudden, unaccountable, panicked feeling of being on the edge of a trap.

"What's it all about, Mama? Why couldn't you say we were coming to Detta's grave? I'd have brought her some flowers."

Mama sighed and her face was heavy with something not quite sadness. Brin realized with a shock that she was getting some obscure dramatic pleasure from the whole performance. She felt an acute sensation of distaste.

"Sabrina. I have to tell you something and I have to tell it to you here above your dead sister's grave, because it was above her tiny corpse I made the promise."

"What promise?" She longed to be away; never to have come. Mama was behaving with all the high drama of a countrywoman at a wake, screaming of the banshee hurtling through the night above her doomed roof.

"For goodness sake, Mama," she couldn't help saying, and Mama looked grieved and patient. In the hawthorn tree a robin began to sing, and Brin envied him his freedom.

"I have asked you," Mama went on heavily, "to please me by entering the convent."

Of course, Brin thought wearily, but why here?

"You told me, Mama," she corrected, and saw at once the shadow of rising anger. "You told me. You didn't ask."

"It's my place to tell you and my duty, and yours to obey me."

Her navy costume was edged with wide braid, and a cockade of the same braid, stitched and stiffened, rose from the side of her hat. Brin had a demoralizing impression that it had risen there at that moment with her anger. Carefully she steadily herself and stood silent until Mama began again.

"When Detta died," she said, and now there was in her voice an anguish she could never repress or forget, "I promised God."

Cold, sick fear took Brin as if the sun had gone from the sea and the robin ceased to whistle. She knew now what Mama was going to say, and looked down stunned at the little marble angel.

"You promised me," she said thickly, appalled. "The next one."

"I did. I vowed to God that if my next child was whole and sane, I would give it back to Him."

There was no triumph in Mama's eyes, only a sort of sick sadness that Sabrina had driven her to tell her this, after which there could not possibly be any further refusal.

Brin looked at her and tried to capture some of the pain and sorrow of that dreadful time. Ulick had told her of the baby, with legs like sticks and a poor tiny body, the slavering head the size of itself. Bernadette. As real as the rest of them for her short life. She understood the horror and even the sense of shame that must have seized her proud, perfectionist mother. The desperate love over all the others that she would have given the poor little creature, as though her own intensity might heal it. But no one, surely, could bargain with God.

"Mama, you had no right!" she burst out, and her mother stared at her, as shattered as if she had started to tear open the small grave with her hands.

"No right?" she said hoarsely when she could collect herself.

The girl should have been in stricken tears, touched to her obstinate heart by having been promised to God even before she was born. It was the most beautiful gesture a mother could make over the body of a dead child. Saints had come of it. But here was the vowed child, facing her across the very grave itself, with eyes like flints and the obstinacy set in her face like plaster.

"No right?" she said fiercely. "Didn't I bear you?"

"Mama, how could you promise my life to God? It was His already. He gave it to me. In any case," desperately she summoned her courage, "I don't believe in it."

"In what, miss?" Pure fury was rising, Mama driven almost to frenzy by such soulless indifference.

"In promising away someone else's life."

They argued furiously and angrily across the head of the weeping angel, who stood apathetic to all they said, lost in suitable grief while they fought above her. Suddenly Sabrina was touched by the ludicrousness of the situation, she and Mama battling fiercely in an empty graveyard. Mama alone could have achieved this falsity while reaching for her deepest beliefs. Brin fought down the appalling desire to laugh that had pursued her through so many of her mother's most serious rages.

An old man stopped and leaned on the wall to watch them with amazed concentration, picking his yellow teeth and storing the strange scene in his mind for endless retelling in the shebeen over a pint of porter. Only when Mama noticed him did she collect herself and with a twitch of her skirts walk away through the tangled grass, the blue hat high.

She made one last effort at the door of the church.

"Will you come in and say a prayer with me for your vocation?" she asked, and Brin shook her head, touched by the plea.

"All the prayers are for the same thing, Mama," she said gently, "and I cannot do it."

As she watched the straight back marching to the trap, she wondered how long she could hold out. She must see Gerrard before, from sheer pressure, she found herself enmeshed in the web of her mother's determination and creeping along the walls of some cold wax-smelling corridor in the ugly black dress of a postulant. At the moment she knew deep pity for her mother, and longed to reach out and touch her, but Mama was unreachable, except for children who were good.

The drive home was in total silence, no sound but the clatter of the pony's hooves and the faint whine of the rising wind that was piling soft unstable clouds above the hills. In that twenty minutes of frozen silence Brin decided almost angrily what she must do.

At the front door Mama handed her the reins and asked her to be good enough to take the pony to the stables. She looked down at the polite severe face. Mama would never be so undignified as to lose her manners, no matter what the argument, and Brin suddenly felt her throat close with unhappy tears.

Mama, she wanted to cry, you are *making* it all happen. You are *making* me deceive you. Why can't I just be myself? There could be another chance. Maggie might *want* it—like Sue.

But Mama only smiled carefully and frostily and picked up the blue skirt of her costume to climb the steps. As she shook the reins to start the pony, Brin saw Cousin Anna open the door, throwing her a glance of crushing satisfaction, certain of Mama's victory and ready to rejoice with her.

Brin drew a deep breath of splendid pleasure, feeling

immediately better. At least that one had a severe shock coming.

She was aware that she was being childish but couldn't help it, smiling as she went through the archway to the stables.

In her room, Teresa was putting away the clothes that had come back from Kilfenora, and Brin closed the door carefully behind her.

"Teresa, are you going home today?"

Teresa didn't answer directly. "And what'll you do after I'm married and I'll not be here to help you?"

Teresa never stopped thanking the good God that they had got away with it so long, and expected every letter to be found out, and herself sent home in disgrace to a mother neither to be held nor bound. But she looked up at Sabrina's face and knew this battle to have been worse than usual.

"I am," she said then gently. "In fact I'll do better. My brother'll be home too, and I'll give it to him to post in the city this evening when he goes back."

Sabrina was too distraught to thank her or to tell her the letter was not to Gerrard. From her shelves she took down her red morocco address book, still wondering at the impulse that had made her write down the address at all, since she didn't even like the girls. But anything in the city seemed close to Gerrard. Even to write the name Cork, was something to be grasped at.

She sat down at her little mahogany desk.

"Dear Euphemia . . ."

She had judged the Misses MacRory Glynn to the last detail. Their great big hearts and their soft foolish snobbery that would make them do anything for Sabrina Heron from Abbeygate. Their giggling romanticism, sloppily encouraged by their vast sentimental mother. Their delight in anything that would make them feel involved in a world they thought smarter than their own.

"Oh, my! Genia!" said Euphemia when in their overcrowded bedroom she ripped open Sabrina's letter. Her protuberant blue eyes grew big as saucers. Eugenia grabbed it, hurling yet another costly blouse onto the foot-high pile of discards on the lurid carpet.

"Well," she said, with a certain deep satisfaction. "Willy listen to that. Did you ever beat it? Her proud Mama'll be eating the fence posts with fury, does she ever find out!"

"She mustn't," Phemia cried urgently, so filled with horror that she put down half-eaten a delicious handmade chocolate cream with a real violet crystallized on top. They had not yet had breakfast. She showed real alarm because she knew that although every butterfly in Munster seemed to be flying round her stomach, there was nothing she would be able to refuse Sabrina. Now maybe they'd be real bosom friends, and Brin—she flushed with embarrassed excitement at the idea of calling her Brin—would tell her all her secrets about the Moynihan boy. She eyed the other half of the chocolate and left it. Brin was so slender. Then she thought of what Genia had said and turned on her.

"You'd never tell!" she hissed fiercely.

"Ah, for God's sake," said Genia, dismissing it. "And she'd never find out either. She and the Mama don't even know the same people."

The next morning Margaret went off from Abbeygate for her first term as a boarder in the convent, a little forlorn in her uniform that was, as Mama promised, largely made up of things outgrown by her two sisters. Her escort was Cousin Anna, and Sabrina could see that under her nervousness the child's mouth was tight with distaste and even shame at being sent off with the old crow. She felt a pang of compunction that her own unsatisfactory life had occupied her so completely that she had given little time lately to the small ones. She gave Maggie a specially warm hug and promised to come and see her soon, and resolved to see much more of Denis Mary before he went away in the term after Christmas. Already he construed painful Latin with the parish priest and did elementary mathematics with a smattering of geography and much biased history that was to confuse him deeply later on, when he went to school in England. Nurse, bereft, moved like a haunt around the house, searching desperately for an occupation to show she was still needed.

Three mornings later, over her toast and lightly boiled egg in its initialed silver cup, Mama gazed suspiciously at a letter addressed in the loose, ungainly hand of Mrs. MacRory Glynn. She frowned and dabbed her lips with her napkin.

"Someone, Sabrina, inviting you to attend a sacred concert. And to stay the night," she added, her eyebrows rising. "In Cork. Do we know them?"

Brin held her breath at the immediate note of doubt and disapproval. Beside her, Con took her attention from the fastidious dissection of a kipper and looked at her with lifted brows.

"Well, aren't you the bold one," she said under her breath, and Brin was furious, unable to stop herself blushing.

"In Cork," Con said then. "Who with, Mama?"

Fortunately for Brin, Mama was having trouble with the signature, and Papa was paying his customary careful no attention.

"Posy MacRory Glynn," said Mama in the end. "Who is she? Posy," she added reflectively, as if trying to imagine that she could know anyone with such a name. She took up the envelope and sniffed with controlled distaste at the lining, as Mother Angela had done. "I can't think I know them. What *very* self-conscious notepaper."

"Ah, Brin and I know her, don't we, Brin?" said Con, and once more Brin felt the scarlet flame her cheeks, ready to strangle her sister. But Con was not letting her down.

"You remember, Mama," she said smoothly. "They took us on a picnic to Summer Cove. Oh, very nice people. It was delightful. Very generous."

Brin listened to her sister with awe, recalling their host prostrate on the sand in his braces with a newspaper over his head, doling out half sovereigns to all the runners in the races; and Mrs. Posy, snoring under the tartan rug in her pink satin blouse while the man Peter happily swallowed the last of the warm champagne. She took courage.

"Very nice people," she said, and knew it true, although her mother might not agree. "We had a lovely day." And that was true too.

"Ah, yes." Mama remembered that Mother Angela had sanctioned the picnic, and after a few objections clearly aimed at guarding a girl about to become a nun, she gave her permission. The dogcart would be sent for Sabrina the following evening if that was suitable to Mrs. MacRory Glynn.

Genius, thought Brin, to have made it a sacred concert. She wondered if there really was one.

Her mother echoed her.

"Very suitable," she said, "for it to be a sacred concert."

Brin had to ask to be excused to get a handkerchief, partly because either she or Con would explode, and partly for the fact that she had begun to shake in a storm of released emotion she could barely hide. Con flicked her a sharp glance.

"Show me that impossible envelope, Mama," she said quickly, and occupied Mama with happy disparagement of the MacRory Glynn notepaper until Brin was safely from the room.

CHAPTER 9

The upholstered kindness of Mrs. MacRory Glynn almost undid all the planning. When Sabrina arrived in the dogcart before the tall cream-painted house on the fashionable summit of St. Patrick's Hill, she was enveloped by Mrs. Glynn in a vast Parma-violet-scented hug to the mild but unconcealed astonishment of her mother's groom. Matt would accept his end of the social world, and that of his mistress, but the off-key middle registers he held in suitably snobbish disapproval. Brin extricated herself with the best possible grace, seeing his eye, and asked if it would be convenient if she was collected at five o'clock on the following evening.

" 'Tis entirely," Mrs. MacRory Glynn said warmly, the girls beaming behind her. " 'Tis entirely for you to say. The month or the year would be all the same to us, and the longer the better."

Sabrina felt a little shamed, knowing she meant every warmhearted word of it.

"Five o'clock then, please, Matt," she said, and hoped

no echoes of his astonishment would reach her mother. She dismissed that. Mama would listen to no servant, not even MacGinnis. The front door closed behind her and she turned to the girls, mouthing and gesticulating out of their mother's sight. Phemia had a great purple bow in her sandy hair, and drifts of pearl sheen powder conflicted unfortunately with her usual high color. Both of them began to speak at once, but they were no match for the mother, who led the way in a gust of perfume along the hot and overfurnished hall, talking as she went.

"Well now, Sabrina must be tired after the long drive, the creature. Take her up, girls, and she can have a cup of tea and a biscuit or two in her room and rest there until the concert. You'll like that now, Sabrina, and you beat off your feet."

Brin had an appalled vision of some monstrous meal among the pillows and no chance to meet Gerrard. Helplessly she looked at the girls and they almost leapt on their mother as she tried to keep the disappointment from shattering her face. Already a plump little country maid with a saucy eye was vanishing round the corner of the stairs with her traveling basket, looking forward to going through the possessions of as much Quality as would ever come to this house.

"But, Mama," Genia was first, her voice almost a shriek. "You know we have an appointment with the dressmaker. We wanted Sabrina to come with us and see our new dresses."

Her mother dismissed her with a massive hand.

"Leave the woman. Leave her. Don't I pay her enough not to have Sabrina driven into the streets in the very moment of her coming to the house!"

Brin managed to hide her smile, but it took them almost a quarter of an hour. In the end she had to take her gloves off because of the damp palms of her hands, protesting as strongly as she dared.

"I'm not tired. Honestly, Mrs. Glynn. And I'm not often in Cork now. I'd love to go with the girls."

She had no idea even what they'd planned. Whether there was a dressmaker or even a sacred concert, but her heart was soft to them for their efforts. In the end Mrs. MacRory Glynn gave way. There were repeated instructions that they must walk along the river so Sabrina could get a bit of fresh air and some good out of her visit after all and if Sabrina didn't mind she wouldn't come herself but would put the feet up for half an hour on the chaise longue on account of the bunions were killing her. Gravely Sabrina said good-bye for the moment and the two girls swooped like hawks on the hats and gloves already laid waiting on the hall stand.

"In the name of God," Genia said when she had them at last going at a fast clip down the hill. "I thought we'd have to get her a drop of chloroform. Euphemia, you have your hat on backward."

Fiercely Phemia tore off the hat, maddened that she had put Genia in a position to find fault with her before Sabrina. A lump of hair came with the hatpins in reversing it.

It was to Brin that she cried "Will it do now?" and Brin smiled at her reassuringly.

"Perfect, Phemia, and thank you for arranging everything. Is there really a dressmaker?"

She was galloping along after Genia, who lost ground to turn on her with disapproval.

"There is indeed. Would you have us lying to the Mama? But you don't have to come," she added more gently, and Phemia's big blue eyes glowed under the tattered hair.

"We have it all arranged," she panted, carrying the most weight, and so most severely taxed by Genia's pace. "For the love of heaven, Genia, will you not ease up a bit."

"The Mama mothering away like that has us late," Genia said firmly. "Would you want him gone?"

Brin stopped dead, and an interested woman tacked around her, looking at the three hopefully as if she expected a row.

"I'll not go another step until you tell me. I can't stand it."

"Brennan's Tea Shop," said Genia, and hurled herself on again, and now Brin was barely aware of them, given the unbelievable reality of a place. Brennan's. She knew it well, of course, the setting of many a sedate outing from the convent with Mama, and a pang of nervous fear touched her that some one of Mama's friends might see her.

" 'Tis the only possible place," Eugenia said, pushing a damp strand of hair off her scarlet face. "You couldn't go anywhere else," and Brin knew she was right.

"We'll keep old Nellie talking as long as we can," Phemia said.

"Keep her going mad with the pins," her sister said tersely. "Tell her nothing fits."

Brin tried to say a word of thank as they pounded along the walls of the River Lee towards the center of the City, and the sweet bells of Shandon Church pealed gently through the "Londonderry Air," the music falling soft as the autumn mist along the dark river.

About herself she was past thinking, her mind a knot of sick apprehension that even now something might happen to prevent it all. But they arrived safely at the double doors of Brennan's, with the famous name crusted in gold along the beveled glass, and Genia and Phemia vanished like the witches in *Macbeth*, crying in sibilant whispers that they would see her in about an hour.

Looking after them along the street, she envied them for a few moments for some untouched youth she had already lost, and felt shamed to use them. Then she remembered who was waiting for her inside, and faced what Mama would think the unseemly and improper conduct of walking into Brennan's on her own. Two ladies, glossy in their autumn furs and talking each other out of existence came along at that moment, and gratefully she followed them through into the warm glitter of light.

She saw him at once and forgot everything else; he was standing beside a potted palm under a cluster of electric globes, and the first thing she noticed was the light in his brown hair, as she had long ago seen it under the gas lamps in the gallery. There was a delighted grin on his face. He had been watching her come in and knew all her doubts, and although he was laughing at her he came at once, standing very close to her and for a few moments not speaking, and all she could think of was a book she'd once read about some people caught in an earthquake, and it had the effect of sucking the breath from their bodies. She recovered hers when he spoke.

"You look exactly," he said, "as if you're going to rob the place."

"Me? I've never robbed anywhere."

"No?"

The touch of his hand under her elbow told her he was real and she smiled at him with pure happiness. In all her lonely dreams, brought to desperation by their impossibility, she had pictured every possible circumstance of such a meeting. Even in the last wordless stages of the race into town, she had thought of dumb emotion and clasped hands and a tremendous struggle to speak of all that had nearly defeated her through the empty months.

Never in one of those longing dreams had it occurred to her that they would simply laugh. At once. Swamped to the exclusion of everything else by the wild delight of seeing each other. So easy. So immediate. As if it had been yesterday they had met. Talk coming bubbling as he led her to a discreet table that hid its convoluted legs and spindly chairs behind another potted palm. But only talk of silly simple things like the canter down the hill and Mrs. MacRory Glynn almost putting her to bed.

"It gives me a weakness to think of it," said Gerrard, in Genia's voice.

There were the clasped hands of her dreams simply because they didn't seem to be able to keep them apart, reaching across the table as they searched each other's smiling faces. She saw him infinitely more handsome, the fine planes of his face firmer, with a look of strength under the grin he couldn't wipe away. His brown hair was still fiercely smoothed across the top, but broke to mutinous feathers round his ears that made her fingers long to reach out and smooth them. And his eyebrows still went up and down and his grey suit was smart and suitable to a young solicitor, very smart, with a pale paisley tie, and she remembered the handkerchief she had given him and hoped fleetingly that his mother still hated it.

When the elderly waitress came with a clean pink cloth, they had to loose their hands reluctantly to let her lay the table, but their eyes could not unlock. She had grown, he thought tenderly, and was thinner, and wore her pale blue costume with a beautiful self-confident young elegance, but in the hilarity of the grey eyes and in the small damp ball of gloves she laid beside her on the table, he saw still the girl who would think always first of what she did and only later of how she looked. He noticed the pearls of her first mutiny at her throat and knew she had come far from the tousled bridesmaid with the cream of the stolen wedding food crushed against her dress. But not too far, thank God, for her long-lashed eyes rested on him with delight and love she would never learn the deviousness to conceal. He felt humble and blessed, and wild with power and pride.

"Oh, Brin," he said, and then the waitress was standing over them with a tray again, and a notebook, indifferent to currents of emotion she saw almost every day.

"What would you like?" Gerrard asked Brin, and she had trouble in remembering where she was.

"Muffins," said the waitress flatly, unwilling to wait.

"Muffins?" said Gerrard.

"Oh, yes, muffins," said Brin and found it intolerably funny. What was funny about muffins? Gerrard's grin spread again and they found it almost impossible to choose between two such ludicrous words as Indian and China.

Then as abruptly as it had begun, their laughter died and they stared at each other in rising sadness, facing the hopeless reality. She told him everything then, all the pressures that were being put on her, even the fearful blackmail of Detta's grave, and he gripped her fingers until they hurt, and when the muffins came, they not only found them no longer funny, but forgot to eat them, and the melted butter ran from them and congealed in cold yellow rings around their colored plates.

Gerrard's face grew dark with an anger she had never seen on it, changing him, making him older. But he would not speak to her against her mother.

"You won't give in, will you?" was all he said, and tried not to burden her with his own bleak horror at the thought of her being wrenched from him and immured behind some monstrous wall with all her hair cut off, which was about the limit of his knowledge of the ways of nuns. But Brin's grey eyes grew soft, all anxiety gone from them, and she smiled, tightening her fingers around his.

"Not now," she said. "Not now that I've seen you. I just had to, to give me courage."

His own smile warmed, and they sat in silence, gathering from each other the strength to go back to enduring their separation, until the gaunt waitress passed them and glared in disapproval at their untouched food and tea.

"We'd better have a cup of tea," Gerrard said then, "or that gorgon'll come and pour it down our throats. I'm sure she's thinking we'd do as well on a bench on the green as taking up one of her tables."

As, indeed to God, he thought as she poured the tea, impeccably trained by Mama, indeed to God, I wish we were on a bench somewhere, so I could get her in my arms. Get her—

Determinedly he closed his mind to the longings of his body, for Brin was not the girl you took to a park bench. Or anywhere else come to that, except the altar, and please God, a long life beyond it. He thought fleetingly of his father. All the pictures in the house showed him as a tall young man whose strong character was written in every line of his face. Had he lived, would it have saved his mother from the professional widowhood, the ingrown possessiveness, both for him and for Sabrina's mother, that dominated her life?

"Gerrard," Brin said suddenly, above the congealed muffins, the world outside intruding with the reality of the teacups. "What about the war? Will you go? John's gone, you know, but he's a soldier. I expect he's in France by now."

He saw the fear in her face and reached to touch her hand, holding the flowered teapot.

"He'll be all right," he said gently.

"Mama," she said then and didn't finish, and there was a moment's silence.

"Will you go?" she asked again then, and tried to say it calmly.

"I want to, my love," he said, and seemed suddenly older. "Of course I want to. But Brown McCaffery feels I'd be mad to go rushing off in the middle of my articles for a war that'll be over in a few months."

Brin thought of the newspapers she slipped into the gun room to read. Both sides digging themselves in into the cold autumn mud. Trench warfare, they called it. All for a few months?

"So I've promised," Gerrard said, "to qualify before I

do anything. Like marry." He grinned. "We'll see. My mother doesn't even acknowledge there's a war."

"I know," Brin said, and her own eyes brightened and she told him of Con leading his mother on to talk about him and all the torrents of praise. Gerrard grimaced and pushed his cup away.

"But she's very pleased," Brin said gravely, "that you've too much sense to have a girl."

He didn't smile back, and hers faded, and they were still sitting like that, their hands joined again among the buttery plates, when Genia and Phemia bustled in, full of self-importance, their round faces flushed with the cool evening air and the wild excitement of successful conspiracy.

"Gerrard," Brin whispered as they edged out through the crowded tea room. After the crushing answer about the dressmaker, she didn't dare ask the girls, "Is there really a sacred concert?"

His hazel eyes gleamed at her.

"Indeed there is. And we have to sit through it. We wouldn't want to deceive our Mamas, would we?"

Brin smiled back at him, delighted at the echo, and he paused beside the high mahogany desk where a plump lady in rimless glasses and a high-necked blouse presided over her kingdom of bills and spikes. As he paid the bill, which she accepted with an air of severe distaste, Brin thought of what he and the girls had said. Of course, of course they wanted to deceive their Mamas. That's all they were trying to do, and if they were found out they might as well go off to the Western Front together, for all the chance they'd have.

She took his arm without thinking as they came out into the dusky street, all the new-lit lamps gleaming pale through the river mist, and sauntered quietly behind the two girls with no thought but for themselves, until their roads parted. Close together, their hands locked, Brin was oblivious, in the sweet contact of Gerrard's fingers, that she had left the crumpled ball of her gloves on the pink tablecloth.

"I shall see you," Gerrard said when he left them, "at the sacred concert," and although Brin tried to smile, she knew they were lucky to have that.

Mrs. MacRory Glynn had her victory the next day, when Brin had hoped to meet Gerrard even for a few desperate minutes in his dinner hour from Brown McCaffery. Determined to have her social triumph fully recognized, her hostess had arranged a girls' luncheon, for all her daughters' friends to meet Sabrina.

"But, Mama," Phemia said in last hopeless protest, knowing what Sabrina wanted to do. "Aren't they all convent girls, and don't they know her already?"

"Not under my roof," her mother answered with deep satisfaction, hitting the nub of it, and all the morning rushed her vast velvet-padded bulk through preparations for a meal that would have been no disgrace in Dublin Castle for a bit of foreign royalty, as Genia observed bitterly. But Brin tried to accept it with good grace, a little shamed by all of it, and honest enough to acknowledge that Mrs. MacRory Glynn had a right to something in the heel of the hunt.

Almost before it was over, and the young ladies up in the bedroom straightening their hats to go home, the dogcart was waiting below the steps, the young groom in his brass-buttoned coat carefully lighting the candles in the huge brass lamps against the last dark stages of the journey.

Mrs. MacRory Glynn came thundering down from where she was boasting happily to the mothers in the drawing room, and heavy with unwanted food, Brin kissed her and gave her the box of crystallized violets that Mama regarded as an obligatory part of the packing for any visit.

"Well, sure to God now," screeched Mrs. Glynn, and as Brin accepted a large damp kiss, the smell of whiskey wafted across her face. "I've nearly as much of that stuff as I'd have of Turkish delight, and isn't it odd now that the city of Cork is the place it all comes from and you'd think it from those haythens with the veils themselves, is that young fella with the buttons safe now with the horse?"

From all of which Brin assumed she meant thank-you for the present and a safe journey home, and she waved once more at the girls, accepting gratefully when Matt offered her the rug against the chill Irish miles back to Abbeygate. The mist was creeping again from the quiet river, and as she looked back at the city, thinking of Gerrard, every early light was haloed pale in gold, luminous as memory.

Mama and Papa were gone out to dine with friends, so thankfully she had the evening to herself, tried by nothing more than light answers to Ulick's undemanding questions at dinner. In the morning the glances Mama shot her at the breakfast table were sharp and critical and Sabrina braced herself for the detailed inquiries that in the end she never had to face.

She was in the conservatory after breakfast, doing the house flowers with Mama, a task whose quietness and remoteness from the household had often been used for some of the most difficult pressures and discussions. She had done her best to isolate herself in the small room off the big glassed dome, where a tap ran in an old shallow trough and a long marble bench for doing the flowers had shelves above it for the pots and vases. Left alone, she loved it, and sniffed happily at the conservatory smell of damp moss and loam and water, dominated at this time of year by the sharp spice of the chrysanthemums, almost waist high, massed in colored pots. She heard MacGinnis come into the room outside and speak to her mother, and after a pause Mama answered quietly.

"Sabrina," she cried then, and her voice held some urgency that brought the girl out at once with dripping hands, her eyes falling immediately on the orange flimsy of the wire in Mama's hand.

"John," Brin said, and felt as if some giant hand had hit her, knocking her off balance, surprised that she didn't move. Mama recovered at once, but her voice was still a little uneven.

"No," she said. "Thank God, no. It's Gran. Go and find me Teresa, please, Sabrina, and tell her to come to me. And if your father isn't in the house, go and search the stables. We must catch the midday train."

"Can I not come?" Brin said. "Can I not come?"

Just, she didn't add, just to see her once more. Just once. Her eyes rested pleading on her mother's face and for a moment Brin thought she was going to soften.

Then, "No," Mama said briskly. "Your father will be enough. Please, Sabrina, I don't have much time."

Nor probably does Gran, Brin thought as she walked through the house, already unfamiliar with the impact of impending sorrow. Poor Gran. No, Gran doesn't mind. Poor us. Poor me. Poor Mama, she thought last of all, with sudden compassion.

"Keep in touch with Mary Rose," Mama said as she went past her up the stairs, and she realized the wire must have torn her in two, but Gran was alone, and Mary Rose a married woman with her own husband and family round her. Brin warmed to the first faint hint of responsibility ever offered her.

Never before could she remember the house without either of her parents, and with Ulick out round the land, she unashamedly spent most of the morning in the kitchen, where Cookie plied her with endless cups of tea, strong and dark and brown, and also plied her, in what she thought to be a suitably muted voice, with lugubrious tales of death and sorrow and the howlings of the banshee, while MacGinnis looked on with puckered disapproval.

It was he who sent her over after lunch was done, to Mary Rose.

"She should know, Miss Brin, and your mother had no time to think of it, nor Mr. Ulick to go himself. Go on now and put on your habit and I'll speak for the horse for you."

He watched her go out of the stableyard, his long face full of sad affection and his coattails flapping in the damp wind. Get her away at least, from that oul' harridan in the kitchen, heart set on holding the wake before the old lady, God have mercy on her, was even dead.

Brin clopped slowly along the country road below the leafless trees and up through Dermot's untidy park, her mind full of her own piled-up thoughts, offering nothing but sorrow and frustration; but there was little comfort for her with Mary Rose, except for the happy clamor of the children and their warm sweet kisses. Even they were not allowed to stay long, as they tired their mother, and when they were led reluctantly away, Brin promised faithfully to come up and see them before she left. She turned back to her sister. Mary Rose was only a week away from the birth of the baby she had been told would almost certainly kill her; she lay mute and exhausted on the sofa in her overheated drawing room. The velvet curtains were already drawn against the misty afternoon, and a crocheted afghan lay across her swollen body.

"Oh, poor Gran," said Mary Rose when Brin told her, and for a few moments sorrow for her grandmother dispersed the terror for herself that darkened her blue eyes. "I wish I could have seen her again."

Brin felt trapped and overwhelmed, her emotions already drawn to threads by the brief meeting with Gerrard. The lovely, happy Mary Rose looked old and sad and frightened, and Brin felt on every side of her grief and sorrow and distress she was unable to assuage, and not the least of it her own. Desperately she did her best to make bright chatter to the seemingly indifferent Lady Fitzjames across the tea table, miserable and overly hot in her heavy habit beside the roaring fire, and every polite word she tried to say about the sacred concert and her two days in Cork brought her to the edge of tears.

As soon as she decently could, she stood up and made the excuse that she had promised MacGinnis she would be home before dark.

"Of course, darling," Mary Rose said. "You have Tatty?"

"Yes."

Mary Rose smiled for one moment as if she remembered happiness, and as Brin bent to kiss her she knew she left her tears on her face and that she shouldn't. It wasn't fair. The last thing Mary Rose needed was someone else's tears.

"You'll miss her," Mary Rose said, and wouldn't allow the tears were for anyone else than Gran. "You and she were always special."

They took her death for granted. And Mary Rose? Brin looked down at her through blurred eyes and went clumsily from the room, forgetting to say good-bye to Lady Fitzjames and to the children.

The great red sun was sliding away behind the pale mist, and even the world itself smelled of dampness and decay, the dead leaves thick and soft, unswept, under Tatty's hooves. Suddenly Brin kicked her heels into the horse's sides, and Tattybogle seemed to understand and acquiesce, shaking her head and giving a little whinny. Beyond the demesne gates they crossed the road, and for the length of a long stony lane Brin held her to a canter, until they came through the open gate at the end of it.

"Now, my beautiful," she said, and let her go, flying off into a wide country circle that would bring her round and into Abbeygate from the back. Over the sheep-dotted land and through the walled pastures, Tatty taking the grey stones like a bird. Across the river where it was narrow enough for one great leap, and Brin laughed aloud with the tear marks still on her face as Tatty landed in the spiky sedge. She slapped her silken neck.

They went across a lane bounded by two stony banks ablaze with gorse, and barely space for a hoof change in between them, disturbing an astonished laborer fiddling with a slane along the side of the ditch, a sodden sack across his shoulders against the mist. Past the kennels, setting the hounds in uproar at the sound of Tatty's hooves, and Brin grinned and Tattybogle tossed her flying chestnut mane as if to tell them come and catch her; and then they were in the dark avenue of the larch-woods and out into the light again, pounding up the long sloping pasture where Ulick's cattle lifted indifferent eyes from the sodden grass; along the narrow back boreen where they must slow down a bit before the gate that led into the stables past the cottages and the coach house and the round black clock below the cupola that was just sweetly chiming five and the dusk coming down and light pouring from the kitchen. She rode in gently, flushed and calm, and Tatty rolled her a pleased conspiratorial eye as she dropped from the saddle under the mulberry tree beside the well.

Only Matt came out, chewing on a long straw, and he looked at the horse with cold disapproval.

"Get a rug on her, Matt, she's hot."

"D'you say so, Miss Brin," he said scathingly, but she didn't apologize and felt sure that Tatty didn't want to either. She dropped a kiss on her damp velvet nose and went in to the house; nor did she stop in the kitchen, content now to be alone.

When the wire came the next afternoon to say that

Gran was dead, her tears were tears of sad acceptance, no longer the miserable clamor of a child who demanded that its world remain unchanged.

But, oh, God, please God, help Mary Rose. Help Mary Rose.

It was over a week later that Mama and Papa came home, the funeral over and all the tedious business cared for, and even before she had properly kissed Sabrina, Mama asked the sharp anxious question.

"How is your sister?"

"Well, Mama. Well indeed. But frightened," she couldn't help adding, and got a withering flash from Mama's eyes for daring, an unmarried girl, to offer an opinion about such things. But Brin noticed the strain ease from her face, and realized she looked pale and tired, although her hair gleamed with brilliance against the unaccustomed black of her feathered hat. She longed to be able to offer her one word to reach her and comfort her, understanding that she must have been trapped between grief for the loss of her own adored mother and desperate anxiety for Mary Rose. But Mama drew herself up, and began issuing clear, precise orders to MacGinnis, presuming without asking that the house had fallen into chaos in her absence. It was Papa who put his arm through Brin's and drew her off up the stairs.

"And how's the mistress of the house?" he asked her, his blue eyes warm with pleasure at her youth and beauty after a week of age and grief and death.

She squeezed his arm.

"Never, oh, never," she said, "like Mary Rose, Papa. But Cookie said I didn't make a bad fist of it."

Mary Rose took them all by surprise, Dermot himself driving over only two mornings later through the hazy sun of early day, standing in the hall to wait for them all to come down to him, his ulster beaded with the silver damp. He had the vague bemused smile of a man who has been pardoned the sentence of death and taken the night to celebrate it, his black hair rumpled and the shadow of a beard on his soft chin.

Mama and Brin arrived together in a rush, and he could hardly answer their unspoken questions.

"N-nothing," he said, looking in astonished relief from one to the other of them. "N-nothing happened after all. Nothing."

"For pity's sake, Dermot, what do you mean, nothing?" Mama could not hold her patience.

He focused her with dark eyes that held some violent deep antagonism and swayed a little. He had an air of exhaustion, as if the fear had been too great almost to allow for celebration when it lifted.

"I mean, Mrs. Heron," he said slowly and deliberately to Mama, "that I have another fine son, and no trouble to Mary Rose at all. No trouble at all."

Clearly his manner said that it was the women, and only the women, who had caused the nightmare of guilt and fear he had lived through for the last nine months.

Brin flung her arms about his neck, unable to bear his face, which should have held nothing but pride and happiness. A little astonished, for Mama did not encourage demonstrations of affection in her family, and he knew it, he kissed Brin back warmly, accepting then Mama's formal kiss of congratulations, warm too, almost against her will, with relief and delight for Mary Rose.

"Oh, Dermot. She's quite all right?"

"Yes, Mother." Dermot began to expand himself. "She's all right. She's wonderful." His eyes filled with tears below the bull curls.

Full, delighted celebration flowered when Papa came thumping down the stairs in his tartan dressing gown, tears also misting his eyes uncontrollably when he heard the news.

"Ah, my Mary Rose," he said. "God bless them both. What'll you call him, Dermot?"

"Barry, sir," said Dermot, smiling, and Papa moved off to ring the bell for MacGinnis.

There was champagne then on the breakfast table, among the willow-pattern plates and the silver dishes of the kippers and the kedgeree, and not even Mama could stay proof against the almost imbecile grin on Dermot's face and the atmosphere of rejoicing and relief.

"And when can we see her, Dermot?"

He was taking his damp coat from MacGinnis in the hall, going off, back to his wonderful new world.

"Any time. Any time at all. I tell you, she's as fettle as a spring filly."

When they drove over that afternoon, they found she was. Radiant, with a fair, beautiful, healthy son, and her smile was Mary Rose again, tranquil and loving against her lace-bordered pillows.

"Took me no time at all," she said to Brin when Mama had left the room, forgetting she was talking to her unmarried sister. "And Brin—"

"Yes, love?"

Brin smiled into her triumphant eyes.

"The old lady's to get out. And horseface. Dermot told them there's too many children now."

"Oh, Mary Rose."

Her heart was full that Mary Rose should be so happy, lifting the fog of sorrow that had bound them all. She took the child when she was allowed to, a soft and yet astonishingly heavy bundle, and remembered when she had held her sister's first son in her arms. Tentative and uncomprehending, something alien to herself, belonging to some other world that was Mary Rose's. Now she understood the little warm creature as something vital of life itself. Some stage that she and Gerrard had not yet reached, but would, with God's help come to. She was already in some secret place from which Mama was struggling to exclude her. Illogically she thought of the caper with the MacRory Glynns in the tea shop, and Gerrard's hands in hers across the table, and smiling, she kissed the sleeping baby. She laid him gently back beside his mother.

"He's beautiful, Mary Rose. Beautiful."

"Tch-tch," said Mama, coming at that moment into the room. "Do be careful how you hold his head, Sabrina. You must learn—"

She checked herself with an obvious sad pride, leaving unspoken the statement that Sabrina, please God, would never need to know how to hold a baby. Brin kissed her sister quickly and left the room.

The whole household, crippled with fear for Mary Rose and the sad wait for Gran's death, expanded with relief and happiness, right down into the kitchen, where Katty

Ann stared sentimentally into space above the vegetables in the stone sink.

"Ah, God," she said, "the little fella. Fair they say he is, like his mother. Wouldn't I love to set eyes on him."

As if in her own sod-roofed home little fellas did not arrive with all the predictability of falling leaves or spring.

"Well hold your scrap of a mind on what you're doing," roared Cookie, "in order I don't put you out on the streets, and I have no doubt that in God's good time you will."

Katty Ann's scrawny face was unperturbed as she bent over the carrots. Mrs. Cook was always yelling about putting her on the streets, although God knew what streets and there only the one bit of road running past the house. Yet there wasn't an evening she went home empty-handed from that kitchen to her swarming family.

"The little fella," she said again.

The cautious doctor, uttering warning words about one swallow, however welcome, not making a summer, was brushed aside, and a few days later, Mama was in high fettle as she set out in the trap for Castle Brackett, where Padgeen's mother was inaugurating a committee of ladies of the district to organize the provision of comforts for their representatives in the trenches of France.

"And may I not come, Mama?" Brin said, and felt she was forever saying it. "You know how interested I am in anything like that."

"Quite unsuitable," Mama said briskly at once; her confidence in the defeat of Sabrina had been vastly increased by the correctness of her judgment over Mary Rose. There was nothing wrong with Dermot. An excellent young husband. And there would be nothing wrong with the convent either, for Sabrina.

"I'll take the umbrella for the trap, please, MacGinnis. It looks a little grey." She buttoned the wrists of kid gloves so fine they were a second skin on her hands. Almost as an afterthought she turned to Sabrina. "You will stay here and get on with your spiritual reading, which has been badly neglected. You have barely begun it."

Brin looked at her expressionlessly, thinking of the piles of dreary books on the lives and piety of dreary saints that had been appearing in increasing numbers in her room, marked at special passages with little slips of card painted with holy pictures. She recognized the far-reaching hand of Reverend Mother.

"Mama," she said quietly and patiently, and from the corner of her eye saw MacGinnis effacing himself. She nearly told him it was all right, there wasn't going to be a row. "I am not going to be a nun."

Mama didn't even offer her any attention, sweeping off through the front door, with MacGinnis behind her with the colored umbrella, which he fitted to the socket of the trap. She gathered the reins into her hands, and Brin watched her drive off, erect and elegant in a violet coat and skirt suitable for the days after Gran's death, the black band of mourning on her arm and the gleam of pearls at her throat. A small smile of satisfaction and content warmed her face as she flicked the pony to a start, the filtered sun gleaming on the polished trap and the brasses of the lamps and harness, a dark rug spread neatly on her knees. Beside her, erect too in his brass buttons, Matt looked positively proud of her.

And who wouldn't, thought Brin, shaking her head. She'd take the blue ribbon for style in the Dublin Horse Show any day you'd put her there. She turned and went off up to her room, where Teresa had lit a welcome fire, and firmly she put away Saint Teresa and Saint Augustine of Hippo, and curled herself with sinful pleasure on her bed with an apple and a lurid novelette belonging to Teresa, until MacGinnis should call her for the lunch.

She heard her clearly when she came back in the late afternoon, careening across the gravel like the charge of the Light Brigade, and as Brin ran to the top of the stairs, filled with the inevitable fright for Mary Rose, Mama swept into the hall. Through the open door Brin could see Matt, leading away the astonished and outraged pony, looking himself ruefully at the mud spattered on his gleaming trap.

"Sabrina," Mama said at once, and Brin thought, Oh, Lord, what now?

It was clear that Mama could not and would not wait to do battle anywhere other than on the spot, and after one quick comprehending glance, MacGinnis faded away behind the stairs.

"There's storm cones flying upstairs," he said to Cookie in the kitchen, shaking his head, and Cookie lifted her vast face from the evening's pastry.

"The madam?" she said.

"Indeed."

"And Miss Brin?"

MacGinnis nodded.

"Ah, the creature, she'll need her wits about her." Cookie picked up the pastry and slammed it down again as if she hated it.

At the foot of the stairs Brin stood and watched her mother fumbling furiously in her reticule, and when she saw a crumpled pair of pale blue gloves emerge, she felt for a moment actual sickness and a sense of dreadful weary boredom at what she knew she must go through.

"I am not afraid," she told herself, and put her hands at once behind her back to hide their trembling, and locked her knees. Never once had she thought about the gloves, but now Mama produced them, she could see them clearly, lying on the pink tablecloth as she walked out with Gerrard, oblivious of the very world, never mind a pair of gloves.

But who? Who had been there that she didn't see? Or had Mrs. MacRory Glynn got them somehow and given them in all good faith.

Mama cut her speculations short, icy and accusing, her color high.

"You know where you left them?"

She began walking up and down the hall carpet in the sheer nervous energy of her anger, and Brin felt it wrong her footsteps were so soundless. Such rage should make a noise. She felt too curiously tired. All too easily might she say, Mama, I have decided to go into the convent rather than face another row. After the strain of Gran and Mary Rose I cannot stand it.

Then she felt all tiredness slip away, replaced by the new confidence she had gained from the brief meeting that was the trigger point, after all, for this outburst. This was the moment when deceit must end, and all the petty subterfuges Mama had pushed them to. Quietly she took her hands from behind her back and stood with one of them on the carved newel of the stairs, the other at her side. There was something in her attitude and quietness that halted Mama, who looked her up and down sharply. Brin's level gaze met hers.

"I know where I left them, Mama. And thank you for bringing them back."

"Bringing them back!" Her lack of guilt seemed to throw Mama into fresh paroxysms.

"In a—a—common eating house! And alone with a young man! Alone. You of all people to be alone—"

Brin's eyes told her not to start that one again.

"In an eating house!" Mama finished for want of better.

"Who gave them to you, Mama?" she asked.

"Who gave them to me? Padgeen's mother gave them to me. The most respectable of my friends, and does it not bother you to be destroying your sister's chances? And you so lost to all decent behavior that you walked out without them and left them on the table behind you."

Brin sorted that one out. She couldn't think either Con or Padgeen would have any marriage broken because she went out to tea with Gerrard. But Lady Brackett? Never saw her, she thought, and couldn't help a smile, knowing she had seen nothing. She saw her mother literally rear up in outrage at the smile, and spoke quickly.

"She was there?"

"She was there," said Mama fiercely, and too late saw that she had placed Lady Brackett in a common eating house, and Brin saw it too, but was past laughing. Mama rushed to the attack.

"And who was this—this—gallant? Sacred concert indeed. A pack of lies from start to finish to arrange this assignation."

"In a common eating house, Mama." Brin said coolly. "And with Lady Brackett watching. It couldn't have been more public. And there was a sacred concert." And a dressmaker, she almost added, from sheer nervous fear now that she must speak. She took a deep breath but it seemed to reach no further than the cameo of Gran's that pinned the ruffled jabot of her blouse. The shadows in the hall had grown unaccountably darker and closer around her, and she felt very much alone. Facing my mother, she thought, and I feel alone.

"Gerrard Moynihan, Mama," she said, and hoped that might make it a little more acceptable. But Mama's voice was a hoarse whisper and her green eyes enormous.

"Anna's son. That boy. But they know—they know—"

"Not from me, Mama," she said with desperate courage.

"Cousin Anna's son!" Mama said again, appalled as a queen might be at the treachery of a favored subject.

Four foot high with warts and Brin remembered how she and Con had the giggles at the thought of him, and in reality, of the feathers of hair above his ears. She felt like a rock that had been since the beginning of time, immovable at the foot of the stairs, and at the same time weightless, as if she might, unless she were careful, rise up and float away, up past the pampas and through the house, to lodge like a gas balloon against the ceiling outside Denis Mary's room.

"And how long?" Her mother's furious, incredulous face, close to hers, brought her back from fantasy. She had no chance of floating away, like some scarlet fugitive with a dangling string, blown away at a fete. "How long," gritted Mama, "have you been conducting this sinful liaison behind my back? You—you—almost ready for—"

"No," said Brin flatly. "No, Mama."

Sinful liaison, she thought wearily. Are these the sins of the world that take people like little Sue away forever to pray for them? Surely only in Mama's mind. There must be more to it than that.

She took a deep breath.

"Mama," she said, then, astonished at the calmness of her own voice. "You must understand I will never be a nun, not only because I don't want to, but because I have promised to marry Gerrard. A long time ago. As soon as he is through his articles. I shall be older than Mary Rose and there's no trouble about money. He'll inherit a lot from his father when he's twenty-one. And his mother is your friend."

She knew she was rushing a bit at the end, troubled by the disintegration of her mother's face. She almost pitied her, and would have begun an appeal for softness, moving a step towards her, but Mama's stricken silence was only because she had provoked more words even than Mama could get out. She stuttered with fury and derision.

"Married! To Anna Grant's son! To anyone, against my wishes!"

"I love Gerrard, Mama, and he loves me."

Deliberately Mama ignored this childish platitude and regained control of herself, taking off her small toque of violet feathers and smoothing her hair as if the exchange had ruffled it. Her breathing was a little hard, furious with herself for her loss of dignity, and that one of her children had so far escaped from control.

"We will say no more of this, Sabrina," she said, picking up the braided hem of her skirt with a gesture that lifted it in distaste from more than the dust of the stairs. "Clearly you have allowed yourself to be carried away by unfortunate influences. And I am to blame for not exercising more supervision. But there's nothing that can't be settled. Will you please go to the kitchen now, and see what you can do to help Mrs. Cook with the dinner."

She went on up, with immense dignity to compensate for her lapse, and as she vanished past the pale feathers of the pampas, Brin slid down to sit on the stairs, hands around her knees and her eyes wide, weak and shattered, yet pleased now that battle was declared and everything was out in the open.

For one moment she put her head down on her knees.

"Gerrard," she whispered. "Gerrard." Not quite sure if it was a plea or a promise.

Never had she felt more close to him, and never for one second did she think to doubt him, no matter what the opposition. For after all, in spite of all the threats, what could they do? If she and Gerrard chose to wait long enough, there was nothing any of them could do. Nothing. She began to smile a little.

When the Maneen came slithering in his big boots through the shadows with the taper for the lamps, she was still there. He stopped, peering at her through the pale light, his wizened face bright with curiosity, the hint of the row having seeped by now down into the kitchen and MacGinnis saying to Cookie it was the worst ever.

"That's a strange perch you have there, Miss Brin," he said. "Have you taken a weakness?"

Rather to his disappointment, Sabrina stood up and, as well as he could see in the little bit of a light, looked well content with herself.

"Thank you, Manny," she said, and then grinned. "As a matter of fact, I think I've just taken a strength. I was thinking."

Thinking, thought the Maneen in disgust. That sort of carry-on never did anyone any good.

But Brin had been thinking that she would write to Gerrard that evening and tell him everything was out. It would be a relief to him too, and they could plan together, although God knew it would be unlikely the Mama would make it easy.

With an excited flick of her red skirt, she was gone, off round to the kitchens, and the Maneen shrugged and moved along the hall to the warm comfortable plop of the next gaslight. Down at the back door, Denis Mary came banging and shouting home from his lessons.

CHAPTER 10

Cousin Anna's house gave the same impression as herself of immobility and overstuffing.

All the furniture was out of date and heavy, solid gleaming mahogany with the appearance of being screwed to the floor as if on a ship. Fine pieces so crammed together that Gerrard found difficulty in reaching the fire between them. All the tables were draped and bobbled to the ground, and blinds and lace and velvet curtains hung in braided layers to close the world out from the rich and airless gloom. On lace doilies on the tables countless photographs in velvet frames jostled priceless porcelain, snuff boxes, musical boxes, and collections of shells of long sentimental memories. Along the draped marble mantel, Dresden nymphs simpered at their shepherds, and below them, with the same look of permanence, Anna filled her high-backed chair of black horsehair, crocheting with placid concentration beside a careful fire.

The doorbell brought a crease of disapproval to her

low forehead, and she glanced at the French clock between the nymphs. Who could this be, who didn't know she disliked afternoon callers before the stroke of four? She heard the voice of her servant in the hall and thought how she'd scald the heart from her if she didn't dispose of them. As she said to Gerrard later, she little thought it to be her friend Honor Heron, bursting in like the very Germans themselves. She hadn't even the goodness to wait for the poor maid who gawped nervously behind her, expecting just the heart-scalding her mistress had planned.

Anna straightened with slow deliberation in her chair and laid the crochet carefully on the table at her side with an air of patient interruption, moving aside two gull's eggs in a papier-mâché nest and tightening the wool before she looked up.

"Go on away, Pegeen," she said then. "Mrs. Heron will announce herself."

Mama didn't even acknowledge the rebuke, nodding her own dismissal to the woman and settling herself at once in the identical horsehair chair on the other side of the fire, and taking off her gloves, smoothing them fiercely in her lap.

"Anna," she said, and offered no greeting. "Something very distasteful has come up. I must speak to you."

Anna ignored her friend's tension in the chair, her flushed face under the violet hat. Her own grievance must be settled first.

"I don't know quite what to offer you at this time of day, Honor," she said pointedly. "It's too early for the tea. Would you like a small glass of sherry wine?"

She managed to put some subtle emphasis on the word small, to imply that if Mama did accept it, it would be no more than one more step along some disastrous road already embarked upon by anyone who would come calling at three-twenty in the afternoon.

Mama looked at her sharply then, but she was running at too high a pitch for her friend's subtleties. Any of Honor Heron's children could have told Cousin Anna that when Mama had anything to say she said it, and only if the victims rose from the floor and struck back did it occur to her that there might be two sides to any question, and even then the other side was only of academic interest. Earlier in the day, Papa had tried vainly to dissuade her from making the visit at all, full of sentimental ridiculous notions that the two young people concerned should be allowed to have some say, and that indeed there was little wrong with what they wanted to do.

She had tossed her red head with contempt, and whirled off alone in the dogcart, reflecting that her husband had always been a milksop, especially where his children were concerned. She lifted her head now from the gloves in her lap and regarded her friend with severity.

It was all over in no time at all.

Right from the accusations of Gerrard's getting Sabrina drunk at Christmastime and in answer Didn't the whiskey come from Abbeygate itself? through to the kind of young man who would go compromising—

"Compromising, is it?" interjected Anna.

Compromising a girl who was about to enter to become a nun, and the derisive snort in answer that that one would never be a nun this side of the Resurrection, having obviously other things on her mind, and in any case Gerrard was in no need of bits of girls and he not qualified. When the time came, there'd be some decent girl found for him to marry and settle down with.

Anna looked round her with satisfaction, seeing the decent girl moving docilely around a room she would never be allowed to disturb, but Mama was beside herself.

"Decent girl!"

Anna's face was red now, and the uncut hairs on her warts stood out like bristles. You'd think she'd clip them, Mama thought, but at least managed not to say that; but said enough for the row to sweep on like an avalanche, tearing all the years of interdependence away with it, all the fragile needs that had made them so long friends.

"You were always conceited, Honor Heron. Always the great lady." Unconsciously Mama sat up a little straighter. "Right back to the time you used to make me brush your hair at school."

Mama knew it had gone too far but was caught in the avalanche and unable to stop it. She had a fleeting memory of the small opaque mirror and the long strands of red-gold hair lifting with the patient brush, behind them the fat pale face of Anna Grant. With warts. But always admiring. Always there with the whispered word to feed the self-doubting vanity of the lovely Honor. Like the mirror itself.

Then Anna said it.

"You never had any need of me at all, Honor Heron, except for the admiring of you and the telling you that every mortal thing you did was right. Although," she added with shrewd unkindness and a rapier dart of the small black eyes, "when you wake in the night, you must ask yourself often if it is."

Mama's lips trembled. With shock and rage. Untouched now by doubt, the certainties of the years invulnerable. Only filled with the recollection of all the occasions she had had this warty, fat little creature visiting her house and all the family furious, and only for herself, poor lonely creature that she was, and she fool enough to pity her and try to give her a bit of pleasure.

She stood up abruptly, and in her indignation stumbled over the corner of the brass fender, and without even looking at her, Anna's face managed to convey that she had been, of course, quite right about the sherry wine.

Mama was gasping with indignation, struggling to find words, but Anna forestalled her, solid and controlled in the release of jealousy that had eaten her for bitter years. Her anger now was remorseless.

"I'll pull for Pegeen to see you out," she said, and reached for the tasseled pull beside the fire.

"Have no fear," she said then, "about your daughter and my son. I'll soon put a halt to that particular gallop."

Until Pegeen came she sat there with her button eyes inimically on her friend. There was nothing more to be said, their unknowingly fragile friendship cracked across, all the jealousies and resentments showing through like bones in the darkness of a broken tomb.

"Mrs. Heron will be going now, Pegeen."

"Good-bye, Anna."

Anna didn't answer, Pegeen flicking them both with a curious glance from the door, and Mama threaded her way out through furniture and from Anna's house into the grey chilly day. She refused to acknowledge a nagging, bewildered feeling, curiously like the blind terror of the smart and beautiful little Honor Joyce, who could only face the black fears of the convent nights because of the whispered endearments of the fat little girl in the cubicle next door, risking fearful punishments if she were heard.

Ridiculous. What an ill-bred performance the whole thing had been. She collected herself and put her head back in the air where it belonged, the heels of her kid boots beating firmly in the quiet street as she made her way back down to the stable where she had lodged the pony.

Put a halt to that gallop indeed! What was a person like that supposed to do. The only halt to that gallop would be for Sabrina to do as she was told.

Gerrard came home in the frost-touched dusk, exhilarated by the chill air, and found his mother still sitting in the dark beside the dying fire.

"She wouldn't let me light the lamps, Mr. Gerrard," Pegeen whispered to him hoarsely in the hall. "She's after having some kind of a dispute with her friend Mrs. Heron."

Gerrard stood very still for a moment, and then with slow deliberate movements gave Pegeen his coat and hat and muffler.

"Ah, Mr. Gerrard, you can smell the cold in them. There'll be no good of a fire in there."

Gerrard smiled at her.

"I'll see to it, Pegeen. It's all right."

"What's all this, Mother?" he said as he opened the door, his voice holding the practiced calm of many scenes of melodrama. With the same practiced care he threaded his way through the furniture and took a taper from the velvet-covered box on the mantel. "Why are you sitting in the dark?"

The only answer was a long trembling sigh, and he put the taper into the last embers of the fire and pulled the chain of the gas. It lit with a cheerful bang, and he looked down at his mother, uncommonly, he thought, like an old black spider, bright eyes and all. She had dropped her ball of wool and more than once, for threads of pale fluffy pink crossed and recrossed like a web over her black skirt. With weary boredom he realized that all the danger signs were there. The overbright eyes that watched him in silence except for the deep sighs, the crochet hook tap-tapping on the arm of her chair.

"That's one very poor fire you have there, mother, for a cove to come home to."

He moved over to the coal bucket, with a moment of surprise that she didn't answer to the cue. It should have brought some shriveling answer such as that the likes of her had little good from the cheerfulness of fires, and so on. But she remained silent and he knew an exasperated anger. Work had been hard at the office and he could do without this, and the real labor it would be to bring her out of it.

He raked together the dying coals and blew them into life with the bellows, piling on fresh coal from which a small, enthusiastic flame burst at once. B'God it was a good chimney.

In the small interest of relighting the fire he had forgotten her for a moment, but looking up, he found her eyes fixed on him in some bitter speculation.

"What's the matter, Mother?"

She didn't blink, the crochet hook still tapping.

"You've been seeing the Heron girl."

He felt a greater weariness than any caused by Mr. Brown McCaffery's clients and their complex business. Slowly he sat down where Brin's mother had sat, resolution flooding him. His instinct in the hall had been right. Well. It had to come sometime. He hitched the knees of his fine herringbone trousers and made his voice quiet and steady.

"That's correct, Mother. Would there be anything wrong in it?"

"Everything."

"Why?"

"Do you not know she's to be a nun, and you cavorting in the tea shops of Cork city with her for all to see."

Poor Brin. Poor love. Someone had seen, obviously. It wouldn't be the two fat girls, that was certain. But who? And what murder was raging round her head by now? He had to curb an impulse to seize his coat and race down to the stable for the pony, to drive at once to Abbeygate. A smile touched his lips. No doubt he'd be as welcome there as a virulent case of the plague. He looked at his mother quietly, and the black eyes snapped back at him.

"Mrs. Heron says Sabrina is going to be a nun, Mother," he corrected, "but it's time you knew that she is not. She has promised to marry me as soon as my articles are through."

His mother looked at him expressionless, and Gerrard was again surprised. His announcement should have rated at least a weakness, with cries for smelling salts and whiskey and threats of a failing heart. He'd had it all for far less. But this time she merely eased herself in her chair and looked with disapproval at the crackling fire. Did he not know the price of coal?

"The mother told me," she said, "of that. But it's always as well," she added enigmatically, "when you make plans, to be sure you can carry them out."

"No one, Mother, can compel Sabrina to be a nun. Not even her mother."

"'Tis not the girl at all I'm thinking of," she said heavily. "She must settle her own affairs with her mother. Although," she added tartly, "I'd not like to be any young creature coming to contention with that one."

Gerrard was lost, but unable to keep back a smile at the change from all the sugary years of "my friend Honor." What fur and feathers had flown here today?

"Will you ring for Pegeen to come and put a bit of wet slack on that fire before the house is burnt round us," his mother said, but Gerrard's mind was on one remark. He gave the fire an encouraging poke and forgot to ring the bell.

"What did you mean, Mother, about it not being Sabrina you were think of. Something about me?"

Gravely his mother nodded, and a cold thread of alarm wound suddenly through his brain. All the money gone? Not that that would matter. He could make enough. Probably it was no more than that he was scheduled to look after his widowed mother for the rest of her black-clad days. His handsome mouth hardened. There was clearly no lack of money now, for all her parsimonious ways, although she refused ever to discuss it with him or to tell him anything of her financial state or her inheritance from his father. Nor would they ever neglect her. But he and

Sabrina were going to live with neither mother, no matter what custom said. Their life would be their own. His face softened even at the vague thought, and he held his hands out to the crackling fire, smiling a little.

"You do well to smile," she said portentously. "While you can." And he grew irritated.

"Mother, for God's sake, what is this?"

She looked over at him, and under the act of heavy tragedy, he could see her eyes were sharp and calculating, filling him with uneasiness. As so often, her next words were irrelevant, surprising him.

"Tomorrow is Saturday."

"It is."

"You'll not be at the office."

"No."

"Well, I want you to drive me somewhere."

He controlled his impatience. He had other plans.

"Is it important?"

"You may well think so. You'll know then what I'm talking about." She pulled the bell herself for Pegeen to damp the fire.

He could get no more out of her, more baffled by her even than was usual, and her spirits seemed completely recovered, without any smelling salts or the little tent of the John Jamieson. With faint alarm, he sensed some triumphant air of decision, and God knew where that might lead him, concealed though it was by the occasional bout of heartfelt sighs. All evening she was benign and benevolent, eating a hearty dinner of roast beef and proposing a hand or two of whist before they went to bed.

Gerrard drew his curtains thoughtfully, looking out as he always did, toward Abbeygate, over the roofs of the city and across the frosty fields. He didn't trust his mother, and she tired him more than a day's training with the militia. And she was always at her most dangerous when smooth and friendly as she had been this evening.

Where did she want to go tomorrow?

The only real excuse on which he could get out of it would be a drilling day. Unwillingly respecting Mr. Brown McCaffery's wish that he wait to qualify, he was nevertheless drilling regularly with the Militia of the Leinsters.

But tomorrow no drilling. So no excuse. He could only

hope it wouldn't take long. As for the drama, his mother couldn't live without it, and it would all probably turn out to be nothing at all. He yawned, dismissing it, and lifted the towel from the copper can that Pegeen had placed on his washstand, almost marked like fingerprints with her unfailing astonishment that he should want hot water to wash himself at night as well as in the morning.

The next morning had all the transient beauty of November in County Cork, with an arch of sky as clear and blue as summer, and out of the wind a sweet sun that would deceive you. Gerrard found it hard to keep up his resentment of the outing as they bowled along the grey roads between the stone walls and the fields, where many of the trees still hung with the splendid colors of the dying year, safe until the first gales of December. Far away, the sea stretched like milk, pale into the misty distance.

"Topping day, Mother," Gerrard said, looking about him with satisfaction. "How long?"

Let her have her melodrama to keep her happy. He would enjoy the drive.

"Two hours."

"Two hours? Where on earth are we going?"

"The other side of Dunveague."

Deep in his mind some forgotten chord struck. Dunveague. Way back when he was very small he seemed to have heard the name, spoken over and over again in grown-up conversations far above his head. Way back. No memory of happiness there, nothing of good memory in the name.

He knew little, for all his name, of the Irish end of his family, having grown up in a spacious old Georgian house in Windsor, left to his father by *his* father, who had been something vague and eminent and very respectable in the service of the old queen. Spiffing place to live, Windsor, on the edge of all that parkland, and the lake and everything. Then there was school, and lots of holidays spent with his father's parents, pretty ancient now, in a rather grand old house in the Midlands. And in Yorkshire, with his father's sister, not very far from school, where they always seemed to be shooting things and had a cockfighting main in the stables. He sighed. All jolly good. He'd had great times. But Dunveague?

"Ah," he said then suddenly. "Didn't my father—wasn't there a little estate somewhere out here?"

His mother made a vague jerky gesture.

"Over there. Ardmore House. It's let," she said shortly.

"Since my father died?"

There was a long silence.

"Yes," she said shortly, again.

"That's good business," he said. "Must bring in quite a nice bit of money for you."

Her lack of response was deliberate, her eyes apparently fixed unmoving on the ribbon of road running away before the trap into the folded hills, her black-gloved hands in her lap, and her head nodding a little to the bouncing from the road. He glanced at her and then shrugged away his irritation, flicking up the pony. When he was twenty-one she would have to tell him. Unless he was already dead in the war. And what then? his solicitor's training asked him sharply. He felt a certain deep anger that his mother would give him no more confidence than she would give a child, and resolved that when this day, whatever it was, was over, he would try to put pressure on her to tell him at least something of what would be soon his own affairs.

He gave his mind to enjoying the beautiful day and to the endless speculation as to what it would mean now that both mothers knew of his intentions for Sabrina. At the back of his mind all the time, uneasiness crawled, wondering where they were going, knowing his mother not ever to set anything aside. There would always be a time of reckoning.

After long miles through the golden country, bleak grey houses with flat fronts and slate roofs began to scatter at intervals on the sides of the road. Straight gravel paths led from iron gates up to the doors, and a few weedy borders held the last of chrysanthemums blackened by the frost. A cool wind had come up from the west and beat against their faces.

"Dunveague, wouldn't you think, Mother?" Gerrard was beginning to be tired of the whole thing as the sun faded and the wind grew cold.

The houses grew closer, and the gardens vanished, the half doors leading straight through into the dark rooms, and he stared round him, touched by some elusive familiarity, some memory flickering at the edges of his brain. His face creased. Someone crying and crying and crying. What in God's name could that have to do with Dunveague. To his recollection he'd never seen the place before, and he'd be quite glad never to see it again.

They clattered down the long wide street, where few people moved, only a couple of ass carts, turned patiently nose to wall, waited for their owners, but even he was aware of the eyes that watched them from the shadows of doors and windows.

"Curious, aren't they?" he said, as he steered the pony round a flock of sheep that had burst onto the road from a boreen between two houses, a dirty black-and-white collie snapping at their heels.

"We're strangers," his mother answered, and "G'on outa that," she shouted at the collie, who had left his sheep to bark and nip between the pony's feet. "Isn't any stranger meat and drink to them in a place like this. Take the side road to the right at the end here, Gerrard."

"Have I been here before, Mother?" he asked her then, frowning. The town had fallen away with startling suddenness, and the rough country road wound off between wet overgrown ditches, away before them for the length of a shallow, almost treeless valley. But for the bright sun that had come back to draw the green and yellow colors from the land it would have been desolate and bleak. In the distance, some vast institution sprawled its buildings along the slight rise of land at the valley end, and even from here he could see they were all contained by the thread of a long wall.

"Why would you?" his mother answered him, and he was struck again by her unusual silence. He glanced at her and saw her eyes fixed, dark and withdrawn on the grey buildings beyond the valley, and knew an immediate and unwilling certainty that there was their destination. God knew, there was nothing else.

"Mother—" he said.

"Keep going." She wouldn't let him speak, and formless apprehension trembled through him. "Keep going, and when you reach the wall, watch for the gates."

The wall? The gates? What was it?

He knew for certain as soon as they reached the wall, high and grey, stretching like a curving snake away from them along the road, closing out from whoever lay behind it all the green sunlit world that flowed away below it on their left. Yet the gates still took him as a shock.

And the tall metal letters, painted black, that curved above them in a arch.

"St. Joseph's Asylum for the Insane."

"For God's sake, Mother." He stared up at them appalled.

"Stop, will you, Gerrard."

He had already stopped, in sick certainty. But who, or why? It seemed a place of nothing but grief and sorrow, and his mother's face was stiff and set, yet he caught in her eyes a curious sparkle that had taught him caution long ago. But surely before God, such a place as this was not for mischief, even for his mother.

He watched as a porter with the upright look of an old soldier stepped out of his square office at the side of the gate, touching the peak of his shiny blue cap. The sun glinted in the silver buttons of his jacket, and Gerrard had the terrible feeling of being thrust awake, into a dream, able to awake properly sometime and thank God that none of it was true.

"Good-day to you, Mrs. Moynihan, ma'am," the porter said, and although he was old, the waxed points of his moustache snow white, his faded blue eyes were sharp, and he examined Gerrard with curiosity, like something entirely unexpected.

"Good-day to you, Rooney. Would you open the gate, please."

Unwillingly, his eyes on the young man and his lips ready with a load of questions, Rooney accepted the repression of Anna's eye and reached for the huge bunch of keys hanging on a chain from his belt. Slowly and heavily he pushed back the iron gates, and with infinite, sick reluctance, Gerrard shook the reins and drove the pony through.

He heard the clang behind him and the tumble of the heavy lock, and knew a moment when he almost leaped from the trap to run and clamor at the gates before they kept him there forever. He cursed himself for a fool and looked ahead, with no idea what he must expect.

The parklike look of well-kept grounds somewhat reassured him, with wide roads and walks threading between tall trees, but then he saw away to his right a railed enclosure and within it there was no grass. And no trees. Only a waste of grey asphalt, and the only figures he could see. Walking, some of them very fast, or sitting down, and many of them simply standing in the cold wind, no more than dark shapes in the sunlight, yet touched, even at that distance, with some searing sorrow.

"Watch the pony, Son."

He was driving up onto the grass.

"Mother, if you'd only tell me what it's all about. Why are we here, in this place?"

"Go to the left here."

Her voice was flat, as though she too protected herself against emotion.

The place was enormous, and he turned as instructed, past the big main doors with glass panels meshed with wire, and on along the front of the central block. The narrow road passed through another gate, standing open, and across another stretch of grass to a separate building, itself huge. He wondered in dumb astonishment where they all came from. Were there that many lunatics in Ireland, let alone in County Cork?

He hitched the pony to the iron railing curving round to the front door. Everywhere gates and railings and the sense of division and enclosure.

"This is where the paying ones are," his mother said as he helped her from the trap, and he glanced up at the windowed clifflike wall. Her plump face was pale and impassive, and told him nothing, no more than her words, and she went steadily on up the shallow steps to press the round brass bell set into the brickwork at the side of the door. From behind her through the meshed glass, he could see a large dim hall, with corridors opening at the sides and a wide stairs going up straight opposite. From a door somewhere at the side came a man with a too-long blue overall flapping round his ankles, and a large bunch of keys on a chain clipped to a belt underneath it.

Like the man at the gate, he knew Anna, and as he lifted his keys and unlocked the door, his eyes flickered over Gerrard with the same surprised curiosity. He let them in, bidding them good-day, and moved behind them at once to close the door. Gerrard listened to the falling of the second heavy lock. He couldn't help glancing back at the green world, but his mother was already moving, unconcerned, across the bare, highly polished hall, furnished only with a few benches of varnished wood along the walls. Gerrard noticed that the head of the stairs had a wall across it and a closed door in the wall, and doors barred the corridor on either side. Each section was in itself a locked cell, and his mind shrank in revulsion that it should all have anything to do with him. For any reason. Such things were for other people. Surely not for him.

"I'll want to see Dr.—Jamieson, is it? The new one." his mother said, and added perfunctorily that she was sorry to hear of Dr. Daly's death.

The porter nodded his almost-shaven head familiarly.

"Ye knew him a long time," he said, and unlocked one of the side doors, which led on to a wide, clean corridor smelling of polish and a faint mustiness from lack of air. It stretched to its end at a barred window, and closed doors lay along its sides. Behind them the door clanged, and the porter turned with his bunch of keys and another lock fell between them and the world.

Jesus, thought Gerrard. Imagine being on the top floor, and how many locks there'd be between you and getting out.

"You'll wait," the shaven-headed one said with scant ceremony, ushering them into what looked like a doctor's office heavy with shelves and books and papers, and a small bright gas fire in a black japanned frame, popping merrily like a message from a more cheerful world and filling the room with a smell of hot paint. Gerrard looked round in relief to see the door left half open, and wondered what was going to happen next. Could not think of it.

His mother was silent and curiously still, only her small eyes darting round the room, searching perhaps for possible changes in something long familiar. He knew it useless to question her. Whatever she was at would get the full theatrical treatment, and he must wait. He sat down on the chair opposite her, also in silence.

It was some time before they heard the clang of the passage door and keys jingling along outside. A youngish man in a long white coat came into the room. He looked intelligent and controlled, and his thin fair hair was already receding over observant blue eyes behind pince-nez. His gaze rested briefly first on Gerrard, and then shifted to Anna.

"Mrs. Moynihan?" he said, and his voice had the flat softness of the west. "Please don't get up. I'm Doctor Jamieson. I'm afraid I've not met you before. I took over from Doctor Daly."

"Good-day to you, Doctor." She shook hands with him and then gestured towards Gerrard. "This is my son, Gerrard."

The doctor shook hands with him pleasantly. Gerrard felt sure his damp palms had not gone unobserved, but Jamieson only smiled briefly and turned to reach for a file brought in by a fat girl with her hair twined in two lumps over her ears. Gerrard was distracted for a moment, and then his eyes followed the file. A thin one, he noticed. Whoever it was had not been here long. Or nothing much had happened to him, came the other thought, chill and fearful.

Jamieson opened the file.

"Now what can I do for you, Mrs. Moynihan?" He glanced down. "I see this is an extra visit."

The blue eyes were urbane but cautious and Gerrard had a wild impulse to leap to his feet and tell this nice man he damn needed to be cautious of his mother, but out of her stillness Anna spoke.

"We'd like to see Mr. Moynihan."

Her black eyes fixed him, and Jamieson stared back at her completely expressionless, but Gerrard felt certain that behind the blank eyes, his brain was racing to cope with the unexpected and to calculate the reasons, exactly as his own was doing.

"To see him, Mrs. Moynihan?" the doctor asked carefully. He glanced down again at the file. "I thought it was long ago agreed—"

Anna gathered herself together, straightening in the chair.

"I think it is time my son saw him and understood."

The blue, magnified gaze switched to Gerrard, who felt cold and sick, looking desperately for some sense of escape to the clouds that raced now past the high, barred window. Saw who? Was he then never dead? Only dead to the bright world beyond the locked doors. A fearful certainty crept over him like the first shivering tremors of a fever.

Gerrard brought his eyes down and found that the doctor's had never left him. He made a small steeple of his fingers.

"How old are you, Mr. Moynihan?"

"Almost twenty, Doctor," he said, grateful for the Mr. Moynihan.

"And do you wish to see him?"

"Yes." He nearly shouted. Whatever it was, let them get it over with. Try as he might, his voice was thin. "My mother is right, it is time."

No discussions, please God. The talking could come afterwards.

The doctor seemed to sense his need, rising at once to his feet and moving to the door on his silent rubber-shod feet.

"I'll take you," he said, and inexplicably, Gerrard's mother gave a long sigh. Jamieson paused.

"You don't want to come, Mrs. Moynihan?"

Anna gestured him away with a black glove.

"No reason," she said. "No reason. It's for the boy."

Gerrard found out then what it was like to be on the top floor. Up through door after locked door, and every single flight of stairs sealed off behind them. He lost count of the number of locks between him and the world of green fields and racing sun and shadow that he glimpsed occasionally through barred landing windows. His feet clipped with embarrassing noise in a total silence. They were walking in a sealed core, with anguish and sorrow and madness held carefully in check behind the impenetrable doors. You'd need to be insane, he thought, to stand it.

Jamieson apologized gently.

"I'm sorry about this," he said, on the fifth floor. "But

you'll understand we have to keep the most violent cases highest up for safety."

Gerrard managed to speak as evenly as he.

"And he's . . ." He still could not manage to speak the name. "He's one of the most violent?"

The doctor paused a moment and looked at him, as if he had expected him to know, trying to assess a situation he didn't quite understand. Then he turned and went on up the last short flight, unlocking the last door onto a square landing. Through a big window here, the stone-walled fields were visible far below, and in the distance, the small white human habitations of Dunveague.

He pressed a bell beside one of the two plain doors that faced each other across the polished landing. Three short rings. Then one.

He gave Gerrard a small smile.

"Even I," he said, "am not allowed in here alone."

The attendant who opened the door a narrow gap had the build of a knuckle fighter, cropped hair, and a very flat heavy face without expression. Having checked who it was, he automatically glanced back behind him and then opened the door wider to allow them in.

The first thing to touch Gerrard's apprehensive nerves was the quality of the silence, which was not completely silent, but a straining for half-heard sounds. Muffled. A thin voice, crying on an endlessly rising thread. A steady drumming, soft, without impact. Faint but unmistakable shrills of senseless laughing. The doctor kept his face expressionless and did not look at Gerrard.

"The padded cells," he said, "for the most violent."

They stretched the length of a long, wide corridor, and three of the huge attendants sat on chairs at intervals, each one beside a brass bell in the wall. No more than watchers. Nothing was needed for them but their brute strength, to match that which madness had given to their gentler and more intelligent brothers.

Gerrard felt his feet glued to the floor, and his appalled mind screamed that he wanted to go no further. Wanted to be a child again in whatever ignorance they had thought fit to keep him, content in whatever lies they had seen fit to tell him. Not to know. Not to know. He found he was muttering prayers he had forgotten since he was a little boy, and had half turned back toward the door.

But the young doctor was gone ahead of him and had paused at the fourth door, before one of the inch-thick panes of glass that was also reinforced with wire. He glanced in, and stood waiting for Gerrard to reach him, and there was compassion in his level eyes. With sick reluctance Gerrard forced himself to follow and to look, unnerved again by a sudden wild shriek from the cell next door, muted by the thick wall and heavy glass. And by the deep padding which was the first thing his mind accepted as he peered through the little window. It was stitched in lines all over the walls and even the floor. No bed. No chair. Nothing at all through which those who craved death might possibly be fortunate enough to find it.

Cool dim light from the autumn day crept pale through the barred window from another world, and it was some seconds before he saw the figure crouched against the wall in the angle of the far corner. It was impossible to see the face, and only a few rags of clothes hung from the emaciated body, the rest in shreds, savagely torn, lying across the padded floor. The hair was lank and dead, brown, the color of Gerrard's own, and the skeleton hands hung limp, palms upwards, as if relinquishing all his known life, relinquishing for the moment even the violence that had exhausted him.

This was the paying wing; even the attendants were protected somewhat from the horrors of their task, for who knew when visitors might come? But nevertheless, even through the thick glass, Gerrard knew with nauseated certainty that the smell inside the lonely cell was animal. No more.

"Jesus," he whispered. "Oh, my gracious God."

Ashen-faced, he turned away, and the doctor signaled the attendant to let them out. By the tall window on the landing, when the door had clanged behind them, Gerrard stood and stared out blindly through the bars at the spread of country, where the dark clouds were piling from the west, chasing the sun across the gentle fields. He leaned against the iron bars and felt their coldness on his forehead gratefully and struggled against sickness.

Patiently the doctor waited, and in the end Gerrard turned his shattered face.

"He will never get better."

It was a statement. Even he knew better than to make it a question.

The doctor shook his head.

"He will never get better. Tell me." He couldn't contain his curiosity. "Did your mother never tell you of the condition of your father?"

Gerrard looked back at him, pulling himself together, still stunned with shock.

"She told me," he said, "that he was dead."

Exasperation puckered the doctor's face. Another of them. It was as big a problem to combat as the patients themselves. This feeling of shame and secrecy in the families, as though mental illness were some fearful mark among them of God's displeasure. Why could they not understand it was only illness, like any other. This boy's father had never had a chance, diseased since the day he was born. It had only needed something to trigger off complete collapse. A shock. Something the normal mind might accept without disaster. He looked with pity at the young man. Such a person should never have a child.

He sighed. He was before his time, and knew it.

"Are you all right?" he asked Gerrard. "I think we should go down and talk to your mother."

"I am all right," Gerrard answered, although all the inferences of what he had seen were beginning to seep in grief through his paralyzed thought.

They went down again, door by door by door, through the sealed-off core of sanity in the mad world, setting away his father, and with him everything he had put his heart on.

"Well?" said his mother as they came back into the office, and he knew a moment of surprise that there was neither grief nor pity in her eyes, only some guarded question. Dr. Jamieson settled himself back behind his desk and watched them both, aware as Gerrard was, of some unnatural detachment in the mother. But Gerrard had collected himself on the long key-haunted journey downstairs, locks clanging on the end of happiness. He knew the answer before he asked his one most urgent question.

"Doctor," he said, "there is naturally something very important to me. It is hereditary?"

"The boy has some idea of getting married," his mother said, as she might have said of him at seven years old that he wished to drive a train. But the doctor didn't look at her, only at Gerrard, meeting his eyes with a directness that did not hide his pity.

"I am afraid so," he said quietly. "It is quite normal for it to skip a generation, but—"

"But my children if I should have any," Gerrard finished for him, and he nodded. Gran and Grandpa, thought Gerrard. Normal. And me. Normal. Then my father in between. And, oh, God, Sabrina's children could be like that poor animal upstairs.

He buried his head a moment in his hands, his fingers through the feathery hair, and then he lifted his head and still fought back despairingly, his mind clamoring as the mind will clamor against death. That there must be some mistake. He clamped his hands together and looked at Jamieson, the mobile eyebrows low above his eyes.

"Can I see the entry of my father's admission, please, Doctor?"

His mother at once grew restless.

"What matter is that," she said sharply. "Isn't he here and you've heard the doctor say he'll never be out of it."

"Please, Mother," said Gerrard, and found it difficult not to shout at her. But it was to her the doctor spoke.

"He will, Mrs. Moynihan," he said gently. "Quite soon. He won't live much longer."

He met Gerrard's gaze of pure shattered grief. The young man was thinking of all the photographs of the handsome man who had been his father. Very like himself to look at.

"I'd still like to see the entry, Doctor," he said and Jamieson nodded patiently.

It took a long time and his mother fidgeted all through the waiting, sipping restlessly at the tea they brought in thick white cups and rearranging her skirts and folding her gloves and looking pointedly at the little gold watch with an enameled face that she wore about her neck.

Gerrard could not bring himself to talk to her, even when they were left alone, baffled and appalled by the cruelty with which she had brought him face to face with it.

"Why didn't you tell me?" he burst out in the end. "Why did you do it like this?" He went over and laid down his cup on a varnished table at the wall, looking back at her as if she had become a stranger.

"It was time you knew," she said evasively and became busy searching for something in her purse.

"I should have known long ago," he answered curtly. "But now, now it's because of Sabrina, isn't it?"

"Because of any girl," she said fiercely, and snapped close the purse, her mouth as tight as the clasp.

He stared at her for a long time, nagged by the feeling of something false. But nothing, nothing could obliterate the reality of the poor damaged creature upstairs. There was no way she could have invented him.

Sighing, he moved to the window and turned away sharply when he reached the bars.

"You're quite right about that, of course, Mother." His young face had grown in the last hour thinner and sharper, pale under the brown hair. "There can be no girl, if that's what you were after." He stared at her until she dropped her eyes.

When the admission book was brought, for all those years ago, the entry was there, in neat copperplate writing. Tidy and unhurried epitaph for a man committed to burial alive.

The signatures of two doctors.

The signature of his wife, who was committing him. Anna Moynihan.

But.

"I thought you always called my father Ned," he said sharply.

Antony Edward Moynihan, said the tombstone in the ledger.

His mother answered tranquilly.

"Don't we always call you Gerrard?" she said. "But if you go back to your certificate of baptism, you'll find it was Antony Gerrard given to you at the font."

And he was there, Gerrard thought, barely able to

withstand it. He was there. Tall and good-looking and bursting with pride, no doubt, because he had a son.

Abruptly he closed the big ledger and looked at both of them.

"I was no more than a baby," he said.

His mother seemed suddenly agreeable, willing to tell him all, leaning toward him brightly.

"Yes, yes," she said, "It was the time your—" She gave a little gasp and started again. "It was the time just before your second birthday."

For a moment her eyes were filled with some panicked fear, but he was too preoccupied to notice it.

"Thank-you, Doctor," he said. "Thank-you. Is there anything else I should know about?"

The sniff from his mother asked clearly what could a child like himself do, but Jamieson answered him quietly.

"Well, not now, Mr. Moynihan, but I understand from your mother that when you come of age you will have total responsibility for Mr. Moynihan."

That would be natural, Gerrard thought, leaving it until he came to it. There had been enough for today and all he wanted now was to get out of the place. To be alone to think, and decide what he must do about the inevitable and heartbreaking consequences of this day's work.

"And there is nothing to be done?" he said finally, and the doctor shook his head, his eyes on the desk. He was sorry for this young man, who was taking it all with great dignity and control, but what was the mother about to make it such a deliberate shock? And looking almost pleased with herself now she had done it. There were, he thought, for far from the first time, as many odd ones on the outside as on the inside, if not more.

The mother was now in a hurry to be gone, gathering up purse and gloves and standing up.

"Wouldn't you give me credit, Gerrard," she said, with a pained side glance at Jamieson to share the pathetic foolishness of children, "for doing all that could be done and long ago? Well, thank you now, Doctor, and we'll be off. It's been a sad day for me and I'll be glad to be back into my home."

"We'll see you on the first of January as usual," he said, and she nodded.

"You will," she said. "You will. Today was for the boy. Only for the boy."

Her son glanced at her and felt he still had a great deal to find out.

The first thing he found was that his mother's desire to be back in her home after this sad day, faded sharply between the asylum and Dunveague. Much against the desires of either his will or his stomach, he found himself shortly facing her over a grey, gravy-spotted tablecloth in Garvin's Hotel, an opaque window at their side looking over the wind-whipped lake; waiting for the mutton chops with swedes and cabbage and potatoes that was the compulsory menu for the day's dinner.

"And a little drop of John Jamieson for me, please, Gerrard, and tell the girl now not too much." She settled her black bulk into her chair in comfort. "It's been a hard day. A hard day, God help us all."

He couldn't make head or tail of her, though God knew that was nothing fresh. He looked at her pale untroubled face, uttery indifferent to the thunderbolt she had just delivered, preoccupied only with the comfort of her chair and the length of time it would take to get her dinner and John Jamieson. Wedging herself a little tighter, she peeled off the black kid gloves from her plump hands, easing them over the rings, and looked with bright curious eyes around the empty dining room. Gerrard followed her glance round the red-faded walls hung with lurid landscapes and big clear sentimental pictures of animals and little children taken from the Christmas supplements. Below them a huge sideboard ran the clear length of one wall, arrayed with tarnished cover dishes big enough to hide a year-old baby, flanked by cruets and pots of drying mustard. Seeming satisfied, she nodded, and turned back to her son.

"They'll not mind us being late," she said. "They'll all know we're after coming from the madhouse. Half their custom comes from there."

"Mother!"

He was appalled by her callousness, and the curious deep excitement of her black eyes troubled him. As if she knew she had gone too far, she heaved a deep and stricken sigh.

"Ah, Son," she said. "You'll always understand I'm glad when it's over. It's a terrible strain."

"But, Mother! You haven't seen him for ten years. All you do is pay the bills!"

The plump face grew sharp and malevolent.

"Who told you that?"

"The doctor, on the way down. He couldn't understand why you wanted me to see him. It would have been enough to tell me. And long ago at that," he added.

"He had a long tongue on him."

Visibly she controlled herself. When she answered her voice was full of self-pity.

"When you have children you have to do many things for them you'd not approve of," she said enigmatically, and her face changed. "You know now," she said, "what your children would have been like with the Sabrina one."

His eyes closed against the naked satisfaction in hers, and again some deep doubt troubled him. He turned away and looked out at the darkening day. Across the road a few hens cowered under a ragged hedge, sheltering from the rising wind, and he looked at them with fellow feeling, thinking of the long, cold journey home and nothing at the end of it.

"Can I put the dinner down now, sir?"

Sharply he drew back before a heavy smell of perspiration, and a red-faced girl with straggling hair and a dress too tight for her slammed down his mutton chops. On the thick plate they swam sadly in pale grease, the swedes a cheerful orange mound beside them. Unpeeled potatoes came piled in a tureen of fragile Coalport, and as she laid it down the girl gave a yelp.

"Ah, Jaysus," she cried, "didn't I forget the skin plates."

She clattered from the room in her heavy laced boots, and Gerrard watched her unbelievingly as one of the lesser parts of the cold nightmare that had overtaken him.

The skin plates came and she skimmed them onto the table like flat stones across the lake.

"Wouldn't I forget me own immortal soul," she cried cheerfully, "were it not for the prayshte to remind me of hell fire."

The John Jamieson was in a glass thumbprinted from

her hand, a small stone jug of water at its side. Anna looked at it all with relish.

"And a cup of tea, miss, for after it," she cried. "Would you like tea, Gerrard?"

Gerrard would like tea as little as he liked the dinner or, at that moment, his mother's company.

He was far too shocked for rage, and, indeed, years of dealing with his mother had taught him that anger beat on her as helplessly as waves against a bastion of cliffs. But he was sick. Sick with disgust at her deceit. With sorrow over what must happen between him and Sabrina. With pity for his father. Unable yet to frame words for any of it, all he wanted was to be alone and think, knowing even before he started that there would be no answer.

"Thank-you, Mother," he said. "I'll take tea."

CHAPTER 11

That night he never slept at all, sitting through the hours looking over the silent city towards Abbeygate, unaware of any time in the rage of grief and disappointment and loss that was roaring through his head. At times he searched his mind for pity for his mother, who seemed to have no real pity for herself, or for his father. He told himself he mustn't blame her. He would have done the same for his own child. But not quite as she had done it.

In his mind he set her aside. The present grief was for himself, and for Sabrina, and the children they would never have.

He went down early and asked Pegeen for a breakfast only for himself, telling her not to call his mother.

"Will I tell her where you've gone? Is it Mass?"

"Mass?" He stared at her raw, decent face. Mass. He had never even thought of it. To thank God, no doubt, for all his blessings.

"No, Pegeen, I'm not going to Mass. But I'll be back for the dinner."

Even the immobility of the trap was too much for him, to sit and watch the passing of the loved miles to Abbeygate, undermining his courage. He took instead his bright new bicycle, and in the hard chill effort of the ride, endeavored to close off his thoughts until he must face them. When MacGinnis opened the door to him, he was flushed with wind and exercise, but determinedly composed.

"MacGinnis. Good-morning. I'd like to see Miss Sabrina, please."

Now what have we here? thought MacGinnis and stood back to let him in, and the madam not in the house and no callers for the young girls without permission anyway. But this one! And the lad grown so tall and good-looking.

"I'm afraid Mrs. Heron is at second Mass, Mr. Gerrard. I—"

"Thank-you, MacGinnis, but I don't want to trouble Mrs. Heron. It's Miss Sabrina I came to see. Please tell her I'm here."

Away with the bit, thought MacGinnis. Away with the bit over something. He closed the hall door slowly to give himself time to think, and his eye caught the glitter of the bicycle propped below the steps and he shook his head. Ah, dear, but the madam wouldn't care for that at all. That would be no help to anything that was at stake. He'd get one of the lads to come and whip it round behind.

But when he turned with more excuses on his lips, for the madam would flay him letting any callers to the girls, he found in the young man some still authority. Standing there with his cap in his hand, and he almost as tall as MacGinnis himself, and some strength in his eyes that made the old man do exactly as he had been asked.

"Yes, Mr. Gerrard, sir," he said, as if it had been Papa. "If you'll just come up to the drawing room." And God knew nowhere could be more public than that and he'd not close the doors behind them. "I'll go and get her. She's down in the hothouse with the flowers."

Gerrard followed him along the warm red-carpeted gallery to the double doors of the drawing room, and in his mind it was again the first evening he had come, in all the excitement of her sister's wedding. She had been standing there beside the door, alone, in a sort of cream dress and the light behind her in her hair, and those marvelous pearls around her neck. Remembering, his feet in the same steps, he was shriveled with such barren sorrow that he knew a vision and a withering understanding of old age. When, as for him, there was nothing left to happen that could matter, and all the gold of life was done.

"Will you just wait now, Mr. Gerrard," MacGinnis said, "and I'll tell her."

Gerrard stared at him with sightless eyes.

In a few minutes she came running, flying along the gallery with her blue skirt in her hand, her eyes alight, beautiful and excited because she felt his presence here could only mean that everything was all right. With her into the room came the fresh cool smell of flowers.

"Gerrard!"

Before she could reach his arms, she saw his face and stopped, and the light died from hers.

"Gerrard?" Her arms fell.

When Mama came home from the second Mass of the day, Teresa told her that Miss Sabrina would not be down to the lunch, as she had a headache.

"A headache?" Mama frowned, unpinning her hat and handing it to Teresa with the two long pearl-handled hatpins. And not down to the lunch. Her face registered that it was all very disorderly.

"Thank-you, Teresa. I'll go and see her."

"Ma'am, I think she's asleep," Teresa said quickly, and Mama's frown deepened. What was the matter with them all? Even Teresa looked pinched and red about the eyes as if she were coming down with a cold, and that would be very inconvenient. But Sabrina asleep in the middle of the day. Either you were well or you were ill.

When she looked into Sabrina's room a little later, Sabrina did appear to be asleep, and on the counterpane at that. Mama clicked her teeth in disapproval, but the girl didn't move, her face turned toward the roses on the wall so that only her hair was to be seen; Teresa had covered her up with the soft pink rug normally folded on the back of her armchair. She made another small sharp noise of displeasure and then went out and closed the door. How could the girl be well when she wouldn't settle down. A bottle of Parrish's Food would do no harm. From her waistband pocket she took her small gold watch. Just time to do those letters for Lady Brackett's committee before MacGinnis brought the lunch.

MacGinnis was down in the conservatory, his long face creased with pity for some sorrow he didn't quite yet understand, replacing the pots and sweeping up the scattered earth of the unfinished task, muttering unhappily to himself.

Sabrina came to her mother in her sittting room in the late afternoon. Mama had been resting on her curly-ended sofa, propped on her special cushions and a fluffy green afghan thrown across her knees, and MacGinnis had not yet come in to light the lamps. The soft purple dusk of the autumn evening held the little room, and beyond the windows the sky trailed wisps of chilly copper. Over the trees, the last light lay pale on the distant sea.

Brin knocked and came in quietly.

"Mama. I'm sorry. Were you asleep?"

Mama sat up at once, touching her hair to tidiness.

"No, dearest. Of course not. And are you better for being asleep?" Reproach was implicit. "Is your headache gone, or would you like a powder from Nurse?"

In the cool light from the evening outside, she could see the girl was unnaturally pale, her eyes enormous, and her hands clasped in front of her in an attitude of careful stillness. Almost of submission. Mama's sharp eyes raked her. Something had happened to the child, but what? No one had felt it their duty to tell her of Gerrard's visit.

Brin took her eyes from the treetops, moving in dark freedom against the sky, and brought them down to her mother's face.

"Thank you, Mama. It's all gone. And Mama—"

"Yes, pet?" Where was MacGinnis, she thought irritably. She could hardly see the child.

Sabrina's voice was expressionless. "I have decided to do what you want, Mama," she said. "I'll enter the convent as soon as they are willing to have me."

There was a moment of amazed silence, only the wind sighing round the house.

"My darling!" Mama tossed aside the fluffy afghan and got up at once. "My dear, dear daughter, I knew in the end that you would do what was right. You have made me very happy."

Even in the dim light the girl could see the tears in her mother's eyes, and allowed herself to be kissed and kissed and kissed again, thrusting away the bleak thought that these were the beginning of a lifetime of barren and unmeaning kisses. Four hours ago in the drawing room, through desperate and protesting tears, she had received the last kisses that would ever matter to her heart.

It was almost Christmas before Mama discovered the reason for Sabrina's capitulation, blissfully immersed in the preparations for her postulancy. She appeared as absorbed and as supremely content in the gathering of plain white underwear and thick woolen stockings and ugly blunt-toed shoes as she had been in the accumulation of all the piles of silks and ruffles and laces for Mary Rose's trousseau.

Con and Margaret had come home from the convent for the Christmas holidays, Con expressing grim determination never to go back there, even if it should mean marrying Padgeen Brackett in the morning. She was filled with baffled fury at the waste of her beautiful sister, and could not think what had possessed Sabrina to give in. A waste of a beautiful young man into the bargain, she thought bitterly. All she knew was that a radiant Mama had descended posthaste on the nuns, to be showered with ghostly kisses at her announcement. As if she had endowed the establishment with the certain makings of a saint, Sabrina having not told her of the one unshakable condition of her entering. Firmly but absolutely she refused to enter where she had been at school, but would go instead, if they would take her, to the fully enclosed house of the contemplative Augustinians, over to the south of Dunveague, where Tomasheen dug and planted through his silent days.

Con was already ripping off her school uniform as she came across the hall, followed by the ever correct and dutiful Maggie, who was laden with most of her sister's belongings. Teresa came racing down to intercept Con, collaring her at the bottom of the stairs.

"Don't go near Miss Brin," she hissed authoritatively, "until I talk to you."

Con, her hands full of tie and boater and costume jacket, widened her eyes and tossed her brown head, but listened, as they had always listened to Teresa.

"Come on up to my room then," she said.

When Teresa finally left her, she sat a long time on the edge of her bed, swinging her school hat by its elastic and staring at the pink flowered wallpaper chosen long, long ago by Mary Rose.

She stood up in the end and flung the hat into a corner, using one sharp word more favored in the stables than the house.

"And where now," she said aloud. "Where now would the poor thing get the strength to fight?"

Mama was still radiant, looking with benevolence on everyone. She bent her head to look at Con above her reading glasses when Con came in to kiss her and tell her they were back. Mama only wanted to talk about Sabrina.

"I knew," she said, winding away at coarse black wool from which Nurse was going to knit Sabrina's stockings. "So much better than the bought ones," Mama interjected comfortably. Con looked at it with disgust and refused when Mama asked her to hold it on her hands, waving it away with a distasteful flip of her delicate wrists. "I knew," went on Mama, "that she would find the grace in the end to do what was right."

Con hesitated only a moment, looking at her mother's self-satisfied face, and turning away to fiddle with the things on the mantelpiece in an attempt not to be too blunt. She caught her reflection in the mirror and carefully smoothed an eyebrow before she turned back. Even then she was sharp.

"Grace," she said, "had nothing to do with it. Nothing whatever to do with it."

And told her.

Mama's hands grew still a moment on the thick black wool, the heavy ball ugly between her delicate fingers, her eyelids dropped. She took her glasses off then and rubbed her eyes, but did not look at Con. Away down in the back hall, MacGinnis pounded the gong for dinner, but for once, Mama, fanatic for punctuality, didn't seem to hear it. She put back the eyeglasses and resumed the winding.

"I always knew," she said, and her voice held a deep satisfaction, "that that woman had some skeleton in her cupboard." She sighed contentedly. "Ah, well. God's grace comes in curious ways. Wasn't it well it came to Sabrina before it was too late?"

Con stared at her and had to get up and walk away. "Constance," Mama cried after her, seeing nothing wrong, "did Papa tell you John is gazetted captain? Isn't that wonderful? Thank God. He'd never have got it without the war."

"Why did it happen?" Con wanted to ask. In the convent they were told nothing of the war. Only made to pray for the brave soldiers, and the fools like her had to knit them ghastly khaki scarves, since only the smarter ones could put a heel into a sock. Now with sick dismay she had been catching up on the papers in the gun room. Were all the others killed? she wanted to ask.

She turned at the door, poker-faced.

"Wonderful, Mama," she said. "You must be very proud. I think MacGinnis wants us for the dinner."

Mama came up to Christmas touched with the sanctified aura of the convent, full of ecstatic liturgical expectancy suitable to the grey waiting days of Advent. Not even the true greyness of the days, nor ice-cold winds and lowering skies did anything to trouble her serene content in her affairs and in her family.

In that one gesture, Sabrina had given up all her trying obstinacy and was preparing with admirable piety and devotion to enter the convent in March. By then all her spiritual preparation should be complete. It had been embarrassing when she obdurately refused to enter in Cork, but even Mama had known when to bow to the inevitable.

She was now reassured and confident in her soldier son, rising successfully in his career. Not even to Papa would she confide the doubts that had ridden her for some time back, over his light-mindedness and even possibly loose behavior.

Mary Rose and the new baby were both thriving, she and Dermot alone now in that very satisfactory house and getting a nice little position among the younger people in the county. Dermot was proving after all a perfectly successful choice as her daughter's husband. Good and responsible.

Terry was content in God's grace, as he had always been once his feet had been placed on the right road.

And Ulick of course, God bless him, was Abbeygate itself.

Con was coming up now, but she foresaw little trouble with her as long as she didn't damage herself with her smart tongue. No one liked too glib a woman. By the same token, she must see to it to foster the friendship with young Patrick Brackett during the holidays.

All this was running through her mind as she dressed on Christmas Eve, screwing into her ears the topazes her husband had given her when they became engaged, and thinking how well they went with the new brown velvet. Looking at her reflection in the mirror with calm satisfaction, her home and children all safe and prospering beneath her hands, she told Teresa she could go home for the night.

They all smiled at her as she came down the stairs from the last lights beside the pampas into the shadows in the hall where the huge Christmas tree stood waiting to be lit. The bronze velvet echoed the glowing color of her hair that was only beginning to be touched here and there with grey, still warm gold beneath the lamps.

"Darlings," she said to Constance and Sabrina sitting at the bottom of the stairs, and took a long wax taper from MacGinnis. With grace and pleasure she moved through the little ceremony of lighting the candles on the tree. Papa stood and watched her, indulgent, and a little to one side MacGinnis waited, lest, as had been known to happen, there was some little slip that needed a quick leap for the buckets of sand and water hidden in a corner, or the help of the Maneen, hidden away behind the stairs. With every kindled candle, the shadows of the hall receded, and Christmas came glowing and glittering to life. Mama turned to Papa, smiling, and he came forward to take her hand, sharing the taper to light the last few candles, his heavy, handsome face gentle, pleased to find some simplicity in which they could be one.

Brin and Con sat close together on the stairs, both of them very much aware of all the special efforts being made for this, Brin's last Christmas in the world. Con's mouth was narrow with anger, but Brin watched smiling, aware of everything, but with the feeling that never left her now, of a sheet of glass, opaque and cloudy, between her and the world through which she moved in conscious and determined perfection. The glittering tree held all the sweet magic and excitement of remembered years, but she had to tell herself that this was so. It had receded, like everything else, to some carefully watched distance. She sat tidily, feet and knees together, in a navy skirt and plain white blouse, completely without ornament.

"We might as well put all the jewelry away now, darling," Mama had said. "As well get used to some things early."

In this far distance Sabrina had watched herself carefully putting away the pearls, and all the other loving gifts of years. Even the small gold cross of the first Communion. Mama looked at her with smiling approval. Once Sabrina had been more trouble than the lot of them at Christmas, sitting on the banisters, wildly overexcited, as like as not with tinsel in her hair, clamoring for the taper to be allowed to light the candles for herself. Now it was being said in all the drawing rooms of the county that already the girl was showing the makings of a born nun.

When the tree was lit, Maggie and Denis Mary would be called from the top of the house, where they were already threatening the health of Nurse's heart by hanging head first over the banisters in the gaslit shadows sick with excitement and begging her to let them come down. At any moment Ulick would be in from the chilly stables, and Mary Rose was coming, with Dermot and the little children.

With a small secret smile, MacGinnis drew aside the heavy velvet curtain over the long window at the side of the door.

"I declare to God," he said, "I'm after seeing a flake or two of snow. 'Twill be a white Christmas."

Papa regarded him with benevolent cynicism, urbane and handsome in his grey Glenurquhart suit, the red waistcoat of his old regiment, his gesture towards Christmas, matching the candles on the tree. MacGinnis, the decent fellow, he thought, could always be relied upon to play his part. MacGinnis himself had looked a little longer than his part required, watching, somewhat puzzled, a small light wavering through the big gates beyond the lawn. A little unsteady and uncertain. 'Twould be, he told himself, and let the curtain drop, another one to add to the gillevrang already down in the kitchen, drinking themselves foolish on the sir's whiskey. He turned back to the family and the tree.

Through the door from the kitchen stairs, Ulick came, the cold of the winter evening hanging to his clothes, and a marvelous smell following him through the swinging door, of game soup and plum pudding, wafting up to join the sharp odor of the fir.

"Ah, Ulick," said Mama as he beamed contentedly round the hall, delighted as always to be in the middle of his family. She began thinking sentimentally of John and Terry, the only ones absent now from this last of family Christmases. They would drink a toast to them when they all came back from midnight Mass. Sad not to have them, but they were where God and duty had called them, and He would reward them both.

"There!" She sighed in deep content, well pleased with her ordered world, and the last small candle flamed to life as the bell pealed at the front door.

"How perfect." She turned, the smoking taper in her hand, and every one of them was touched by the happiness of her face. "That will be Mary Rose and the children. Let them in, MacGinnis."

As he opened the inner door, MacGinnis saw the single light down by the steps and thought, Merciful Mother of God, it can't be Mr. Gerrard again on the bicycle in the night and the cold. A small wind trembled across the hall and all the candles moved in it, touching the dark branches of the fir in pale shifting light and catching the folds of

Mama's dress. She looked at the tree in triumph, waiting to show it to Mary Rose and the little ones.

"Isn't it beautiful, girls?" she said. "The most beautiful ever, I think."

"You say that every single year," said Con indulgently, even she at that moment unable to resist one of Mama's rare moments of complete simplicity.

Mama turned smiling as the door opened again behind her, but it was not Mary Rose. MacGinnis came back in alone, closing it carefully, a terrible stillness on his face and the orange envelope of a wire in his hand.

Mama froze where she stood, the taper smoking, and after a few seconds Papa stepped forward and took the wire. He got his reading glasses on their black cord from his pocket and perched them on his nose, moving closer to the candlelight. When he opened it they watched ten years of age move like a sudden shadow down his face. Mama didn't speak, staring from his face to the orange flimsy, and slowly he moved over to her and took the taper and blew it out. All her life, when she allowed herself to remember, Sabrina would recall the silence and the stillness, MacGinnis standing as if he had been carved, and the hot, sweet smell of burning wax.

Papa didn't look at any of them. He took Mama's unresisting arm and led her toward the stairs, and with her normal automatic grace she lifted her soft skirt to go up. As they passed, Papa handed the wire wordlessly to Ulick, and when he had read it, in silence he gave it to Brin. Numbly she read it, as if she had never seen words before.

"Deeply regret to inform you that your son, John Barry Edmond . . ."

Standing before them, his face a mask of misery and shock, MacGinnis spoke.

"He said," he whispered, "the lad on the bicycle said that God help you all, there'd be no answer to that one. 'Tis Mr. John?"

Sabrina nodded, and he turned and stumbled away toward the kitchen. Ulick had sat down in an armchair, staring blindly at the tree, and from her frozen world, Brin looked out and tried to reach untouchable sorrow locked inside her.

John, she told herself, and saw him, in the dark drawing room on that winter day. John. John is dead.

She heard her sister's gasping, stricken cry and turned at once, instinctively to gather her into her arms, cradling her head on her shoulder. She understood her bitter grief, and felt the hot salt of her tears on her face, but her own eyes stared dry and hopeless at the dancing candles, and search as she might, she could find no grief of her own.

Up through the dreadful silence of the house came thinly the sound of keening in the kitchen.

The colonel's letter came after their sad, muted Christmas, eased a little by Terry's presence, allowed by the unexpected compassion of his ceramic priest to join his family for three days. He comforted them all as best he could, with all the love and hope and words that he could find. And he watched Sabrina with growing unease from dark, speculative eyes.

John had died of wounds in a base hospital after a skirmish south of the Menin Road, subsequent to the main battles of Ypres itself. In the actual battle, the colonel wrote, and was glad to do since he was an old friend of Mama's, John had distinguished himself with outstanding gallantry, and he had felt privileged to recommend him at the time for the Military Cross. A fine soldier, he wrote, and an admirable young man, understandably a severe and bitter loss to all his family.

In due course, the contents of his will were made known to them, with considerable embarrassment, by Mr. Brown McCaffery. He had left personal mementoes with loving messages to all his family. Beyond that, everything he possessed had gone to a Miss Grace Mary Meehan of Cabinteely, County Dublin. This included the small slate-roofed house with green-painted doors and windows and a summer garden fragrant with the smell of mignonette, where she had kept house for three years, and for two had tended John's baby son with all the same devotion she had offered to the father.

Mama listened, and her chin lifted, her head tilting a little to one side. She never mentioned it again.

When the Military Cross came home, with sad pride she had the blue-and-white ribbon mounted against red velvet in a gilded frame, and hung it in a place of honor, with John's photograph in dress uniform, beside the fire-place in the drawing room.

Nor did it ever occur to her to think that Grace Mary Meehan might have had some right to it.

CHAPTER 12

One of the last things Sabrina did in the world was to go and see Teresa married to her Jonas on a cold, damp Saturday at the end of February. Teresa had wanted to postpone it, but Mama wouldn't hear of it, saying in the gentle sadness she had assumed as the mother of a dead hero, that Mr. John would never have wished it.

The little chapel that had glowed with flowers and summer for Mary Rose was dank in drizzle of early morning, and the small congregation more like mourners than a wedding party, in their shawls and hooded cloaks and good dark shiny suits. Even Teresa looked cold and thin in the plain, suitable costume that Mama had given her for the wedding. MacGinnis had been given leave to come, and Katty Ann, and Cookie, who provided the only properly festive note with a vast hat of purple velvet topped with a full-blown rose and what appeared to be a pair of pigeon's wings.

Tomasheen had escaped for the day from his nuns. Tall

enough now to stand at the back and see over the heads of the lot of them, he tried with his natural good manners to stop looking all the time at Miss Brin. Shaping his wordless thoughts. More beautiful than ever, as God himself could see. But in the old days there, she used to shine somehow. Not anymore. He thought of the flame of his candle dying between his fingers, and the light gone. So it was with her, but then maybe, and who was he to know, it was the same with all the shapeless figures he saw in the distance. Pacing the walks of the garden he must only touch when they were all locked inside the grey building praying and singing or whatever they did there.

When they all came crowding out after the quick ceremony and the low Mass, glad to be in even the pale glimmer of the sun, Brin came to Teresa to say good-bye. Suddenly and uncontrollably Teresa began to cry, the tears falling on the white hyacinths from what MacGinnis called the hothouse, and the long streamers of white satin ribbon with which Brin had tied them. Jonas got even redder in the face and looked embarrassed, and Mama's face grew sharp with irritation at the lack of self-control among the lower classes. She knew it had been her duty to come. They had had the girl since she was a child. Nor must her deep mourning for John be allowed to cast a cloud, but the whole sentimental affair, full of red, cold faces and the reek of camphor from their Sunday clothes, had been a great trial to her.

Her foot in its neat glacé boot tapped disapprovingly and flustered Teresa through her tears.

"Good-bye, Miss Brin, and God bless you."

That was another thing. There must be no more "Brin."

"Good-bye, dear Tesa. And thank-you."

Teresa's eyes opened, drowned with tears.

"Thank me, Miss Brin? What would you thank me for?"

Sabrina's eyes looked at her long and gently, full of affection, and could have reflected the years of love and selfless care given to a child by another very little older than herself. Of tangled hair and dirty boots and hidden tears and secrets from Mama—

Abruptly she closed her mind. Of all the training she

was going through for the convent this secret discipline was the most intense. And the most treacherous. The destruction of memory. The iron-fast closing of all doors that could still swing open in unguarded moments onto past happiness. Everything must be obliterated except the present. And that to be lived day by day by day, until at last it became acceptable as life.

Outside the churchyard gate, the fiddler had already scraped into a tune to lead the wedding party to the breakfast, and the guests were inching past to follow him.

"For being yourself, Tesa," Brin said quickly. "For being yourself."

She kissed her, and said good-bye to Jonas, and then turned to follow Mama to the trap.

Jonas watched them go with deep relief, easing his stiff collar on the strong, short neck that barely gave room for it, and speculating on how far would the day be gone before he would dare ask Teresa if he could take it off. He was deeply glad Mrs. Heron and the young lady had come, and never in his generous heart was he to question his new wife's loyalties. His was the great good fortune in getting her at all, and he knew well it was the ways of the big house that had made her the neat good creature that she was.

But at this moment, and he up fasting since the dawn to get the work done before the wedding, all he could think of was a good plate of streaky bacon and a few eggs, with the thirteen dozen of black-bottled porter and the six of Jamieson that constituted the main business of the day. All waiting up there at the end of the boreen in the big room belonging to Teresa's uncle. They'd robbed themselves, the decent people, to provide the wedding. And the fiddler into the bargain, who would drink the entirety were he not watched.

The fiddler was as impatient as Jonas, screeching wildly up his strings, howling on the battered fiddle for them all to come. Teresa laughed and rubbed away her tears, and then turned to Jonas, her thin face tender, looking at him as if she saw him for the first time that morning.

"Well, Jonas Higgins," she said, "what is it you're waiting for?" He grabbed her hand, and together they ran down the muddy pathway to the gate, to follow the capering fiddler at the head of their guests, half dancing, half walking, up between the grey stone walls and the sodden grass and the tribes of wet shrieking children, to their wedding breakfast.

In the green distance the big umbrella a point of aching color in the mist, the trap turned the corner onto the road to Abbeygate, and a week later to the day, Sabrina entered the convent as a postulant, still adamant that she would not go in where she had been at school. Secretly fearful that there it would be too easy for memory to trail sudden treacherous fingers over the blank palimpsest she was struggling to make of her mind.

Mama had in the end been delighted, discovering that the convent below Dunveague was the Irish house of an order very fashionable in Europe among the daughters of the nobility who sought enclosure.

"Very old," she was soon telling her friends smugly. "One of the oldest. Founded in the Middle Ages, if you please, for the daughters of princes! Sabrina is very fortunate to have been accepted."

To herself she kept the still rankling resentment that in fact Sabrina's acceptance had been far from automatic. Having achieved it, she couldn't keep the satisfaction from her face and voice, and it was soon whispered over the tea tables of the county that Honor Heron seemed to have come out on the top of that one anyway, after all the trouble. Although it was as well, if the place was so exclusive, they'd heard no word of all these rumors going round about the dead son.

This convent held only one treacherous thread for Sabrina. Tomasheen. Beyond the high thick hedges of the nuns' garden, and beyond the limits of her world. But there. To be stripped, like home and childhood and all the associations of heart and mind beyond her own immediate family, into nothingness.

When she had been there a week, it was as if she had been there forever.

The very act of entering had helped her, filling her with a sense of security to be alone with those exactly like herself in all their aims and thoughts. Before the plump little portress closed the big door, she waited a moment for the girl to turn back for a last glance at her mother. With selfless sympathy she had long watched the sad scenes of parting on this doorstep, and waited for the usual last poignant moment. But this lovely child, and she was little more, only lifted her hand in a vague gesture of farewell, and her eyes were cool and empty as the door thudded into its frame behind her.

Papa had refused point blank to leave the trap. He sat in it in the outer courtyard, which was as far as they would allow the conveniences of the world, and square and heavy in his plaid Inverness cape, he stared from sad pouchy eyes at the long, high wall behind which his child had vanished. Before God, he asked himself, should he not have put his feet down? He could still feel her cool small kiss against his cheek. Gone from him even before she left the trap. In all their practical interests, he'd not failed one of them, and even that poor lost girl going in there now for no more than love she could never have—even she took a dowry to bring a gleam to Reverend Mother's saintly eyes. But when it came to standing up to Honor . . . He looked blindly around him in the bright spring day and wondered if one day God would ask him to account. And if He did, he felt he would deserve it.

Even Mama looked a little shocked and subdued when she came back, aware of the gesture that had amazed the nun, and of Sabrina turning away without another glance, leaving her to get herself off the doorstep before the door was even shut. She had looked as if she were fleeing to some kind of safety, and Mama's rigidly unimaginative mind was troubled, for not even she could be unaware of the impression.

Ponderously and courteously Papa climbed down to help her into the trap, the pony straining under the change of weight. He settled down again opposite her and took the reins.

"I'm sure she will be very happy," Mama said then firmly, and thrust aside the moment of dismay, settling the rug over her knees. "Very happy."

Papa didn't answer, taking the pony out under the great stone arch that was the last bastion between the convent and the world.

"Will we take lunch in Cork?" he said.

Nine other girls had left their worlds behind them on

the same day and delivered themselves in varying agonies of homesickness through the great door into the overwhelming silence of the convent. Bleak and beautiful in its austerity. Spotlessly clean as human hands could make it for the love of God. Stripped as far as the human mind could strip it of warmth or evidence of human love. The building, like the spirits of the nuns, was emptied of everything of worldly triviality, and open only to God's grace.

Sabrina neither felt nor showed the smallest curiosity about any of the other girls. She spoke to them, as Mother Mary Margaret instructed, in the periods of recreation, about the small, unimportant things of their surroundings, not only ignoring, but completely unaware of, blank faces, numb with longing for all they loved, and young eyes, red-rimmed with weeping through lonely nights on a lumpy bed of straw.

At the beginning Tomasheen was achingly aware of her, positioning himself carefully so he could look through the budding leaves of the hedge that screened his vegetable gardens from the distant walks of recreation. He realized immediately that she had become no more than any of the other shapeless young figures in a black dress and a sort of cap thing, clustered like fledglings round the old one in the white habit. He never even knew which one she was, and soon went back where he belonged, his blue eyes hazed with anger. Dead, she might as well be. Dead like all the rest of them. What was the mother about, and even to his poor knowledge, the whole country knowing Miss Brin never wanted to be a nun. A clutter of children would be more to her mind.

With total concentration Sabrina dedicated herself to the dictates of Mother Mary Margaret and the learning of the Holy Rule. In the cold beauty of the enclosure, the silence and the remorseless discipline, she thought of nothing save the drills and habits of behavior that would in the end set her, with God's help, beyond the reach of anything that had ever happened to her. Always neat and observant, she put herself in cold and silence to be the perfect nun. She mastered rapidly the physical rules of silence and control, learnt very quickly to be silent in her every movement, never to be in haste, to accept the most demeaning penances and tasks with sweet cheerfulness for God, listening to the words of Mother Mary Margaret correctly as if they were the words of God, leading her in humility towards the holy gifts of poverty and chastity and obedience.

Nor did she even recollect, as she kept herself humbly along the passage walls, how she and Con had hooted with repugnance at this very custom.

With her shrewd and rapid assessment of all her charges and their potential use to the community, Mother Mary Margaret was not long in finding out the gifts of Sabrina's neat fingers. Beautiful needlework, and formal exquisite handwriting, carefully cultivated by the nuns in Cork. Very soon she found herself summoned often from more ordinary tasks to ones where the beauty of her letters was of value; copying old records of the Order, already fading on the pages of ancient books; writing formal addresses for the grand occasions of the convent; inscribing prayers and invocations with decorated capitals on vellum, for Reverend Mother to give to the Sisters as small gifts on their feasts. All this she was allowed to do in a small untenanted cell beside the lay sisters' chapel, enjoying an unusual degree of solitude, so that the griefs and difficulties of her struggling sisters touched her even less than usually.

She was unaware of the slow breaking of the winter and the young leaves bursting on the boles of the elms along the walls; of the blue and yellow flowers of spring coming ordered into the garden borders, and down in Tomasheen's orchard, the first surprised cuckoos calling in the budding trees. Determined discipline had taught her not even to lift her eyes to where the swifts squabbled around the building of their little houses under the grey eaves of the roof, her eyes dutiful on the pages of her spiritual reading, until some bell should summon her in the very middle of a word.

Successfully she had begun to close her mind and her world about her, withdrawing into the nothingness which the Mistress of Postulants told her was the first step towards the achievement of the grace of God. It was almost with resentment and a certain confusion that she looked at one of the postulants who slipped late into recreation one afternoon, kneeling to offer her apologies to Mother, but unable to conceal her air of shock and the appalled tears still wet on her cheeks. Dismayed, Sabrina saw the composed face of Mother flicker with some shock, and after a brief whispered conversation, the nun laid a compassionate hand on the girl's head, and she got up and went, uncontrollably weeping, from the room. Sabrina stared after her with all the others, her mind concerned with trying to understand that anything should cause such grief. Then Mother called them stiffly to order and they bent again to their sewing, recreation continuing with its customary stilted talk, as if nothing whatever had occurred.

In the evening, however, before Compline, she called them together again in the bleak community room. Before whispering began in corners she said, and her very immobility seemed to accuse some of them of the fault already, Reverend Mother had decided they should be told of what had happened. They stared at each other, bewildered by the break in their ruthless routine, curious eyes forgetting the Rule.

There had been, Mother told them in a quiet voice, a most dreadful tragedy, in which Frances had lost her father. The previous afternoon, in full daylight, off the Old Head of Kinsale, the Germans had torpedoed an Atlantic steamer. In clear sight of horrified watchers on the land.

They all gasped, except Sabrina, who heard only the reality of the place.

The Old Head of Kinsale.

The beach at Summer Cove, and the Atlantic steamer marking the line between sky and silver sea. Oh, God forgive me and kill my memories.

Slamming her mind closed against her recollections of the place, she slammed it shut also against awareness of the tragedy. Not that she could know of Gerrard, and hundreds like him, racing through the streets of Cork towards the quays, to wrench his little dinghy from its moorings and go tacking out in his white collar and his city suit, in hopeless searching of the placid sea. Survivors were numbered on his two hands, and later he was to help in the dreadful task of collecting and bringing in, for days to come, the floating dead.

The *Lusitania.*

She heard the name, and later in the chapel, the cool sad voice of Reverend Mother saying that they would recite before Compline the Litany of the Dead for all the poor drowned souls and sing the "Dies Irae" for their eternal rest. In her humble place, kneeling upright on the floor of the gallery above the choir, she listened to the hundred voices of the community, reciting antiphon and response in the ancient words of grief, and numbly, to the climbing agonies of the *Dies Irae,* threading in sorrow through the gilded rafters of the roof.

Astonished, she knew the girls around her to be crying, and searched with a sense of hopelessness for the reality of little children screaming in the sea, of couples torn from each other's arms, the fearful horror of the explosion and violent death.

She could only pray dutifully for them all, since Mother had told her to, making her prayers as perfect as possible.

Since it took even the nuns by surprise, they had been told about the *Lusitania,* but apart from that they knew nothing of the progress of the war. They prayed, as they were taught to, for all souls in trouble, and special mention was made of those dying in the war, but nothing was said of the fearful size of their numbers, of the trenches being dug away in some different world, a network across the fields of France, where men were doomed to live and fight and die like moles for years to come.

Day followed ordered day, and hour followed planned hour, divided by bells demanding instant obedience as the word of God. An entire life devoted to the meticulous observation of every detail of behavior, allowing for no single individual thought. Sabrina followed it so perfectly and so carefully, and took such cool pleasure in her own perfection that she didn't even realize it wasn't happiness, nor that her own shock and grief, without release, had forced her already to a peak of mindless detachment that was dangerous.

Only Mother Mary Margaret, Mistress of Novices, was aware of this empty perfection, watching with quiet, experienced eyes the flawless behavior, all the lessons so rapidly learned. The apparent spiritual content.

The absent heart.

In the high days of June, Sabrina was called to the parlor for a visit from Mama and Con. It was Con's first visit, and Mama was finding her difficult company. Con lifted her head in its daisied hat and surveyed with shivering horror the bronze grille dividing the chill, polished parlor into two. Only a small shuttered square was left available, through which they might speak to Sabrina. To the right of it was a sort of turntable, and Màma explained that anything they brought must be put onto it, and it could then be turned round into the enclosure. And, of course, given at once to Mother.

"For goodness sake, Mamà," Con cried. "It's like Dublin Zoo. Even school wasn't as bad as this."

"Constance! Hush! You never know—"

"If you mean there's probably one of them lurking behind that fence, listening to every word we say, I'd think you're right. They read all her letters, don't they?"

Con was the one person against whom Mama was almost helpless. After Christmas she had refused to go back to school, and was now completely defeating Mama by never doing anything actually wrong that Mama could lay a finger on. But she could never feel sure of her. She bought her suitable, well-bred clothes as she had bought for Sabrina, but by the time Con had them on—well, no one could call it fast, because no daughter of Mama's could be thought fast, but they had some look that Mama thought quite unsuitable and was powerless to alter, since Con would just lift an indifferent shoulder and point out, quite rightly, that she chose them.

It was only in Con's company that Mama ever looked uncertain, and she was on the edge of being nervous as the shutter slid back and Sabrina sat down on the other side of the grille. It was only to be hoped that Constance would behave.

"Mama! Con!"

She seemed genuinely pleased to see them, touching their fingers through the grille, which was all that could be managed, her smile sweet and warm.

"It's ridiculous," said Con, and Sabrina only smiled again. It was against the Rule to speak against any custom of the convent.

"How are you, child?" Mama said, asserting herself after a moment in which she felt lost and unsure. It was, after all, only Sabrina. Mama still wore black for John, but her toque was held by a glittering silver buckle that caught the light from behind Sabrina and flashed fire. There were pearls at the neck of her blouse and for a moment they meant something to Sabrina. Quickly she suppressed all thought. Any thought.

"You are thin," Mama said then, and Brin smiled again.

"That hat! For goodness sake, Brin!" Con said.

Next month, thought Mama, she will have to call her Sister Carmel, and that will make it easier.

Brin touched the small construction of black net, strings tied under her chin.

"What's wrong? Is it on backwards?" And memory bit again.

Someone would have told her if it was wrong. What did Con mean?

"Haven't you looked in the mirror?"

Con was derisive, unbelieving. Brin couldn't look like this. This wasn't being a nun.

There was a pause.

"We don't have mirrors," Sabrina said then.

"Not *ever?*"

"No."

"You mean, you'll never, ever, see yourself again?"

There was a long silence, as though Sabrina had never thought of it.

"Jesus, Mary, and Joseph," said Con, and Mama reared in outrage.

"Constance! Behave yourself." Desperately she tried to recover what should have been the tone of the visit. "Sabrina. We have come to see you today because your sister has some special news for you."

Sabrina's eyes moved round to meet her sister's and for one second surprised there a look compounded of triumph and something close to shame. But detachment had become so easy a habit that before she could secure the moment it was gone, and Con was holding out her hand with a self-satisfied smile. On her engagement finger was a large square sapphire, glowing even in the dim light of the parlor, bordered with the chill fire of diamonds.

Brin stared at it and knew it should mean more to her than it did as her sister put her hand up to the grille.

"Padgeen," she said at last.

"Who else?" said Con. "Didn't I tell you long ago?"

Long ago. Something about beating Mama at her own game. Long ago. Kilfenora. Deep inside Brin some violent protest stirred. Some knowledge of wrong, and she stared through the bars, helpless, at Con's beautiful, bright-eyed face, and tried to shape words she was being trained to forget.

"Aren't you happy for her? It's a very good marriage."

A shadow crossed Mama's face.

"A mixed marriage of course. You'll know the Bracketts are Protestants. All the new families are, and they're only here a hundred years or so."

She didn't see Con grin, and having got rid of her barely acknowledged doubts, she repeated the important part again.

"It's a very fine marriage for your sister."

"Of course, Mama. Dear Con. Congratulations."

Brin clasped the ringed hand through the grille, and her grey eyes were clear and loving as she let the comfortable numbness envelop her. What was it to her, who was concerned only with God? Daily she was told that all she left behind her was as nothing.

Nothing.

With careful grace, for it was a fault against the Rule for a nun ever to be awkward or at a loss, she wished her sister happiness with Padgeen Brackett. Then asked carefully after all the others.

Well, Mama told her. Very well. Margaret particularly was most happy at the convent, and the nuns felt her an extremely holy little girl.

Sabrina avoided Con's derisive eye, and drew back a little into the shadows beyond the grille.

"And Mary Rose?" she asked quickly. "And the children?"

Mama beamed, still rejoicing in having been proved right. Her voice was smug.

"Mary Rose is in excellent health, I'm glad to say. And the little Barry is the pick of the bunch. She will be having another child, DV, in September."

She was contentedly gathering her gloves and purse, but felt a sudden awkward gesture from Sabrina. Looking up, she found her staring eyes uncontrollably filled with worldly anxiety and remembered fear. Irritably she clicked her teeth.

"My dear Sabrina. All that is over. Mary Rose is as happy as only a good marriage can make her. As Constance will also be, I'm sure. And well. You must think only of your duty here."

There was a moment of silence, the three faces, alike and yet so different, lit by the one light behind Sabrina, evening gathering deep through all the rest of the large, cold room. Mama was serene and satisfied, and Con smoothed her gloves, her lovely face expressionless. Sabrina looked from one of them to the other, and then sprang to her feet with unseemly and grateful haste as a bell rang somewhere deep inside the enclosure. She would not meet their eyes.

"I have to go now," she said rapidly. She barely smiled and touched their fingers before sliding closed the shutter of the grille at the same moment as the portress came to the outer door to let Con and Mama out.

It was days before Con could bring herself to speak more than the minimum of words to her mother.

"And how was she?" Papa had asked her in the evening when they came back, and Mama had issued her subtly evasive report across the dinner table.

He had cornered Con on the gallery outside the drawing room, and she boiled with fury at the way his eyes watched the stairs warily for Mama, the sort of resigned doubt that held his face. When they were children they had thought that he was God. Perhaps it was better for him like this. The new sharpness faded from her face and she leaned to him and kissed him, her dark eyes soft.

"Dear Papa," she said gently. "I'm sure she'll be all right. It's all a bit new to her, you know. Like going away to school."

He accepted her loving reassurance for what it was worth, and nodded heavily, valuing the love and offering her back his own with a helpless gesture of his heavy shoulders. She watched him off along the gallery and round the turn of the stairs, making for his own private security in the gun room, where Ulick already sat sprawled with the day's paper before a roaring fire.

Con swore unsuitably and, as the only available person, spoke to the Nubian slave beside her.

"Truth to tell, blackie," she said, "she was glad to be rid of us, God help her."

Blackie stared past her, white eyeballs gleaming, and she herself went on down and knocked with cool politeness on the door of Mama's sitting room. Mama had finished with the square-toed shoes and the cotton bloomers, and was now up to her neat ankles in the next pile of wedding lists and ladies' journals and swaths of white silk and satin, all gleaming rich under the warm lamplight.

"Ah, Constance." She peered over her reading glasses, oblivious of any strain. "I'm glad you came in. Now, let me tell you what I have decided."

Con listened politely and let her go on, having nothing in her own mind to decide other than when she would move in with her own, and final, decisions about everything.

She had taken one that she hoped Mama would never know about.

July sixteenth was the feast of Our Lady of Mount Carmel; a cloudless brilliant day, when it would seem a mortal impossibility even to consider relinquishing the world. Before eight o'clock, Gerrard slid quietly and unobtrusively into a seat in the rear of the guest section of the convent chapel.

The feast of Our Lady of Mount Carmel, when Sabrina would receive the habit and take the first vows to sever her from the bright world held at bay, like sin itself, beyond the convent walls.

Unlike her, he had closed his mind to nothing, remembering like a fading dream every word they had spoken together, every smallest incident. Stringing them together through his mind like a rosary of loss and pain. At the time of the row over his letter, he had told her he knew nothing about convents, so as his knees banged on the hard bench that morning, he had no idea what he must expect. While grateful to Con for the small note and the card, for which no doubt she might well be murdered by the mother, he had at first recoiled violently from having anything to do with it. Only slowly did he give way to his longing, intolerable desire, to see her just the once again. No matter what the circumstances.

What he could not accept was that this was the first step to close her away forever. He clamped his mind against it. Not Brin. His. Wide grey eyes and the quick grin. Beauty and tenderness and hilarity. All the things she was.

Terror consumed him lest he should be seen himself, huddling into the extreme corner of a bench, up against the wall, numb and disinterested through the long Mass. Across the polished aisle and up the white walls, the sun laid golden stripes from narrow windows, even its dusty brilliance bringing thoughts of prison to his protesting mind.

Among many others, ahead of him, were the familiar backs of her family, more flowers and feathers among them even than for the sister's wedding. Although the mother was still in black. God pity them, he had heard the second son was dead already in the war. God rest him. Even the priest was there, and Gerrard fought back an impulse to rush up there and grab him and shout that surely he should know some way to stop it.

Beyond them was the blaze of light and gold and color in the sanctuary, and in the whispering organ there was an air of jubilation that confused him. What was there to rejoice about? But high brilliant festival was implicit too in the glory of the altar, the ranks of candles, the flowers. Taken by surprise, he cringed against the wall as the organ stopped whispering and took a breath to break into triumphant processional. He saw a few children turn their heads and was horrified to find himself trembling. What was there to see?

At first, nothing but another blaze of light and color, but then it resolved itself into the gorgeous orphrey of the bishop and the copes of his attendant priests; the haze of jewels from the tall, gold-shafted cross; little boys in pleated surplices, deep with lace, and cassocks of pure scarlet. Two priests, chill in black after all the color. As they filed past him he waited in a confusion of longing and sick reluctance for what he must see in the end.

"Anyone can come, really," Con had said in her letter. "But the family sends cards, so I enclose one." There were indeed a small scattering of the curious with him in the benches at the back. "Not," Con had added, "that I suppose you will want to come to the breakfast."

Indeed. Although even a while ago, his mother would have been trailing her black skirts there with the best of them.

So, it was nothing he shouldn't see, but why, for God's sake had she not warned him it would be this travesty of a wedding coming next past his astonished eyes.

He could not have known her, lost in the clouds of her veil, had it not been for her father, who had her white-gloved hand resting on his arm, exactly as he had done for Mary Rose. But today there were four brides. And behind each one a flock of pretty children crowned with flowers and carrying baskets of them. Finally the cold, remorseless presence of four older nuns, habited in white and veiled in black, bringing back sharply the knowledge that this was no ordinary wedding; to his outraged eyes they were no more than jailers to his girl.

It would have been easier, he thought, to have watched her being married to some other man. Probably he'd have marched up there and taken a puck at him, but it would have been more normal than this perverted drama. Why did they do it? In a storm of rebellion he watched her father lead her to the altar steps, to the blaze of candlelight and color that awaited her, and for one bleak moment saw her face as, eyes downcast, she turned and swept her father a last deep curtsey of farewell.

Dear Jesus God, thought Gerrard, can you really ask it of him?

He saw the tears open and unashamed on Papa's face as he moved down to his place with the family, and blind rage took him for the benign figure of the best Christmas he had ever known.

She handed over her blessed candle, the symbol of her

renounced life, and knowing himself part, if not the most, of it, he bent his head into his hands, letting the exquisite singing and the long litanies wash over him for what seemed like hours. And then interminable Latin prayers he had no mind to listen to, watching his own memories of Sabrina move across his covered eyes. After a long time he was arrested by a complete silence and drove himself to look again, and may God forgive him for not watching, she had become a nun. Nor could he even tell which one. How fast in the end. After all the processing and the singing and the prayers, how fast the last impossible act. The bridal dresses were being carried from the altar by an acolyte, and he tried desperately to decide which of the white-veiled novices would be Sabrina. No more now than a nun shape. Like all the others, closed in the secrecy of the white thing round her face.

No longer Brin. No longer even Sabrina, and not even they had ever been quite the same. For a bitter moment, he suspected Con of heartless cruelty, but then knew that was wrong. She wanted him to understand and accept. Really understand. But what matter anyway. No need for her to have become a nun. She could never marry a man whose father was an eejit.

He flailed himself with his own grief and loss, listening to them all singing and praying away to God as if He was going to be some use to them, staring at it all from the chill shadows where even the prison stripes of sun had gone, barren with desolation.

From somewhere high above him a voice of celestial purity soared out into the vaults of the painted ceiling, underlining loss with its exquisite certainty.

"The kingdom of this world and all the ornaments of
time,
Have I despised, for love of Jesus Christ my Lord—"

The four girls on the altar began to sing in joyous answer, and he could stand no more. He knew he made a noise stumbling out, and in the garden of hats at the front, saw Con's face turn slowly, carefully, and was aware of the glare she got from her mother.

Like a man blind, he waited in the outer courtyard, staring at nothing while the big deaf-mute brought the pony and trap from some secret place where he had locked them. As he drove away, he gave him a shilling and nodded his thanks, astonished and taken aback as he looked down, to see his own black rage mirrored in the young man's dark blue eyes.

It was still early morning, barely half nine, as he set the pony's head for home, allowing him to take his own pace. Low shafts of yellow sun pierced the green woods along the road and lit tall foxgloves hiding in the shadows, and in the ditches the grass was long and green and starred with flowers. In the small walled fields, men were lifting and clamping the last of the potatoes, and with the sun in their long scythes, were starting on the first of the hay, praying for the good weather to continue and pausing to wave to the young man passing in the trap. When he reached the long clear flank of the hills, all the summer country lay green and gold below him, drifting into the distant haze of the milky sea.

He saw none of it, his eyes fixed unmoving between the pony's ears, abandoned in the grey winter of his own future.

Toward the end of August, Con was married to the Honorable Patrick Aloysius Brackett, by special dispensation at the foot of the altar instead of furtively in the vestry as was the proper ruling for a mixed marriage. This small brief ceremoney was attended by the families only, after which they all drove to Castle Brackett for a blessing by the Protestant incumbent in the private chapel of the castle. This pleased all parties, and more particularly Con, for it gathered all the guests at Castle Brackett, making it then obviously simpler to have the reception there, rather than at Abbeygate. Which was what Con had intended all along.

Mama considered her white satin bridal gown to be of almost indecent simplicity, and showing far too much ankle, although her own taste was too good for her not to acknowledge its undoubted elegance and the restrained correctness of the few lilies of the valley which were all that Con would carry. Most of the arrangements had been skillfully removed from her hands, and she stood in slightly outraged hauteur between Papa and the Bracketts, receiving guests to a wedding that had almost taken her by surprise.

A few glasses of champagne and several successful conversations with the "county" had restored her self-confidence, and she stood more happily with Mary Rose as the richly dressed crowd poured out onto the gravel to watch the bride and groom drive off for the Scottish honeymoon (My dear, too bad this wretched war, stopping them from going to Italy.) in the white Rolls-Royce, upholstered in scarlet leather, that was the bridegroom's present to his exquisite bride.

"Don't they make a lovely, good-looking couple," Mama said, sighing with satisfaction. As indeed they did, Con remarkably beautiful in a costume of pink ribbed silk, and a tousle of roses for a hat above her shining eyes. Padgeen had grown very tall, with a lanky uncoordinated grace, a fine leg for a boot, and a pair of devastating aquamarine eyes that crinkled in a lopsided grin of immense appeal and charm. Among others, he held the reputation for being one of the finest riders over the sticks in Ireland. In a beautifully tailored suit of fine tweed, he steered his bride towards the new motorcar under a shower of petals and confetti.

"I'm sure she'll be very, very happy," Mama said with satisfaction, marvelously elegant herself in cream lace, her hat looped with coffee-colored ribbons. She moved back a little sharply as the motor exploded into shaking life. The dust-coated chauffeur adjusted his goggles. "Very happy indeed."

Such a pity Father Terence couldn't get away. It was of course really quite improper for Mary Rose to be there, so close to the birth of her child, but she was so wonderfully well and in such good spirits they had decided it would be permissible for a family occasion like this. Mama purred at the thought of being family with the Bracketts.

"Very happy," she repeated again as the motor moved off with great shouting and waving of hats and parasols and handkerchiefs, and pretty, shrieking girls racing it with the bags of rose leaves.

Mary Rose may well have been tired. For the concealing cape she had to wear the sunless August day was hot. Her answer had uncharacteristic sharpness.

"Well, if she's not," she said. "she has only herself to blame. She chose him. And not yesterday either. She's had plenty of time to think."

Her blue eyes were enormous in her thin face as she watched the white motorcar disappear, down where the rhododendrons piled themselves below the fir trees at the far bend of the drive, Con and Padgeen waving until they were out of sight, and the pursuers giving up and trooping back hilariously for more champagne.

"Excuse me, Mama," she said then.

She was aware of Dermot, tacking unsteadily through a flowerbed, smashing the red snapdragons and the blue lobelia underfoot, his hands still full of the pink and white rose petals that had cascaded down the front of his dark suit.

"Are you the bride now, Dermot?" someone shouted at him, and even to laugh almost brought him down. Mary Rose reached him before he fell, and he swayed against her and grew quiet, looking down at her with his red face soft with all the loving apology of a dog that knows he has misbehaved, and also that no matter what they say to him he'll do it again.

"Could we go home, Dermot?" she said. "I'm tired now." He went with her at once, letting the colored petals scatter in a trail behind him on the grass.

Mama and Maggie, who had been a bridesmaid, went to visit Sabrina, to bring her all the news of the wedding and to hold the stiff pictures up for her against the thin bronze railing of the grille. She looked at them long and carefully, and admired Con's dress, and listened to all their descriptions with sweet, disciplined attention, her face half hidden by the shadow of her coif. She promised she would pray for Con and Padgeen and their happiness, and then turned with a gentle glow in her eyes to Maggie, gladly answering with all the detail she was permitted the child's enraptured questions about the convent.

She promised Maggie in turn that she would pray for the vocation she felt that she already had, promised Mama she would pray for Mary Rose, and was gone like a moth almost before the first stroke of the bell had sounded for the end of the visit.

Nowadays she was always glad when visitors went away, releasing her from the effort of contact with the world outside and allowing her to retreat back into the mindless discipline, in whose nothingness she had begun to find some sweet promise of safety and content.

In late September, on a day of golden air and gusting winds, the portress came to her as she was walking in the garden with her book of spiritual reading, rapt in the complexities of the soul of Mother Theresa of Avila, who appeared to find the welfare of her pigs and the scrubbing of her floors as important as the battle for the immortal soul of her king.

"Excuse me, Sister." The small fat soul was panting a little from unsuitable haste, and with the sympathy bound to be due when she had delivered her message. Sister Carmel put her finger in the place and closed the book, smiling to show Sister Eulalie that she did not, in God, object to being interrupted, and giving her her full attention.

"It is nothing, Sister."

"Reverend Mother thought, Sister," panted the little lay sister, "that you might wish to have this now, so you would be alone to read it."

From under her scapular, she produced a black-bordered letter, looking as apologetic as if she herself had caused whatever sorrow it contained. After a moment's pause, Sister Carmel took it, and there was no sound but the wind stripping the dry leaves from the elms and the hens cackling away happily in the run beyond the hedge.

Mama's writing. But who? John was dead. Papa? She remembered Mary Rose, and even against discipline her heart grew cold.

"That was very kind of Reverend Mother," she said. "Thank-you, Sister." With a steady gentle gaze she dismissed the anxious curiosity of the eyes; defeated, the little lay sister turned and trotted off along the neat walks.

For a moment, Sister Carmel thought of imposing on herself the penance of leaving the letter unopened until she went to bed that evening, laying, for the love of God, uncertainty on top of the burden of grief. Then she recalled that Reverend Mother had sent the letter to be opened here, and even the mildest suggestion from Reverend Mother must be God's command.

Delaying only to commend to God the news inside it, she opened the envelope.

Mary Rose had been delivered of a dead son.

With God's help, after terrible anxiety, Mary Rose herself was now safe, but would be very delicate for a long time to come. With a note of unaccustomed humility, Mama begged Sister Carmel's prayers for both of them.

For a long time, Sister Carmel stood staring over the impeccable garden, the wind tugging at her veil and the little black-edged paper fluttering in her hand. A tall nun and very beautiful, who wore her habit with ease and grace, thinned in face and figure by the practice of austerity to what Maggie thought to be the image of a perfect religious.

Another little grave like Detta's, the white immortelles gleaming through the green of the baby's grave glass. For one unbearable moment she felt in her arms again the soft, astonishing weight of the little Barry, warm against her, milky eyes staring up from the edges of contented sleep. She made a violent physical gesture with her hands, as if she pushed the image away, gasping with the effort of self-discipline required to block it out. As everything must be blocked out. Lest she allow herself the vulnerability of even one memory. Everything cleared from her mind and the shell laid bare for God. All that was required now was for her to pray for her sister and the soul of the little child, and all the other suffering souls of God's world.

By the time she went in, she was calm, and was able to lift her eyes from her darning at evening recreation and tell them quietly and without visible reaction what had happened, to ask them calmly for their prayers. All with a cool detachment that brought the eyes of the Mistress of Novices to bear on her for a long assessing moment.

In late October, when Con and Padgeen were not long returned from their honeymoon, a naval officer in a uniform of conspicuous newness came bicycling unsuitably up the winding drive between the fir trees, to dismount at the front door of Castle Brackett.

And God knows, he thought, looking about him, it was no place to come other than in a carriage. Or a white Rolls-Royce. He surveyed with interest the beautiful old grey house with its mullioned windows, solid and dignified against the cold wind from the sea. He propped his bicycle against the boot scraper and felt like apologizing.

Castle Brackett gained the dignity of being a castle by reason of the square Norman keep left standing from the original castle, incorporated into one end of the L-shaped house. The present Lady Brackett had converted the empty tower with great success into stables, the tack and fodder raised to the first floor, where the conquerors of Ireland in their day had feasted and thrown their bones to the wolfhounds in the straw.

Olive Brackett had been deeply satisfied with the result, until some local wag was heard to say that in the present structure of Castle Brackett, it was the horses had the Castle, and poor old Eustace was banished to the attics.

Shivering a little from his cold ride, the naval officer pulled the glittering brass bell pull and stood admiring the solidity of the polished oak door.

A few minutes later, a maid knocked at the door of Con's new sitting room upstairs.

"Ma'am, there's a Lieutenant Commander Heron down the stairs asking to see you."

"Heron?" Con's dark brows drew together.

"Indeed ma'am, that's what he said. He'd be some sort of a sailor."

"Thank-you, Kitty." Con crushed further speculation. He'd be some friend of Papa's no doubt. "Bring him up, please." She sighed unwilling to have the peace of the afternoon given over to polite chat.

The girl went off, and very soon Father Terence walked smiling into the room that was so very much Con's, with the plain curtains and the olive-colored wallpaper looping with white lilies, long after William Morris, and the frail silk-covered furniture that even he knew was the rage of Dublin. But a bright fire danced in the tiled hearth, and beside it sat his sister in a yellow dress, on a spindly little sofa heaped with cushions, showing a considerable length of long beautiful leg, her embroidery frame between her fingers.

"You look," he said, when all the kisses and the hugs and the pleased cries were over, "you look like some picture in a women's magazine." He looked at her and then appreciatively round the charming room.

"Darling." She took his hand and led him towards the fire. "I *am* the pictures in the women's magazines."

Her warm brown eyes smiled her delight in seeing him.

"And when do you read them, anyway?"

"But what's all this?" she added, taking his overcoat and touching the gold buttons and the rings around the sleeve. She surveyed him admiringly. "Handsome. Handsome indeed. But since when?"

He settled himself gingerly in a fragile armchair, and found it agreeably comfortable, holding his cold hands gratefully to the blaze. He looked up at her, firelight gold in his hair.

"Not long," he said. "Not long. I'm the lucky fellow who has managed to get the best of both worlds. But I wanted it all cut and dried before anyone got wind of it. Easier that way."

There was a small pause and they both knew who he meant.

"You know I always wanted to go to sea," Terence said then.

Con didn't, but she nodded, not to interrupt him. Probably Brin would know. They were always thick as thieves.

"But the Mama won that round," he went on. "Well, now there's a war, and don't the poor sailors need priests like anybody else." He grinned. "What Brin always called my porcelain priest was very understanding. Very amenable when I asked him for permission from the bishop to volunteer."

Con smiled and set the embroidery frame aside.

"Perhaps you weren't much good." She folded her hands in her lap to give him her full, delighted attention.

Terence sat back and smiled too.

"No," he said. "I think it was he that was better than I understood. He saw the bishop for me. I think he realized my heart would never be in parish work. It was either that or the foreign missions."

"My dear Terry." Con looked horrified. "What a dreadful choice. Nightshirts or woolly scarves."

He didn't understand and didn't bother. It was always more restful to let Con rattle on. Then her lovely face sobered and she looked at him intently.

"And the Mama, what does she think?"

There was no dissembling between them anymore. They all knew where their trouble lay, only Mary Rose still suffering in sweet loyal silence and attributing it all to the will of God. Terence met Con's eyes squarely and there was bright mischief in his own.

"She's a very confused woman," he said. "I'm still a priest, so she has no complaint about that. And now I'm one of the brave boys she's always going to committees for, so she can't really grumble about that either. But I tell you, she's not pleased. She feels I've slipped through her fingers somewhere."

They both laughed helplessly and Terry shook his head. "She'd kill us if she knew we were laughing at her."

His sister's face hardened. "She should laugh with us a bit more," she said sharply. "I'll ring for some tea for you, Terry. How did you come?"

"Oh, on a bicycle."

He lay back in his odd, comfortable chair, enjoying the fire and her scandalized face.

"A bicycle! You must be frozen!"

The maid opened the door, looking at the sailor with great attention, having been asked downstairs who was he, was he a flame of young Mrs. Brackett's or what? Con told her to get tea and toast and muffins and boiled eggs and ham, and she went out reluctantly, her questions still unanswered.

"Would you like more, Terry? Will that be enough? It would take no time at all to do you a bit of steak."

"Can I put my feet on the fender?" he asked her. "They're still a bit cold."

"You can too, and I'll not make you polish it."

As Mama used to do when they were all children, if one of them were caught with forbidden feet on the high brass rails of the playroom fender.

"But, Terry, a bicycle!" She couldn't get over it. "Have

you seen my sister?" she asked him then, and he looked at her questioningly.

"Maggie?"

Con snorted. "Ah, no. That little prig. I've no concern about that one. She has a natural instinct for doing the right thing to keep Mama purring."

"That's the one to be a nun," said Father Terence.

"Well, how is she?" It was Con's lovely, affectionate face that looked with concern for his answer, not the brittle beauty of Mrs. Patrick Brackett, and she deserved an honest answer. He was a long time giving it, staring into the fire.

"I'm afraid," he said in the end, "she's in mortal danger of becoming happy."

Across the white hearthrug, Con regarded him levelly. "That's a very strange remark for a priest."

"She's my sister."

Con smiled affectionately.

"Your most precious sister. What do you mean, Terry?"

"I understand that people are happy under—chloroform's the old word—anesthetics they call them now. Brin's in that condition. Not really aware of anything she's doing. I imagine she hasn't allowed herself to think since she said good-bye to that boy. She's allowing the Rule to do all her thinking for her."

"I don't know if she'd have been able to hold out against Mama anyway. Gerrard or not."

"I think she would. But don't you see, Con. The convent is a natural place for her, or anyone like her, who wants to blank out and construct a new life. In essence that's what they ask of them. In the end she'll believe she really wants to be there, and you know Sabrina. Anything she does, she'll do it perfectly. She could end up being a Living Rule."

"What on earth's that?"

"That's a nun so perfect, they say that if they lost the Rule of the Order, they could reconstruct it just by watching her."

Con shivered.

"Inhuman." She picked up the brass poker and thoughtfully stirred the fire to a brighter blaze. "And supposing she's happy doing it? Isn't that all right? Don't burn your shoes and mark my good rug."

"I'm frightened," he said somberly, "of her coming round after she's taken her final vows. Though I can't see what would bring it about. Every time I see her she's deeper in."

The maid knocked again at the door to say the tea was down there ready.

"Put it by the fire," Con said. "There's only the two of us."

Sharp as a warning, rain gusted against the windows, and Terry looked out at the grey racing clouds, touched here and there with torn shreds of copper and small unexpected blue.

"I can't be too long, Con, love. I still have to get to Cork, and I've no lamps on the machine. It belongs to the groom lad Matt, and I've promised he can pick it up in Cork on Thursday."

Con looked at him as she neatly rolled up the bright folds of her embroidery.

"For goodness sake, Terry, was there no one could take you in? We'll leave the machine here and I'll drive you in myself. What a nuisance Mama won't have the telephone, and we could let the boy know where the bicycle is."

Terry grinned. "Ah now," he said, "that would be too grand altogether, even for Mama. And I enjoyed the ride."

He didn't add that he had seized his moment, on hearing fortuitously in the stables that Padgeen and Lady Brackett were off buying horses that day in a sale up in Mallow. He had wanted to talk to Con alone, troubled by a deep certainty that some day Brin might need her sister.

They had a large companionable tea, set close to a roaring fire in a dining room as large as a church hall and with the same lack of warmth, and Terry told her how, at Papa's request, he had been to see John's young woman.

"No trouble there at all," he said. "No trouble. A real little bright Dublin girl, almost a bit of a gypsy, and all set now to marry a widower with a small girl. A butcher. They have a good bit to bring to each other. She moved to the city, and said she was a widow."

He paused, thinking of it.

"She was grateful to me for coming, but she'd not want to continue it. I think now John is like a dream to her. Best let it fade."

Con nodded. "I can imagine. Take another egg, Terry."

And they spoke no more about it, and when the last light was gleaming cold away over the distant sea, they rumbled richly into Cork through the purple dusk in the white Rolls-Royce, the hood up against the gusting rain, and a beaver rug drawn up to their chins.

"It's like getting out of a warm bed, to leave this," Terry said as they drew up below the lamp-lit steps of his hotel.

"Well remember," Con said, "I don't have to get up yet. So don't let the cold in."

They both laughed.

"Terry," she said then. In the shadows of the hood, her eyes were huge and grave under her sable hat, and all the frivolous chatter of the journey had faded. She laid her hand on the sleeve of his coat.

"Dear Terry, take care."

He put his hand over hers and smiled at her.

"Don't worry, Con-Con," he said. "I'll probably finish up saying six masses a day at some monstrous depot. And if they do send me to sea, it'll be in one of the big fellas. Only the big fellas have padres. In the small ones they have to die as best they can."

She smiled then and kissed him, and he held her tightly for a moment, feeling her furs soft against his face, touched with the sweet sophistication of her perfume, and thinking of another sister.

Reluctantly he started to get out and the chauffeur leapt to the door. Terry stood a moment when it was open, the lamplight of the hotel picking brilliance from his buttons. Then he leaned back into the car.

"Con, dearest," he said, "say a prayer for your sister."

Which one? she almost asked him, for God knew, there were two in need of it. But Father Terence, she thought, would be more familiar with spiritual problems than the sorrows of stillbirths. In which she wronged him, not understanding the wide meaning of the word *Father*, in a backward country parish.

For a long moment she looked at him somberly, then

reached out and laid her hand against his cheek. Her eyes gleamed, a little lamp in each of them from the pillars behind him. Her face was alight with mischief, and reassurance too.

"But, Father Terence, darling," she said. "I was given to understand that my sister went into that place to pray for me."

He laughed then and went, and still smiling, she watched him up the steps and through the spinning door of the hotel. When he was out of sight, the smile died. She thrust her hands back into her muff as if she searched for safety.

"Home, please, Connelly. Home." she said.

CHAPTER 13

April 19, 1916, and Gerrard woke to pale yellow sunlight beyond the blind, aware, even before his mind cleared of sleep, of the importance of the day. He didn't move his eyes from the ceiling, where the map of cracks he had traveled through his childhood provided a familiar pattern for his waking, his mind roaming with resigned sadness over all that should have happened today, his twenty-first birthday.

Today, in full possession of his inheritance, he should have asked formally for Sabrina's hand, and even if the mother had been difficult, with God's help he could still have had her in the end. The father, he sensed, would have been on his side. With an effort, he turned from dwelling on it. His mother had offered him celebrations, and he had looked at her with sick disgust. Celebrate some sort of position he had acquired by reason of a non-human, witless creature closed in his own unending nightmare in the cold building beyond Dunveague. And a beautiful young girl also lost to the world in circumstances he found just as fearful.

Celebrations.

"No, Mother," he had managed to say, knowing she wouldn't understand him. Seeing in the opaque eyes the certainty that since he was himself all right, then everything else was all right also. Wasn't he getting all the money and the houses? What more could he want? Indeed.

His forehead furrowed and he stirred, thinking of all the money and the property that would come to him this day. But how? Earlier, he had questioned little, in the manner of the young, who take their world for granted. But he had been puzzled since the day he saw his father. How could he inherit money and property from a man not yet dead. His solicitor's training had shown no precedent as far as he had gone, and he shied away from asking Mr. Brown McCaffery direct, lest he appear indecently eager for his inheritance. All questions to his mother had been blocked by answers as thick and woolly as her own crochet. Nor did he pursue them very far. He knew all he had to do was wait until today, and being of patient and steady disposition, he had not found it very difficult.

Thinking over it all, his eyes grew dark, lost in the distance of useless memories. What did it all matter? Without Sabrina, the rest of it was dross. With a quick defensive gesture, he threw back the bedclothes and got out of bed.

He was early, taking Pegeen by surprise, coming down the stairs very much the young professional businessman in his grey houndstooth suit and high white collar, his father's chiming hunter looped across his well-cut waistcoat. That was another thing. The hunter and the seal ring. He had them. Did his mother just dismiss the poor man as dead and hand him everything? Since Dunveague he had not felt happy in their possession, owning them with an irrepressible sense of guilt, but pushed by his common sense into realizing it would help nobody if he refused to use them. They didn't need gold hunters in St. Joseph's Asylum for the Insane.

At the foot of the stairs Pegeen heard him and came flustering from the dark kitchen, thrusting her red frizzy hair up under her cap. Behind her the range roared scarlet, newly open to the windy day.

"Ah. Mr. Gerrard sir, you're early. I haven't the breakfast on yet. Sure, sir, it'll be the excitement. Can I give you the wishes of the day."

He smiled at her flushed face.

"You can, Pegeen, and thank-you. And don't hurry the breakfast. Have you just a cup of tea?"

"I have. I have that ready, Mr. Gerrard. And there's a big letter been handed in for you. The post isn't here yet."

He smiled again. Brown McCaffery was prompt on the task. One of the poor clerks, no doubt, deputed to get out of bed at dawn to see the thing delivered. Not that it was Brown McCaffery's affair. He was only receiving it for the solicitor in Windsor, where they had lived. Before his father died, his mind was going to add, and shied away.

The letter lay on the breakfast table, thick and bulky, and he recognized it with amusement as one of Brown McCaffery's best manila envelopes. For the richest clients. He picked it up and sat down beside the new-lit fire that spat and crackled, filling the room with acrid smoke. Pegeen came in with the teapot under its pink velvet cosy, covered with little lumps his mother called French knots. He used to get into trouble as a child for picking at them. If your nails were long enough, you could unravel the whole thing with one quick twist.

"Put it down, Pegeen. Thank-you. I'll pour it myself. And don't bring the breakfast until I ring for it."

Pegeen withdrew, bobbing and respectful, full of an air of portentousness, and with an irresistible stab of excitement, Gerrard took a knife to the bulky letter. There was a second envelope inside it. Windsor had not shared its secrets with Brown McCaffery.

The legal terms and phrases offered him no difficulties, and he understood it clearly and at once. Yet because he couldn't bring himself to believe in it, he sat awhile when he had finished, staring incredulous into space, attempting to form a reaction. Blind rage was not enough. There must have been some reason for it all. He could see his hands were shaking, and to give himself something simple to do, searching for calm before he should read it again, he walked over to the window and parted the heavy layers of lace and velvet. He could see nothing but the house across the road and, two houses along, a maidservant sweeping the doorstep in the chilly shadows. But the direction he stared in was that of Abbeygate. Piercing the bricks and stone to see through them to the grey, gracious house beside the sea. Where, because of this, she no longer lived.

Bewildered, he let the curtains fall, to run his hands across his hair, smoothing fiercely at the feathers Sabrina loved, and then walked slowly back to his chair, where the fire too leaped and snapped as if it had been stricken by amazement. Slowly and carefully he read the whole document through again, and then reached over with deliberation and pulled the red plush bell rope at the fireplace.

Like a clown from a box, Pegeen shot in with his breakfast, smelling delicious under the silver covers. A pleased smile wreathed her face that now the day, thank God, was going normally. There'd be letters in the post, please God, for the lad, and it'd be more like a birthday.

"Oh. No thank-you, Pegeen. I'm sorry, I didn't want my breakfast yet."

Breakfast. Like celebrations. There were a few things to settle first.

"Keep it hot for me," he said to her thwarted face. "But first, Pegeen, please ask my mother to come downstairs. I want to see her. Now."

"Now, is it?" Pegeen nearly dropped the tray. "At this hour? It'd be more than my position would be worth, Mr. Gerrard. Why don't you—"

She started forward again with the breakfast.

"Pegeen. My mother, please. Now. She'll come," he added, and at some grimness in his tone and his young face, she backed out, full of curiosity and alarm.

"I declare to God," she said to the indifferent gardener who had just come in the back doorway with no other interest than his cup of hot sweet tea and ten minutes before the range. "You'd declare to God, he'd be older than herself. My mother. Now. That must be what being twenty-one does for you."

But she left him supping his tea and went rapidly upstairs to knock on her mistress's door, while Gerrard stared out at the muted sun through the curtains and reflected that it was usually nice for his birthday. Though once, he remembered, in Yorkshire, at his aunt's, it had snowed.

When his mother came in he was still holding the will. She looked serene and cosy in a long grey woolen dressing gown with collar and cuffs of quilted velvet, the high frill of her nightdress peeping out at the neck and her hair hanging neatly into two thick plaits of peppered black and grey. No trace of anxiety or guilt troubled her benign smile.

He stared at her, unbelieving.

"Well, Son, you have me up early enough to wish you a happy birthday," she said, with the faintest hint of reproof. "But sure, it's one day in a lifetime." She lifted a vague hand to the document he held and looked for her right to the most comfortable chair close to the fire. "I see you have it," she said. "Would you pour me a cup of tea like a good boy. Is it hot, or will I get Pegeen to get more for us?"

Mesmerized, he watched her settle herself beside the hearth and draw her warm skirts round her knees, completely preoccupied with her own comfort. Not for the first time, it crossed his mind that it was she who might be more than a little mad.

"Mother," he burst out, "I have more than tea on my mind."

She sighed with her familiar air of being weary of the vagaries of children, but willing to humor him for that one day.

He tapped the heavy paper.

"You know what's in here?"

"I do indeed. Why wouldn't I?"

Wariness was beginning to cloud the bland expression.

"My father," he said slowly and distinctly, "died when I was twenty months old. Exactly as I have always been told by everyone."

"He did, the poor creature. He did."

Gerrard took a deep breath and moved over to sit close to her. Obviously it was going to be like getting blood from a stone. Nor could he stop staring at her, trying, baffled, to understand what she had done. And why? Had his father's death turned her brain?

"Mother, *who* was the man in the asylum at Dunveague?"

He tried to keep his voice level, because he knew this was the best thing to do, although he longed to take the comfortable grey shoulders and shake the whole dreadful story out of her until the bones came rattling with it.

She gave him a long defensive look, still absolutely calm.

"He's your father's half brother. Antony."

He nodded. So it had said in the copy of the will. He had wanted to hear it from herself. Unbelievably. From herself, who had said he was his father. A sharp sudden thought caught him. Had she actually at any time said so? Always Mr. Moynihan. He began to go back over the conversation at Dunveague and then left it. That could come later. At the moment he must have the facts. Before God, what facts.

"No relation of mine whatever, by blood," he said to her, intent and deliberate.

He spoke very slowly, too shattered even for anger.

"So there is not, and never has been, any insanity in my father's family."

"No. Indeed there has not." She tossed her mottled braids as if she had been insulted. "'Twas another wife. A weak poor thing who died when the child was born."

She had the look of gathering her square bulk together in the chair, summoning strength for the moment when he would force her to tell him everything. But the black eyes still held little more than bored annoyance. At any moment, even now, she might rouse herself to tell him to put away all that paper like a good boy and get on with his breakfast.

"Will you not pour me a cup of tea?" she said, a little querulous.

He ignored her.

"There was then no reason, no reason at all, why I shouldn't have married Sabrina. Or anybody else."

She seized on the last part.

"Oh, anyone else, Gerrard, son. If you'd brought home

a suitable girl, and you settling to the right age, I'd have told you."

The right age. Fifty or more, thought Gerrard. But actually never. He tried to crush the grief and rage pouring through his mind so that he could barely bring himself to look at his mother lest he do her some harm.

"But that Sabrina one," she said comfortably, "was going to be a nun. She'd have been no use to you."

He looked at her bleakly, trying to believe in her.

"But you knew," he said wearily. "You knew I had to find out today. And I might have gone to England and found out there."

The glance she shot at him was shrewd and black with satisfaction, her currant eyes bright.

"Ah, yes, well that was a risk. But until today was long enough. Long enough, wasn't it, to get her into the convent. Wasn't it?"

Gerrard felt very tired. He got up and walked over again to the window, ignoring another request for a cup of tea. When he turned, she was pouring it herself.

"Ah, it's cold," she said, as if he were to blame.

"Mother," he said quietly, "I think you have to settle down and tell me everything."

The bald facts were there, in the heavy sheets of paper, but as he had realized in Dunveague, there must be much more he had never been told. Enough to send his mother mad?

She sighed again and eased herself against her cushions, settling to the unavoidable task.

"Well give me another cup of tea, son."

"It's cold now, Mother. You just said so."

"No matter."

With infinite patience, thrusting down an insane feeling that the whole thing was never happening at all, he poured a cup of tea for her in her big favorite cup the size of a small bowl, with ripe crimson cherries on the sides of it. And had to wait again while she took two long eager gulps, knowing it grey and scummy with cold, and that she was only playing for time.

"Mother."

Obliquely she looked at him over the rim of the cup,

and knew from his face she could prevaricate no longer.

"And, Mother. Tell me the truth."

"Why would I not?" she cried, indignant, and handed him the cup. She fell silent, and her eyes grew even darker and more opaque, forced to look backward. He waited.

"You see, Son," she said in the end. "Your grandfather had two wives."

"Yes."

"The first one, I was telling you, was a wan bit of a thing, it seems, and herself only tenpence in the shilling all along. But a great bit of a beauty and took your grandfather's fancy, but she was only eighteen when she died having this boy."

"Antony Edward Moynihan, now in Dunveague Asylum."

Her eyes flared, dark points of light.

"Will you wait and let me tell it."

He felt the sun come into the room, golden with the promise of a lovely day, and waited, holding his patience as best he could.

"You have the child now, is that understood?" She was not to be rushed. "And he not right in the head from the minute he was born. Well, your grandfather soon married again. Your grandmother.

"At Broadgate?" He named the Midlands mansion.

"Exactly," said his mother, and he could see she was warming to her story, nodding a little as she put each fact into place. "Three years after the eejit, you father was born. And then your Aunt Eleanor. Just the two of them."

"Aunt Eleanor in Yorkshire."

He had too keep it all clear in his mind, but she grew irritated.

"The same. Who else? Isn't she your father's sister? Now listen to me. The first child, Antony, was little more than nothing there at all. Ah, not too bad, but you had to be careful with him, or he'd cut loose entirely. They had him in and out of some place there near Northampton all his life, but they'd have him home when he was able, and it seemed always the one person who could handle him was your father. And the eejit thought the light of day shone out of Ned."

"His half brother. Three years younger," said Gerrard

carefully. "And, Mother. Don't keep calling him the eejit. He had a name."

This time she didn't seem to notice the interruption, coming toward that which she remembered, her expression distant, lost in recollection.

"Antony's mother," she said, and used his name, "the first wife, well she was an only child, and there were no relations on her side cared to know about the mad boy. Her father was sick worried about what would happen to the boy when he was dead and no one to look after him, so when your father was about sixteen, didn't he settle all he had on him, from the age of twenty-one, with the one condition that he would look after the eejit —after Antony—for as long as he should live.

"Do you understand me?" she asked him, as he made no comment.

He nodded, feeling a sharp flash of the tragedy that had left his father dead almost twenty years, and the poor witless one living out his hopeless life behind locked doors.

"Ah, God," he said. "Go on."

"Well," said his mother. "So it was when I met your father. And when I married him. He had full care of the Antony one, and a fortune for the doing of it."

She met his eyes then, and there was no deviousness.

"God knows, no one could have been better. He was still the only one could handle him, and with Ned, he was always quiet as a lamb. After we were married, we used to bring him over here to Ardnateely for the holidays."

"Ardnateely?"

"The house and the little demesne out near Dunveague. 'Twill be yours now. 'Tis a lovely place, Gerrard. Lovely."

Remembering her long widowhood, she touched her eyes with a large white handkerchief, pulled from her velvet cuff. He knew a moment of compunction when he saw the easy tears, and then remembered Sabrina.

"Yes, Mother."

She stared at him, breathing a little heavily, and he almost expected to see pictures reflected in her eyes, so intent was her expression.

"We came over here when you were a year and a

half or so, and Antony came with us. It was unnatural cold for Cork, even at that time of year."

He sat quiet.

"Just coming up to Christmas, and there was a frost. A white, heavy frost. I mind telling Ned to be careful. They were off together driving in the gig. Your father, you know, was always a great hand with any horse, ridden or driven, and no weather would keep him in."

She was seeing it all. The hard, sunless day and the ice black in the puddles on the gravel sweep beyond the lovely portico. The high yellow wheel of the gig. And looking down at her, the thick-mouthed, unsmiling face of Antony, only half-aware. Squat above her against the cold sky.

"Take care now, Ned," she cried across him. "Take care. It's treacherous."

He had raised his whip in confident reassurance, smiling good-bye. The same smile she had lived with ever since on Gerrard's face. And spun off down the long drive between the frosty fields. When he was out of sight, she hugged her shawl round her and went gratefully back to the fire.

"God alone knows what happened," she said to Gerrard now, and her eyes rested on his, holding no more than amazed speculation. "For we never did." She shook her head. "It could be some fool fired a shot behind a hedge or something, for your father could handle anything. Or maybe the eejit gave him trouble and he couldn't manage the horses as well as him. He could be violent."

She paused and Gerrard stared into the dancing fire, stilled by a story he had never heard before. Feeling the long-gone tragedy, the present sorrow. His father. He knew he should feel pity for her.

But he could not forget Sabrina. Or how she had used the eejit, as she called him.

"Anyway," she went on, "when it was pitch dark and they not home, I sent the servants out to search for them."

Another pause.

"They found your father where the road turned at the foot of Power's Hill, gone cold already and his neck broken. The mare was eating the grass beside him, and the bits of the gig still hanging to her from the harness."

"And—the other one?"

"They got him. In the early hours of the morning, five miles away. Running the fields like a mad animal. That was the end of him. They said it was the shock. He's been the way you saw him from that day to this."

She lifted her eyes and met his again, and they were black as jet, the pupils pinpointed, boring into him as though daring comment on anything she had done.

"So there I was," she said, "this black winter's night, and the one of them dead and the other as mad as a March hare, and you yelling the head off you with the sense of trouble, and the servants useless, wailing and screeching like a flock of banshees themselves. One of them," she said, after a long gap, "got the doctor in the end from Dunveague. And the priest from Clonfin down beside the gates. Your father was as dead as he would ever be, and we buried him in the chapel on the demesne, where we were married and you baptized." She paused again. "They took the other one away in a sort of van, in a straitjacket. I never saw reason to have him moved."

"Mother."

He should have been appalled for her, touched to the heart by such a tale of sorrow. But there was in her recital some terrible flatness. As if she told the whole story about someone else she little cared for. He was shocked for her and yet repelled. There seemed no emotion in her, either then or now. Nor had there been pity for Sabrina.

"And?"

"And," she echoed, "your father left all he had to me on the same condition. That I'd look after the other one as long as he lived, or until you were twenty-one."

"Look after him." Gerrard remembered the unvisited cell. The twice-yearly trips to Ireland he had never understood. He glanced again at the document, frowning.

"The houses?" he asked. Especially the one in Windsor. He had loved it and been happy there, and would like to think of it free of tragedy.

"Nothing to do with it," said his mother. "The both of them were your father's own, through the Moynihans."

"You said Ardnateely was let."

"It is. To Protestants. I believe they use the chapel for playing games in. I tell you, Gerrard, you'll find nothing wrong. I wanted to come back home to Cork to a small house. But both houses are well let. I've managed well for you," she said with satisfaction.

Except, he thought, in the way I wanted.

"I'm sure you have, Mother," he said, and it was the truth. She had never been mean with him, and yet the present total of the estate stunned him. He felt he hardly knew her. So much tragedy and so much sorrow, and yet now that she had got it off her mind, she was looking at him with bright self-satisfied eyes, certain it would absolve her from all blame for her deception and destruction of his life. And Sabrina's.

"So there you are, Son," she said briskly. "You have it all now."

"No, Mother. I haven't it all."

She bridled.

"What more do you want? Do you want the bit left to me to live on?"

"I wanted Sabrina."

Her contemptuous gesture of dismissal roused almost uncontrollable anger.

"You used that poor fellow out there in Dunveague to get rid of her, without honesty or scruple."

"I did." The overbright glance rested on him with pride. "You were much better off without her." Now she was self-confident, and more than content, her object achieved and her conscience eased by confession. "Much better off without her, Son."

"That was for me to decide, Mother."

"Can we not have breakfast now Gerrard? I declare I'm famished with being up so early. And I have a small birthday present for you."

For her it was all over, and Gerrard gazed at her in the certainty of defeat. There was no purpose even in trying to have a row with her. He felt a spasm, not of compassion, because there was nothing in his mother to be pitied, but a numb, resigned tolerance to all she was. The emotion would, however, know certain well-defined limits that were already shaping in his mind.

Being his mother, he felt, must be like going along forever in a train, with the blinds drawn down. Thumping through life completely indifferent as to what was happening outside, with small interest even in the welfare or happiness of the few she admitted into the warm and comfortable compartment of her mind.

"How did you meet my father?" he asked her then, thinking of the few people in the carriage.

She looked relieved. That was a harmless one.

"Hadn't I school friends out round Dunveague," she said. "From the convent. I used to go out there and stay with them, and Honor Heron sometimes too, Honor Joyce she was then, although she was married and gone before I met Ned. And one night, Christmas it was, there was a bit of a dance in one of the country houses, and a party of us went. Wasn't he there and three friends with him. We were married in six months."

To this day, her face held the settled amazement that she, the dumpy Anna Grant with the two little birthmarks—for her mother all her life had forbidden her to call them warts—and not a penny to her name, had in that winter landed one of the finest catches in County Cork.

"We were," she said again as if she still didn't believe it, "we were married in July in the chapel in Ardnateely."

Gerrard had thought of something else.

"The admission book, Mother, in Dunveague. It says you were his wife. Anna Moynihan. Wife."

"Ah that." She dismissed it as nothing. "It was only a bit of a clerk, writing it all down, and I beside myself with it all, I never bothered to contradict him." She paused. "But didn't it," she added, "come in useful after all?"

It did, Gerrard thought grimly. The one thing that had convinced him. He had been running through the conversation in his mind, and realizing himself right; but his mother spoke first, voicing his thoughts.

"I never, you know, Gerrard," she said self-righteously, "said even once it was your father. It was you and the doctor decided that for yourselves."

She looked aggrieved.

"Oh, Mother." He put his head in his hands. He had had enough. In a few moments he lifted his head and reached over for the bell pull, clicking open his father's watch. His watch, now, thank God. Well, the office wouldn't be seeing him today.

"We'll have breakfast now, Mother," he said quietly. "And then I must go out. I have a lot to do."

Oh, Brin. Brin. It need never have happened.

"Thank you, Pegeen," as the long speculative face appeared at the door. She wasn't dragging in any more unwanted trays. "We'll have breakfast now."

He was polite to her during breakfast, listening in amazement to her bright birthday chatter, as though nothing out of the ordinary had happened. Everything had been arranged as she wished it, and thank God, it didn't seem the boy was too cross. In no time at all he'd forget that Heron girl, and they'd settle down comfortably as they had always been. She bent herself with attention to her solid breakfast, and was spreading her toast systematically to its very edges with McGovern's Orange Marmalade, the very best in Ireland, when Gerrard excused himself.

She looked at him, her knife in her hand.

"Go on away, Son," she said indulgently. "Don't wait for me. Do you know when you'll be back?"

His look told her nothing as he answered her.

"No, Mother. That I cannot tell."

In Brown McCaffery's he was closeted in the private office for two solid hours, while the old clerks outside wagged their heads and speculated as to whether the pupil was getting the door, or what.

"Well, that's all in order, Gerrard," said the old man in the end, looking at him long and hard over his rimless glasses on their black ribbon. "But I am bound to say I don't understand you. To be doing this at this particular moment. I hope you have a good reason for it."

Gerrard looked down at his hands, locked together below the desk.

"The only reason I can give you, sir, is that just at this moment, I don't think I could do anything else. Would you allow me, please, to use your telephone for a private call before I go?"

Mr. Brown McCaffery was lacking a little of his usual smooth self-confidence, not quite knowing how to behave toward an articled pupil who had just become one of his richest clients.

"To be sure," he said, "to be sure," waving a hand at the tall instrument that still filled him with a certain amount of fear. He secretly admired Gerrard's ease in handling the yoke, but stiffened in his seat when after a long delay of clicks and whirrs and hums, he got his connection, and asked for a name.

"Can I speak, please, to Mrs. Patrick Brackett," he said.

So that was the way of it, thought Mr. Brown McCaffery. So that was the way of it. Barry Heron's girl, and all Cork ringing already with the gossip that she and the young husband weren't getting on. His bloodhound face grew even more lugubriously stern as he heard Gerrard, to whom it would never have occurred to dissemble, asking Con urgently to drive in and meet him that afternoon for tea in Brennan's.

"Would you, Con. It's very urgent, and I haven't much time."

"Before what?" said Con curiously, and sounding as if she were speaking in an empty church.

"Tell you when I see you. Please, Con."

In a voice grown more hollow, and overlaid with whoops and whistles, she agreed, and as he put the instrument down, the old solicitor sighed deeply. He'd known them all at Abbeygate since they were babies, and he'd thought this young fellow above such carry-on. Well, he seemed to be doing the gentlemanly thing about it anyway. When Gerrard held out his hand to say good-bye, his fleshy face was stern and disapproving, but the young man was too preoccupied to notice.

"I'd better be away, sir, if that's everything."

He gestured to the pile of papers on the desk.

"That's everything, young fellow," said Mr. Brown McCaffery, and took his hand a little unwillingly. "And may I say now that I think you are doing the right thing."

"Oh." Gerrard was taken aback, not understanding his change of attitude. "Oh. Jolly good. May I go out your door, sir?"

He left Brown McCaffery's. Quietly and without going through the office; out into the April sunshine that was giving him a birthday as good as most, clicking open his hunter to see the time. There was a monstrous lot to do, and he had no idea how long his next errand would take him, before he could go and meet Con.

When at last he reached Brennan's, she was waiting for him, and for all his determined composure, he couldn't escape a sick lurch of the heart to see her sitting there in her easy elegance, so like Sabrina in the tilt to her head, gloved hands folded on the pink tablecloth. He had never come there since.

But she was not Sabrina, and he thrust memory away and threaded between the palms and the clattering, chattering tables, to take the chair opposite her.

"Con," he said. "I'm sorry I'm late. And it was very good of you to come."

She smiled, a gleam of beautiful teeth.

"I'm incorrigibly curious," she said. "Mama was always reminding me of what happened to the cat."

For a few moments they looked at each other. He found Con grown vastly beautiful, a real stunner, and dressed to stop your breath. But there was some sharpness in the lovely face that hadn't been there before. Some look of astonished defensiveness about the eyes, watching for trouble she had never expected.

He smiled at her again, warmly, genuinely pleased to see her, and sensing also that she was in need of kindness. And Con thought Jesus, Mary, and Joseph, just look at him. And that sister of mine is shut up in a convent, and I have Padgeen Brackett. There was strength in Gerrard's face that drew her at once, a calm steadiness. Yet the eyes were warm with a quick laugh in them, and the long mouth smiled easily to match, lifting at the corners. And dear God, the way the hair grew wild above his ears.

"What can I get you for tea?"

Reluctantly, she took her eyes off him, and looked at the menu.

"Oh, anything. Crumpets would do. Thank-you."

It was the same horsefaced waitress, and loss was tearing Gerrard's heart, almost confused as to which girl sat opposite him, groping with lunatic dreams that there could be a miracle and time turn back, and it be Sabrina in her blue dress, her gloves in that treacherous ball beside her on the table.

"You're keeping me waiting."

But she could guess his thoughts and her brown eyes were gentle as she spoke. "I came a long way for your secrets."

"I'm sorry," he said. "I'll tell you."

And folding his hands on the table in front of him, not looking up until he finished, he told her. When he did look up her cheeks were flushed and her face alive with baffled rage.

"The—the—old *besom*," she cried. "We always hated her. She's nothing but a monster. A *monster*!"

Gerrard had done his thinking about his mother, and knew her, pathetically, to be nothing as grand as that. No more than a lonely and completely selfish woman who was going to hold on to the one person she had, no matter what it took. But Con must not be denied her very proper rage.

"The old crow," she went on. "That's what we called her. The old crow!" Then her face changed abruptly and she fell silent, staring at him appalled across the table.

"But, Gerrard," she whispered then. "Gerrard. What about Brin? And you? What can you do? Oh, God, what a mess."

They had to wait then for Horseface to lay their teacups and the silver cover dish of crumpets. Oblivious to her, moving automatically from her way, Con watched him, and with a cold heart knew from his face what the answer was going to be.

"Nothing," he said, as she expected, when they were alone again. "Nothing. That's why I wanted to see you. My mother calculated nicely that Brin would be well into the convent before she found out. Or before I found out. She's a nun now, and there's nothing we can do about it."

Con stared at him, full of baffled sadness for both of them, and automatically picked up the teapot.

"She must never know, Con."

Con's hand moved sharply and she filled a pink saucer.

"No," she said, after a long pause. "I suppose you're right. It would destroy her." She beckoned the waitress for a clean saucer, instinctively looking after the table while her mind dwelled with sorrow on what he had said. "No," she said then again, more firmly, thinking of her conversation with Terence. "She must never know."

"Cork's a small place," Gerrard went on. "It's bound to leak out that I've come into money and all that. My mother will see to that. But Brin can't have many visitors, I'm sure."

Con shook her head.

"Well then," he went on, "I'd be grateful if you'd see that none of them tell her."

"Maggie's the only one, and I'll threaten her to within an inch of her life." She looked as if it would be a pleasure. "But I don't think she even knows about you," she added then.

The crumpets were cooling, forgotten in the silver dish as they sat looking at each other, mute with unnecessary misery that nothing now could set aside. Gerrard gave a lopsided grin.

"There's something about this place," he said. "I never seem to get my tea."

"Oh, Gerrard," she said. "I'm so sorry. So sorry for both of you."

Tears filled her brown eyes, and he put a hand over hers on the table, unable to say anything lest he should weep himself. As he knew that somewhere, at some time, he would. It was Con who smiled with swimming eyes and squeezed his hand.

"We'll need to be careful," she said. "My mother-in-law might be hiding in a palm like the last time. It was really she who started it all off. Then our Mama needled yours, and that was it. Not to be unfair to poor Ma Brackett, I think it was the last thing she meant to do, to make trouble. She's very kind to me."

They were silent, hopelessly reviewing it all.

"Is she happy?" he asked then, with difficulty.

"Sabrina?"

"Yes."

Con thought again of her talk with Terry that windy afternoon last autumn. The last time she had seen him.

"My brother Terence thinks," she said carefully, "that she is happy."

"That's something."

"Did you know," she said, turning the conversation before it overcame them, deftly pouring him some fresh tea and grimacing at the crumpets. She handed him back his cup. "Did you know that Terry has become a naval chaplain? He joined the navy because he always longed to go to sea, and now they've got him in a depot in Portsmouth! He said they would."

Both of them laughed and then Con's face grew sober again.

"You knew John is dead. Killed."

"Yes. I did. I'm sorry."

"It's a war." She gave the smallest shrug.

"And how's Ulick? He was always good to me."

"Growing vegetables and bored to death. But he'll never change now. Denis Mary's at your old school."

He smiled, pleased.

"Is he now? He'll like it, I'm sure."

"He seems very happy. He's a nice little sprat."

He had been watching carefully the play of her expressions, her face regularly and exquisitely beautiful, set off by a little folded hat of some pink stuff, soft and fluffy. He could not fail but notice an edge of wariness about her, a brittle control that saddened him. Only occasionally did the old lighthearted Con break through, making the change more apparent. In the end he leaned across the table, breaking into her chatter of her county neighbors with which she was trying to set aside all that had gone before, looking into the dark eyes, his own serious and gentle. Con stopped chattering at once, and thought again of Sabrina wasting in the convent in her woolen stockings.

"Yes?" she said, knowing it would matter.

"And how about you, Con?" he said. "How about you?"

For one moment she looked back at him, misery naked in her eyes, and then her chin went up in a gesture that rocked him, so like it was to Sabrina's. She answered him with dark brows lifted, as if surprised at the question.

"Aren't I Mrs. Patrick Brackett?" she said, "The Honorable. And isn't that what I wanted?" Then she grinned suddenly. "Although to tell you the truth I'm a bit cheated. I thought by now I'd be Lady Brackett, but all I've done is give the old old fellow a new lease of life with the excitement of chasing me all over the castle, hoping for a pinch or a squeeze. He's a new man indeed."

Gerrard laughed.

"But you do have Padgeen," he said then, groping for some right thing to say in answer to some elusive sadness. Being Lady Brackett couldn't matter all that much to Con Heron. There must be something else. He was unprepared for her wild flare of temper, eyes black as sloes with anger.

"I do," she said, almost mimicking him. "I do indeed have Padgeen. And to my certain knowledge he has every maidservant in a range of thirty miles, and unless I'm much mistaken, my best friend at the moment into the bargain. That's my Padgeen."

She looked like a girl who had walked long with care on the edge of a precipice and then suddenly fallen over it. Both of them knew there was no answer. She spoke first, wryly.

"I'm sorry," she said. "I suppose it's because you're half a stranger I let loose. I haven't done it before."

And because, she could have told him, you look strong and steady and gentle with it all and what woman could resist telling you everything, and if I were my sister I'd climb the walls themselves. He took both her hands and said nothing at all, asking himself silently had there ever been such a day of shattered lives.

"And you, Gerrard?" she asked him then into the silence. "What are you going to do now you're a rich man?"

Gerrard let go one of her hands and reached into his pocket, pulling out a bright silver shilling and spinning it on the table between the plates.

"That's my fortune as of today," he said.

"What do you mean?"

"I signed on this morning with the Second Leinsters," he said. "They gave me tomorrow to settle my affairs. I've been drilling with the militia a good time back and I should get away sooner than most."

"Get away. To France."

"Yes."

Only then did Con weep, her hands in his and the lamplight glittering in the tears sliding uncontrollably down her cheeks.

A month or so later she was talking to Aunt Tessa, who was on a visit to Mama. Con had driven over from Castle Brackett.

"And how is Sue?" she asked her.

Aunt Tessa was as warm and sweet and charming as ever, but her face was etched now with the lines that had first crept there in those brilliant mornings in Kilfenora when they had raked the papers for news, in the days after Sarajevo, their eyes on their sons. Three boys were gone now, and the next one praying the war would last forever.

"Well," she said, "she's only allowed to write twice a year." Her careful cheerfulness screened another aching wound. "But I am sure she is happy."

She made no mention of the heartbreak of the empty letters, in which even the handwriting no longer belonged to Sue. What, in her life, had the child to say? Nuns' letters, on the cheapest of thin paper, in turned envelopes, careful phrases of affection and duty. Seeing even her close family now through the eyes of God.

Yet they still held some air of the serene and confident radiance with which Sue had left them.

"Yes," said her mother, "I am quite sure she is happy."

Con smiled at her, loving her, as they all had always done. She looked at her for a long time, speculating. They were alone in Mama's sitting room, Mama gone off to some committee. Running the county now, Ulick said dourly, since her children were beginning to escape her. No one would disturb them for a long time.

Con made up her mind, and drew a deep breath.

"Aunt Tessa." she said, and her aunt looked at her, recognizing some importance. "Aunt Tessa. If she wasn't happy, could she come out?"

There was a long silence, and a blackbird fluted in the elms across the lawn. Aunt Tessa answered her slowly, her eyes watchful.

"Sue couldn't," she said, "because she has taken her final vows. Any nun can come out, though, before she has made her final profession. It's a hard thing to do, but she can."

Across the pretty room they looked at each other like

wrestlers searching for a hold. Then Aunt Tessa sat up very straight.

"Mind you," she said, "I have never heard of it happening. In my own experience, I mean. I think for the girl it would be almost impossible. Where would she fit in afterward?"

I could imagine where, Con thought. She played with an ivory paper knife on the top of her mother's desk, staring out over the garden to the dark blue sea. Along the little road the hedges were white with hawthorn like a scattered snow.

"I think, Con," said Aunt Tessa gently. "You had better tell me what it is all about."

Con turned round, meeting her eyes.

"I'd be glad, Aunt Tessa. But it must be between us. I want advice and no one to know."

Both of them knew she meant her mother.

Aunt Tessa nodded. Often in the black nights when she awoke, thinking of her children, she remembered the day in the late summer garden, when Sabrina had come to her, and asked her to speak to her mother and make her understand she didn't want to be a nun. This deep into the holocaust, she knew she would not give her so dismissive an answer. Knew that the happiness of even one of them was worth more than any old principle, for who knew in this dreadful world how long they were going to live?

She moved over and sat on the buttoned satin of the long desk seat beside Con, taking her hand in hers and listening silently until it was all done. Her gentle face had grown pale and pinched with pity, her eyes wide and unseeing on the tender sky outside.

"And now Gerrard is in France," she said at the end of it.

"Yes."

"No address."

Con shrugged. "Only Cousin Anna, and I would never trust her."

"No address. And the odds against a future." Aunt Tessa sighed. "Leave it, Con darling," she said heavily then. "Leave it. Tell her nothing and let her find what happiness she can."

Dumbly and sadly Con nodded. It was what she had thought herself, but felt the weight less heavy to have shared it.

"Thank-you, Aunt Tessa," she said, and leaned and kissed her.

Aunt Tessa patted her hand, and they went on then deliberately to talk of other things.

"Did you see any of the fighting in Dublin last month?" Con asked her.

"Oh, no, mercifully no. We were only there for three days, and we left on the Thursday to go home for Easter. It was all a bit strange, but it was only on the Sunday the whole thing broke out. I believe the Post Office is no more than a skeleton. You'd think one war was enough."

They went on then to talk vaguely, for they know little of it yet, of the Sinn Fein rebellion sweeping Ireland. Neither of them dreamed that in due course, because of foolish things like Mama's London clothes and the boys' English schools and John and Terence, the civil lads with the paraffin cans would arrive on the lawns of Abbeygate. Waiting with patience for the family to get out before they sent the grey house flaming to the skies.

CHAPTER 14

The hot July sun slanted through the round window, falling in a beam of gold on the folded hands of Sister Carmel as she knelt beside the desk of Reverend Mother. Apart from the one bright lance of warmth and light, even in high summer the room was chilly and implacably austere. The wooden floor, its knots laid bare by years of heavy shoes and scrubbing, was still damp from the onslaught of the morning, smelling bleakly of coarse soap and Lysol. Only a beautiful tortured crucifix above Reverend Mother's head broke the blankness of the walls. And in an alcove stood a little statue of the young Virgin, in terra cotta touched with gold, one perfect dark red rose in a crystal vase before her feet.

The carven, immobile face of the elderly nun presented the same gift of unexpected beauty as she raised her heavy lids, disclosing eyes dark with charm and humor and astonishing youth. Beyond that, some magnetism so deep, one glance could give courage to the struggling, or its clear penetration could reach down scathingly into the souls of the inadequate.

She looked now at the young nun kneeling at her side, her face severely beautiful and correct in humility and selflessness in the shadows of her coif. The shaft of sun caught a glitter from the ring that bound her to her heavenly bridegroom. Reverend Mother gave a small sigh and summoned her words carefully. It was always difficult with these ones who had so much to offer. And yet were held by some thread from the world too deeply buried for acknowledgment; held from giving anything at all. One word too harsh and they were lost forever, so fragile was their balance.

In her precise musical voice she began speaking her prepared words.

It was a year since her clothing as a novice, and in three days time, Sister Carmel was due to begin the eight-day retreat preceding her final vows. Already the four to be professed had begun to draw apart a little in the noviceship, closing in upon themselves before their last irredeemable step.

The day before, the Mistress of Novices had sought an interview with Reverend Mother. As was the custom with the more senior of her nuns, she gestured her at once to rise from her knees and take the upright rush-bottomed chair on the far side of her desk.

Mother Mary Margaret sat down and folded her hands quietly into her sleeves.

"I have come to see you, Reverend Mother," she said, even her voice disciplined to perfect pitch, carrying only to the one addressed, not even breath wasted from the service of God. "I have come to see you about Sister Carmel. It is my opinion in God, Reverend Mother, that she should delay her final profession. For some months at least."

Reverend Mother's remarkable eyes were wide open and intent and grave. It was a very serious decision, deeply precarious in its potential for discouragement. A shattering trial and disappointment for the soul concerned. Reluctantly, she knew she must agree.

"I am of the same opinion, Mother," she said unwillingly. "Yet I feel she is one of our best nuns. Tell me why you think she should wait."

Mother Mary Margaret inclined her head. She was a small woman with a thin face of great dignity and intelligence, every movement and gesture a lesson to her novices in economy and perfection.

"With your permission, Reverend Mother."

When Sister Carmel first entered, she had been very hopeful for her as a postulant, feeling she brought much to offer to God, and should in time, with His help, approach good understanding of the lifelong struggle for perfection that was the burden of every nun. This understanding was an essential before any nun was ready to be professed.

But for Sister Carmel there appeared to be no struggle, right from the beginning. The grindingly humiliating penances, inflicted for the smallest faults, were accepted sweetly and seemingly without embarrassment or anguish, as due punishment for her infringements of the Holy Rule.

She appeared to have no battle for detachment. Parting with her family and setting aside of all her worldly possessions—even her hair, which seemed to wrench the hearts of most of them—had all been accomplished with a controlled calm worthy of a long-professed nun.

Acceptance of nothingness provided one of the most grilling struggles of the novitiate, the laying aside of all personal pride, and even identity. To Sister Carmel all that appeared to come as simply as all the other losses. She was always willing to accept the most ruthless disciplines, the most menial work, without distress or resentment.

Gradually but unshakably, Mother had come to the conclusion that this excellence had nothing to do with the necessary subjugation of a strong will. Rather was it the complete indifference of a frozen heart.

The sun moved round and the same beam of light struck through the window. Mother Mary Margaret moved slightly, avoiding the singularity of being sought out even by the sun.

"She is not ready, Mother. She is much happier, but she is not ready."

Reverend Mother nodded slowly, looking down at her folded hands. These two intelligent and acutely observant women had little need for the medium of words. There were many reasons, they knew, why girls and women came into the convent. Both of them were aware that if Sister Carmel's detachment and humility could reach deep enough, past the mind, past even the spirit, down to break open the closed, sad regions of her own heart, then indeed she might become one of God's rare chosen. Brought to Him by His own incalculable ways. The nun as perfect as any human being attempting total unity with God could be.

A Living Rule.

But that was not yet, and as Sister Carmel knelt beside her, Reverend Mother studied her carefully for the signs of disappointment and rebellion that such a setback usually produced in even the most successful and disciplined of novices. But Sister Carmel only bent her white-veiled head a little lower in acquiescence, subduing instantly the temptation even to ask why. The pattern of obedience and perfection.

"God wants everything we have to give, dear child," Reverend Mother said gently. "But all the rest is nothing if we do not offer Him our hearts."

She reached out and made the sign of the cross on the young nun's forehead with her thumb, light as a moth, minimum human contact.

"Go with God, Sister," she said. "And I shall pray for you."

Sister Carmel walked with even, silent steps along the white wall of the passage leading to the cloister, her eyes down and her hands clasped in the depths of her sleeves. There was no anger or disappointment. Only humble sorrow filled her that in some way she had failed God, for whom she tried so hard. Obviously even more was needed before she was worthy of Him. She slipped into the shadows of the choir where the smell of incense hung heavy in the air like the ghost of Mass itself, and on her knees begged God to help her understand what more He asked. The dark red curtains moved a little in the draft at the windows, and a captive bee droned along the stalls, noisily searching for the sun and his warm harvest in the flowers.

She didn't notice him, locked in contrition for her own imperfections; nor did God seem to have any answer, so in the end she rose, and went back soundlessly to her duties in the refectory.

God may have offered neither answer nor consolation, but her own efforts were so intense that when another black-edged letter came, a couple of weeks later, she was able to take it calmly from the portress after only the smallest pause, and put it in her scapular. Steadily she continued setting the wooden bowls along the bare tables, vigorously preparing herself to accept in quietness of her heart and spirit the news of Father Terence's death at sea.

She had not thought of Mary Rose. Dead in the hopeless effort to produce another child, not due to be born until October. She stared at the small black-bordered sheet, written in Mama's neat and upright hand, until the refectorian came quietly up beside her.

"Sister," she asked her gently. "Would you like to go to your cell awhile to be alone? Or into the garden."

Tomasheen was in the garden.

The thought struck sudden as a crack in a dropped bowl; not understood, and gone as soon as it had come. She looked at the older nun and her face was composed, but her eyes were enormous and dark as night, their disciplined quiet touched by sudden bewilderment.

"No, thank-you, Sister," she said then. "I shall stay here."

She moved on down to the kitchen hatch for another pile of bowls, prayers already on her lips for the soul of her dead sister.

Through the long days of that summer, the distant and unheeded war continued to ravage the world she had abandoned.

Jutland.

The tragic, monstrous losses in the battles of the Somme.

The death of Lord Kitchener at sea.

She listened dutifully to what the little Mother saw fit to tell them in the novitiate, and prayed, as she was told, for all those engaged in the dreadful conflict, never knowing that she prayed for Gerrard with them. She prayed also for the dead of her own family, including now one of the twins from Kilfenora, lost in the carnage of the trenches. But in reality she knew the turning days only as fresh hours to devote to her own endless struggles for perfection.

Through August, thin clouds held the heat low above the sprawled buildings of the convent, wearying as fever, pasting their heavy habits to their bodies and melting starched headbands to soggy rags around the forehead. Demanding every ounce of holy resolution to endure the discomfort and manage to keep even reasonable charity in God toward each other.

Grateful for the dim refectory, where the drawn curtains and stone floor gave an illusion of coolness, Sister Carmel was engaged in the monthly task of changing all the coarse unbleached napkins for clean ones, fresh and smelling of the air, from the long lines in the laundry yard.

Through the open door, Reverend Mother's chaplain glided in like a shadow, almost disembodied, so light her touch upon the world.

"Sister."

Sister Carmel looked up, faint certainty of some fresh failure shadowing her eyes.

"Yes, Sister?"

"Reverend Mother wishes to speak to you. In the library."

A summons from Reverend Mother was as commanding as the bells themselves. At once, Sister Carmel laid down her pile of linen, not even completing the change she was making.

Sister Gervase inclined her head to indicate that her message had been delivered, and was gone as smoothly as she had come. Searching humbly for faults, Sister Carmel made her way along the walls of the empty corridors, over to the library on the far side of the cloister.

But in the high-ceilinged, airless room, packed with the orderly accumulations of years, Reverend Mother was smiling, standing beside one of the tables. As soon as the young nun had knelt for her blessing, she signed her to get up.

"Sister Carmel," she said encouragingly. Her smile did not prevent her noticing with concern the strained pallor of the novice's face. Please God, this small unusual task might prove a diversion to help her lift the pressure from herself.

"I have something special here that needs rewriting. As always, Sister, I am sure you will do it well." She gave a small gentle smile. "I have brought you in here because I'm afraid the sisters making flowers for the fete have taken over your small kingdom for the moment."

Sister Carmel nodded her acquiescence and silently reproached herself for relating everything with such presumption to her own affairs. It was only another task like any other. She must do penance most humbly for so singularizing herself.

But why, Reverend Mother? she wondered briefly. Why not Sister Bonaventure, the ancient and incredibly wise nun who sat in the shadows at the far end of the room, her head withdrawn into the carapace of her coif like some old tortoise?

Reverend Mother picked up, a little carefully, a thick hardbacked journal from the table at her side, where in the brilliant polish even the inkpot rested on its own image upside down. The book was obviously old, the red cover faded, and along the top of the pages and halfway down the side was a purplish-brown stain.

"Poor old Father Fitz," said Reverend Mother gently, and smiled again. "He has such rheumatism in his fingers. He dropped a bottle of altar wine and it spilled all over his parish journal. He brought it to me in great distress, and I promised him we would copy it for him quickly before any records became destroyed."

Father Fitz was an old white-haired priest with an emaciated face and saintly eyes, who did duty sometimes for the convent chaplain, creeping round the altar so slowly, it disrupted the timing of the offices for half the day. She remembered hearing when she was a postulant and gathering information about her new world, that he came from some minute village in the country not far from the convent. A handful of parishioners and a big house that no longer needed him since it had gone to

Protestants. When he died, there would never be another priest.

She took the book, smiling herself, gentle towards the old man's troubles. The pages of at least a third of it were clinging together, sticky with wine.

"Ah," she said. "It will need to be done quickly. He is right. It could be obliterated."

What a difference, thought the older nun, a light of interest made in the child's face.

"When would you wish me to start, Reverend Mother?" she asked.

"Now," Reverend Mother answered. "Now." She indicated the table with the clean new journal and the pen and inkwell. "The sooner it is done the better. I will settle matters in the refectory. You need do nothing else until that is finished. I am sure you will do it well," she said again.

Before she had brought it down, she had glanced through it, knowing the neat fingers of Sister Carmel the right ones for the task, but wondering briefly whether these records of the living world might trouble memory in the young nun. Both she and Mother had decided that the real detachment of Sister Carmel was sufficient to withstand it. Indeed it seemed more likely that it would need all her concentration and discipline to keep accuracy through the monotony of the records of the tiny village.

She inclined her head, indicating that the conversation was at an end, and once more Sister Carmel dropped to her knees until the door had closed behind her. With a small bow toward the indifferent old Sister Bonaventure, and the prayer to ask God's blessing on her work, she arranged the new book on the table, careful not to bend the stiff covers. Putting pen and inkwell to her hand, she opened the first mulberry-colored page, where the ink was already going pale, with a curious copper sheen.

When she had mastered the old man's sprawling hand, more collected in the earlier pages, and understood that marriage, birth, and death were all laid down in the order God sent them, and not in any formal columns, then names to her were nothing more than another shape of duty. Automatically she closed her mind to the human stories in the old records; the clear path of a family through generations, marriage, birth, and death all under the same roof. Happiness and grief. She ignored it as in the garden she would bend herself to her spiritual reading, never lifting her eyes to the racing clouds, nor heeding the sweet chattering of the small birds in the hedges.

On the third day, she eased apart two difficult pages where the wine was thickest, wiping her fingers on the piece of cloth she had got from the vestiarians for the purpose. She was well pleased with the amount that, in God's name, she had done. She examined her nib, deciding she could use it another day, the pressure of holy poverty extending even to such special tasks as this, and felt grateful for the rare privilege of being alone, even Sister Bonaventure missing for some reason from her distant table where she muttered and rustled through her days.

Manners, she copied carefully, taking pleasure humbly in God, in her exquisite writing. A son. John Joseph.

The next one was difficult, almost black with wine.

Moran. She made it out at last. A death. Nora Patricia.

Moy— The first three letters were already on the page before the name crashed into her shuttered mind with so physical a jolt that she looked round bewildered to be sure she was still alone. Absolute stillness followed. The correct thing to do was to rise at once and go to Reverend Mother and tell her that some other sister must take over the task. She felt her body begin even to lift from the chair, so strong was the compulsion of obedience, and her hand laid down the pen, the small prayer coming to her lips to ask the blessing of Almighty God on the end of any task.

But although she had written only three letters, the rest of the entry had engraved itself on her mind.

A marriage. Edward James Moynihan. Anna Mary Grant. Chapel of our Lady. Ardnateely House. Clonfin.

Beyond her will, as if they belonged to someone else outside the Holy Rule of obedience, her eyes moved down the page past the other couple of entries, to Gerrard's baptism in the same church. She turned it over, not exactly knowing why. The entry sprang out at her as if, like all the visions of the ancient saints, it was ringed with dancing fire.

A death. Moynihan. Edward James. December 22, 1896. As was his custom all the way through the book, Father Fitz had added the cause of death in brackets, like an afterthought: (Carriage accident).

Slowly, accepting her own sin, she went back and read it all again. Her mind seemed to be splitting open, charged with light, almost in pain, at the simple efforts of reading something that could give her facts that were not concerned with Almighty God or directed at the well-being of her immortal soul.

She was like a child, spelling it out.

The marriage. It must have been in the big house near the village where Father Fitz came from. She put her hand up to her head, dazed with the effort of logical thought.

Gerrard's baptism. As yet the name meant little. A name. Information she must follow up. For there was something wrong. Wrong.

The third entry was the one. The death. Painfully she read it and reread it, comparing all the names. Even to her shattered mind, there was no doubt.

Gerrard's father had died, exactly as Gerrard had first told her, when he was little more than a baby. Here, somewhere near enough for Father Fitz to come for Mass. From a carriage accident.

She assembled it all, and then suddenly lifted up her head, the gesture now so unfamiliar, it hurt her neck. Wide-eyed she stared at the shelf of ancient books before her, and through them to the drawing room at Abbeygate, on that October day. The leaves whirling past the windows.

"I have to tell you," he had said, and her hands began to tremble as she gave way to the recollection of his voice. "I have to tell you something my mother has told me."

My mother. Cousin Anna. As long as she remembered, she had mistrusted Cousin Anna. Why had she believed her then? Inside the rigid guimpe she came close to a shrug. Because it never occurred to them that a mother would actually be lying. Dear God, she thought, we were only children. They could do as they liked with us. Did

Mama know? And who was the man in the asylum that Gerrard had told her about. Not his father. His father was dead.

Dead. Not mad. For nearly two years, she had thought only as she had been instructed, closing all reason and intelligence from her mind, and all the influences of her earthly memories. Her head hurt intolerably, and she clasped her hands on the two sides of her white veil, trying to reassure herself that it was not going to affect her mind before she could find out the truth.

Find out. Be sure first. Carefully she lowered her hands and stood up, carrying the old book close to one of the barred windows, frosted above eye level since it looked out onto the treacherous world beyond the walls. She pulled the curtain back and let the warm white light fall on the stained pages, reading it carefully with all her re-awakened concentration.

She looked up then slowly to the milky sky above the bars, and clearly to her ears came the happy chirping of the sparrows in the gutters. Turning quickly she laid down the book again on the table, and left the library with deliberation. Had Sister Bonaventure been there, she would not have remembered her. In sinful haste she made her way along the middle of the great gallery and down the wide shallow stairs into the cloister, around the flagged sides of it, past all the closed doors where discipline still reigned unchallenged, past the tired asters in their ordered beds, and along the polished passage to the garden door.

Sister Carmel was set aside. It was Sabrina who heaved back the heavy bolt with an uncaring crash and threw open the double door, coming to a halt at the top of the flight of stone steps outside it. The hedge beyond the walks was so thick and tall, it was impossible to see through it into the kitchen garden, so she set off down the steps toward the wooden door that would be unlocked, since at this time all the nuns were within the convent walls. Except herself. It was Sabrina who raced along the neat paths, her heavy skirts held up and her veil lifting behind her; the training of two years exploded, the air sweet on her face.

As soon as she was through the gate, into the rows of

cabbages and beans and swedes, she could see him. In between the orchard trees, tending a bonfire of rubbish from which the smoke rose straight into the light, windless sky.

"Tomasheen," she said, although she knew he couldn't hear her, and ploughed straight toward him over the rough grass, scattered with the first of the fallen apples, busy with wasps.

Tomasheen. In the end she had to touch him, occupied to the exclusion of all else with his bonfire.

"Tomasheen," she said again, uselessly, but laid a hand on his arm.

She saw the mute astonishment sweep his face, followed by fear, and realized he didn't know her. Had probably forgotten that she was there. He glanced up at the blank windows of the building as if for help, and gestured to her to go back.

"Con," she said then rapidly on her fingers, thanking God she hadn't forgotten. "Tomasheen, I want Miss Con. Tell Tesa. Tell Tesa I want Miss Con."

The amazement passed slowly from his face, and she was surprised for a moment by a look of pure anger. And by a half-noticed realization that he was far taller than she was. And big. Big.

"Tomasheen," she said again then, and he reached out his big dirty hand and touched her gently on the shoulder, as he might reassure a frightened animal, and his fine eyes were full of sorrow. The bonfire hissed and snapped and the wasps whipped past them searching for more apples, and Abbeygate and all their shared childhood lay between their eyes.

The big deaf-mute took charge then, and told her urgently to go back. To go back at once before she should be missed. As fast as he could go to Teresa, who knew how to talk on the wires, she would get Miss Con. But to go back now, before there was trouble for the both of them. Go back now, Miss Brin, for God's sake.

Obediently she did, as if strength and impulse had suddenly forsaken her, going much more slowly over the rough grass and past the vegetables, not quite clear what she had done. Tomasheen blessed himself, and watched her through the garden door, then went back to his fire, unaware of how, on the way back through the nuns' garden, Sabrina had reverted to being Sister Carmel, acquiring again the level, sexless walk of the nun, and sliding home the bolts of the garden door in careful and perfect silence.

It was only when she stood again before her table in the library, accepting the little nod of greeting from Sister Bonaventure, who had arrived in her absence, and was beginning to shake uncontrollably, did she realize she had not been missed. And probably not seen. The walls were not the only enclosures in the convent. Every nun was trained to her personal enclosure, so bent to the custody of the eyes and mind to the exclusion of all except the task in hand, that the wild flight of Sister Carmel through the garden had gone completely without witness.

Carefully she settled herself down again in her chair and took up the pen, willing her hand to steadiness.

A marriage. Moynihan. Edward James.

In the kitchen garden, with many anxious glances towards the buildings, as if he expected some fearful hue and cry, Tomasheen made his bonfire safe—no matter what they were, you wouldn't want the creatures burning to the ground. Satisfied of their safety, he changed his boots in the little shed where he kept all his tools, and put on his cap, preparatory to his own flight. He pulled his turnip watch on a piece of twine out of his waistcoat pocket. Nodded. Into Cork city first on the bicycle, and time then for the late train to Passage West.

The black crows would never take him back after it, but what matter? Bad cess to them, they'd never get another like him, with the best vegetables in County Cork.

Miss Brin. The creature. His bony face was dark with settled anger as he let himself out through the wicket in the big back gate, which the portress normally locked and double locked and bolted behind him every evening. He had the sense he wouldn't be coming back, somehow, and a grin of sardonic pleasure touched his mouth as he flung his leg over his bicycle, leaving the door flapping on its hinges.

Habit and training had become so deeply impressed, the imprint doubled by her own frenzied determination, that through that day Sabrina reverted blindly and impeccably to being Sister Carmel, humbly following, like every other day, the smallest edict of the Rule. It would never have occurred to her to associate herself with a day when she was small and she and Terry had been down at the fowl runs when two farm boys came to kill chickens for some party of Mama's. They had a hatchet each, chopping the heads off two chickens at the same moment, and laying hilarious bets as to which of the unfortunate creatures would run longest, headless, round the pen.

Headless and mindless, still running, not understanding they had stopped living with the crash of the hatchet.

Sabrina was in vespers when the understanding came, kneeling upright in her place with all the other white-veiled novices down the center of the choir. Shapeless in their heavy choir mantles, shrouded in their hoods, the professed were a faceless frieze along the carved stalls on either side. The choir bell for vespers was still ringing, and clear shafts of the sun that had hidden its face all day were laying carpets of color on the marble floor through stained glass windows above the altar. Automatically she stood, with all the others and recited the prayer before the office, and in the silence when the bell had stopped, her own silent Pater and Ave. It was the pealing organ that seemed to summon her to something she had forgotten, and she threw up her head and kept it up, a grievous infraction of the Rule. Her eyes, wide open, saw the frail clouds of sunset rose-red in the clearing evening, through the high windows, and she felt again the air on her face as she had run through the garden. And the sharp early autumn smell of Tomasheen's fire. Around her she could feel a stir of shock, although none of her sisters moved to look at her.

In the same moment, she became unbearably conscious, as if she had never known of it before, of the ridiculous discomfort of her archaic clothes. Layer upon layer of linen, in this hot evening drawn tight about her head, squeezing sense and reason from her brain, the wide starched coif reducing her vision to the range of a blinkered horse. Garment over garment of coarse sweat-sodden wool covered her inadequately washed body, and as she gave way to all her repressed senses, she realized with a physical sickness that she could smell all her sisters round her, and knew that on this suffocating August day she must be just as they. The drawstring of her woolen stockings grew intolerably tight, and the weight of each brutish shoe impossible. Her guimpe around her throat was choking her, the careful folds fallen to a damp string.

There was no thought of Gerrard, nor any reason for her revulsion in her mind. Her intelligence was so nearly broken to the endless repetition of mindless obedience that would insult a child that she was not yet capable of thought. The Rule had come close to obliterating Sabrina from the face of the earth, and in near stupor she gazed out through the windows at the fading clouds as if she gazed at life itself.

In the enormous pockets of her habit was a little black book, with a stub of pencil that was all that holy poverty would allow. A wild thought demanded where all the new pencils got to. Did they cut them into stubs the day they were bought? Was there a stub-cutting nun secreted somewhere in some one of the endless nooks and crannies of the convent? In this little book, with this stub, she must enter every smallest infringement of the Holy Rule. Hysterical laughter welled inside her, and she was aware that although not one of them lost custody of the eyes, all the professed were realizing there was something wrong with Sister Carmel.

Sister Carmel herself was shaking with suppressed giggles that in the last five minutes she had committed enough faults to fill the little black book from cover to cover. And in the morning enough to fill a shelf and wear the stub to nothing.

Vesper and response flowed back and forward between choir and nuns in sweetly practiced beauty, the calm prayer of the day's end, and Sister Carmel felt her laughter die; and slowly sweat gathered cold underneath her headband, and her body felt as chill and shattered as if she had brushed with death itself. Her sliding mind told her that she had. With death. With living death.

The eyes of Mother Chantress were boring into her from where she paced in the center of the choir, aware that she was distressed, willing her to overcome it, and

Sister Carmel compounded all her faults by staring back blankly into her vexed eyes and missing a response.

If I faint, she was thinking, they won't stop. They never stop for anyone. They'll just go on singing as if nothing had happened. It was taking on the character of the nightmares that even now could wake her in the pitch and solitary dark on her narrow straw mattress in her cell. Even the curtains drawn firmly closed, by order of the Rule, lest a lonely and homesick girl might take comfort from one solitary star, or the moon that shone above her home.

Not even the nun beside her would turn her eyes as she fell to the floor. Until the infirmarian should slowly, and with due and proper ceremony, leave her stall and touch the nearest novice on the shoulder, to ask help in carrying her out.

I could be dead, she thought, and darkness swirled in her head and her singing sisters wheeled and lurched and fell away. I could be dead before they get to me. And never get out. Never—

The nuns on either side of her went on, carefully enunciating the age-old lovely words of their responses, and the infirmarian allowed them to finish the psalm before she laid down her Book of Hours, and left her stall, bowing deep and formally to Reverend Mother before she moved down the sun-touched aisle and laid a hand on the shoulder of the nearest novice to Sister Carmel, asking for help in carrying her out.

CHAPTER 15

When Brin first left the convent, there was some difficulty as to where she could go, inasmuch as she was a creature outside everyone's experience, and an object of morbid curiosity to many.

And of violent disapproval to some. Like Mama, who would have nothing to do with her.

In well-chosen words that she had obviously been rehearsing, she made it clear that any daughter who behaved with such disgraceful lack of responsibility in the eyes of God and the world could expect neither sympathy nor shelter from her. Listening, Sabrina thought privately that the world was much the more important to her of the two.

Mama tossed her burnished head, silver now across her temples, for Mama would never be anything as common as plain grey. Beside her, Maggie looked down her pretty little nose with an air of appalled smugness. Sabrina gave one glance at her weight of lovely long fair hair, and thought with a mean and unbecoming pleasure of it falling under the shears on the community room floor. Mama's little echo. She turned back to her mother, and the last two years of training taught her not to show one hint of hurt or sorrow, or even the flash of cheerful malice against her little sister.

"You mean, Mama," she said, "that I cannot come home."

Her face deep in the coif was impassive.

"As an example to this child here?" Mama said severely. "It would be impossible, Sabrina. She is so anxious to be a nun, and to do it properly." Maggie assumed an expression of protected righteousness. "How could she achieve a vocation with you coming and going from the convent like a cuckoo from a Swiss clock."

She could have said nothing to make it easier and blunt the shock, and laughter welled up in Sabrina, dying quickly as she realized with sorrow that the last long loss would be her mother's.

"I'll be glad," Mama said, and as usual didn't realize when she had become impossible, "I'll be glad any time to hear from you that this nonsense is all over and you have settled down again, and I can hold my head up with my friends."

Sabrina sighed.

Mama used not, she thought, to be so obvious. She was more subtle in trying to get her own way without being so obvious about why she wanted it. Used to pretend it was always for the good of her children.

She began to say that she hoped she was going to settle down now. That that's what it was all about. That she was still thinking of being a nurse. She stopped, knowing Mama wouldn't listen.

The beautiful young nun in the starched veil who had so excited Maggie's admiration still looked out from the shelter of the bronze grille. But it was Sabrina's wide-open grey eyes, focused once more upon the world outside, that gazed out at her mother's lifted chin.

"No, Mama," she said, and sighed as she said it, feeling for far from the first time, that it was almost the only thing she ever said to her mother.

Mama swept up her purse and gloves.

"Then there is no more to be said. Margaret, say goodbye to your sister."

It seemed to Brin, too, that Mama had always been sweeping away from her in some kind of rage or disapproval. She must have been a very unsatisfactory daughter for her. But she couldn't help it. She watched the smart figure in the biscuit-colored linen suit and the wide straw hat to match it go out through the parlor door, the priggish little Maggie padding at her heels, the set of her sailor hat already whispering of the convent. Brin sat where they had left her, her eyes wide and sad, until the bell rang for the official ending of the visit, knowing it would only be the first of many similar scenes.

Con, faced with the direct question and staggered at how Sabrina had found out, had told her the whole story of Cousin Anna's lie. And that Gerrard was in France. She made no attempt to conceal her frank delight when she heard that Sabrina had started the necessary long proceedings to come out. But when the moment came, she could be of little use.

"Darling," she cried, now totally uninhibited by the gloom and shadows of the parlor. "You know I'd have you to stay with me like a shot. And Ma Brackett couldn't mind less; being a Prod she thinks the whole thing is a rubbish anyway. But."

She waited for the full impact of her news, her head tilted a little defiantly in its high striped collar.

"I've left Brackett, Brin. I'm getting a divorce."

Brin literally gasped and gaped, and not for the first time Con felt real warm pleasure to see normal expressions chasing each other across her sister's face that had grown still and empty as some marble woman on a tomb. Excitement and apprehension were mixed on her own expression as she waited for Brin to manage a reaction.

"But, Con—" It was only a few months since the old Lord Eustace had obliged by dying, and even in her shuttered world Brin had allowed herself enough understanding to hope her sister might be happier. She had always wanted to be Lady Brackett. The full impact sunk into her mind. A *divorce.*

Con looked down at her beautifully kept nails, avoiding her eyes.

"Yes, I know. Mother Church and all the rest of it. But Mother Church did nothing at all to help me with Brackett. Bear your cross, they told me, and God will reward you. So there I was, bearing my cross and Brackett cavorting with my maid in the next room. Or thereabouts." She grinned, acknowledging the exaggeration.

"I'd rather live in sin and be happy," she went on, "if all I can get is a half divorce. Or whatever they give to a mixed marriage. And I'll need to hurry up about the whole thing, in case the Sinn Fein win. There'd I'd be marooned in a Catholic state with no divorce. We have the petition filed in London."

Brin noticed the word we, but let it pass, and through the grille the two girls regarded each other gravely, both of them seared and damaged by what they had been through, yet touched with an inescapable sense of the excitement of change. It was from both their thoughts that Con spoke.

"So she won't have you home."

Brin shook her head, speaking lightly to cover the wound.

"She said I am not respectable. She said," she added, and the smile came, "that I was in and out like a cuckoo in a Swiss clock."

Con snorted. "God save the mark," she said, and could have been MacGinnis. "It'll take her a time," she added, "to swallow a renegade nun and a divorcée. Although I think I can get away with it a bit. Divorce is very smart now."

Brin's face creased with pity. The brittle Con come back, covering every hurt with barbs sharper than the wound.

"At least," Con said then, "I chose Brackett."

Brin's look was level.

"You didn't, Con."

Con looked back at her wryly.

"You're right, of course. I was so damned if she was going to choose for me that I took the first one came along."

There was silence between them, wrapped in the

greater enveloping silence of the convent, and then Con shrugged.

"Anyway, the fool settled a great mass of money on me that he can't take back. But at the moment I've no home. I'm staying with Clare Mellor. What can we do about you, Brin?"

Brin smiled, her face full of affection.

"Tesa. She offered at once, God bless her. She has her parlor with the bed in it. It could be just the thing, Con."

Unspeaking, they acknowledged all the readjustments that Brin would have to make for her future back in the world; and that for the start of them, the isolation and quiet of Teresa's little house might be the best possible place.

"I have to grow my hair," said Brin, as though that was the sum of it.

And a great deal more than that, Con thought privately, well aware of all the nervous fears that lay behind Brin's calm face. And the sorrow.

Con grasped her courage and blurted out the one question she was desperate to ask. "Brin. What about Gerrard?"

She saw her sister, as she had expected, withdraw visibly into her coif, swept by a defensive look that came close to fear.

"What of him?" She wasn't even ready to discuss it.

"Will you not write to him? Can't I write for you?"

"Where?"

At that Con threw out her hands in exasperation, noticing at the same time that Brin, who had begun to relax from many of the formal positions of the nun, had thrust her own hands back into her sleeves, withdrawn and closed once more against the world. Con ploughed on.

"We'd find some way. Through the War Office. Marcus Mellor was there, you know, before he got this asthma business that put him out. He'd know. They'd give you a number or something to write to."

Brin sat in silence, her eyes down, and Con could have kicked herself. She wasn't ready. God knew it would take enough just to learn not to be a nun.

"But it'd do no harm for him to know you'd come out," she couldn't help saying.

Brin took a deep breath. "I couldn't have him see me till my hair grew."

Con snorted and then grew gentle as she realized her sister was trembling.

"Ah, I'm sorry, Brin," she said. "I'm rushing you."

"Yes," said Brin, and as she lifted her eyes the lashes were bright with tears. She spoke with an effort.

"I've come such a long way, Con-Con, from the Brin who loved Gerrard, that I can't come back all at once. And if you wrote to him, he'd want to see me. Please. Give me some time. Be patient with me. And of course," she added sadly, "he may not come back at all."

Con could say nothing to that, remembering with a chill the day in the tea shop, when without so many words, Gerrard had made it clear that that was what he hoped for.

Brin smiled suddenly, easing the sadness. "I've more to do to myself at Tesa's than grow my hair, you know."

Con reached quickly through the grille and laid a hand on Brin's arm.

"I'm a thick-headed meddler," she said. "I'll say no word again until you tell me. But he'll come back. And when he does," she added with a grin, "I'm not sure I'll keep any promise not to meddle then."

They smiled at each other, a long moment of affection, and across their silence the bell pealed for the end of the visit.

"Tell them to go to hell," said Con fiercely.

Brin grinned, quick and cheerful as she ever was. "I have," she said. "But nicely. I can't hurry them. They've been good to me."

But she stood up, and Con stood too. Brin noticed that her parasol was in the same smart stripes as her high little collar and her cuffs.

"Very smart," she said. "Is that the new fashion?"

She was a little apprehensive about the length of leg she would obviously be expected to show when she came out.

Con put the end of her parasol on the ground and

twirled round it, floating her short skirt and tilting her lovely head.

"The latest," she said. "Well, good-bye, Brin dearest—and race you to freedom!"

Brin reached and touched her fingers through the grille, and as she watched Con open the parlor door, she couldn't help a small secret smile in the shelter of her coif. Con would be simply furious if she knew how exactly like Mama she looked, walking out that door, head in the air, both of them ready to do battle with anyone for the world as they saw it.

Slowly and thoughtfully she walked back to the community room, going from habit along the wall, thinking of what she had said to Con about not being willing to hurry the nuns. She could just walk out, but as she said, in their lights they had been good to her. And to be honest, she had come in there of her own free will. Rearing to go, as Papa would say. It must have seemed immensely unreasonable suddenly to say she wanted out, and as fast as possible, especially since she knew that even that desire was not quite wholehearted. Much of the order and discipline and stark beauty of the convent life had appealed to her, and she had gained deep pleasure and satisfaction in conforming to it. But in the ultimate end, once the paralysis had fallen from her mind, she knew that for all her good performance, she had failed utterly in proper observance of every aspect of the Holy Rule.

Nor was there any question now of trying to do better. Coldly, clearly, and with a feeling of deep guilt for having wasted the time of these dedicated women, she knew what she had always known. That it was not for her. She did not belong. Her reawakened power of reason could never subdue itself again to the almost senseless discipline and obedience exacted by the convent, and deep within the shelter of her coif she was finding sudden difficulty in things like watching a file of nuns pasted up along the wall of an empty corridor without a smile, remembering how Con loved to imitate them back at school. Sliding along in her holland pinafore, her eyes cast down.

Even then, as a child, she had known she didn't belong. Her whole shameful performance had been a hypocrisy.

For a time, she had been deceived by the deadening anesthetic of pain she had found insupportable, allowing herself to be washed in here on the tide of a lie.

About Gerrard she never spoke at all, never mentioning him to Con again after the first desperate inquiry. To the nuns, she only asked forgiveness for giving them trouble, and would say no more than that she had discovered her religious life to be founded on a deception, making it impossible to pursue it.

Mother Mary Margaret and Reverend Mother had struggled long and hard, unwilling, as they saw it, to lose a soul of such promise. But in the end, when she was even considering the indignity of running away, they had given in, and Reverend Mother had written the necessary letter to the bishop, asking for permission for her to leave the convent.

It was only at the very end that she discovered that the time of kindness passed with the hope of keeping her. Her going was without farewell or regret, turned back bleakly into a world they had no use for. She was directed, when she had changed her clothes, to go to a small door down a passage, and she had nodded dumbly to the little portress, who seemed already to have become a stranger, observing Brin through her thick glasses as if she had undergone some strange physical change.

She was too nervous too react in any way to the clothes, discarding the unwashed wool and the starched linen for the pretty scraps of underwear that Con had brought, with no more thought than that surely it would have been more sensible to put them on when she got up. From training she automatically folded her habit in the same perfection in which for two years she had left it every night on the chair back in her cell. Nor did she look at it as she went out, groping in the short dark passage for the door, thinking still she would come into some unfamiliar parlor of the convent, where there would be someone to say good-bye.

To her shock and amazement, the door opened straight into a road, and although she had seen no one when she had come through it, it slammed shut on her heels, and she could hear the crashing of the bolts and locks, as if in fearful haste they closed out something dangerous.

Sickly, she thought the whole arrangement must have been constructed for the ejection of such as her.

She looked round her, awkward and unhappy in the costume Con had brought for her, firmly having the skirt shortened first.

"Dearest Brin, you may be a renegade, but you cannot be a frump."

She felt her legs as long as a giraffe's, and knew the oddness of the small close-fitting hat that still had spikes of hair sticking out from under it. She was on no more than a lane below the convent wall, and she thanked God for the early hour that had few people yet about. With some sad need for shelter, she slunk, still nunlike, along the bottom of the wall, gripping the dreadful cardboard case they had given her, for she had been told to take away all the woolen underclothes and stockings and the fearful stubby shoes. Only the habit was the property of the House.

As long as she kept walking, she worked out, she must come to the outer courtyard, where Con should be waiting. At this time of day, with the colors of dawn still hanging in the sky? It would be unheard of for Con to drag herself from bed at this unholy hour.

But Con was there, and only she would have come to meet her renegade in the scarlet de Dion Bouton that had succeeded the white Rolls-Royce. As Sabrina came timidly through the archway from outside, the blaze of color and Con's glowing face below her motor veil were like an outrage in the grey impersonal place. Only then did Brin admit to herself the secret terror that she would not be there, and begin to relax, catching some of Con's excitement. By the time they thundered out the archway she had thought never to see again, she had begun to smile herself, turning in her seat like a child to look about her at her new world.

They could get nowhere near Teresa's cottage, and had to get out of the motor in the one street of little sod-roofed houses filled with turf reek and the smells of cattle dung and clean salt wind. The car was surrounded at once by the entire population, silent and well mannered; too civil to ask questions or to crowd, all of them pretending that it was only the sheerest chance or running a message for this or that, that had brought them out at the moment the red machine came roaring down the street. In their silence and politeness they managed to ensure enough information for the embellished story of the coming of the red motor and the brass lamps on it as bright as the candlesticks at Mass and the one in the pulled-down hat a runaway nun, to linger round the embers of their fires for generations.

Embarrassed, Brin turned at once with Con to climb the stony hill, the grass brilliant in the clear October day and the limestone rocks cropping grey up through the difficult fields. At a respectful distance behind trooped all the children of the village, whipped hotfoot from the potato picking by their mothers, and sent after the gentry to find out all they could.

"Con," Brin said when they were clear of it all. "I'm bothered about my legs."

Con whirled her lovely eyes at them, and Brin was aware of a fresh softness, even happiness, in her sister. The look of devilment was the Con of long ago.

"You have no reason to be," was all Con said, and then Brin laughed aloud and stopped walking.

"Con," she said, "I laughed."

"More power to you," Con said. "You must do it more often."

"You've been very good to me, Con-Con," she said then. "I'd never have managed it without you."

With immense distaste Con circled deep, water-filled cattle prints outside a gate, fastidiously placing her narrow strapped shoes on bits of dry ground.

"I imagine you would," she said, and Sabrina, her own head down, trying to find space to walk, knew in her heart she was right. But she had a long way to come back, and there were places, God knew, she would never reach again. She lifted her head and looked at the tiny house above her, sheltered from the sea by the shoulder of the hill. Teresa was waiting in the gap of the wall.

The little house was sparse, but spotless as anything of Teresa's was bound to be. A wooden table blanched with scrubbing took up most of the floor, with four straight wooden chairs, no two of them the same. Beside the hearth, one armchair that was Jonas's right, set against a rug of colored rags. A wall was taken up by the sliding wall bed and the rattling door that led out to the yard. Above the damped-down fire, the mantelpiece was ranged with glittering tins from tea or biscuits, and a small smile touched Brin's mouth to see them, knowing that they would have come as Christmas gifts from Abbeygate. In the center of them glowed the tiny crimson lamp below a picture of the Sacred Heart, soft in the dim room. A fat red kettle sang on a trivet over the sods, and beside the hearth a baby slept in a wooden cradle. The whole house was full of the soft turf smell and the sense of serenity and peace.

Brin took a deep breath.

"Oh, Tesa," she said, and at her door Teresa stood with her hands folded on her spotless blue apron, her hair drawn back from her thin face, her small son clinging to her skirt.

"Our house is yours, Miss Brin," she said.

Despite their raging curiosity, the village people were tolerant and good-mannered, and in their small world Brin had all the peace and quietness she needed to feel her way back into living, needing almost as much discipline to resume it as she had needed in learning to give it up.

She passed her days in reading the piles of what Con thought suitable literature to help her to "catch up"; and with fearful grief she read the old newspapers she'd asked for, realizing for the first time the full and dreadful horror of the war she had ignored. Now she prayed for all of them, and understood, appalled, what she was praying for.

She took the little boys and walked with them on the windy autumn shore, gathering shells and pebbles to make a path for Mammy's garden, where between the house and the stone wall of the boreen Teresa struggled in a losing battle for a few windblown fuchsias and dispirited yellow roses.

She walked down the long hill for Teresa's messages in the one small shop, and sat on windowsills in the thin November sun, chatting to the village people, who with infinite courtesy never asked her one question of herself, behaving always as if she had come recently from somewhere like Australia, and couldn't be expected then, the creature, to know anything about anything.

In the evenings she talked with Jonas and Teresa before the glowing hearth until Jonas gave notice with his mighty yawns that farmers must be early up and it was time to open the wall bed and for Brin to go next door into her own warm room.

Blissfully she climbed at the end of every day into the deep featherbed, with the bedspread of white crocheted lace and another larger Sacret Heart bleeding above the brass rails at its foot, the pride and grace of and only picture in Teresa's parlor. Nightly she looked at it over the top of her sheets and replaced it in her mind with the little Virgin that had stood in Reverend Mother's room. Jonas would have carried in a few sods of turf on the shovel, from the kitchen fire, and in the small black grate they pulsed and glowed and turned the uneven whitewashed ceiling to a warm shadowy rose; filling the little room with their nostalgic, haunting smell. Immediately beyond her window, she could hear the small comfortable night noises of the animals in the yard, and knew she would finally wake in the morning to the boasting of the bright-tailed cock on the hen-house roof.

Practiced discipline thrust away thought, and she always slept at once, but the struggle of heart and mind came with each day at her first waking, in the dark before the dawn, as irrevocable as the convent bell.

Teresa had been cutting Brin's hair to thicken it, and rubbing her neglected hands with goose grease. Slowly her hair began to grow again, flattened and thinned by the binding of the coif, and they laughed together as they had laughed long ago, to see it growing in a crop of tawny curls.

"In faith, Miss Brin," cried Teresa, "you're no different from young Jon Jo in the cradle."

But Brin wouldn't go out, even to the village, without her cap.

"They'd be asking to come up and feel it," she said. "in case a nun's hair grew any different from other people's!"

Chattering and laughing with Teresa and playing with

the babies, she gradually became free of the long silences that had seemed impenetrable to begin with. Color came back into her pale, sun-starved face, and by the time Christmas was close, she looked much as she had always done.

But never once to anyone did she mention Gerrard's mother, or the reason she had left the convent; nor Gerrard himself. Nor Mary Rose nor John; and Teresa, who knew her better than she knew herself, clipped the pretty hair and tended the shapeless nails and watched her with anxiety. She knew the closing of the convent door had only freed the half of her, and a great deal was still as locked away as if she had never left the place. She had a long way yet to go, God help her, and no one could say what path it would take.

At Christmastime she went into Cork city in the cart with Jonas to buy presents for the two small ones, and for Teresa and Con and the good kind Jonas himself, who never once had said to Teresa that he would prefer his small house to himself. Firmly she closed her mind to all the memories of the city streets themselves, untouched by the Easter Rising, and also to the thoughts of other people for whom she should be buying gifts. And with whom she should be sharing Christmas.

But she saw them. In the wide street alive with Christmas, the shop windows piled with candied fruits and tins of tea and biscuits, many of them harrowing, with scenes of war on their bright sides. Turkeys hung like frames around the windows of the butchers', and holly crowned the pigs' heads and glittered in the piles of trotters. She saw them first, coming toward her on the crowded street, Mama and Maggie, and Denis Mary, grown so tall and lanky, his hair like curls of flame around the edges of his cap. The huge Christmas tree at Abbeygate rose up before her, and no strength of mind could dismiss it, ablaze with candles and all the children singing and Cookie and MacGinnis and Katty and the Maneen peering round the staircase door. Had her hands not been full of parcels, she would have held them out toward her mother.

Mama chose not to see her.

Maggie needed no prompting to do the same, but Denis Mary had to be seized by the hand and propelled past, wide blue eyes first astonished, and then, Sabrina saw, furiously angry. For several moments, Brin stood where she was, the cheerful Christmas crowd dividing round her like tide against a rock. In a while, she went on slowly down toward the bridge where Jonas had arranged to meet her for the journey home.

When they got there, there was an enormous wicker hamper, sent from Abbeygate in the dogcart with Tomasheen's old father, who did little now but hang about the stables polishing anything that would shine. No doubt, thought Brin, they felt he was least likely to be missed. Her eyes filled with tears as she looked at the cold pheasants and the ham and the tongue and the plum duff and the candied peel and fruit. Not for the gift, although she knew well the difference it would make in Teresa's slender purse. But for the thought of them all packing it frantically in the kitchen while Mama was out in Cork, Cookie and MacGinnis—and Papa nervously supervising the whole thing. He would no doubt be responsible for the bottle of his best malt, obviously rammed in at the end. Shoving the old man into the dogcart and hustling him off, threatening him with little short of death were he not home before the madam.

For all their sakes she hoped he was, and smiled again as she dried her eyes, understanding once more with sorrow that the lonely one was the smart, proud mother in the streets of Cork with the two children still young enough for her control.

Con came down after their quiet Christmas, although the bottle of malt did much to warm Jonas's heart and face. She had had the forethought to wear a pair of high-laced boots, and she and Brin went walking in the green hills where the mild air had already brought the violets into bloom along the banks, and the buds of primroses showed between the stones. When Con was gone, having released the red car and its driver, beleaguered in the village, by hurling a shower of pennies for the children, and roared away laughing in the scramble, Brin came slowly back up the hill to the little house.

Taking one of the scrubbed chairs beside the table where Teresa was up to her wrists in flour in a yellow crock, she absently caressed the soft curls of the baby who staggered up to clutch her skirt. She laughed then and looked down at him.

"Your hair even feels like mine, Jon Jo pet," she said, and the small boy crowed with pleasure as if she had made some marvelous joke. She bent and kissed his small face.

"Teresa," she said then, looking round the spotless room where she had been so content. The sun was pouring through the small window, and the fire glowed crimson under the bastable, waiting for the bread Teresa was mixing in the crock. "Teresa, it is time for me to go away. Con and I have been arranging it. I am going to live in Cork and do some work."

Teresa's hands grew still. She wasn't sure at all it was time for her to go away, but Miss Brin herself must have the say so. She smiled at Sabrina with affection and approval.

"I'm glad to hear that, Miss Brin. Very glad indeed."

Sabrina didn't misunderstand her. "I shall miss you all very much," she said.

"And what'll you do, Miss Brin?"

Marriage had put no weight on Teresa, as thin and rangy as the days when she used to be racing the stairs at Abbeygate with cans of boiling water.

"Miss Con is finding me lodgings." Fleetingly Brin wondered if the habit of calling her Miss Con would survive both Padgeen and divorce. Miss Brin had survived Sister Carmel. "It seems," she went on, "that the housekeeper in Castle Brackett has a sister. She's in a poor way financially as a widow, and she takes in a couple of ladies for an income. It sounds suitable. Very suitable if she has a vacancy. It's near the hospital. I hope she'll think I'm respectable."

Teresa's glance of contempt for anyone who would think otherwise dismissed that one. But she looked then sharply at Sabrina.

"The hospital?"

It could do good to no one, she thought, being barred up like that and they not wanting it. Sabrina read her mind and smiled, reaching out to touch a floury hand.

"No, Teresa. I'm all right. But I am going to train as a VAD."

Teresa's head tilted to one side and she beamed down at Sabrina in open pleasure. Her mind was flying backward to the lovely days in Kilfenora after they said the war was started, although at that time it was little enough she knew of it. Miss Brin had talked a lot then of being a nurse, but it had all blown away in the commotion over being a nun.

"Well now, Miss Brin. Isn't that what you always wanted?"

And could have done long ago, thought Teresa savagely, and been happy and had the boy as well. Were it not for some people. Even if she didn't want the marriage, and what was wrong with the lad anyway, there was no need to cheat her into the convent the way it was done. Please God she wasn't destroyed for life. The girl had hardly known what she was doing at the time, between Mr. John and all of it.

As for the other one. The boy's mother. Well, surely hell and all its torments were waiting in God's good time for that one.

She shook away her thoughts.

"How will you live, Miss Brin?" she asked practically, and Brin for the thousandth time wondered how without offense she was going to recompense Jonas and Teresa for these months, during which they would not take a penny.

"They gave me back my dowry when I came out," she said, and fell silent, remembering the cold face thrusting a turned envelope stuffed with a dangerous sum of money across the table, wordlessly demanding a receipt. And even that was before she realized that no one would offer her good-bye.

"Papa wrote to say that I could keep it," she said, and that letter had warmed her for a few short moments to the tears she seemed to have forgotten how to shed.

"So I'll be quite all right," she added.

Please God, thought Teresa.

"I'm very glad, Miss Brin," she said aloud. "Very glad."

Terence was very glad also, when he came to see her during a leave that began at the end of March.

"You're doing right," he said to her when the small

exchanges of their meeting were over and, oppressed by Brin's drab room, they strolled in a chilly dusk along the river. "You had to have something to do."

He glanced at her face, wrapped in a small close-fitting hat above the fur collar of her coat. Like Teresa, he thought her much improved, but there were strains and shadows that had not yet eased away. A sense that she was still only half-alive. Gently he eased his way toward the all-important question, speaking of the family one after the other.

"Terry," she said suddenly, helping him without realizing it. "What d'you think about Con? And Marcus?" Doubtfully she looked at him, wondering if she should ask him at all. "They're very happy," she said defensively.

It was a while before Terry spoke, raising his collar around his neck against the wind.

"He's a good, decent man, Brin. And her brother Terry is very glad to see Con happy, and well aware of what Brackett did to her. But you'll understand it all raises difficulties for Father Terence Heron."

He put her arm in his and they walked in silence for some minutes, Brin knowing he could give no other answer. Father Terence Heron could never condone a divorce and some civil marriage that would leave Con in his eyes still forever married to Patrick Brackett.

Terry seized the moment.

"And you, my love?" he asked her. "What of your young man. Have you written to him?"

He sensed her immediate withdrawal, and she shook her head, engulfed by something close to panic that seized her even at the mention of Gerrard's name, even though her deep heart was filled with longing.

"No," she said. "Not yet."

"Why?"

His voice was gentle but pressing. He felt the arm in his was trembling.

"I—I'm not ready yet."

"For Gerrard or for anybody?"

She stopped and turned to him in the misty dusk, amazement on her face. "There'll never be 'anybody.' There's only Gerrard."

"Good. Would you let me write to him for you?"

"No, no." He sensed the panic in her voice. "No. I'll do it. When I'm ready."

He took her hand in his and pressed it reassuringly as they walked on.

"All right, love. All right. Take your time."

The convent walls, he realized, were still up around the deep core of her being, and it would take some mortal shock to bring them down. God grant it wouldn't take the form of Gerrard's death, for that might utterly destroy her.

He sighed and turned the talk to other things as they headed home.

"This is only a little visit," he said. "I'm coming back through Cork when I've been to Abbeygate, and I'll stay awhile. I've no idea how long I've got or where I'm going. They'll send a wire for me."

Brin opened the small front gate and slammed away the picture of her home with the discipline still held from the convent. Terry's heart was sick with sorrow for her, but he said nothing, taking her key to open the front door.

"Come back soon," she said to him.

The cold spring winds of that year whistled from the sea and moaned around the cottage, nipping the young crops in Jonas's small acres. And in Flanders they howled across the barren, shell-stripped fields, bringing nothing but the breath of death and misery.

By April, they were pouring the mutilated hordes back home from the carnage of Arras and Vimy Ridge. They raced them from the specter of gangrene stalking the dressing stations and the clearing stations, up to the field hospitals, and then onto the trains for home as fast as they could load them, their wounds barely stitched, grey with shock and the blood still crusted into the dust of battle on their clothes.

The Irish regiments came back into Queenstown, into an Ireland as touchy as a keg of powder. They came wracked by the discomforts of the rough voyage in the hospital ship from Cherbourg, arriving exhausted and many of them already dead, on the long windy quay between the ship with its huge red crosses and the packed, foul-smelling train that would take them on to Dublin. To hospital. To another world. And for many of them to the end of their individual war.

A couple of weeks after Terry had spoken to Sabrina, seagulls were careening around a ship newly arrived, loaded beyond capacity with the wounded of Arras. They wheeled and screeched round the rigging, riding the cold wind that whipped in from the sea, picking irritatingly at the veils of the young VADs who moved urgently among the rows of stretchers brought from the ship and laid along the quay.

Persistently the wind searched its way in under the single dirty blanket covering a young officer who lay, still dazed with the shock of wounds and amputation, wishing to God it were not so cold, and attempting groggily to measure all that had happened to him in the last few days. How many? And indeed where was he? Ireland, he remembered carefully. Ireland, they said it was. Home. As if that were some golden gift that would make up for everything.

His head, wrapped in a comforter too big for him that slipped maddeningly down over his eyes, was pillowed only on his cap, and under the blanket he still wore his greatcoat. As he had been doing when what happened? Where? Nor did he know if in the agony and confusion they had ever taken it off. Probably not. Too busy taking off his leg. No time to take off his greatcoat. Left him that for consolation. And to keep him warm. He shivered and rolled his head, peering out below the comforter, and thought how blue the sky was. And why would it not be, he told himself carefully, in Ireland in the spring? There was little spring where he had come from. Although they said it wasn't all that good in Ireland now, either. It all blew up just after he'd left last year. Easter Rising. There was something funny about that. Brin would see it. Brin.

His coat was buttoned on the wrong buttons and let the wind in round his neck, but he was too exhausted to lift a hand, and the blanket had slipped, and all the nurse girls with the white veils were too far away.

From where he lay, the train waiting there looked high as a cliff, above him against the sky, and they were beginning already to load in the first lot of stretchers, the clanging doors smashing into his tired head. That was stupid. You'd think by now he'd be past caring about noise. He could feel the stubble rough and dirty on his face, and without moving his eyes he knew that the man on the stretcher next to him was dead. Ah, well. Death in Ireland. That was one of the things the old prayer asked for. And the woman of your choice to you, but his mother had seen to that one. Death in Ireland. That fellow had it, and his family to cry above his grave, God rest him, and not some stinking shell hole full of water with pieces of your friends afloat in it, and no one alive any better off than you were yourself.

Jesus, Mary, and Joseph, how could there be such pain in a foot they'd thrown into a lime pit somewhere outside Arras four days ago? Or how many days? You'd think with all these spare limbs God could make up quite a few new fellows and start it all over again. The Resurrection of the Body, they had taught him at school. Everyone perfect again. God would be busy finding some of the pieces after this lot. His mind roamed patchily, and he felt a weak desire to laugh or cry and didn't know at what at all.

There were women now, pushing a boiler on wheels and an urn on it steaming with tea, and the young ones in the veils were handing it out to the men on the stretchers. He could actually feel the tears in his eyes with the longing for the hot mug in his hand, but they would take a year to get to him. He rolled his head again, not to watch too desperately.

A young naval chaplain was coming slowly along the line of stretchers, speaking a word to every man who could hear him, smiling, writing down messages for others. Tell my mother I'm home. I'm sorry I died on the way. Tell my wife I've no legs but what matter to a farmer. His cap was in his hand, for many of those he paused by were already dead, and the wind ruffling his red-gold hair conveyed suddenly some unreachable message to the dazed, rambling mind of the young man on the stretcher. Some good memory of better places whispering round the edges of his shock.

With intense concentration, he watched the priest come

to the man next to him and kneel down quickly to close the dead eyes. He made the sign of the cross on the man's forehead with his thumb and pulled the blood-stiffened blanket up over his face. Then knelt to commend his soul to God.

The thin face, the color of the hair. Dear God, where was it? Somewhere happy before the world blew up. Weakly, the young captain fought to remember, and as the priest stood up from the next stretcher he caught the fierce intensity of the exhausted eyes. He came quickly, bending down.

"Can I do anything for you?" he asked the soldier. "There's tea coming. Would you care for a cigarette?"

He was the same as all the others, dirty and exhausted, the eyes red-rimmed in the shocked face, but this one was looking up at him with some special desperation, groping for words.

"Would you rather see one of your own army people?" he asked him then. "I'm only a sort of visitor here. Will I get you someone?"

The light tone, the humor that so easily lit the narrow face, a sense of security even in the man's smile. The captain stared intently and his lips moved. With slow, infinite difficulty he managed to withdraw a hand from under the blanket, and laid it on the gold braid of the priest's sleeve.

"Don't go away," he whispered hoarsely. "Don't go away. You're Sabrina's brother."

Dear God Almighty, thought Terry, and sat down beside the stretcher on the cold stone of the quay. How could he have recognized him without some help, in the state he was in, and the cap thing down to his eyebrows. But it's him all right. Behind him doors banged and whistles blew and the first train pulled out on its way to Dublin and he could hear the cheering of the obstinate little loyal crowd who still gathered at the harbor gates to meet the ships, despite the threats to anyone who would still show loyalty to the British Army.

But, dear God, what do I do now? Only yesterday he had seen her again to say good-bye, and she was still firm that she wasn't ready to see Gerrard.

"Gerrard," he said, and the soldier smiled weakly.

He played for a few moments' time.

"Have you all you want for the moment?" he asked.

Gerrard gave a small nod, his eyes full of questions, but Terence spoke first, nodding down at the blanket. "What is it?"

"My left leg. Below the knee, but they say they'll have to take it off again."

"Arras?"

"Orange Hill. Beyond."

A woman handed him a tin mug of tea with a photograph of Lord Kitchener on the side of it, and gently he lifted Gerrard's head and helped him drink it, much of it going, for all his efforts, down over the stained overcoat. The hot drink revived Gerrard, and he shook his head at more, no longer to be put off. Terence, beside him, laid down Lord Kitchener deliberately on the quay, his decision made.

At once, he answered all the questions in the exhausted eyes.

"She's out, Gerrard. She came out last October."

Gerrard's lids fell a moment, and Terry thought the shock had been too much for him. Then he opened them again.

"She found out," he said.

"She did." Terry wouldn't weary him with details. He could see he was barely able to speak, his face grey beneath the stubble. He pulled the blanket up round him to cover his cold hand, and still Gerrard didn't speak.

"And me," he said bitterly in the end. "Like this at the heel of the hunt."

"That," said Terry getting to his feet. He was aware of the clanking of the second train along the quay, and that there were others might need him. "That would be the least of it. Wouldn't you know that about Sabrina?"

Gerrard's gaze roamed over the tall figure, well suited by the dark uniform.

"You'll be here?" he asked him, as if for help.

Terry shook his head.

"I'm off this evening to Scapa. Train to Rosyth, and I'll get onto something there. I've been on leave and I heard this ship was in, so I came down to see what I could do."

"In Abbeygate?" The voice was only a whisper, and the priest had to look away from his eyes.

"Yes. But Brin wasn't there." Wouldn't tell him about that now either.

"I have to go now, Gerrard," he said. "God bless you. I'll be seeing you again now you're back."

Gerrard's eyes now were little more than slits, filmy. Terence hoped to God that what he said was true. As he began to move away, the eyes opened suddenly, bright and tender with the memory of amusement and love.

"Father," he said. "How is she?"

Terence paused a moment and then grinned. "Well," he said carefully. "Her hair's a bit odd. Can you imagine Brin with curls?"

An orderly was tying a label to the buttonhole of Gerrard's coat, and they were coming for his row of stretchers.

"It's like going back to school," he said feebly. With curls. Then, "Father."

"Yes," Terry said again.

"Give me a bit of a chance, will you," he said. "Don't tell my mother where I am."

The red-rimmed eyes fell closed, and quickly Terry moved back and read the label, making a note of it before he passed on to the other stretchers.

It was four days before the postman toiled on his high bicycle as far as he could go with it up the stony little road to the farmhouse in the green country beyond Passage West. When he could go no further he got off and mopped his brow with the cuff of his coat and propped the machine against the stone wall. In the bright soft morning he plodded up the last steep slope. So rare a visitor was he that Teresa was waiting for him at the half door, one small son peering from behind her skirts, the baby in her arms. Their big anxious eyes caught the feeling of her fear.

"What is it, Padraic? Is it a wire?"

Sure harbinger of disaster and death.

Well, it couldn't be anything to do with Jonas, and he was up over the lip of the hill in the top field. She had a sudden foolish urge to run up and see that he was still there.

" 'Tis a letter," he said portentously, feeling for it in his bag. "And from England at that."

Professional blankness closed Teresa's face. If it was from England it could only be to do with the family. Who would she know in England to be writing to her?

"Thank you, Padraic," she said, and took it from him. "Come in now and warm yourself and have a cup of tea. The wind is very cold still."

He had earned a small while in the wooden armchair at the fire, and a mug of scalding tea, to discuss the weather and the crops and the latest rumored activities of Sinn Fein.

There was a moment of somber and apprehensive silence in the warm little room, echoing the uncertainty of Ireland's future. And theirs with it, and all like them. Sinn Fein. Ourselves alone. The rebels, with growing strength and support, set on hurling out the English conquerors and taking Ireland back for the Irish. After close on a thousand years when conquerors and conquered had become so mixed that most had forgotten which was which.

"They'll have us all destroyed in the end," said Padraic, wiping the tea from his long moustache with the back of his hand. "Did you know young Matthew Mahon, was a groom over with your family—did you know he's on the run?"

Teresa's face creased with the waste of it. "Ah, no. What for?"

"Taking part in a raid on a police barracks. The father is heart-scalded, being a constable himself."

Correct young Matt, so proud of himself and his tailored coat with the brass buttons. You'd think it'd matter more to better himself. Now it would be prison or America. If he could even get away.

"Well, good-day to you now, Teresa, and I hope it will be good news."

She resisted the hint to open it in front of him, and watched him politely to the gap in the wall. Then she took it from her apron pocket, shushing away the children. The writing was unfamiliar, the address when she opened it a hotel in Rosyth. The letter looked hurried.

Dear Teresa, it said,

I don't exactly know where Miss Con is at the moment, so I would be most grateful if you would do something for us.

Would you go and see Miss Brin, and tell her that Captain Gerrard Moynihan is alive, but very severely wounded, in St. Peter's Hospital in Dublin.

Be easy with her, Tesa, and wait a few days to let the man get some strength. Tell her I'm going north now by sea, and will write to her from Scapa.

My regards to Jonas, and God bless you all.

Father Terence

Teresa looked out the small window above the green leaves of the geraniums, toward the long slope of the hill where Jonas worked, and tears of relief and happiness came hot into her eyes. Oh, thank God, said Teresa to herself. Oh, thank God. She longed for Jonas to come home so she could tell him.

CHAPTER 16

When Jonas's mother came up with the milk later in the day, she made all her arrangements with her, and neither of them, nor Jonas, questioned that she should go. The following evening she took the two babies across the hill to her mother-in-law, and in the next yellow dawn the loving and patient Jonas drove her the rumbling two and a half Irish miles to the halt where she could catch the early train to Cork. His father would collect her here in the evening, off the five o'clock.

Jonas would never shame himself by being seen kissing her, but his blue eyes rested on her with love and pleasure in the blue suit Mrs. Heron had given her for the wedding, and the white blouse she had made herself to go with it. And the gloves. There wasn't another woman he knew, had gloves. The village always said he had married above himself, and he was the first to agree with them, proud of it, and of his wife.

"Be quick now," he said, "and get back."

"And you take care," she said, and in the brightening day she turned into the tiny station that was no more than a platform of planks, and along the palings the bright advertisements that always made her think of the days long gone when the whole happy army of them used to be clamoring their way to Kilfenora. She climbed into the laboring train, the letter in her purse, and the pit of her stomach cold with nerves.

Never, until she lifted a hand to the black japanned knocker, had it occurred to her that Miss Brin might not be home, and the whole day gone for nothing. But the neat grey-haired woman with curious eyes who opened the door to her reminded her that it was Saturday, and on Saturdays Miss Heron had no duties. It gave her obvious pleasure to know more of Miss Heron's ways than did her caller. It was the door on the right at the top of the stairs, if the young lady would like to go up and knock.

Teresa knew her experienced glance had told her that she was acceptable, but definitely not family. She smiled and went up the worn stairs.

"Tesa!"

Sabrina's face lit with pleasure, but Teresa was shocked at how thin she had got, and saw that the strained look was back in her face. She gave her plenty of time for all the news and the questions about the babies, and asked after Miss Con.

Sabrina smiled.

"I think Miss Con is getting over her bad marriage," was all she said. "But, Tesa, what brings you to the city, and it so hard to leave the babies?"

It was the opening she wanted.

"I have a message," she said, and it tore her heart to see fear spring at once into the other girl's eyes.

"It's nothing bad, Miss Brin," she said hastily. "Nothing bad."

She gave her the opened letter, and as Brin took it out of the envelope with nervous fingers, Teresa walked over to the window, so that she might read it unwatched. In the absolute silence behind her, she looked along the shabby and respectable little street, with its small walls around the gardens and cindered paths up to the doors, the few flowers stunted by the cold April. There was no one in the street, and it was like an incident in a dream when the red de Dion Bouton hurtled round a corner further down and drew to an awkward stop outside the house.

"It's nothing bad," she had said to Sabrina, and would have gone to the ends of the earth to bring her the news she had just brought. But as she watched Con almost throwing herself from the motorcar, sick certain misery shrunk the flesh against her bones. There was something in the way Miss Con had scrambled from her seat almost before the motor had stopped, waiting for no help from the tall moustached man in the pale dustcoat who was driving. He caught her as she ran around the bonnet, and Teresa watched him take her hands, clearly pleading to come with her. Equally clearly she refused, wildly dragging her hands from his, and although she could hear nothing, Teresa knew she was telling him no, to wait, to wait, she must do this alone.

Teresa closed her eyes.

Gerrard must be dead, and oh, God, what now, for the sad-faced girl behind her? She didn't turn.

Con had a key. Her high heels clattered up the stairs as fast as she could come, and Teresa turned then as the door burst open. Con was more disheveled than she had ever seen her, her hair blown to pieces in the car without a veil, her eyes wild, and an opened wire crumpled in her hand.

As Brin stared at her, she slammed it on the table and began to pull it flat, too shocked with grief herself to remember to be gentle. Perhaps that's what the man below had been trying to say to her. Be gentle. But Con was past it.

"It's Terry," she gasped. "Terry. Torpedoed. Off somewhere called the Hoxa Sound, wherever God put that."

It took Sabrina a long time to reach out with stiff fingers and take the wire. Even then she didn't read it, staring dumbly at her sister. "He's dead," she whispered.

"Yes. Yes. At least missing, believed killed, and everybody knows that just means they haven't found the pieces. Oh, Brin, I can't bear it. Oh, Brin . . ."

The pert, sophisticated Con was nearly in hysterics,

torn as her sister was by far too many sorrows, far too deeply suppressed. Teresa went to her, and took her in her arms as she had done many times for childish griefs, and Con clung to her, crying wildly on her shoulder, releasing pent-up anguish in her flooding tears. She held her tight, as she might have done to comfort her for some wild injustice from Mama, and felt her growing quieter.

But Brin stood, staring straight in front of her beside the table, the letter from her brother in one hand and the blunt news of his death in the other. Her eyes were dark and overwide, and in the end her silence drew Con from her grief. She raised her head and began to pull herself together, taking the handkerchief Teresa offered, remembering John, and how Terry and Brin had always been special in the same way. Beyond her own anguish, she understood the fearful blow she had just delivered.

Haltingly, she told them all about it.

Some friend of Terry's must have had the Mellors' number from him, and had telephoned. Apparently it happened on the way out of Scapa Flow, where the Germans had submarines to try to catch them getting in. She and Marcus Mellor had driven at once over to Abbeygate, and found them with the wire just in their hands.

"Maybe I should have waited," Con said, "till she was a bit past the shock of it, but, Brin, my first thought was of you. I asked her could I come and get you and bring you home."

Now Brin's eyes left the distance and moved to rest on Con, knowing the answer.

"She said no," Con gasped and began to cry again.

Mama had stood beside the window in the hall, looking with distaste at the scarlet car below her steps, her face pinched and white, rejecting even comfort from Papa, as if to say that no one was going to help her with her grief, and why should anyone help Sabrina.

"I think she's gone a bit from the shock," Con said. "You couldn't credit it. She said you must lie on the bed you made for yourself, and learn to bear your sorrows like the rest of us."

And this is no time to tell that to Miss Brin either, thought Teresa, looking at Sabrina's expressionless face, but Miss Con, poor thing, was past being careful. That man downstairs would have known it, being with her all the morning.

Papa had turned away from Mama, and after one wild incredulous glance at her mother, Con had seized the wire still lying on the hall table and raced back out to the motorcar and into Cork, Marcus a tower of gentleness and consideration that she didn't even notice.

"Brin," she said now, suddenly frightened by the dreadful vacancy of her sister's face, "Brin."

Teresa looked from one to the other of them and thought her heart would bleed away for pity for the two lovely little girls she had cared for in some past happy time. She wondered should she go, and leave them together, to each other, and then Brin spoke, as if her name on Con's lips had broken some spell.

"C-C-C-Con," she said urgently. She had begun to stammer. "C-C-Con. You have the m-m-motor?"

Con nodded, not understanding, frightened now that the whole thing had been too much for her sister.

"I have. Marcus Mellor is driving me."

Brin whirled round and looked at the small clock on the mantel shelf behind her, and then back to Con.

"W-w-would, would it ever g-g-get me to the station to catch the one o'clock?"

"To Dublin?"

Con looked from her sister to Teresa, her own eyes wild now, not understanding.

"K-K-Kingsbridge. Yes."

She looked so unbalanced that Con was willing to promise her anything.

"Of course it would, Brin. Of course. But why?"

But Sabrina was already away, wheeling blindly into the bedroom and slamming drawers. Con's face was blanched and sharp. She looked after her distractedly.

"For God's sake, where's she going? Is she gone mad, Teresa? Is she gone mad over Terence?"

Teresa laid a gentle hand around her shoulders and showed her the letter from Terence that Brin had dropped on the table as she ran. Con began to cry again as she read it, but quietly, not with the same wild anguish. Tender relief flooded her face.

"Oh, thank God," she said, "for something."

"But you must go with her, Tesa," she said then urgently. "Go with her. She's not fit to be alone. Will you, Tesa?"

Fumbling in her soft calf purse, she rammed two ten-pound notes into Teresa's hand. Both of them knew that the presence of Teresa, trained since childhood to be there and yet not be there, was exactly what Brin needed at the moment. Unhesitatingly Teresa pushed the money into her own purse.

"You'll go out and tell Jonas, Miss Con? The father'll be meeting the five o'clock."

"I will. I will."

"His mother will keep the babies. And you, Miss Con? Will you be all right?"

Con's lovely face was ashen, but she smiled then at Teresa.

"Thank-you, Tesa, yes, I'll be all right. I have someone with me."

They both turned to Sabrina as she came racing from the other room, stuffing money haphazardly into her own purse.

"I'm ready," she said. "C-c-can we g-go, Con?"

Con set aside her own grief.

"Would you not put on a hat?" she asked her wild-eyed sister gently, and Sabrina put her hands up to her head as if she didn't understand she hadn't got one. She crashed back into the bedroom to reappear with a soft blue tam-o'-shanter crammed down over her conspicuous hair, curling down her neck, too short still to hold a hairpin.

She was out of the door before either of them, and down the cindered path to the front gate, standing by the motor to stare blindly at the tall man with a soft moustache, who looked at all of them stampeding from the house with gentle and concerned blue eyes.

"This is Marcus Mellor, Brin. Claire's brother," Con said briefly. "Marcus, my sister has need to catch the one o'clock to Dublin."

With a glance and a small gesture she indicated to him to get going at once without comment. The talking could come later. Brin gave him one glance from empty eyes and a small nod, and he didn't look again at her tragic face as he helped her up the high step of the red motor. Only as he laid a plaid rug across her knees did she say mechanically.

"Th-th-thank-you."

Like a well-trained child remembering its manners.

Teresa, asking God when it was all going to end, scrambled in on the other side of her, and Marcus helped Con into the front with a tenderness and solicitude that Brin was past noticing.

At the station, Con was proved right, and Brin stood in numb indifference while Teresa ran to get the tickets. Con went after her.

"Take care of her, Tesa," she said. "She's not herself."

Teresa stared at her. Merciful God. Not herself.

"Miss Con," she said, "will you tell me what in the name of providence will I do if this one's dead when we get there?"

Con put her hands over her eyes. She was trembling from head to foot. She took her hands down and looked over to where her sister was standing with rigid impatience beside Marcus at the barrier. The station was full of the smell of soot and smoke and the hollow clang of buffers and the rumbling of the porter's trolleys.

"If he is, Teresa," Con said slowly. "Then there's no God. Go on now and get her onto the train. Let her feel she's going. And God bless you, Tesa. I'll go and see about Jonas and the babies."

Teresa collected Sabrina and handed in their tickets at the barrier, and Sabrina never even thought to say goodbye. Con slid her hand into Marcus's, and he gave her one quick glance and held her fingers tightly. In silence they watched Brin and Teresa walking through the crowds along the train.

When the train got to Dublin, after some long delay at Limerick Junction that nearly threw Sabrina's reason, the first gas lamps were being lit along the streets, soft with the dark violet dusk of spring. It was Teresa who raced out of the station and got a horse cab, and it occurred to her that if anyone asked Miss Brin for a ticket or money or anything at all, they would be brushed off like a fly. Sabrina sat in the cab exactly as she had sat in the train, rigid, her eyes empty, her hands gripping her purse, and her mind cleared of everything except where she must go. Teresa had been aware of the curious glances and the whispers from the other people in the carriage.

Nor did she now notice the sad, dreadful ruin of Sackville Street, only Teresa gasping with dismay at the shattered shops, the black streaks of fire still marking the walls above their boarded windows, the proud and total ruin of the Post Office, hinge of the rebellion. A crackle of rifle fire was breaking the uneasy truce, and Teresa looked nervously at Sabrina, who had heard nothing, nor smelt the acrid waft of burning somewhere down by Moore Street, where a cloud of smoke hazed the darkening sky.

The cabby sensed her anxiety, turning for a moment from his rangy horse.

"Ye'd need to take no heed of that," he said. "'Tis only banging away for the pleasure of it."

Teresa subsided, remembering with sadness the beautiful elegant street where more than once she had been shopping with Mrs. Heron. And in Grafton Street too, trotting along behind her with all the packages and listening carefully to all the instructions from the dressmakers on how to care for the madam's lovely clothes, many of them brought from London itself.

Below the steps and columns of the hospital, Sabrina leaped from the cab as if she were alone, and once more Teresa thanked God Miss Con had had the sense to send her with her. She saw the blue tam-o'-shanter was down around her ears. Miss Brin, who always cared for everything she wore being right. She herself no longer hurried, knowing limply that there was nothing now for her to do but wait. She paid the thin old cabby, whose lugubrious eyes followed the flying Sabrina with sad speculation.

"There's trouble," he said, tucking away the coins in his layers of overcoats and mufflers. "Surely to God, there's trouble."

"I hope not," Teresa said, and followed Sabrina up the steps. When she got into the big, tiled hallway, she was already out of sight, and Teresa got out her rosary and settled herself quietly on one of the benches along the walls.

When Brin had raced inside, she found a nun at a big desk with a sort of glass fence round it, and a number of people coming and going as if it might be a time for visitors. And what, some last remaining gleam of sense asked her, would she do if it wasn't? Clasping and unclasping her hands, she took her place behind a small fat woman from the country who had trouble in knowing what the nun was saying, and when it came to her turn she was almost incoherent, staring dumbly at the nun for several seconds, unable even to remember Gerrard's name. The tam-o'-shanter had slipped to the back of her head, haloing her distraught face with tawny curls.

With maddening calm, the nun eyed her disapprovingly, obviously thinking her no suitable visitor for anyone, and ran a slow methodical finger down a page of a register behind the desk. Then she told her carefully and precisely where to find him.

"But you are late," she warned severely. "You have barely fifteen minutes left."

She began to repeat her instructions again, but for all Brin cared she might have been describing the bottom of the sea. Her mind had taken it all the first time, and she was already making for the polished corridor leading from the hall, its walls painted a drab green. To the left. She swerved round, never slackening her pace, and then to the right, darting aside from the way of a stretcher on high wheels, throwing just one fleeting glance, reassured by a head of bright red hair against the pillow. To the left again and down a little flight of stairs, skidding on the oilcloth, and the fourth door on the right the woman had said, and she crashed it open in her rush and there was a lot more light and rows of beds and people sitting beside them turning angry faces at the noise she made hurtling through the door. And a nun at the far end of the long ward beginning to get up from a table.

Gerrard saw her before she saw him, and he said to her afterward let no one tell you you can't split the world open like you'd cut an apple because that's what happened to him. She was charging down the polished floor almost at a run, her eyes going frantically from bed to bed, all the beautiful planes of her face sharp and fierce with the repression of her grief. The hat was on the back of her head and the lamplight in all the foolish curls around her face.

He knew then that after all of it, God was good.

In spite of the agony, he raised himself on his elbows, not willing she should find him lying down. She saw him then, and heeled over like a dinghy in a squall, and for one fearful moment, he thought she was going to come down on his leg, or where it had been. It would still be worth it, if he lived to know.

But she had grabbed a chair as she came, hurtling it down beside him, and the nun on duty was coming like vengeance up the ward.

Her overwhelmed and tragic eyes were only inches from his own, and he could smell her sweet fragrance and see the sheen on the pale hair. For a long moment she stared at him, and then drew a breath, no more than a shuddering gasp, and he could see her shaking with it, releasing all her heart had held secret since the day he left.

"G-G-Gerrard." She could hardly speak. "G-Gerrard. T-Terence is dead. Ah, God. And John. And M-Mary Rose. And G-Gran. And Mama won't—"

As if she had only just now heard of it. All at once. She looked at him, incredulous of such despair, as if waiting for God, or someone, to tell her it was all some terrible mistake.

"And you—" she added then, and it seemed the worst of all, "And you—"

He let himself drop back onto his pillows, and the ceiling heaved and roared like the sea with pain. But it freed his hands. He took the tousled head down onto his shoulder.

"Oh, my love," he said. "My poor, poor love."

In late September, on a golden morning with the swallows on the telegraph lines twittering to each other of the winter, and Gerrard well out of the hospital and trying to make friends with a wooden foot, they were married in the little church close to Brin's rooms.

"There'll be no one," she had said to him fiercely. "No one. Only, of course, Tesa and Jonas, and Con for me and your mother for you."

Still finding it difficult to handle memory. Mary Rose's wedding. And that unbelievable morning when she had walked up crowned as a bride on Papa's arm, never knowing that Gerrard was crouched watching in the benches.

"No one," she said again.

"Well," he said, "you'll not keep my dear mother away. She's convinced now she organized the whole thing."

Brin was ready to forgive the world, and tried not to think of Mama, who would not forgive her.

"Well," she said, "it's nice to be someone's white-haired girl."

"Like mine," he said, and she grinned and they sat in happy silence while the bells of Shandon Church launched themselves into the "Garryowen," split a few moments later by one short quick spat of rifle fire. Sabrina jumped, and Gerrard looked toward the city center, his face grave.

"You know all hell is going to break loose here soon, Brin," he said. "It'll come to civil war. I'm glad to get you away."

Immediately after the wedding they were going to the house in Windsor, where they would live, and where Gerrard hoped eagerly to see his children as happy as he had been himself. He saw a wistful expression on Sabrina's face.

"Do you mind leaving?" he said, realizing he had never asked her. "Do you mind leaving Ireland?"

Brin reached out and touched his face with her fingers, smiling into his eyes.

"I'd go to Timbuktu after you, you know that. Didn't I make a holy show of myself following you to Dublin?"

The bells drifted gently to the end of their tune.

"Thank God you did," he said. "Thank God you did."

"Papa is very proud," she said then, "that his family have been in the same townland for almost a thousand years."

"Too lazy to move," Gerrard said, smiling, and then looked down at his feet.

"Well," he said then. "I'm only half-Irish but I'll be damned if I'll follow it through and try and give my second leg for Ireland now I've given the first one for England."

He eased himself into a more comfortable position.

"No," he said contentedly, "I'll settle for being what my father was."

"Yes?"

"An English gentleman with a great love for Ireland and a house to come to whenever we fancy. Brin, it'll be terrific. We'll have the tenants out of Ardnateely in six months. Best of both worlds. We're very lucky."

Very lucky. Mama. The convent. The grim determination of Gerrard's mother to separate them. All the strange thing about the lunatic. Gerrard's leg. Yet here they were after all, and being married in a fortnight.

"Yes, my love," she said. "Very lucky."

She sighed contentedly and Gerrard put an arm round her, hoping he wouldn't tip them both into the river. In a while he stood up awkwardly, leaning on his stick. One of the first things she had realized was that she mustn't help him, or even watch him with any particular concern.

He carried no stick a fortnight later as he limped out of the sacristy to meet her as she came up the aisle with Con. The small church was plain and bare and poor, but the windows along the sides were filled with yellow glass, and with the early sun its ugliness was swamped and defeated by a haze of golden light. She saw Jonas and Teresa, who had spent one grand excited night in a hotel. And on the right-hand side at the front, in the place of honor, was the squat black figure of Cousin Anna. Wry humor was beginning to surface again in Brin, and she thought fleetingly that it was no more to be expected than that she would finish at her wedding with no guest but the old black crow.

A handful of parishioners for the early Mass slid curious eyes from hoods and shawls, growing compassionate as they realized it was a wedding.

"The creature," said a hoarse whisper as she passed. "Willya look at her, and she to be alone like that. And the young fella himself wid' a peg leg."

For one second, memory tore at her, and she saw the village chapel submerged with flowers for Mary Rose, and all the family ranked on either side and her sister

standing in the shadowy hall with Papa as she had drive
off with Mama. Waiting.

Then Gerrard turned with infinite slowness at the alta
and she could see the pain in his face behind the smile
She knew that God had in the end given her all sh
wanted.

Con had firmly managed it all, taking Brin, in spite o
all protests, to her dressmaker, Brin arguing all the wa
that her absolutely quiet wedding wouldn't need suc
grandeur, she could buy herself a dress down in Patric
Street. Con had insisted, and Brin found a long forgotte
delight in choosing the soft dress of ruffled ivory silk, an
the little hat to match it, tipped down over her eyes wit
cream roses gathered on the brim at the back. Her hai
was long enough now to put up, but hopelessly and fo
ever curly.

"Con," she said. "I'd forgotten. Isn't it fun?"

"Of course it is," said Con, who had recovered all he
own bright sparkle. "And you'd better get back to i
all if you want to hold that marvelous man of yours."

Brin smiled softly and didn't contradict her.

Coming up the little aisle, the dress was no mo
than an offset to her lovely face, serene with happines
the grey eyes resting steadily on the young man waitin
for her with such precarious balance at the altar.

"You'll be ready to catch me," he had said the da
before, "if I fall flat on my face. Although, God know
it's not the first bridegroom it'll have happened to i
Ireland."

Guided by Con, he had sent her a bouquet of mo
roses to match the ones on her hat, and the fragile ho
house perfume hung between them as he leaned to ki
her, and she had unobtrusively to put out a hand t
steady him before he could stand upright again. H
winked at her.

He had no idea what she was wearing, except that
was the same color, engraved on his mind, as on the fir
evening he had seen her at Abbeygate. And we, h
thought, but children, and look at all that has happen
to us since. A sort of no color, and the famous pearls
the same evening, for which, did he but know it, he ha
Con to thank, since she had returned all the gifts S

brina had made to her on entering the convent. Maggie had returned nothing.

The young parish priest was waiting already for them, plump and with a calm benignity beyond his years. He surveyed them indulgently through rimless glasses as Gerrard got himself round to face the altar, and his magnified eyes flickered at Con as she moved off and sat in the seat corresponding to Cousin Anna's, who was already genteelly mopping her eyes with one of her black-bordered handkerchiefs. Brin glanced after Con, having some vague idea that she should stay beside her, but having reached Gerrard, he was the world alone and she had lost real consciousness of anybody else. Footsteps on the flagged floor behind her meant nothing. Gerrard was here and she cared no more for anything.

She saw the young priest beam with some conspiratorial pleasure, and had not even time to think about it before Papa was at her side, and Ulick moving in beside Gerrard.

She knew she mustn't cry, and choked the tears back into her closing throat, laying a trembling hand on Papa's arm. He couldn't look at her, staring straight ahead at the gaudy little altar as though the salvation of his immortal soul depended on it.

Ulick was a little easier, and she turned to where he was talking to Gerrard.

"Have you a ring?" he was asking him. "Because we brought this one. It was Gran's."

He fished the heavily embossed ring from his vest pocket, and Sabrina and Gerrard looked at each other, and she could not fail to see the triumph behind his eyes. But they had chosen together a plainer and more fashionable ring and had it engraved with their names and the date. Gerrard took it from his pocket.

"You decide, my love," he said, and the young priest's glasses flashed in the sun as he looked from one to the other.

"Will I tell you what," the priest said. "We'll marry you with the new one, and then put the old one on the other hand to be sure you remember."

They could all smile then, and she could look at Papa, her eyes deep with love and gratitude; but his were still unsteady, fearing to be overwhelmed by happiness when he had for so long been summoning his strength to bear with sorrow.

"The good people back there," said the priest, "will be wondering if they are ever going to hear a Mass today."

"We're ready, Father," Gerrard said, and could have added that before God it had taken some reaching.

Sabrina stood beside him through the mercifully short Mass, since he was unable to kneel down, the cheerful young priest cantering through it so fast the gasping little altar server barely had time for the responses.

When the kissing and the hugging and the signing were all done in the vestry, Gerrard refused his stick for walking down the aisle, although his face was drawn and grey.

"You'd think," Papa said, and he seemed twice as large as when he'd come in, "that it was the quality of Dublin you were going out to face and not a few poor old women with nothing else to do."

Gerrard gave his arm to Sabrina and laughed.

"I can't say I'll lead her from the altar on my own two legs," he said, "but by God, I'll not lead her on three."

She took his weight as best she could and leaned to his uneven step, not looking down the church in her care of his turning at the altar steps. Slowly they left the musty little vestry and turned down the aisle toward the door.

Teresa she had expected, and her good kind man.

But not Dermot, with his hesitant smile below the hanging curls, and the look he would carry all his life of not quite knowing what had happened to him. But he beamed uncomplicated pleasure from his place on the edge of the aisle.

Nor did she expect MacGinnis, trumpeting noisily into a huge red handkerchief and mopping his old eyes, Cookie beside him, sitting down in deference to her destroyed feet, wearing the purple hat with the pigeons' wings and a smile that stretched from one side of her crimson face to the other.

Tomasheen's child's grin looked as if it had come to rest by accident, six foot up on his tall man's body.

And across the aisle, Eugenia and Euphemia MacRory Glynn, dressed to kill, could barely breathe between excitement and the confines of their corsets.

Then Sabrina cried. But couldn't stop smiling either, looking at the enduring love that had warmed her childhood with security, given her the strength to battle through until today.

"But why didn't you tell me?" she asked Gerrard at the door.

He looked at her deeply, tenderly. "Because, my darling, if I'd asked you, you'd have said no. You'd have said you weren't ready to face it. But I knew you were."

And he was right.

Marcus Mellor was outside, with warm delighted kisses, and the de Dion Bouton all aflutter with white ribbons, and when Con ran over to stand beside Marcus, she was as radiant as the bride.

There was a great wedding breakfast arranged at Blake's Hotel, with the Maneen and Katty Ann standing guard over it until they all came, and when the nice young priest tried to say he had other things to do, they almost took him bodily and packed him into the red motor between Con and Marcus, the bride and groom high and proud in the backseat.

The cake was as big and wonderful as anything that Con or Mary Rose had had, and Brin had to go at once with Cookie and admire all the exquisite spun sugar, and listen to the tale of how it had been made, with shrieked interpolations by Katty Ann, hysterical with excitement and complicity.

"And wasn't the poor ould MacGinnis," roared Cookie, "near beaten to his coffin with staying up till four o'clock in the mornings, keeping all the doors in the house open to let out the smell of baking for fear it would waken up the madam."

Proudly and contentedly she put her feet to rest on a chair beside her cake and grandly accepted a glass of malt from the worn-out MacGinnis, whose beaming face showed little of the ordeal of being beaten to his coffin.

Brin found herself beside her father, and leaned a moment wordlessly against him.

"Oh, Papa," she said then.

"Denis Mary wanted to come," he said, "but she wouldn't let him. He sent you his love."

With one long, sober glance they acknowledged her absence, and then set it aside, and no one mentioned her again except Cousin Anna, who, well softened with the little tents of malt, leaned her black bulk confidentially toward Papa later in the morning, just before Sabrina went away.

"Wouldn't you think," said Cousin Anna righteously, and the corncrake voice penetrated everywhere, "that Honor would be here today to see her daughter married. When all's said and done, don't we have to forgive our children everything? In the end, no matter what they've done, we must let bygones be bygones."

There was a staggered silence and from the corner of her eye Brin saw Con collapse convulsively onto Marcus's shoulder. She herself dared not meet Gerrard's eyes. Papa gaped for one long moment, then looked down his nose at Cousin Anna with an expression of dislike so devastating that it moved even her to the understanding that she had gone too far.

Brin came up to kiss him good-bye, and her grin was without rancor. He was still gazing after Cousin Anna as if he did not believe in her.

"She has decided," he said to Brin, "to let bygones be bygones."

"I heard her. She has a great heart, Papa. Do you realize I'll have to teach my children to be polite to her, just like we were?"

Papa looked down at her, and his mild blue eyes gleamed.

"I never was," he said with honesty and satisfaction.

She hugged him then and kissed him good-bye.

"Dearest, dearest Papa," she said. "Thank-you for it. Thank-you."

He said nothing, but patted her on the shoulder, accolade, affection, and consolation from him for as long back as she could remember.

CHAPTER 17

When her eldest child was four and a half years old, Sabrina sat one afternoon sewing in the warm bright drawing room of the house in Windsor. It was early spring and chilly, the fire welcome, but there was a clear vivid light over the stretches of the great park beyond the windows, and in the long front garden Tomasheen was clipping the first straggles of growth from the tops of the yew hedges.

Intent on his work, in his own silent world, he didn't hear, and so didn't see, the approach of an erect and elderly gentleman through the front gates and up the carefully kept walk. With him was a red-haired boy of about sixteen, patiently adapting his pace to that of the heavily built older man. Tomasheen clipped carefully on, convincing himself that there was actually something to clip.

Denis Mary paused and watched him.

"Will I go up and touch him, Pop?" he asked cautiously.

"Do not," Papa said at once. "Do not. I'd be afraid he'd

take a puck at you with the clippers." He had always avoided having to acknowledge Tomasheen's infirmity, kept at a safe distance by the hierarchy of the servants. "Sure," he added, "I could do no more than grin at him."

He arrived on the spotless doorstep and pressed the round brass bell, admiring the Georgian solidity of the house, and then peering impatiently through the stained glass panels of the door.

"There's someone," he said contentedly, seeing the shadow come along the hall.

Both to him and the boy there was something vaguely familiar about the neat little maid who opened the door, but no more than that, so after a small pause, Papa merely asked if Mrs. Moynihan was within.

"She is, sir. She is."

"Well, will you just tell her that Mr. Heron is here. Will you do that?"

She smiled and bobbed and let them in, and Papa gazed with fresh approval along the wide hall, from which green-carpeted stairs led up to a huge bay window on the landing, pouring light into the house.

" 'Tis solid," Papa said. "Solid."

Denis Mary said nothing. To him it was a house he had grown to love and in which he had known much happiness, and before he could raise any comment, Brin herself came racing down the stairs to throw herself into her father's arms.

"Papa! Oh, what a wonderful surprise! But why didn't you tell me? Oh, how lovely."

He hadn't set his eyes on her since the day they had driven off from Blake's Hotel in that red machine Con had at the time, and now he held her at arm's length and felt he could echo her own words. How lovely.

Lovely indeed, as brilliantly beautiful as all her childhood had promised, but the strains gone now, her beauty softened by happiness to a gentle calm. The hint of nonsense was still there in her eyes, the look of hilariousness that had first caught Gerrard.

"We thought we'd surprise you," he said. "I left the bags down at the station for the lad to bring over. We were across, the pair of us, to John's grave."

She glanced at him tenderly.

Ah, she thought. And slipped the leash on the way home.

"Oh, Papa," she said. "Dearest Papa. I am so glad to see you. The children are out, thank goodness. Come on up to the fire and we'll have a few moments' peace before they come home."

She linked her arm into his and led him up the wide green stairs.

"To think," she said, "that Con and Marcus were here only last week."

"I know," he said complacently, but she noticed how slow he was on the stairs. "We had a couple of days with them too."

She grinned, amazed at how he had adapted himself to all the impossible situations, like Con's divorce, determined never to lose the children he so loved, for all that he had never been able to frame it into words.

"Oh, Papa," she said again.

Soon after she and Gerrard had been married, Marcus Mellor had brought Con to England, where the whole matter of their divorce and subsequent civil marriage could be brought about with less comment and scandal among the masses of London. Marcus had obtained some position with an organization for caring for the widows of servicemen, being, as he said, too old and fragile a fellow for racing off with a gun. The war over, they had settled down in Devonshire where Marcus was contentedly farming a large acreage of the soft red earth beyond Honiton; and in their lovely old house, Con offered flippant but delighted love to a small girl who looked like Mary Rose and a little hellion of a baby son who she was compelled to admit was no more than herself all over again.

"You found them well?"

"I did," he said. "I did." Not even to her could he admit the struggle to hold back the tears when the little girl had leaned against him and lifted the dark blue eyes of his Mary Rose.

"Gerrard'll be home about half five," she said as she led him to the broad sofa by the fire, scooping away her sewing. "You get my letters?"

"I do," he said, and there was a note of determination

in his voice, as if perhaps there had once been dispute about it.

"Then you'll know," she said, "that he's back to his grindstone."

Papa nodded his approval. Not his inheritance, nor his wooden leg, had stopped Gerrard from going back to start again on his qualification as a solicitor.

"I'd say this is a sound town for a practice. Sound."

Papa's shrewd eyes had estimated Windsor on his walk from the station, and he gave it his approval.

Brin smiled and settled him by the fire, giving Denis a quick kiss to tell him she'd talk to him in a moment. Sadly she noticed that Papa's thick hair was now completely grey, his movements slow and heavy.

"And how," she asked him then gently, "was John's grave?"

Papa turned his eyes on her, their bright blue dimmed and hazed by all his losses. They grew abstracted, looking back, in the bright room, to the fearful, indescribable harvest he had seen being reaped across the flat wet fields of Flanders.

"It's the same," he said heavily, "the same as all the others."

In the silence, Brin rang and ordered tea from the pretty little maid.

"Who's that?" Papa said, watching her from the room. "Do I know her?"

"Tesa's little sister." Brin smiled. "And I have Cookie's niece down in the kitchen."

"And Tomasheen in the garden," chimed in Denis in his unstable voice. "I always wonder why you ever left home."

There was a dreadful silence and Denis flushed scarlet.

"Sorry," he said. "Boob major," and Brin laid a hand on his and grinned reassuringly. Then she turned back to Papa.

"Did you hear lately from Terry?" he said, and in his company, newly back from John's grave, Brin felt again the sick lurch of loss and anguish that had for so long accompanied the mention of Terry's name. Even for a long time after they knew he was safe. For a long time after the blunt and ragged postcard had come to say he was a prisoner of war, picked up by the very submarine that had torpedoed him. "Though not," he was to say afterwards, "from anything to do with Christian charity or love of their enemies, but that they'd have dragged the devil himself from the sea in that area to try and get information about Scapa. I was a terrible disappointment to them, having never been inside the place. I think they came near to throwing me back, were it not for the collar. And mind you, my cap on all the time. The ship blown to pieces under me feet, and the cap on my head as if it was nailed to it, even when they picked me up!"

"I had a letter last week," she said. "Real Terry. I'll show you. I'm a bit sorry for those abos."

When Terry had been released from his prisoner-of-war camp, he did as he had long ago told Con and requested to be sent to the foreign missions. Secretly Brin felt that the embarrassment of Con and Marcus had a lot to do with it, but he seemed now vastly contented in the lost hot world of the Northern Territories of Australia, grappling through the heat and the dust and the rains to bring the word of God to the aborigines. Happy, Brin realized, as he had not been since he lay before the altar at Maynooth. "Although," he had written, "these small men are such determined characters, I'll need to watch out, or I could finish up as the first white abo from the northern hemisphere, and be back to Abbeygate with a couple of bones through my nose."

"And how is Mama?" she asked then, unable to leave it any longer.

He sighed.

"I don't think," he said, "any more than the rest of us, she ever got over the burning of Abbeygate."

Any more than you, above all, thought Brin, and once more thanked God she had not been there to see it.

Abbeygate had gone up, and Castle Brackett, on the same bleak dark December evening; with them, most of the other big houses of the county, and half the villages; and Schull and Skibbereen and Kinsale and the greater part of Cork city itself. Hour after hour the low clouds had hung scarlet over County Cork, flickering with reflected flames, until in the end, people said, God had intervened, and they broke, the sheets of rain putting a hissing, steaming end to the terrible night's work.

Ardnateely had been saved, partly by the rain, and partly by the natural disinclination of the country lads who had been detailed to fire it and in their hearts saw no good reason for burning something that had been there as long as they could remember and never did them any harm. Their indifference, for which they suffered later, was such that when the rain gave them a chance to back out of it, they didn't even think to take away the paraffin, leaving the cans stacked on the mosaic floor of the portico, from where it was removed with great prudence by Gerrard's caretaker, and used for many a long day to kindle the kitchen range.

Gerrard nevertheless thought it wise to allow a few years to elapse before they took their family to the house, a plan they dared at last to cherish for the coming summer.

But Abbeygate had been burnt to the ground, and Papa's face still grew dark with anger when he spoke of it.

"I asked the fellow," he said quite suddenly, as if it was still on the very top of his mind and he had been waiting only to see her to say it. "I asked him in the name of God, why us? And the terrible thing was, it was a nephew of MacGinnis, and the bit of Sinn Fein ribbon round his sleeve, and MacGinnis the poor man ready to drop with the shame of it I'd sent your mother away at once in the trap with the little girl who looks after her now, and Mrs. Cook, and sent old Patrick to drive them to the other house, and wasn't it providence we hadn't tenants in it. And the boyo says to me, the young sprat and giving himself some military title and he no older than Denis Mary, that hadn't I fought for the tyrant, and my sons as well as myself. And by God, Sabrina, I didn't know what in hell or heaven he was talking about. It was MacGinnis told me the fool meant England. And I asked him then who else would I have fought for, and me in the British Army and my sons with me, was it the Germans, I asked him. He said I was lucky not to be put inside the house when it went up. I mind MacGinnis pulling me away because I was near hitting him, and then we were all running round like ferrets trying to get as much out as we could before they fired it."

He sat breathing heavily, and Brin laid a hand on his. He took his eyes from the fire and looked at her, still truculent, the deepest wound not the loss of his house but to be classed as an enemy of Ireland.

"The Herons," he said then, and to Brin it was familiar. "The Herrings we were then, probably with bits of nets down on the strand for fish, would have seen the English lads with their tin suits coming over here to conquer Ireland, and building Castle Brackett."

Brin choked back laughter for the description of the Normans, remembering she must tell Gerrard.

"Papa," she said to halt him, "you're talking like MacGinnis."

"And if I am talking like that good man," he said, "what better? God rest him." He sat silent a moment. " 'Twas being his nephew doing it that finished him."

Brin thought the last sentence more than ever MacGinnis, but echoed the prayer for his soul. MacGinnis had died two months after the burning, struggling to establish a new home for what he considered his family.

"Anyway," Papa said, and Denis was looking resigned. "The Herrings did well enough before the English came, and we did well by them, and I've no doubt the Herons will survive now they've gone, just as long as all the lads signing their treaties up there in Dublin Castle will remember we're as Irish as themselves."

" 'Tis hard on Ulick," he added. "Hard. He deserved better. 'Tis no matter to Maggie, praying away in her convent, and Denis here is heart set to be a doctor. But 'tis hard on Ulick, who should have had it all."

And never wanted it, thought Brin. Would sell it all in the morning for John's red coat. But she said nothing, and fortunately the children came rushing in then, for she could not bear the sadness of Papa's face, or the settled lines of endurance that had come to mark it. She needed Denis then, to ease their shyness with this legendary Grandpapa whose picture had hung on the wall as long as they could remember but whom they had never seen.

Papa had his own way of bridging gaps.

"Denis," he said, eyeing the two small boys who stood on the far side of the hearthrug with a certain degree of mistrust. The scarlet-cheeked baby clawed up his legs, too young to be troubled. "Denis, will you go down to the hall where we left my small bag, and bring it up to me like a good fellow."

Affectionately Brin watched her young brother from the room. With a bit of juggling of school holidays and a few downright lies, he had managed to see quite a lot of her. A calm one, like Ulick, with a hint of the wildness that had always laid its hand on Terry. Then she noticed with infinite tenderness and an unbearable thickening of her throat, that her baby daughter was turning the seal of Papa's watch chain with plump, careful fingers, her face absorbed. Red to green to red. To green to red. She grunted her satisfaction and lifted her head to give Papa a radiant toothless smile of congratulation that he should own such a treasure.

Terence, her eldest, came to her when all the rummaging and distribution was done, leaning confidentially on the arm of her chair.

"Look," he said, almost with awe. "Look, Mammy." His small face, so like Gerrard's, was rapt with wonder "Look what the Grandpapa gave me. Put it to your eye, and when you move it, it goes all different. Look."

She took the red kaleidoscope and held it up toward the light of the windows, her children about her and her father by her side. Slowly she turned it, and clearly, small and far away, lost in the moving colors, she saw the splendid evening before Mary Rose's wedding, when she had felt herself to be one of these fragile pieces, uncertain of her safety in the falling shapes.

But it was not she, she knew now, who had faded and fallen away. The colors had stilled and the pattern changed with sorrow and tragedy still unbelievable to all those it had engulfed in so short a time. It was not she who could find no place in the new design.

It was Mama, left with her principles and a couple of politely indifferent sons, in the small house almost in sight of the charred ruin of Abbeygate. It was Mama, God help her, for she would never change now.

Sabrina felt the threat of overwhelming sadness, and

then downstairs heard the faint click of the front door closing. Quickly she gave the toy back to her son and set him aside with a kiss.

"Wonderful, pet. Wonderful!"

Quickly she went out of the open door of the drawing room and along the landing to the top of the stairs, where she stood, waiting, and all sadness left her as she listened with never-diminishing joy to the uneven step along the hall downstairs.

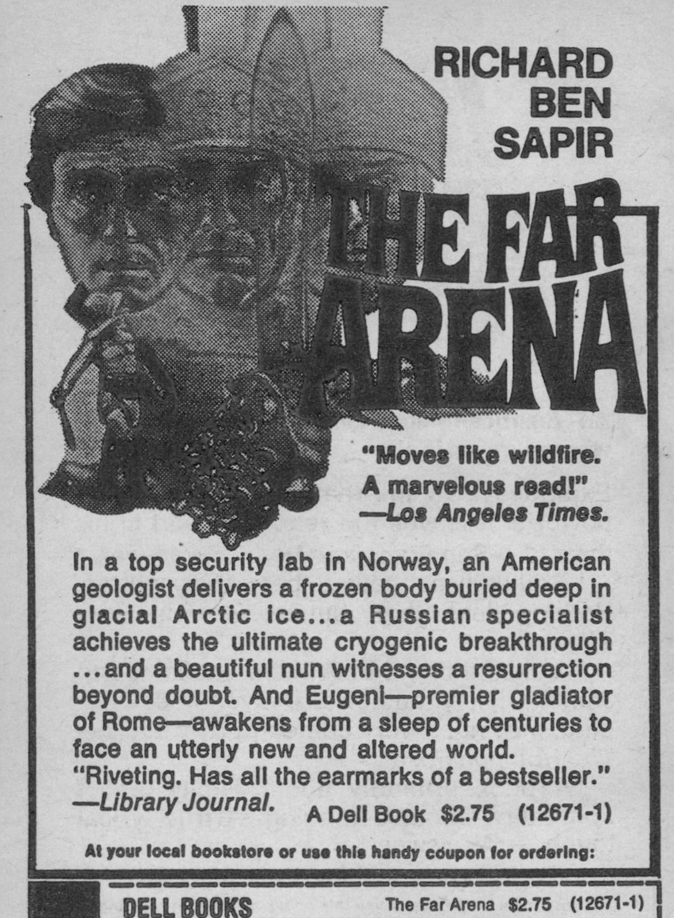
RICHARD
BEN
SAPIR
THE FAR
ARENA
"Moves like wildfire.
A marvelous read!"
—Los Angeles Times.
In a top security lab in Norway, an American geologist delivers a frozen body buried deep in glacial Arctic ice...a Russian specialist achieves the ultimate cryogenic breakthrough ...and a beautiful nun witnesses a resurrection beyond doubt. And Eugeni—premier gladiator of Rome—awakens from a sleep of centuries to face an utterly new and altered world.
"Riveting. Has all the earmarks of a bestseller."
—Library Journal.
A Dell Book $2.75 (12671-1)
At your local bookstore or use this handy coupon for ordering: